The Bastard's Grimoire

Joseph Hirsch

BLACK ROSE writing

The final approval for this literary material is granted by the author.

First printing

This is a work of fiction. Names, characters, businesses, places, events and incidents are either the products of the author's imagination or used in a fictitious manner. Any resemblance to actual persons, living or dead, or actual events is purely coincidental.

ISBN: 978-1-61296-723-3
PUBLISHED BY BLACK ROSE WRITING
www.blackrosewriting.com

Printed in the United States of America
Suggested retail price $16.95

The Bastard's Grimoire is printed in Adobe Garamond

For Jed Ayres and Scott Phillips, in gratitude

Praise for
The Bastard's Grimoire

"Mr. Hirsch is a writer of uncommon talent."
–Tom Kakonis, award-winning author of
Criss Cross and *Treasure Coast*

"Joseph Hirsch is scary good."
– Jed Ayres, author of *Peckerwood*

"One of my favorite writers currently working."
–Scott Phillips, author of the national bestseller,
The Ice Harvest

"I'm not a huge one for fantasy for the most part, but I do enjoy it from time to time…and I really dug this one. Seriously nice stuff, easily convinced me to read the kind of story I normally don't choose to read."
–David S. Atkinson, author of
Not Quite so Stories

"*The Bastard's* Grimoire immediately draws the reader into a pseudo-realistic middle-ages Germany, so vivid, that even the fantasy elements earn their place in history. Hirsch taps into all the senses with his unabashed descriptions and writing style. The story is chock full of historic and literary merit, but first and foremost it is a fun, colorful, and erotic adventure 'down the Mosel'."
–Tina Amiri, *Whatever The Impulse*

The Bastard's Grimoire

In the fifth year that the queen and widow Matina Stovis sits in regency for her son the infant king, Jerome Stovis, named in honor of his father, who died warring with the Slavs and Saracens. It is the third year of her war with the anti-king Robert Stovis, who considers himself rightful heir to King Jerome's throne and accuses the widow Matina of witchcraft, heresy, and of conspiracy against her husband-all of this in the Holy Land with the Holy River, a kingdom forgotten by time and yet remembered by this chronicler.

Chapter One

A Good Wind for Raping

Forkbeard had gathered his men around him and held his block of Icelandic spar toward the sun that was hidden behind the clouds. He grinned with a mouth empty of teeth. "Take note men, and remember the rhyme well."

The other mutineers from the Vitalienbruder League crowded closer to Forkbeard, who smelled like a wine cask filled with sour egg yolk and turned fish. "Mares' tails and mackerel scales make ships carry low sails."

One of the pirates looked upward, struggling with the weight of the frogmouth jousting helmet that he had raided from the armory of the last town they took. "But brother," he said, "the sails are high, and we are no longer under oar."

Forkbeard grinned. "The square sails have been raised to put the fear of Odin into the hearts of the timid. When they see the sails, and if they be not fools, they will abandon their fortress."

He walked past the men gathered around him on the deck of the ship, each of them clutching falchion blades that tapered like cleavers. They gripped their weapons in sweating metal gauntlets by their cross and pommel handles, as if in prayer. Forkbeard walked until he was at the prow of the clinker ship.

Two of his underlings followed behind him, one with blade and the other with crossbow. From beneath the deck there came the thunderous sound of poor, cursed Nephil's footsteps. The half-man, half-angelic beast had tired of torturing the prisoners below deck, and was ascending the steps.

Forkbeard gazed through the coat of fog drifting over the surface of the river. He saw the crenelated enceinte on the horizon. The curtain walls of the Zollschloss stood between them and Koln. It was a castle floating on the sea. Through the mist there came a small deep-berthed vessel drifting in the darkness. Its hull was fitted with shields that bore the Hessian lion, each linked one to the other as close as chains fused in a mail shirt.

"Look!" Forkbeard shouted to the men behind him. "An emissary approaches."

The pirates walked closer to their master, crowding nearer to the ship's figurehead depicting a dragon. Its forked tongue was made of wood but appeared so lifelike that the rain falling on it looked like glistening blood in the half-light.

The oarsmen on the small vessel stopped paddling and came up short just beneath the open maw of the dragon whose carvings were as intricate as a misericord. The emissary in the ship was flanked by several archers with their bows trained on the marauding vessel. The man's voice shook as he read from the whitevine parchment. "It is my duty to inform you that we are willing to pay Danegeld in the amount of one-thousand guineas if you will turn your ship around at this time."

That brought laughter from the ranks swelling behind Forkbeard. Those ranks had not so far swelled that Nephil was counted among their number. If he had been there, the poor wretch in the tiny vessel might be willing to up the bounty.

The men around Forkbeard wore leather tunics reinforced with metal. They sported hauberks and mail shirts, basinets and spiny metallic vambraces that shined despite the clouds covering the sun. Darts, gads, and pointed spikes littered the deck along with shattered bits of the forecastle that collapsed to the deck the last time Forkbeard's crew grappled with another ship and slaughtered most of their number.

Forkbeard's mind was made up on what he would do with this castle before he had even set sail downriver, but he asked, "What if we refuse your Danegeld? What if we take your little castle, and whatever treasure and women be therein? What if we dine on the tripe we slice from your stomachs and quench our thirst with your weak royal blood?"

The parchment fell from the boy's hand, and landed in the cold black water. The bows trembled in the hands of the footmen gathered around him in the ship. Those who gripped the oars seemed ready to turn around. The boy managed to speak. "Then it is my duty to inform you that our keep is garrisoned by Hospitallers who are well-seasoned after a campaign against the Saracens in which they managed to secure a piece of the holy wood from the True Cross."

That brought gales of laughter from the men behind Forkbeard. He choked his ravensbill polearm, and touched the dragon figurehead lightly on the nose. "Awaken!" The dragon went from wood to fleshy scales and its first exhale was a blast of rancid fire that turned all of the men in the small boat to scorched flesh in one quick burst of flame. One of the poor souls shrieked and dived into the water in the hopes of extinguishing himself. He roasted like a pig turned slowly until charred on a spit, and then he bobbed lifelessly in the water.

One of the pirates behind Forkbeard reached his oar into the water and shoved the flaming ship filled with the meat of roasted men back in the direction of the castle. They would quickly deduce what Forkbeard thought of their petty bribe when the charred mass reached the shores.

The entire deck trembled, and for a moment rare fear showed in Forkbeard's face. His visage was too dirty for any to note his terror, besides which no one could blame him for fearing Nephil.

The giant was the son of a fallen angel who mated with a mortal woman, and his head was the same size and nearly the same substance as a boulder. He was a giant among hearty Vikings, and stood several hands taller than the second tallest man among those onboard. He was an unpredictable, ill-tempered ogre who couldn't discern between horseflesh and man gristle. He was also a one man springald who made catapults unnecessary. He could fling a body farther than the second stoutest man aboard could carry one.

"Nephil, my boy." Forkbeard touched his monstrous friend lightly once on the shoulder and pointed toward the nearest bergfried of the Zollschloss in the fogged distance. No doubt archers were staring through their murder holes at the flaming remnants of the ship returning to them, but Forkbeard was confident he and his hearty band were still outside of shooting range.

Forkbeard touched the awakened dragon once with his ravensbill polearm, and the figurehead went from scales to wood once again and slept. He spoke to Nephil. "Can you fling a flaming head from here all the way inside of that old motte and bailey, my friend?"

The half-angel grinned like a sated ape. "Me can."

Forkbeard stroked his pet and shouted to one of the pirates wearing frogmouth armor. "Bring the prisoners above deck, and prepare to light the Greek fire."

"Aye!"

The smell of igniting pitch filled the air, greenwood burning as if a penny preacher were readying to put the faggots to a witch. The air grew dark with smoke and red with flickering flames that shone off the rusted armor of the pirates on deck. This was accompanied by the thundering of wooden ale casks rolling along the ship's deck, until all of those captured in the last raid were brought aboveboard.

The pirates lined them up. They tipped the cockale barrels on their sides, so that the heads of the prisoners protruded, while they struggled and thrashed with their limbs inside the barrels. The mermaid was the first in line, and so Forkbeard walked over to her and leaned down to speak.

"M'lady, you know what desperate and debasing measures we must take when we are in want of women."

A couple of pirates guffawed, and it was clear that some of them preferred buggering a scurvy-ridden sailor to making the beast with a woman. Forkbeard stroked the mermaid's chestnut hair, which was undamaged by exposure to the salty sea air. Her tail thrashed inside of the water-filled wine barrel in which she was imprisoned. "A Lorelei such as thee can as easily change form as a man dining on fairy cakes can join the ranks of the tiny, chaste creatures."

"Never," she said and spit in his face.

Her spit dripped down Forkbeard's dirty face. He waited for it to slink its way through the pits and crags of his disfigured cheeks until the spit was close enough to his mouth, at which point he licked it and swallowed.

"If you do not will away your tail," he said, "then we will forget your fruitful womb, and make use only of your mouth while you flop in your barrel." He held out the hand not gripping the polearm, and tried seduction inasmuch as it was within his ability to woo. He had killed his fair share of poets, but that did not make him a poet. "Take my hand, become mortal, and be my queen."

The mermaid was now too angry to spit or even deny him, and her scaly tail thrashed inside of the barrel. Her fin was starving for the warm blue purchase of the rivers and oceans that were her paradise until one of the Vitalienbruder snagged her in his net. Forkbeard looked up to one of his bruder and nodded. "Take the cunt back below deck."

"Jawohl." The pirate rolled the barrel back down the stairs. Forkbeard lifted his blade toward the first of the remaining men trapped in barrels, their heads peeking out and waiting for his steel.

"Pity," Forkbeard said, "that she would not grant me her hand in marriage.

Otherwise I might on this day grant you a reprieve." He brought the Zweihander down on the man's neck hard enough to split a petrified log, which was more than it took to sever the man's head from his body. Blood flowed like wine. One of the pirates stepped in, grabbed the head by the hair, and dipped it in the flaming Greek fire. The hot head was then handed off to Nephil, who assumed the pose of a glorious Adonis despite his monstrous dimensions. He flung the head sidearm like a discus in the direction of the castle on the horizon.

The men around him cheered as the head cleared the curtain wall and landed inside the motte and bailey. The demonic angel grinned, wiped his flame-calloused hands, and waited for the next head.

"Please, spare me!" the man in the next barrel said.

Forkbeard's lip curled in disgust. He looked to one of the men clad in jousting armor and gripping a falchion cleaver. "Lothar, kill this penny preacher."

"I am a man of God. You …"

The blade didn't penetrate all the way through the neck, but bounced and reverberated like a smithy's anvil striking something in the forge. A giant red set of new lips appeared in the back of the moaning preacher's neck. Forkbeard said, "Leave him to suffer." He nodded at the four remaining prisoners.

He looked over at Nephil and reassured the monster. "There will be more flaming heads to throw. Do not worry, my friend."

"Thank you, Master." Nephil grinned like a dog at a table waiting for scraps, or one of the poor holding hands out for alms.

"Lothar," Forkbeard said, "you are not worthy of the Vitalienbruder name."

"Sorry, my king." He bowed, and stepped away from the moaning and bleeding priest. Forkbeard leaned down to the priest. He lifted the barrel in which the man sat and flung it overboard. The laughter of the men on deck was counterpointed by the burbling of the freshwater around the ship that rippled as the man struggled for air, sank, and drowned.

"We have done so much pillaging on these waters that the feeding fish will be speaking German soon enough." Forkbeard moved on to the next man, and lifted his polearm above his head. He worked the Ravensbill like a farmer threshing wheat, slicing through the head in one swift motion. He curled the decapitated skull in the crescent shape of his scythe for a moment before the head rolled across the deck. It trailed blood like a tail following a tadpole.

Nephil chased the head whose eyes were wide and frozen like those of a perch gutted at market resting on a bed of ice. He walked the head over to the small fire smoldering on deck, and dipped the cranium in the flames where it sizzled. He wound his heavily muscled arm up and lobbed the head in an arching striation that cleared one wall of the castle and made it to the far wall walk.

Forkbeard looked to him with approval. "Would that we had a chronicler among us to record your deeds." Lothar stared down at his boots sheepishly, ashamed of how unfavorably he compared to the offspring of the Nephilim. "Alas," Forkbeard said, "few among our number are literate."

The pirate's blade was slaked with blood, too wet with gristle and all types of matter brought forth from the tracheas and brains of men. He no longer trusted his slimed polearm to do justice to the necks of the remaining prisoners. He was also curious to see whether Lothar's failure to remove a head in one stroke was a failure of nerve, or if it had more to do with the weakness of the weapons they raided from the last town they took by force. He looked among the number of pirates in his midst, and spotted another with an identical blade. He said, "Wolfram, relieve this poor bastard of his head."

"You harrying heathens will face Christ's sword sooner or later," the man trapped in the barrel said.

"Aye!" Forkbeard said, "and once we face his blade, we'll piss on his cross nightly in the halls of Valhalla."

A shrill cry like a hollow wind flew from the man's lips as Wolfram cleaved the neck, bringing a sound like an axe splitting wood as meat and bone broke in a hollow crack. The head spun in place, doing three rotations until it came to rest. The nose leaked blood and faced Lothar's feet.

"Lothar," Forkbeard said, "you have much to learn from your younger brother, Wolfram."

The Viking looked shamed enough now to disembowel himself with his own blade, and he could not meet his master's eyes.

"Wolfram," Forkbeard said, "repeat your performance."

"Aye," Lothar's younger brother said. The waves lapped against the sides of the wooden clinker ship, and the sun peeked from between the clouds. The fog was still heavy, which made Nephil's aim with his next chuck all that more impressive. The pirates watched unbelieving as the head of the latest Christian soared through the air and flew straight into the face of a bowman standing on the castle allure. The bowman staggered, stunned from the force of the blow as he was struck by the phantom head that appeared from the fog without a body. The bowman fell from the wall inside of the castle.

The men on deck roared with laughter. The flaming remnants of the tiny ship that was sent out to bribe them finally reached the edge of the castle. The moat surrounding the castle stunk even from this distance but smelled nowhere near as bad as the men who would soon bring the castle to siege after they beheaded the remaining men in the barrels.

Forkbeard regarded their next victim with a curious eye. The boy in the barrel said nothing. He made no threats and did not beg or panic. "You!" Forkbeard leaned down. The young stoic raised his head as much as he could with his body held captive in the barrel. The prisoner's expression did not alter. Forkbeard asked, "Have you no fear of us? No fear of death?"

"None," was the single word to come from the boy's mouth. Forkbeard gripped the boy's chin in his blood-stained mail gauntlet and tipped the head upward.

Wolfram licked his lips and choked the cruciform pommel of his executioner's sword. He looked from his master to the boy. Nephil watched, his hands hungry for another head.

"And what is your name?" Forkbeard asked.

"Tis none of your concern," the boy answered.

That took Forkbeard from a smile to laughter. "You are a right fresh bastard for one who's been swimming in salt water for such a long time. And though your body's in the barrel, I'd wager your balls are as large as dragon eggs. Come, young man. Tell me your name." Forkbeard's hold on his blade loosened.

"Till Eulenspiegel," the boy said. Those onboard who'd heard of the fool's legendary deeds laughed at this show of insolence.

"It will be a pity to kill you, especially without knowing your name. I am no chronicler as I have said, but I have a good memory and would like to remember the name of one who faced death with such resolve."

The boy shook his head. His thick crown of warm brown hair, a page boy's pudding basin, dripped around his ears. Those pirates who preferred buggery to a mermaid's mouth cast a sidelong glance at the barreled lad. They wished that Forkbeard would spare the boy for reasons that had nothing to do with his courage.

"Casper," the boy said. "Casper Namlos." His eyes glowed like live coals, and he snorted like a bull that caught his cow rutting with another.

Forkbeard stroked the boy's hair, matting his russet locks with rusty dollops of blood. Then the pirate looked to Lothar's younger brother and said, "Send this brave little bugger to his eternal reward, whether it's Valhalla or Christ's

Heaven or the Land where the Saracens dabble with their seventy-two virgins."

"Aye." Wolfram raised his sword and slipped in the gathering puddle of blood that was thicker than that on a butcher's block. He fell toward the ground and his blade flew out in front of him. Its sharpened end cleaved the barrel well enough to split the wooden staves.

Lothar wanted to avenge his own humiliation and the more recent one of his brother. He stepped forward to slice and dice, but Forkbeard ran to the prisoner's aid. "Nay!" He pulled the boy to his feet by his hair, gripping the locks which glistened like a steed's currycombed hide.

"Boy," Forkbeard said, "I believe in dice and divination, and you have earned your freedom." He gripped the boy around the neck. The boy trembled not the least. It was as if he expected this change in fortune and that one bloody head falling after another in his path would not weaken his resolve. He clearly also believed in fated things.

"Wolfram." Forkbeard looked down at the Vitalienbruder struggling to pick himself up off the blooded abattoir they'd made of the deck. "Pick yourself up, slice the rest of the heads, and give them to Nephil to toss at the walls of the castle we will take in a short time."

"And what of the boy?" one of the pirates famed for his buggery exploits asked.

"Bring me the reliquary we pillaged from the last little berg we took."

"Aye," a voice shouted.

There was the shearing sound of a blade brought down cleanly on a less fortunate neck. Then there was the muffled noise of a soft head leaking blood as it rolled, followed by the sound of flames licking into skull. Greek fire seared through skin, accompanied by the *whoosh* of an airborne head floating toward the gray walls of the unfortunate castle.

"Here, Milord."

The pirate held out a box of blue enamel inlaid with beaten gold. There was a latch nestled in the mouth of a cameo depiction of a green man much like that sometimes seen hidden in baptismal fonts of churches or coded in the marginalia of otherwise holy books. The gold glowed, and the pirate opened the box while Forkbeard spoke to the boy whose hair he stroked. Caspar Namlos and Forkbeard gazed inside the chest, where a smiling skull and two femurs were laid like crossbones.

"Before I cut his tongue from his mouth," Forkbeard said, "the parish priest assured me these bones belonged to Saint Nicholas. He is patron saint of all sailors, he whose scepter can calm stormy seas."

Forkbeard walked until he was behind the boy. He played and rutted with his nose in the back of the boy's neck. He stroked Casper's ears until the boy's sphincter loosened as if he accepted catamite status before a single request was made by the captain of this floating Sodom.

"We no longer have letters of mark by the king to pillage. We are no longer corsairs but are now mere pirates whose deeds are as black as those of the famed Eustace."

The pirate with the blue enamel, cameo, and golden reliquary held it up closer to the boy. Casper could smell the chalky, dank scent of the ancient bones. "But you may join our band. You have proven your mettle. And Odin has proven his interest in you by sparing you the ordeal of the others."

Forkbeard nodded in the direction of the other barrels where the last man was parting with his head and his neck spouted blood like a holy stigmata.

"So," Forkbeard said. His propagator grew in his pants, chafed against his mail skirt, and rose with the force of a stone satyr's chiseled cock. "Wilt thou join us in our unholy mission?"

The boy tilted his head over his left shoulder, and then he moved his hindquarters against the Vitalienbruder's massive prick. His open, tiny cherubic lips puckered and he kissed Forkbeard full on the mouth before whispering, "Aye."

Chapter Two

Freeing the Mermaid and Damning the Castle

The battle raged above deck, while below Casper Namlos spoke with the mermaid trapped in the barrel. "I know as a Lorelei that you must keep your word if I set you free." He licked his lips. His mouth was parched from previously kissing the bitter bones of the saint inside the reliquary, which Forkbeard demanded he do to swear allegiance to the Vitalienbruder.

"We of the Sisterhood never break our word once given," the mermaid said. The last time the pirates grappled they fought against a victualling ship on which Casper was a stowaway. The Vitalienbruder had raided the boat for its stores, and the barrel in which the mermaid now sat was surrounded by casks filled with Bordeaux wine and salt from the Bay of Bourgneuf.

"I will free you," Casper said, "but you must help me."

The mermaid's irises glowed like whirlpools leading to another world. She used all of her charm, bringing the power of the sea's tides to bear on the poor mortal's mind. *Free me.*

The boy stared back at her and glowered, sneering at her trick. She thought for a moment that it hadn't worked because he had little genuine lust for women like Forkbeard and most of the others now storming the castle. Casper said, "I am already under the enchantment of another."

The mermaid's tail thrashed and the dry gills behind her ears puckered like hungry mouths. "He must have quite a store of power if my siren song does not work on you. What, pray tell, is the name of this wizard?"

He ignored her, turned around, and walked between the giant barrels of wine and salt until he found what he was looking for. He returned with the sledgehammer. "I will set you free, but you must swim me beneath the castle and get me in."

"What is your business there?"

Casper gripped the wooden handle of the sledgehammer. "My business there is my business."

The pinkish, fleshed gills at the back of her ears continued to suck for saltwater or freshwater that wasn't there. She was dying, and she knew it. There was no way she would will herself into mortality and grow legs to please the men aboard the ship, and she was desperate for freedom.

"Give me your word," the mermaid said.

"What?"

A mortal's word wasn't worth a Cyprian fig, but she would have to trust him. "Say you will take no life except to save your own if I help you attain entrance to this Zollschloss."

"Agreed." Casper stood back and gripped the haft of the weapon until the wood groaned.

"Then free me, and I will get you into the castle."

He swung on the barrel and it broke in half. Stagnant water spilled onto the floor of the hold, bubbles and scum floating at his feet. The mermaid's tail flopped free, and she moaned. "Thank you, young man."

Casper now struck the floor of the ship as hard as he previously hit the barrel that kept the Lorelei prisoner. "Now it is time for you to honor your word," he said.

The wood of the ship's floor splintered, some crewman's work in Flemish ochre now gone to waste. A hole appeared in the floorboards. Water leaked in. The mermaid dowsed toward it with the blue, scaly fins in which her body tapered. It was her first taste of fresh water and of freedom in some time.

"I will honor your request," she said as she moved toward the gaping hole through which water flowed. "But surely this ship will now sink."

Casper walked behind her, gripped her arms as if they were wings. "It is to be hoped." The mermaid slid through the hole in the bottom of the ship through which the water flooded. She kicked her tail hard to force her way out. The boy floated through the dark waters on the back of the mermaid.

Her gills sucked water like a newborn calf nursing at its mother's teat, and

Casper Namlos held his breath. They drifted through the river. They swam through murky algae, past curious fish. They thrashed onward together. All was suddenly illuminated, flaming orange and spangled gold. It was as if they had discovered the vault of a king rich beyond measure in this hidden Atlantis.

Casper saw as he looked up that it was nothing so poetic. Flaming heads were bobbing in the water near the surface. Forkbeard had told Casper after he freed him that he alone knew the secret recipe of the Byzantine variation of Greek fire, the same that was used to defend Constantinople from the harrying of the heathens. It must have been powerful stuff to burn through skulls and yet remain aflame even in water. Bubbles from the gills in the mermaid's neck found their way to the boy's mouth and fed him air. The Lorelei thrashed her tail and swam toward the Garderobe, bypassing the moat. She moved toward the place in the castle where the wastes of those within flowed outward. This would not be the handsomest way to gain entrance to the fortress, but it would work.

Meanwhile above the waterline, Nephil slammed his massive rocky shoulder against the front of the castle's door.

"That's it, me boy!" Forkbeard shouted encouragement to his massive slave from behind the safety of a wall of heater shields he and the other pirates held up against the barrage of arrows coming at them from the castle wall. "Break the door down, and the place is ours!"

Nephil had no shield, but he didn't need one. His back was as callused as the fingers of a seamstress. Arrows nestled in his spine so comfortably that one could swear he wore them in a quiver rather than in his tough skin.

Forkbeard looked to Lothar and Wolfram. The brothers to his left and right also hid behind their shields on the dry land just before the castle's walls started. The rain of arrows was slowing, and Forkbeard guessed the castle would soon run out. That would spell the beginning of the garrison's doom.

"Hospitallers indeed," Forkbeard snorted. "It was naught besides a bluff on their part." Forkbeard could hear all of those inside mustering for the final assault even over the sounds of the shouting and the lick of the crackling flames from the burning heads. Stable boys and men from the workshops gathered their paltry wood and metal accouterments. Once Nephil broke the door down, the men of the castle would all be dead shortly, and the women who weren't killed with them would be raped.

The pirate looked back at his giant, half-angelic offspring as he beat the door with his meaty fists. "Who has need of ballista or trebuchet when such a man is at one's command?"

Lothar laughed. He shuddered as an arrow shot toward him and landed so fiercely in his heater shield that the tanged, cloverleaf-shaped head of the arrow poked through and scraped his nose. The rain of projectiles continued to come. Lothar's brother shouted to Forkbeard over the sound of the metal and wooden ambuscade. "I have seen Nephil punch his way through three men in one swoop, as if their bodies were no more than dried calf bladder."

"He is a treasure," Forkbeard allowed. Then he looked back at the front of the castle, where the door was nearly broken from the assault of the giant's bloody fists. "Perhaps they do have some Hospitallers among their number."

Wolfram worked up the nerve to peek around his shield to see what Forkbeard saw. His brother was too cowardly to abandon the comfort of his heater's protection for even a moment. "Hark," Forkbeard said, and pointed with the mailed finger of his blood-slaked gauntlet.

Wolfram's eyes followed the line drawn by Forkbeard's finger, and he watched in puzzlement as one of the defenders lowered a pole that tapered in a hook in the direction of the giant. Nephil was too busy beating the door to notice.

"What is it?" Wolfram asked. He was less well-travelled than Forkbeard, who had seen as much of the world's seas as Eustace. Wolfram's knowledge of the Levant came only from woven tapestries.

"It is a tool used to flip battering rams invented by the Saracens to thwart the efforts of the Christians." A steel-tipped spear floated toward them, and they both covered their faces with their heater shields. A sound like cookware spilling to the floor rippled through their ranks as the spear touched their shields, dented them, and then bounced off.

Forkbeard lowered his shield in the next moment, and then looked back at Nephil, who was only two or three punches away from bringing the door down and letting them into the castle. "There are thirty Zollschlösser between here and Mainz, and we could have collected enough Danegeld to buy a seat at the Hanseatic Session." He grinned and Wolfram grinned back. "But," Forkbeard said, "it is more sporting to bite the hand that feeds until the fingers pop off, and then to take the treat that was offered." The ground rumbled as if an earthquake was not far away. "And they may surrender and beg for favorable terms, but they will receive only death."

Lothar finally worked up the nerve to lower his own heater shield. He asked, "How far will we go? All the way to Koln?"

"Aye," Forkbeard said.

Lothar grew sheepish. "The town is said to support the anti-king in his war with M'lady Matina."

Forkbeard sighed deeply. He had no respect for Christians or their kings. He had no interest in their popes and priests. Nevertheless what he heard of Queen Matina Stovis from troubadours and minstrels, along with what he had spied with illiterate eyes in woodcuts, filled his heathen heart with song. A goddess like her was something a pagan could respect and adore.

"The town is said to be controlled now by an evil archbishop, who is alleged to be magical enough ..."

The door of the castle came down and a mist of wooden splinters surrounded the bloody giant who had done his share. He turned from the door and marched slowly through the ranks of roaring pirates. They brandished cleavers and forked polearms and rushed in a phalanx of bloody metal that shined in the light reflected from the smoldering Greek fire. Sporadic arrows rained down from the Moorish-capped merlons of the Zollschloss, spears sneaking from the embrasures and falling at the backsides of the men storming the castle.

It was as Forkbeard had suspected. There were no battle-hardened Templars or Hospitallers inside the forecastle walls. There were smithies and butchers who rushed forward and were diced as easily as greased pigs and harrowed by scythes like wheat. Blood flowed as if from geysers and squirted heavenward, counterpointed by cries of misery and pleadings for pity as blades sliced flesh.

Nephil, the boulder of a man, sat and the ground beneath him thundered. He started pulling bloody arrows from his back, wincing slightly. He gazed back toward the ship, whose dragon figurehead was dormant and no longer enchanted. The giant decided that after he finished pulling the arrows from his own back, he would walk toward the prow of the battered ship and pull the arrows from his scaled friend's hide.

He looked closer and saw the ship was listing to one side. It looked to be taking on water. Nephil then glanced back in the direction of the assault, where the bodies of the poor Christians were strewn naked and lifeless, as if the bubonic pest had found them in their sleep. He wanted to tell Forkbeard there was something wrong with the ship, but the pirate was busy sinking a blade to the hilt into the back of a journeyman. He was also sinking his own satyr's one-eyed horn deep into the boy's maidenhead, the kid's pants around his ankles.

The giant didn't do much wondering usually, but as he felt the sting of the arrows in his back now, he did mull over why Forkbeard never called for an escalade when the hemp rope ladders would more than suffice for the job. Nephil's hands were tired from battering. He decided that if Forkbeard asked him to break down another door, he would ask his master to please use the ladders that tapered in gryphon talons the next time they came to a Zollschloss.

Nephil would soak his hands in brine after this raid and maybe eat the mermaid who the others wanted to make mortal for their own purposes. If Forkbeard did not give Nephil his reprieve and the fish-woman as a morsel of a reward, then the giant decided he would squash Forkbeard's head like a muscatel grape and eat as many of the other pirates as he could, until his two stomachs were sated or he was put down.

The remaining garrison force guarded the keeper of the Zollschloss inside the castle's curtain walls. The keeper was one of the Electors of Mainz who had grown fat as a swine on tax collection. Now his eyes were widened in terror. The defenders around him gripped arrows in their bow hands and fired with their other hands, shooting projectiles into the oncoming hoard of pirates who swung their blades like executioners hungry for heads.

Forkbeard wore a kettle helmet he'd picked up from the smithy's shop and he swung a Landsknecht Zweihander he'd found on one of the few genuine footmen among the number of peasants who rushed forward to their slaughter in the moment after the giant knocked the door down. The last of the pigeons had flown from the elector's rookery when Nephil's fists broke through the door. Feathers drifted like snow toward the ground and were spotted with arterial blood that sprayed from the heat of the slaughter taking place inside the castle's courtyard.

Forkbeard waved his sword like a magician casting a spell with his wand, and an archer lost both of his arms. The hands were on the ground, still gripping a bow and arrow and twitching in surprise. The armless man looked on in horror, and the marrow and lumen inside of his body shined.

"Please!" the elector begged. "Spare my wife. She …"

The Landsknecht blade dug between his shoulder and neck and created a gap large enough in the elector for him to be nearly quartered. The tines of his ribs glinted and looked like a right feast for a cannibal, some of whom were actually numbered among the band of Vitalienbruder.

The leader of the pack looked back toward his loyal army and said, "To the main hall. To sup, suck marrow and blood." Forkbeard looked at the ground, where poor Lothar had been stabbed so many times that he was unrecognizable to all but his younger brother Wolfram.

Forkbeard had punctured the elector's intestines with his Landsknechter and he pointed the shit-soaked tip of his blade toward Lothar's dead body. "To Valhalla with him!" The men behind him cheered and rushed toward the great hall. Several women waited with their royal guard behind a barricade of tables and chairs and suits of armor that would hold for some time, now that the offspring of the Nephilim was too tired to batter by hand.

Underwater both the mermaid and Casper Namlos closed their eyes as they floated through the dank and sulfurous moat. The Lorelei moved with the grace of a dolphin, while the boy clung to her back like a lamprey with nothing to offer except a parasite's insatiable hunger. She was eager to be rid of him. She did not like that he was under an enchantment stronger than hers, an enchantment cast over him by a benefactor whose name he refused to divulge. Despite her misgivings though, a promise was a promise, at least when it came to the sisterhood. Men were a different matter, and while he had freed her from the barrel, she had her doubts that he would hold up his end of the bargain and not kill. If he planned to avenge himself against that band of Catamites and he was going to kill Forkbeard, the Lorelei wasn't even sure that she didn't want him to break his word.

An inky cloud of brownish water that was human waste formed. It grew before the mermaid as if it had been expelled from the troubled bowels of an octopus that ate something that didn't agree with its stomach.

The mermaid folded her gills back, and the boy held tightly to her shoulders. He closed his eyes and mouth, and they swam in waste. The Lorelei corkscrewed her way upward into the Garderobe, thrashing through the cesspool. They moved together into the hole in the privy that led into the castle's latrine.

They needn't have worried about someone being seated on the throne, as all of the castle's garrison was either dead from combat wounds or getting ready to die defending the lady of the Zollschloss.

The Lorelei and the boy on her back emerged inside the castle. They were covered in muddy detritus and soiled in vinegary flotsam and pissoir nectar. Casper coughed, gagged, and climbed out of the toilet. The mermaid struggled to speak, despite the eggy smell that made her want to wretch. "I have done my part," she said. "Keep your end of the bargain."

The mermaid pulled a bit of seaweed from her hand and extended her soft, pink digits toward the young cur. "Kill no one."

"I won't," the boy said, and he gripped her slender fingers. He would have kissed them if they weren't covered in waste, and her beauty was such that he thought of gracing the digits with a knightly peck despite the stench.

"Good."

The mermaid dropped back down the Garderobe shaft. He watched until she disappeared, growing smaller until the siren was the size of a mere fairy.

The boy looked around the room. He saw a copper hip bath filled with hot water. It stood there like a half-shell for an absconded Venus. Steam floated from the surface of the warm, soapy perfumed water. Casper Namlos stripped naked and walked toward the shiny vessel.

The lady of the house had probably been preparing for her bath when the raid began, and her attendants and chambermaids had scattered with her. Perhaps they were hidden in secret passages or stowed behind some quarried slab of rock. Casper knew all about hiding. He had managed to go from one Hanseatic clinker or cog to another until he finally made his way onto the victualing ship that had the misfortune to grapple against the Vitalienbruder and to lose.

He walked toward the hip bath and then stepped inside. Warm nettles worked their way over his body in soothing waves. He still ached from the hours spent held captive inside that barrel.

Thank God the poor soul had missed his head with his blade and that he was here now bathing rather than having his body on the deck of the sinking ship while his head alight with Greek fire bobbed in the river and his charred skull washed up on a sandbank somewhere.

It was a pity that the lady of the house hadn't had her bath before the raid began. It would have been nice for her to wash herself, and then to have her chambermaids discard her water into the latrine down into the Garderobe where the perfume and musk of her own feminine smells could help offset the scent of the noxiousness through which they just swam.

Casper Namlos sighed and thought once of the beautiful mermaid. He spoke to himself but wished she could hear. "I will keep my promise to you, freshwater siren, Germanic Lorelei from the land the Romans finally conquered." He dipped his hands into the water of the hip bath, and washed himself with the expert care of one undergoing baptism.

"I will kill no one. I will rape as many women as I can, however. The sower soweth on behalf of his liege, he who granted him eternal powers in the castle at the summit of his mountain."

He drank some of the bathwater. His propagator, small before the wizard touched it with his wand, now grew until it would make Pan himself envious. Casper Namlos was ready to meet the lady of the manor.

Chapter Three

Bursting Forth with Demon Seed

The duchess, late wife of the recently slain palatinate elector, stood in the central branch of the drum tower. It was split into two arteries, one leading to her bedchamber and the other to the washroom and garderobe. The crosswinds beat at the tapestries, and blew a draft throughout. From one direction she could smell the burning hearth, and from the other scents of the moat. The odor was somehow stronger now as if the cesspool were flooding into the castle. Her mind was too occupied for her to give it much thought.

She walked closer to the stained glass window until she was close enough to see her shadow fill the pane. The glass was ruby and sapphire, a rich gothic portal to a dream realm she wished she could enter. She had never longed so much to disappear. The duchess was certain the pirates had made light work of her footmen, and that the only reason they weren't here raping her and her chambermaid was because they were elsewhere engaged with pillage. She could hear them laughing and reveling above the banshee howl of the cold wind that banked off the Rhenish waters and gathered force on the gray ramparts.

For perhaps the final time she wondered what was depicted in the gold and ruby glass. She had spent days walking alone through these chambers while her husband wrote to his guild back in Lubeck. That left her much time to think. The stained glass showed a man stroking a lion on the back of its golden mane, of that much she was certain. The only question was if the man was Charlemagne stroking the symbol of Hesse, or if the artist had meant to invoke Daniel in the lion's den. Perhaps he had meant to suggest both.

The lady of the castle drew her slender hand along the window's sash and carefully opened it. A light snow fell onto the slate battlements. She hoped the river would freeze. That might keep the pirates from passing through the gates and making their way to the next Zollschloss and then the next, until they finally reached Koln.

She gazed toward the black water of the river beyond the moat and wondered where the ship was. The duchess had been too busy fleeing from the great hall when the first alarms came from the belfry, and thus had missed the battle and had not witnessed the ship sink to the bottom of the river. This stretch of the river was shallow enough that even though the ship was wrecked, the dragon figurehead's tongue actually broke through the cresting foam of the jagged freshwater waves. The white square masts were now soaked like harmless canvas, filling with rushing water as the ship herself settled onto the river floor.

The lady leaned out of the window. She momentarily feared a last projectile from the volley could meet her up here, but after a spell she grew more confident and studied the remnants of the carnage below her.

The pirates had killed every man in the lower bailey. They had carted away most of the chickens, ducks, and geese. The birds left a rain of feathers in their wake, enough to fill a royal mattress. Several bloodied peafowl with their tiny necks broken lay scattered among the dead smithies and footmen in the courtyard.

The poor garrison had done what it could to protect itself. When the first of the flaming heads were lobbed over the wall by that monstrous son of a Nephilim, livestock were driven from the buttery on the hoof and the carcass of a previously-buried cow was disinterred and flung over the wall. A lot of good that did. The lady could just barely make out the lines of the giant's form as he sat with his legs folded under him and slowly tore the fetid and diseased cow limb from limb and ate it to his heart's content, while his brethren inside continued with their raiding.

She closed the window, sighed, and the moon splashed against the stained glass. She called softly toward her Kammermädchen, confident her voice would carry through the echoing stones and reach the girl where she stood in the bedchamber.

"Yes, m'lady?" the voice called back.

"I believe I will finish my bath, as intended." The duchess walked toward the room where the padded hipbath was. If she were to die soon, then she decided it would be at the moment of her choosing. She would slit her wrists and stand in the lukewarm water and bid this world *Auf wiedersehen* in her own way.

The chambermaid was ignorant to her lady's designs. She stoked the flames in the hearth by prodding a bit of unspun tow with a brass poker truncating in a shape like the mouth of a Dardanelles canon. The flames licked upward and the chambermaid stood back. She had no doubt that the pirates could see the smoke coming from the chimney. She was certain they would make their way here in due time no matter what measures the two remaining women took to protect themselves.

She had seen one of the raiders tear the throat from a Great Dane guard dog with his teeth. What manner of barricade could keep such a man from a woman he wished to rape?

Eleanor, the chamber girl, walked to her lady's bed and clutched the houppeland by its ermine-lined interior. She rubbed her fingers in admiring circles on the warm fur and carried the garment over toward the fire. She held the ruffed accordion neck toward the dancing flames, turning it this way and that.

She had been preparing her lady's bath before the siege. Now the water was certainly cold, and she would want her lady to step into warm clothing when she emerged from her bath. Eleanor also had another surprise for her lady, something to lift the mood and brighten her spirits a bit before the philistines broke down the door and had their way with them.

Eleanor walked to the stained oak chest that sat in the corner of the room. She'd hidden a small, fresh Nosegay bouquet she picked herself on her walk outside the courtyard wall earlier today. She had been assured that the land around the Zollschloss was safe, but that it was unsightly for a lady to be seen without the wall unaccompanied. She wondered now if Yahweh wasn't visiting this wrath upon their heads for her prior vanity. She was also afraid to fall to her knees in prayer now, since she feared that if she fell that she would begin weeping and never cease.

Eleanor walked toward the bath. She intended to peel the flowers from the nosegay and drop the petals one-by-one into the tepid waters where her lady bathed. The duchess was collapsed in a pile. She was hanging halfway out of the hip bath, with her bloody arms outstretched and venous red streaks dripping along the outer shell of the porcelain bath.

"My lady!"

The chambermaid dropped the flowers and the garment onto the wet floor.

She was ready to weep, but then her wet nose crinkled. She wondered what that horrible smell was, and why the effluvium of the garderobe so filled the bath chamber.

A hand wrapped itself around her mouth, and a dagger pressed its point into the soft flesh of her neck. The point wasn't pressed deep enough to bring blood, but the strength of the man's grip promised death if she didn't listen. Casper Namlos spoke. "I didn't kill her. She was like that when I found her."

"Please!" Eleanor moaned through the fetid fingers. "Let me join her. Spare my maidenhead. Allow me to enter the hereafter with my flower of youth intact, though you may have my life."

At that she attempted to push her neck forward onto the blade, and Casper withdrew the knife before she could manage to impale her neck on the point.

"No," he said. "I have other designs for you."

He lifted the dagger above her head and brought its hilt down on the bone protruding at the back of her skull. She fell to the stone floor in a daze, feeling the ground in the cold darkness as the man above her undressed. He stood naked and covered in the waste from the Garderobe, the bath only having half cleaned him.

"Please," she whispered. "Slit my throat." She held her head upward, presenting her soft white neck to his blade. Casper threw the knife down and mounted her, naked.

"Your life is not mine to take or give." Two of his fingers snuck like snakes onto the hairy mound of her fruit, and he parted the as-yet untouched lips with the skill of a midwife with far less virtuous designs. All soft pretensions were lost in the next moment, as he made a fist and drove it deep into her body with the force of a spiked mace.

The girl shrieked and Casper rammed his hand in and out of her body until he was inside of her up to the elbow. She was broken, as loose as a burlap sack filled with potatoes. He hopped on top of her, thrust in like a battering ram storming a castle. He wallowed on her like a beast and silenced her cries with his dung-covered hand. He cupped her mouth as he forced himself into her.

Casper spoke the words he didn't understand, or rather, the words from the wicked wizard passed through him. They were the words the conjurer had learned from one of the few texts to survive the fire in the Alexandrian Library ninety-seven years before the birth of Christ. Casper recited the spell that the wizard had copied when he was still a young illuminator, before the brothers had found out about his hideous treachery and defrocked him and cast him out into the wilderness.

The cold water where the dead woman sat now began to bubble like a cauldron as he spoke. He was pleased to see the magic was working, and he smiled. "Behold," the boy said, feeling the seed course through his loins, closer now to bursting forth into the pillaged womb of the poor woman. "I am one with the magic power wherever it may be, in the house of any man where it is." He gazed around the room, looking heavenward as if God would ever deign to speak with him after he had made his blasphemous pact.

He then looked down at the form of the woman beneath him. He rubbed his dirty hands across her heavy white breasts, staining the alabaster with pitch and manure he'd brought with him from the Garderobe. He tarred her breasts with his filth and sulfur. He belched and saw the pain on her face.

Casper spoke the words as the seed left his body. It was blood from the brain as Galen had put it, churned white by the milling motion of his hips as he rollicked against her like a ship upon a stormy sea.

"No," she said. Her pink sheath pulsed and glistened with sacred nectar, the moist dew she intended for her eventual-betrothed, a prince she dreamed of during the days while her lady paced the battlements and pondered the ruby and sapphire stained glass. Now this monster had ruined her dreams.

He belched again, a coarse piggish roar coming from his putrid core. "It is faster than air," he said, "swifter than the light."

"What?" she asked. "What have you done to me?" The veins on her neck cabled, and she gazed upward, forsaken by God and abandoned by her lady who had slit her wrists. She felt the living seed wriggle through her like a tadpole, as it latched onto the purchase of her fertile womb and grew. It swelled like a golden egg in a Hausmärchen. It moved too fast, and nine months elapsed in the space of a few blinks of an eye.

Casper Namlos had been trained and prepared for this evil work, but even he was not ready for the transformation. He had seen the wizard turn wine into blood, and with one flick of his wrist bring two succubae from the ether who then pissed golden liquid onto desecrated host. Casper wondered then why he was he so terrified now to see that his seed had done what the man said it would do.

The girl's belly grew as if stoked by a bellows. Casper burped once more, and this time vomited a sheet of papyrus on which the evil illuminator and copyist had scribed something before placing the parchment down the soulless boy's throat.

He thought of the poor stupid Vitalienbruder who'd set him free, and how now the men would pay for their folly. He spoke as his priapic wand dowsed and more seed spilled onto the ground forming a milky puddle. "While Israel was staying in Shittim, the men began to indulge in sexual immorality with Moabite women."

The chambermaid knew the Good Book as well as anyone, and cited chapter and verse as her stomach continued to swell. "Numbers, twenty-five, one."

Casper cackled. He was surprised to hear himself quote the book the wizard had entreated him to shit upon. The chambermaid's stomach exploded like a wineskin filled beyond capacity. Blood and organs shot in every direction, like rays from a doomed crimson sun. Casper Namlos drank whatever blood reached his lips, and he spoke a greeting to the monster that emerged from the ripped hull of the dead girl's body.

He admired his first creation. The demon had a face nestled in its groin, a hissing monster with a forked tongue. Other gargoyle mouths licked at the air from the joints at the knees and elbows of the demon with a black pointed tail and horns like dark gnarled shofars. The wings of the monster weren't leathery like those of a bat or a dragon. Rather they were thin like gauze, nearly transparent in the moonlight that crept through the snow-laced windows. The skull and crossbones motif was one Casper recognized from the many skin-bound grimoires the wizard kept on his shelves.

The spawn of Beelzebub flew upward, ripping through the stone of the ceiling as if it was rotted cheese. It shouted as it streaked through the sky. It flew lower, and fluttered its way toward the cellar where the gluttonous pirates now sated themselves.

"Burn!" Forkbeard shouted. He and Wolfram had managed to throw a full live ox into the fire, and it shrieked as if it was a man trapped inside a heated bronze bull. So sure of their success were the pirates that they had discarded their arms and armor and now danced as if around the maypole.

"Look, Forkbeard," one of the pirates shouted. He held lobes of Moroccan sugar in his hands. The cones were like mini-Giza pyramids, wonders to behold. Another pirate licked the sugar from his compatriot's hand like a deer doting on a saltlick. His friend's licking of his palm stoked the pirate's catamite instinct, and his propagator grew flush and tented against his doeskin trousers. He was too addled by pleasure to even speak, let alone calculate. Another of the pirates did the math for him.

"Such fine sugar is now fetching eight shillings a pound since the Lubeck embargo." He crowded closer to the white gold. He had nothing to fear from its rotting effects, since scurvy had parted him from his teeth a long time ago. His wonder gave way to rage. "All men are pirates," he sneered. "Some just wear a crown."

"Aye," another pirate seconded. "One could buy twenty-four dozen eggs for what these princely types waste on one lobe of sugar."

Yet another pirate returned from the pantry with his own, even more impressive haul. "Cinnamon," he shouted.

A voice came from behind the raiding throng. None of the pirates recognized it, and they turned to listen. The red demon stood there and said, "Cinnamon was used by the Egyptians in aiding the process of embalming." The demon's viperous fangs protruded as it spoke. "The Hebrew priests used it in anointing."

The demon stepped forward. The tail was forked like a trident, and it swayed from left to right behind it as its hoofs clattered on the cellar's mossy cobblestone.

"Shite," one of the pirates whispered. He had nothing close to a weapon on his person. He was ready only for an orgy, not for another battle. The other pirates were also unready and undressed. They guarded their bodies from the demon's sight like chaste maidens. They dropped their spices and sugars they'd raided from the cellar guarded by the pantler they previously beheaded.

The demon laughed, the ox sizzled in the fire, and Forkbeard finally worked up the nerve to speak. "State your purpose, and your lineage." The pirate wished to Odin that the demon before him had deigned to appear while he was still within enchantment distance of the figurehead. If he could awaken the dragon, the fire-breather might give them a fighting chance. That giant son of a Nephilim could help too, if he wasn't busy eating fetid cow meat in the courtyard.

The demon's grin grew wider, and it obliged. "I serve a master whose name is none of your concern, whose mission is also none of your affair."

Forkbeard wanted to appear indignant at this, for men never talked to him this way. He was too terrified to feign anger, and this was no man or ordinary monster. "As for my lineage," the demon said, "I am a composite. I was scribed, scrolled, and imbibed by an otherwise useless cur of a lad who just sired me."

The demon took a few more steps forward, and the pirates stepped back until they were nearly in the fire where the ox roasted now until blackened.

Forkbeard spoke not but suspected the ox's fate was light compared to whatever now awaited him and his band.

"I am made from the Supreme Chief of the Infernal Fire, he who founded the Order of the Fly."

"Beelzebub," Forkbeard muttered. Wolfram looked at his captain, confused. He wondered how the pirate knew such things. He'd never read the Good Book. What the others didn't know was that Forkbeard had been captured and imprisoned in a monastery for several years, where he'd had no choice but to endure the holy rituals and sermons of the men who held him captive until he managed to sneak a skeleton key from a monk's habit and free himself.

"I bear the bones of behemoth, sturdy as iron or brass." The demon reached one of its black claws toward the ground where Forkbeard had pitched the sword he stole from the smithy. It was the same blade he used to slice his way through the elector. The demon bent the sword until it shattered like the cooked carapace of a grasshopper that had the misfortune to jump into a campfire.

"My God," Forkbeard said, for the first time in his life.

The demon snapped its fingers and the roasted ox awoke from the fire behind the pirates. It roared, snorted, and lashed out. It snagged two men on its flaming horns and brought them into the fire where they roasted and blackened like gamey rabbits. The men's screams were drowned in the shouts of terror coming from those still living. One pathetic pirate picked up his patera and hurled the cooking pot impotently at the demon, who laughed. The demon hissed, spit a venomous libation that landed in a globule on Wolfram's face and burnt deeper than any Greek fire a mortal alchemist could conceive. Bone cracked, marrow popped, and the demon waved its tail which swept with the strength of a cedar tree. The tail split six pirates in half as it lashed from left to right.

Forkbeard tried to run with tears in his eyes. The demon was unaware of the pirate's newfound cowardice, but the face nestled in the monster's crotch whispered to the faces lodged in the knee and elbow joints of the monster. "He is getting away!"

The demon heeded the advice of the little heads and turned. It gored the catamite in a most ironic way, running one of its two gnarled horns deep into the poor soul's bunghole. Blood and exquisite milk leaked from the pirate's torn rectum as he gasped and died where he was impaled. The men around him ran shouting in all directions, screaming as they slipped in the blood of their fallen comrades and the pissoir they'd made of the floor in their terror.

The bull jumped from the hearth, and the dead flaming beast danced. It reared up on its hindquarters and stomped the head of one of the unfortunate remaining pirates until his skull was as soft as summer squash in the dead of winter. The demon cackled. The bull looked like a Minotaur while reared on its haunches, and snorted until brimstone flared from its nostrils.

Casper Namlos ran down a spiral staircase in another part of the castle. He fled out of the stone Zollschloss and across a field. He would live to see another day and to sow another one as well.

Chapter Four

The Cockaigne Betwixt the Legs of the Giantess

It had been many years since Roderick the Dwarven Illuminator had passed through this region. He avoided it because it was painful to remember his past years of slavery in the mines, and also because he didn't trust himself not to brain the first man who mistook him for a gnome.

The staff that might do the braining was made of strong beech. It was glazed in the same Prussian amber that covered the rosary beads he wore around his neck. The staff was capped by what looked like a pinecone plucked from the Bayern snow, but the history of the little object was quite storied.

It was a story that Roderick rarely told, but it went like this: One day the young dwarf slave snuck off from work in the mines on a dare. He travelled to the nearby cave where the giantess and the dragon were said to live together, and supposedly slept side by side. Roderick stole into the dank cave, his footfalls lighter than the plunk of moisture as it fell from the stalagmites and dripped into copper pools of water. The young dwarf reached a small, coal-stained hand beneath the scaly belly of the dragon. He stole one of the dragon's unborn and took it with him out of the cave.

Roderick then hand-carried the egg with the care of the Magi cradling the infant Son of Man. He walked until he came to the place of eternal ice. He held the egg over the cool waters of the pool. The egg turned blue, petrifying. It was a frozen memento of his bravery, and his repudiation of the life of a slave.

The dwarf gripped his staff now, pulled his fur-lined dalmatic closer over his undertunic, and then he burped. He tasted the bitter remnants of the last meal he'd had at the Wattle and Daub, an ancient fachwerk inn that looked like a giant chocolate box. His repast had been Keschde chestnuts and vineyard snails that tasted like they'd sucked up more than their fair share of Riesling over the years.

The burp was shortly followed by a fart, and Roderick was grateful no one was about to hear or smell the sulfurous flatulence. *Things*, he thought, *have changed quite a bit since I've last been here*. Some things hadn't changed, of course. The land was still dark with alder and pine, spangled red here and gold there with thriving maple that gained its color from the sandstone mountains. The blue maare craters still yawned, dark as the gunpowder of which Marco Polo wrote in his travels.

He as a dwarf had been allowed to sup among men, however, and that was certainly different from the last time he was here. He was the only dwarf he saw in the Wattle and Daub, and no one commented on his tiny person or spit in his direction. They didn't do as much as sneer at him.

A light wind picked up in the valley where he now roamed, and he pulled his hood lower over his head. His nose filled with the scent of basalt, and the aroma brought back memories. He saw himself working in a column of enslaved dwarves, shackled together on the Hunsruck Mountain. He was breaking stones with his pick. He and his pack were quarrying for the Koln Cathedral, which he refused to see even to this day despite the tales told of the place that made it out to be the eighth wonder of the world.

"Work, rock heads!" He felt the sting of the cat-o-nine tails, the flagellation counterpointed by the clink of a pickaxe on stone creating its own dreadful song. The rock that wasn't bound for Hanseatic ports stayed in the region, and was used to help straighten the river beds.

Roderick now made his way along the Hunsruck Mountain, plunging along the dog's back nestled among the larger range of the Rhenish Mastiff. He saw spots where he was sure his own pickaxe had once found purchase.

The mountains and hills were like one of Alighieri's outer rings of Hell, but the mines themselves were the center of a satanic Fibonacci spiral. Cave-ins were a common occurrence below the earth. At least when one quarried stone in the mountains, the journey to and from the destination took one through field and forest. There a dwarf could admire a deer as it bound over the heather or he could watch the rare Fledermaus beat its wings through the dark branches of the gathering trees with their outstretched arms.

He was sure he was getting closer now. The Teufelstisch rock stood alone among scree and a scattering of bones picked clean by vultures. His father had told young Roderick that this giant boulder was where the Devil dined, and he supposedly used the craggy surface of the rock to sign pacts with men who would trade their souls in exchange for riches and women. Roderick the First said a dwarf's soul could not be bought, for it was already promised to Odin. Also dwarves were creatures of the underworld, and they already knew the location of the Earth's precious metals and could not be bribed with jewels. It was true. Young Roderick himself had worked the silver mines in Rammelsberg and made the fortune of many a Guild member by the blisters on his own fingers and the sweat of his brow. He'd chiseled and carved his way clear through to the upper Nahe near Idar-Oberstein without once seeing the light of day. Vampires saw more sunlight than dwarves, it seemed.

"I hope you were right about what you shewed me," Roderick said to the dragon egg that tipped his staff. He walked toward the hollow, that same black cavern where he risked his life to steal that dragon's egg so long ago and made up his mind that he would no longer be a slave.

His scrying skills were rusted, since it had been years since he'd espied a grimoire. He was still close to certain that he discerned through the opaque fog that the dragon was now dead, along with the giantess. The humungous female had given birth to a daughter who lived in the cave, according to the vision. Now it was time to see whether or not he had seen true.

Two fruit bats flew out of the cave as he entered, beating their leathery wings as they shot off in the direction of the small village where he'd last broken fast. "Hello!" he shouted and his voice echoed. This was certainly a far different approach than he'd used the last time he was here. Had he shouted then, he would not be here now.

The truth was that he wanted to die, and he had chosen death by giantess.

"Yes?" The voice was deep but rich-timbered and honeyed. There was nothing manly in it.

"I have come to die betwixt thine thighs," Roderick said. He reached into the pack on his back for a spermaceti candle, but the giantess outdid him by lighting a torch which smelled of incense. The walls of the cave were spangled in gold and glowed. The dwarf's sight was failing but was still strong enough for him to know at a glance that it wasn't pyrite nestled in the crags and outcroppings of the cave walls.

"You have no desire for gold?" she asked.

Roderick shook his head. "None." The devil might not have ever gotten a dwarf to sign over his soul at the Teufelstisch for something as petty as precious metals, but Roderick was sure that if his old father's words were anything but a Hausmärchen, then many a dwarf from the mines would have traded both his mortal life and immortal soul for one night with a beautiful woman.

The Carolingian Church forbade congress between humans and dwarves. In the rare instance where a woman consented and a lucky dwarf managed to burst forth with seed, the offspring that resulted were said to be monstrous in form.

"Did you work the mines?" The giantess set the torch in a steel cage, and the flames danced against the gold-speckled walls.

"Yes," Roderick said, but he could say no more.

The giantess was standing now, her lustrous black hair the color of a raven after swimming in egg yolk. Her locks were dark and yet glistened with brilliance nigh on blinding. He looked at her hair parted at the middle of the scalp, and he thought of stars and oceans. Her lips were a perfect cupid's bow laid sideways, red as rubies. Her breasts were ample, white and milk-filled. They were heaving and fat enough with life for him to believe she could feed the whole of the world and all could live in peace from her sustenance.

She noticed his poetic appraisal, and turned so that he could admire her further. Her posterior was like two giant, smooth orbs of the type that gypsies used for scrying. They were as unblemished as marble and white as alabaster. She turned around again. The scent of her womb was captured in the black hair particles rising almost to her naked belly. The smell reached him and drew him toward her.

Roderick's tongue fell from his mouth, he set his staff down, and he walked toward her. "Kill me," he said. His life had been nothing but confusion. He was born a heathen hybrid who worked beneath the ground. He had somehow escaped and lived long enough to make it to a monastery where he learned to read, copy, and illuminate. He had converted to Christianity and was sure his father was fed to baying wolves in Valhalla on a nightly basis to atone for his son's conversion to the weak faith.

"Come to me," the giantess said.

She lay on her back, and smelled fresh from a recent bath in the natural mineral springs. Her fingers were large as giant wurst. They rustled through the black forest above her fruit, and she exposed the seat of her love. It was a giant pearl that was larger than Roderick's head. He knew this for a fact because he now pressed himself fully into the rubbery pinkness, smothering himself in her juices and trying to fit his open mouth around the slimed and delicious button.

It tasted of strawberries, and he felt a moan rumbling like an earthquake from deep within the stomach of the giantess. It carried like the screams of Hyiciquiron the Rapacious, whose roar could pull buildings down to their foundations and shake mountains to rubble.

"Die for me," the giantess whispered. The dwarf attempted to unhinge his jaw. He opened his mouth until a painful crack accompanied the slithering of his tongue and he licked from the giant pink pearl down to the very bottom of the glistening sheath. The lips were larger than his body.

He let his form go slack and commended his soul to her. "Die," she said, "but die well." Her giant, warm thighs closed around the dwarf. He didn't fight his death. He used his final breath not to breathe life, but rather squandered it to smell her. He tried to drown in her taste. The ambrosia leaked from her womb, and carried him to another place as the vice of her thighs tightened. He felt each bone in his body on the verge of breaking. He was a mouse in the jaws of a housecat, and he was about to die happy.

He closed his eyes and was in that legendary land. It was dredged from the stories Roderick the First told him in the mines.

A Pandian flute sang melodiously, and men walked across a sun-kissed valley as if buoyed on air. There were columns of marching dwarves, his father among them. One of the humans lashed old Roderick on the backside with the bullwhip, but the dying dwarf's father turned to his son and displayed a back free of scars and lacerations.

"Their whips leave no mark here, my son." His father then tilted his son's head upward, toward what were once gray slabs but were now mountains of Italian parmesan. The dwarves ignored the lash of the useless whips branded by the overseers, and they dipped their hands into the powdered cheese as if it was a sacristy font.

Roderick the Younger stroked his beard and asked his father, "What extramundane realm is this?" He wondered if he'd already died between the thighs of the giantess. If so, he wondered also if this was Heaven.

He stared around and saw in this land shades of the Garden of Hesperides, the land of the Egyptians he'd read of in one of the tomes, which it was forbidden to copy in the monastery. This place also bore a striking resemblance to the Sumerian Land of Dilmun. There were cooked pigs marching around with carving knives stuck in their backs, which made it improbable that this was a land for dead Saracens.

"Come son." The elder Roderick grabbed his son's hand and walked with him between the parmesan ranges.

"Ah," Roderick the younger said. He gazed at a flaming sword, a Zweihander that floated easily in the air. Images flashed in the fire as if by Pyromancy. "We are sealed in this Eden," Roderick said. He guessed at the nature of the place where he found himself by using the Good Book. It was one of the first books he learned to read and was always a good point of reference.

"What?" his father asked, puzzled.

Roderick averted his eyes, embarrassed at his father's illiteracy. He was embarrassed also at his own Christianity. "Genesis," Roderick said, "3:24." Then he quoted. "The Lord drove out the man, and he placed at the east of the Garden of Eden cherubim and a flaming sword, which turned every way, to keep the way of the Tree of Life."

"Yggdrasil is the only tree I know," his father said sternly. He slapped his son across the face, and tears formed in Roderick's eyes. The drops fell like crystals into the rough fur of the dwarf's teenaged stubble. "And it is the only tree you should know."

"I'm sorry, Father." Roderick wept, and his father patted him on the shoulder with his own coal-stained hands.

"It is alright, my son. I should not have slapped you. Tears and pain are not things for this world." His father laughed of a sudden, and shouted, "Cover your head!" Roderick the elder then shielded himself, as if from hail, and his son followed suit. Gold and silver coins rained from the heavens.

"We need mine no more," his father said. "The more a dwarf sleeps here, the more he earns. Come," his father bade him. "Come into the house where you will dwell with your father for the remainder of eternity."

Roderick did not ask questions. He followed his father. They walked past a river that flowed with fruited Riesling that leaked from Eibling and Auserrois from the steep slate vineyards of the Upper Mosselle.

Nightingales and songbirds now preceded them on their path, where the grass was spun sugar dyed green. The songbirds carried flowers in their bills and dropped them softly as snowflakes to make a path for the two men to follow toward the house, which smelled of strong fish even from this far away.

The two dwarves walked behind birds that carried flowers in their bills, and bees rushed to pollinate the flowers as they were dropped. Roderick was curious, and bent down to pick up a flower. It was a gentian, its light purple lips funneled like a miniature angel's trumpet. The curvature reminded Roderick of the intricate wrinkles in the womb of the giantess where he drowned in ecstasy. He was almost dead, and would remain here forever after.

The gentium brought to mind some bit of marginalia he'd read while illuminating. The iced lands of his forefathers were known as *Vagina Gentium* because they were believed to be the lands from which all other men came. He was a Christian now, though. He could not reconcile how it was possible to be born of the eternal womb and to die of the same, unless Mary was not only the mother of God, but also God herself.

Such theological concerns melted into ecumenisms in the next moment, for his father gripped the doorknob of the house where they would now dwell ever after. The doorknob was a singing shad, a herring that greeted them. Its mouth opened as the dwarf's strong palm, calloused even in paradise, gripped the doorknob and held it open for his son.

"What wonders!" Roderick exclaimed. "Such extravagance and abundancy!"

He gazed upward, saw the rafters of the home fashioned of linked, scaly sturgeons. Glazed ham upon glazed ham was piled in the kitchen in the shape of a pyramid. A dog sat guarding the glistening meats, untroubled by its own hungers. Seabass and salmon were laid like tile into the walls.

His father spoke. "All the lathes in this land are fashioned from sausages. The fields are ever ripe with grain and hedgerows are of roasted meat. Ours is a land without violence, except where deserved. For instance," his father said and grinned, "it can be observed that doves will tear wolves limb from limb if the beasts should so much as growl and disturb the slumber that lies upon our land."

Roderick the elder opened a door to another chamber, where his son could see his mother in bed riding another naked dwarf. Roderick could see even from this angle that the man she made the beast with was his uncle. Roderick looked to his father, expecting to see a bit of the wolf rise in the old man and to see the blood color the ancient Viking's cheeks. His father only grinned. "Here all men hold wives in common, and there is no jealousy."

"But ..." Roderick stammered, trailed off, and glanced back at his buck-naked mother riding his groaning and sweating uncle. Her rear faced him like two glistening overripe honeydew melons. He thought back to what he had learned of theology. Woman was never to be atop man during congress. That was akin to a witch riding a broom to Sabbath, the devil's very own hobbyhorse that inverted the natural order of things.

The giantess brought him out of his thoughts and out of paradise. She brought him away from his father and the land of fish and meats and endless delights. He left the land of gold and wine, nectar and songbirds. "Is it the natural order of things," she said, "to let a giantess break your skull with her powerful legs?"

Roderick breathed for the first time in what felt like a good long while. He was brought back from the brink of death, angered because the Danse Macabre was all he wanted. He exhaled, choked, and spit out some of the berried juices he'd sucked from the delights of the giantess's womb. "Why did you bring me back?" He glanced at the torch mounted in a steel cradle on the wall of the golden cave.

"For I scryed something in that dragon's egg you purloined from this cave so many years ago." The giantess held up her perfect white finger. She pointed a sharpened black-painted nail in the direction of the staff where the dwarf had laid his implement upon first entering the cavern.

The frozen egg was cloudy with visions, the unborn dragon's spherical form revealing strong images that told the dwarf that his life was not over and his work not done. He sighed and placed his head against the soft fleshy pillow that was the giantess's leg. Her limb was as large as an ionic column but soft as eiderdown. Her thigh was sticky with the humid warmth his tongue had brought forth from her giant pink button of gloriously wrinkled flesh. He felt himself trapped against her skin like a fly against a spider web.

"Very well," Roderick said, and groaned. "I will live, and do as the prophecy commands. Please let me sleep here a few hours before I resume my journey, my goddess." The winds could be heard howling outside of the cave, and the land was covered in white blankets of snow.

"You may rest before you journey again," the daughter of that ancient giantess said. "Then you must go to Koln."

He shot up so fast that a bit of the skin of his face peeled as he tore himself free from her thigh. He didn't notice the light speckling of blood that came from being exposed to frostbite followed by the warmth of her womb. The drastic change in temperature was so sudden that it caused him to bleed, burn, and chafe not a little.

"I swore the day my father died that I would never set foot in the city whose cathedral we slaving dwarves quarried for stone until our backs broke and our fingers bled."

The giantess smiled, her eyes downcast, and her eyebrows arching. She parted the lips of her womb, as large as the flapping wings on a gryphon. He breathed her tart and pungent scent, and she said, "You have no choice. If you will not obey the vision, at least obey me."

He allowed his arms to hold fast at his sides, and straightened himself until he was as rigid as a ramrod flechette. "You know I am powerless against you."

She picked the dwarf up and rammed him deep inside her body. The voice of the giantess carried to him as he nestled and burrowed into the wet flesh of her innards, his tongue flicking and lashing like a mad dervish on the walls inside of her body.

"A powerless man in the service of a woman is the most powerful creature there is."

He knew she was right, and he licked and sucked to let her know he knew. Of a truth, he was not exactly Jonah in the belly of the Great Whale at this moment. Of another and equal truth however, this was perhaps an even more holy ritual.

Chapter Five

And May the Reader Meet the Bastard Without Further Delay

The forest of masts could be seen high above the tops of all the other buildings in the city, except for the spire of Koln Cathedral. That loomed above all else. Thus it was easy for the idea of seafaring to take root in young Martin Stolzer's heart and for it to linger there like a worm.

Witziger the Chandler could smell the docks on the boy when he came into his shop. The inside of the shop was dim and golden brown, like dunkel brew. "Lock the door," the chandler said. Martin did what was asked of him. The sounds of the market grew dimmer as the door closed, though the smells were as strong as before. Witziger made most of his candles from Berkshire pig tallow, and the guild had allowed him to set up shop within spitting distance of the slaughterhouse. That put him downwind of some bad smells. There was a famine in the land, and there were many mendicants who would come begging not only for bones, but also candles to eat.

"Boy," the chandler said, as Martin got closer, "you primp, coif, and pamper that hair like one of the harlots in that convent of yours." Martin set his leather gispere sack on the counter next to a silver candelabrum. "And you treat your coarse beard like a right old goat."

Witziger cackled at that and took the coin. "You've got a fine set of pickled eggs to talk to me like that. Mother Inferior pays well, so I let it slide." The chandler took the coins. "You should give up this nasty business in the forest, and come work for me."

The boy slid the baggy arms of his shepherd's tunic off his shoulders and reached down to his feet. He extracted some thorns from the leather thongs guarding his legs. The chandler had hidden the coin in a purse, and he came back over to the front of his shop. He saw Martin picking the thorns from the leather and said, "You see? You see what working for that lot gets you?"

The chandler set two handfuls of candles on the counter before him. There were a few fine beeswax jobs mixed in with the tallow ones. Martin gathered them up and placed them in his sack. The old man with the goat's beard persisted. "Do you really want to live on the sea?"

Martin looked through the greasy window of the shop covered with iron bars, toward the street. "Aye."

Witziger scoffed. "He answers like a pirate, even." He leaned across the counter and addressed the lad. "You ever eaten maggot-ridden biscotti?"

Martin said nothing. His features were soft, even when the light wasn't as dim as it was now in the shop. There was something unsure in his movements, though he was not nervous or skittish. His uncertainty was deliberate, like a first-year apprentice who wanted to make a good impression. He could have belonged to any man who came to the stewhouse, from a burgher to a vicar. Whoever sired him was obviously a slumming noble. It annoyed those craftsmen who knew he came from the convent, to think that one whose station was so low still had a better pedigree than they.

"You ever sleep a day outside that fine whorehouse of white lace and feathers?" Witziger asked. Martin shook his head and the man continued. "Do you know what it is to sleep on a lice-ridden straw paillasse? You ever been awoken by a sailor with a prick the size of a bull's?"

The boy was getting tired of this. He had his candles, and there were other chores that needed doing. The other little bastards needed tending. "Why do you ask me all of these questions? What other chance do I have?" The boy gazed through the greasy window again. "I need to go where no one knows my origin, and the sea is a good place to start."

"I ask," Witziger said, "because I know you are a good lad, for all the unseemly and unchristian things you must do to keep your belly fed. I don't need to read your denstbreve."

Martin adjusted the satchel on his back. "The Maschopeien wouldn't let me work for you. I couldn't go from Kinder to Knappen without someone finding out and us both ending up in stocks."

Witziger lowered his voice. "You could bohnhaserei, and work nights for me. I'd pay you just as much as a journeyman once you learned your trade."

The boy's voice was just as low as Witziger's now. "We'd both be growing mandrakes beneath the gallows then if someone got wind."

The chandler nodded toward the front of his shop. "That's why the door's locked."

"Well, I'm going to unlock it." Martin doffed a nonexistent cap, unlocked the door, and touched his hand to the brass handle. The smells of the market assaulted them in waves. There was the rich fetidness of lanolin ointment from sheep fat, the heavy musk of hooves melted into glue, and the smells that came from bones pounded into meal to give bread heft.

Martin held his place in the doorway. "I will sail," he said. "I will alight for Novgorod and Bruges, from Hamburg to Flanders."

"The seas are filled with robbers, privateers, and corsairs," the chandler hissed like a charmed snake. "Beneath the water it is even worse." He shuddered as he thought of the monsters, the slinking and scaled poisonous leviathans with pincers and hard crustacean shells that were ancient and evil and older than the Bible.

"Still," Martin said, "I'll sail." He looked back at Witziger with eyes that were more kind than defiant. He liked the old man and was happy that he was willing to risk everything just to give the young bastard a chance at a life that fate would otherwise deny him. Martin Stolzer now only had eyes for the sea and he would escape the stew at any cost. The only other option was to be a gentleman of leisure, and pimping was for the birds. It was lower even than penny preaching. "The sea will provide," he finally said.

The chandler pointed up the street, his hands waxy as votive candles. "That pig provides, boy. Do you know how much meat a Berkshire swine can furnish?"

Martin shook his head, and his amber hair fell before his eyes. He swept it away, tucking it behind his ear. Witziger said, "You've got a minimum of one-hundred pounds of usable meats, excluding organs and bones and fat."

"Bones?" Martin had seen the piles gathering in the city like the remnants of a plague that had swept the land or the aftereffects of an ancient battle between Romans and barbarians. He had no idea what was done with the bones or what purpose they served.

A dormouse scurried across the dusty floor of the shop, and the chandler said, "Bones, my boy. Not everyone has a houseful of common mothers to sell their maidenhood in return for finery. The poor live by the bones they brew in their pottage."

Martin shrugged. He didn't want to cross swords too hard with the old man, but he'd never seen the chandler in the stewhouse. Martin thought the man didn't rightly know how the fallen girls lived. One thing the man did know was his trade, and Martin lifted one of the candles from the sack and asked, "How do you make them just so? That they burn evenly?"

The chandler smiled a secretive grin. It was his doing that actually earned the fallen women of Koln the sobriquet of "girls by the candle," since each man who came into the house could make the beast with a woman for as long as the candles burned. The tallow or wax always smoldered for the same amount of time, about as long as it took for a lethargic cloud to pass from the face of the moon.

"If you want the secrets of my trade, come work nights for me."

The little whorehouse denizen shook his head. He gazed toward the array of wooden masts peeking on the horizon, high above the city wall. "The sea's for me."

"Balderdash!" The chandler shouted, and unwound a bit of peat that'd gotten lodged among the coins the boy had given him. "You've been to the docks and that's as far as you've gotten, collecting moss in the woods for the ships."

Martin squared himself to the old chandler. "It pays well. They need someone to plug the strakes and caulk the deckboards, and that gets me close enough to the ships."

"If they were wise, they'd use heather and pork fat."

The boy pointed up the cobbled alley. "Your friend won't sell to them. Nor will he give me sheepskin to make mop heads for greasing the hulls."

The chandler laughed until the loose skin of his face danced like a reddish turkey waddle. "We all know why too."

Martin couldn't help but smile with him. There wasn't a wedge of gossip that didn't reach Martin's ears on account of the way men loved to talk to his many mothers after the candles had burnt their way down to the bases of the wicks. Koln was a big town, but everyone knew that the butcher's wife had left with a sailor some years ago. It was on that account that the man hated seamen.

"Auf wiedersehen, then." Martin waved once to the old man, who shouted, "May the road rise to meet you, and then give you a swift kick to the rear!"

Martin damn-near sprained an ankle as his felt covered feet went from wood to cobblestone. He righted himself. He moved among the throng of the mendicants, the working poor, the foot soldiers, and the merchants. He saw a few striped hoods but didn't say a word to any of the whores when he was outside of the convent.

The streets were dirty haustein, an ugly limestone color that reminded him of aged cheese. Wilted lettuce, feces, and other rubbish caulked the spaces between the cobblestones and stained the bottoms of his curl-toed shoes. He turned right, away from the Gerberstrasse section. He worked his way upwind toward the fairgrounds where things didn't smell as bad. The lapping wind from the Rhine was strong enough here to make the air fresh, but there were also enough burned brick abodes to mute the gale and keep it from chilling him to the bone.

The banner with the red nettle leaf sewn into its fabric beckoned in the near-distance. It marked the beginning of the market district, where it hung from a protruding oriel. A man with a crooked wooden staff slapped several Jutland cattle on the rump, and Martin stepped aside to let the herder and his beasts go through. He turned once more. This time he went to the right and finally made his way home to the convent.

He opened the door to the cellar, and stepped inside. The room was made of stone and was cold. A draft flowed from the padstones to the arched ceiling. Martin loved looking up at the cross-ribbed ceiling, which reminded him of the hull of a boat that had fully capsized and sealed him in its overturned berth. The sound of the fatherless children playing up above came through the wood and brass door at the top of the stone stairs. He crept silently past the door, into the other room of the cellar.

Merlin meowed as he entered the pantry. The cat licked his calico paws once and then chased after a roach creeping across the floor. "Hello, boy!"

Martin went to the shelves filled with crockery, and poured the contents of his pack onto a shelf where jellies and jams sat. He hung his leather sack on one of the nails where herbs hung. He breathed in the scent of lavender and rosemary and smoothed the tallow candles in a neat row across the pig bladder that covered the shelf.

He spoke to the cat. "Keep the little buggers away from the dry goods." He leaned down to stroke Merlin, who now stood sentry in front of the burlap sacks filled with grain and dried peas. The cat looked up with its jade Egyptian eyes toward the ceiling, where gammon hams hung dangling from the rafters. Merlin prayed with his little brain that the cured meats would strain on their hemp tethers until they broke and came tumbling down into his tiny mouth, but it was to no avail.

Martin checked the cat's saucer, saw that there was still milk there, and then he started for the stairs. He pressed his face to the door, pounded it thrice like a giant in a Hausmärchen, and shouted, "Kobolds, brownies, and gnomes! I be here to grind ye for me bread." He opened the door and saw that four of the six fatherless had scattered and hid in various quarters of the room.

He saw tiny feet behind the lacquered cabinet, and he counted another pair behind the washbasin. He heard giggling from behind the table where a lily-filled majolica vase caught light streaming through the double-shuttered window. Heat from the large oven filtered into the room, and only young Oliver with the newborn in his hands stood out in the open.

Oliver wore fine samite braies and white cotte, and he ran his finger in and out of the suckling babe's mouth as he looked up at his older brother. "Will ya read to us?"

"If your chores are done." Martin left the room for a moment, and he walked into the ashlar-dressed chamber where the bread oven was brimming with risen pandemain. He returned to the room where the other bastards hid. Oliver still stood there in the middle of the room and let the baby use his finger as a pacifier.

"Olly, the bread is done. You and the others can eat till your bellies burst, but do it inside."

There was still a bit of the famine on. If the rowdies of the town saw the sons of whores wearing finery and eating pandemain at midday while they still suffered under the embargo and ate acorn bread, then the boys might all end up dead.

"Aye!" Oliver said, speaking like a pirate. He wanted to be a Vitalienbruder because Martin did.

The promise of food brought the other children from their hiding. Two or three wrapped their hands around Martin's legs. The rest went to help Oliver, who had set the baby down in the bassinet while he went to cool the bread and kill the oven embers.

David was the third eldest after Martin and Oliver. He made his way to the babe in white cloth. "What will happen to him?"

Martin took the heads of two younger boys in his palms, and spun them around like a toymaker's tops. "We have five beds, so when young Marcus is too large for his bassinet, he will have to go to the orphanage."

"No!" David's mouth was a frozen "O," like that of a cherub in a fountain.

"Either him or you," Martin said.

David's eyes turned away from the bassinet. If it was as simple as Martin said, then his sympathy for the tot was already at its end. A question still loomed, though.

"What of his mother?" David asked.

Martin stayed the tears in his eyes and refused to let them fall to his cheeks. "Lyudmila is fat with milk, and so she will wet nurse for the royals."

They all loved her, though not as much as him. The two children in his arms squirmed like snared hares yanked from their traces, and the other boy walked over from the bassinet. "Then what will happen to her?"

"If she's smart," Martin said, "she will learn midwifery while among the royals, and will not return to be a girl paid by the candle."

None of them were old enough to notice her breasts heaving with milk or to feel their own vital life sapped by the succubae at night. They knew nothing about candles except that they burned. They understood enough to know that Lyudmila wouldn't be coming back once she was gone, and that this was somehow better than living in this house that was a sort of heaven for them and a hell for their many mothers.

"She will learn much," David said.

The others returned from the kitchen with the cooked bread in a wicker basket covered in white linen. "She can read," Oliver said. The children gathered around the basket and tore the bread and ate like tiny disciples crowding around blessed multiplied loaves.

David said, "We've seen her reading that *Roman de la Rose*."

Martin shot the little one a stern look, snatched a slice of bread from his hand, and placed it in his own mouth. He talked as he chewed. "You are too young to gaze on those woodcuts." None of them could read, but they could see well enough. He thought them too immature to understand what the "Rose" of the *Roman* was, or to understand why they shouldn't read the book.

"If your chores are done, then we can start on *Parzifal*." Martin finished the bread he'd stolen from the little one, and the babe cooed from the bassinet. The poor child didn't know it would soon part from its mother forever, and would also lose the only brothers and sisters it might ever know.

"The pots have been emptied in the cesspit," one of the little ones said.

Martin leaned down to him and took a deep breath. He smelled fetidness on the young boy's clothes. "I can tell you did journey to the pit this morning."

He coughed and the little boy giggled. The boy threw a jab at his elder brother's groin. Martin intercepted his fist and spun the boy around and rubbed his towhead with his knuckle until a cowlick rose and danced. "You," Martin said to Oliver. His voice was stern again.

Martin was only thirteen, but he was the eldest male to call the convent home. If he was not tough, the rough men who visited the stewhouse would take advantage of him and his many mothers. "Aye?"

Martin played at Eustace of the high seas. "After ye swabbed the decks, did ye scatter wormwood through the bedding straw to keep the bedbugs at bay?" Martin kissed a phantom parrot on his shoulder and pretended his leg was peg for a moment.

His show made Ollie laugh, and the boy who lisped on account of being breastfed too long said, "Aye, captain."

"Good, then." Martin once more opened the door to the basement, snuck down the stone stairs, and walked to the shelf in the room where the cat meowed. Merlin tilted his head and watched his master quizzically as the boy took the kid-bound volume down from the shelf and carried it slowly up the stairs in two hands.

Martin walked the Eschenbach work over to the escritoire, and laid it open on the writing desk. The smell of wood and ink filled the air with its enchanted musk. The children crowded around the book, but kept their hands at their sides without Martin having to instruct them.

He kept his thoughts to himself, though he wished there was someone his own age with whom he could talk. Lyudmila lorded over his dreams, with her breast bunched like grapes and white as porcelain. He had committed the sin of Onan, coming not onto another man's wife but onto the straw and wormwood as his mind grew fevered with visions of the young whore. Her pregnant stomach was not a thing of shame for him, as it was for the other men of Koln who scorned the striped-hooded girl at market. The stomach was for him a swollen mound of fertility, the mark of a goddess whose fat contours he wished would drape over all of Christendom and conquer it and its flaming swords, with naught but soft belly and breasts.

Martin cast his thoughts aside and lightly touched the gold leaf foliate borders of the page of the book he held. Little Oliver's eyes drifted to the bas-de-page, where a monk played a bellows with a distaff he held like a catgut bow. A donkey danced in the margins to the monk's music. Martin started reading from the first letter, an oversized "F" lavished in a thicket of inked blackberries.

"Flegetanis the heathen could read in the heavens high how the stars went on their course and circled the skies."

"What's a heathen?" David asked, for what must have been the hundredth time. Oliver pinched him and the boy hushed and filled his inquisitive mouth with bread. Martin continued. "The lot of man is hard, and he wanders without end. If he be smart, he may read the stars and see strange secrets there." Oliver couldn't read but had heard the story enough times by now that he could mutter along word for word under his breath. He spoke without sound to keep from throwing Martin off-course. He measured his cadences so that they kept time with the verse of the eldest bastard. "Though heathen, his heart was good. Thus God granted him a vision of the Grail in the stars."

Martin turned the page. "A host of angels once bore this marvel of heaven to the Earth. But the sons of men now hold it, and guard it with humble heart."

"And the best of mankind," Oliver said, louder now, "shall be those knights who have in such service a glorious part."

David and the other young ones laughed at the synchronized rhyme that just occurred between Martin and Oliver. Martin took a hand from the page and patted Oliver on his head.

"My mother says my father was a Templar." Oliver gave up his pretentions of being a buccaneer, and now struck the stance of a warrior for Christ. He held an invisible longsword pitched into an equally invisible rock lain at his feet.

David spitefully flicked the little bastard on the earlobe and said, "You don't know who your mother is, so what makes you think any of the candle girls here could tell you who your father was?"

Martin couldn't abide a fight this close to the precious book. It was one of three in the house aside from Lyudmila's secret copy of *Roman de la Rose*. He covered the kid-skinned tome with his form and said, "Calm yourselves, boys. If you want to go at it hammers and tongs, do so in the garden, but not in the room where the babe sleeps." Martin looked over toward the bassinet. "And not so close to the book." He closed the tome and dust clouds fluttered into the air, catching light that streamed into the window from the sunny courtyard.

Both of the younger boys looked toward the window, wondering if the bread was well-enough digested yet to let them punch at one-another. Then again, they wanted to hear more of *Parzifal*. They looked back meekly toward Martin. "Apologize," Martin said to David.

The boy stared at his leather shoes and said "Entschuldigung" to the bells on his curled toes.

Martin's voice took on that fatherly tone again. "Did you do your feet offense, or did you do offense to your brother? How do you know that his father didn't fight the Saracens?"

The boy's face was no longer a mask of shame but was lit by the light of curiosity. His imagination glowed like a tiny fire in his skull. "So is the Grail real then?"

"I don't know," Martin said, and he was being honest. "Some say it lays in Muntsalvasche, which is many days' journey from here. Some say that the Grail isn't a cup, but is a lapis lazuli of some kind."

"What's that?"

Martin struggled to describe the blue, metamorphic jewel that was like a bloodstone mixed with the green-blue of a mermaid. It was something whose beauty was beyond the words he knew. "It is a rock," he said, and he sighed. Words, which were so important to him, had failed him now.

Oliver looked out the window, though now his eyes were not on the courtyard where he might box to get revenge on the other lad who impugned his father the Templar. His eyes and his mind wandered far above the limestone wall that kept the boys safe from the hatred and stares of the townsfolk, toward the high wall that guarded Koln from the rest of the world. "Will we ever travel beyond the walls of this town?"

Martin answered his younger brother. "I leave almost daily."

"I mean farther than a couple of stadia to collect a bit of peat and moss for the ships at the dock."

Now Martin felt like boxing the boy's ears. He would give little Michael some sparring lessons to prepare him to win his boxing match with Oliver, should he goad his older brother with further charges of bastardy. "Don't disparage my trade," Martin said. "It earns me extra coin, and it gets me closer to the ships."

Oliver might as well be old Witziger himself if he was going to caution Martin against his dream of eventually taking to the sea. Martin stood and walked to the two ancient swords crossed over the hearth. "One of these days I will take to the sea," he said, making the promise more to himself than to any in attendance.

The bells from the church suddenly rang. All grew silent, except for the sounds of the babe who wept against the ugly dissonance. He cried also for the taste of milk that wasn't forthcoming. Each of the boys in the room looked at each other and shuddered because they knew what the bells meant. That old archbishop who called himself a man of Christ but more probably served Baphomet was about to preach. The people of the town were going to gather in the shadow of the steeple and listen to his rancid poison as he poured it into them.

Martin walked into the kitchen, took up a willow broom, and began to sweep up bits of bread that lay scattered in crumbs on the floor. He spoke over the sound of the bells. He wished that they could all ignore the ringing, even though the din struck fear deep into their very marrow. The younger boys had only been to market a few times, accompanied by their mothers in striped hoods. They had heard how the archbishop spoke of the candle girls. He put them in the same company as Jews, Saracens, lepers, and sodomites. All would burn according to the archbishop. Thus the boys loathed him, for one would have to be quite loathsome himself to want to see his own mother burn.

"Open the door to the cellar," Martin said. Oliver ran to the door and pulled it open. Merlin stopped pawing at the rotted, wainscoted board on the other side of the door and padded softly into the room. The cat bounded quickly for the crumbs of bread on the floor. It would eat those to help sop up the milk it had lapped from its tiny saucer.

Oh, Martin thought, *to be a black cat in a whorehouse. What a life it must be!* He stopped sweeping, braced his chin on the wooden handle of the willow broom, and he thought some more. He thought of grails and pirates, of corsairs and sea monsters. He thought of Leviathan and Behemoth. Above all he thought of Lyudmila.

Chapter Six

The Archbishop's Sermon

He preached to the wealthy from behind the altar, and to the masses on the steps of the church. It was better to speak to the poor in the full light of the sun, where his jewels and vestments could glow.

Archbishop Torner had finished preaching to the throng of merchants, bankers, and nobles within, reading verbatim from a Latin missile. Now it was time to talk to the ragged masses of the Hanseatic Freistadt.

The Bell of the Three Kings ceased ringing. The echo of the last gong carried toward the flying buttresses of the church, which reached high enough in the sky to slice the white clouds. A ray of sunlight splashed against the stained glass windows of the cathedral, filtered through the nave, and glowed in the water of the baptismal font. This made the inside of the church look like the heavenly city of Jerusalem in the Book of Revelation.

"People of Koln …" The dirty masses crowded around the archbishop. He held his golden scepter in one hand and two volumes bound in the virgin skin of an unnamed animal in the other. The books didn't look to the crowd like Bibles from where they were standing. The people moved closer to get a better look at the tomes even though few of their number could read.

The archbishop managed to adjust his chain of office, the golden clinker-built cog on the medallion bearing the arms of the Hanseatic Guild in radiant enamel. The faces of the audience were so completely covered in soot and dirt that they could be mistaken for Moors. The clothing of the archbishop was lamb-white down to the last exposed bit of fabric on his miter.

He raised his books in one hand and his staff in the other. The reflection of the sun off the gem-encrusted rod forced some of the throng to close their eyes, but they could still hear his words. "Today," the archbishop said, "we must speak of evil."

A soft zephyr picked up, lifted the hood and mantle of his vestments, and made the budge fur of his collar rustle like grass in a field. One man in the crowd found that his eyes burned when he focused on the jeweled staff, and yet he could not take his eyes away from it. Topaz crystals glowed along with inlaid emerald chrysolites. Those spots on the staff where there were dark onyxes banded with milky white did nothing to dim the bright effect of the holy staff. It was so animate and alive with tinted beryls and gemstones that more than one among the number of the ragged crowd thought there was a chance that if the Archbishop cast the staff to the ground, it might become a living snake and creep off to warn pharaoh of his hubris.

The last of the gems in the staff were of sardius, so red that they caused sinful thoughts to bubble in the minds of the men who secretly frequented the convent on occasion. "First," the archbishop said, "let me caution you people against abstention from pork."

"Why, Archbishop?" someone shouted. Their words were only meant to further prompt him on the subject and thus weren't regarded as insolence. The eyes of the holy man nevertheless fixed their colorless force in the direction of the interloper.

"You will note," the archbishop said, "that if you venture far from the walls of our town, the lepers in the colony count a great number of Jews among their pitiable ranks." His voice was shrill. "It is because the Jews abstain from pork that they are susceptible to leprosy. For pork fortifies the Galenic humors with strength."

"Pork is hard to come by during the embargo. A Holstein goes for more than I earn in a year."

He ignored the protest of the man in the crowd. The bishop gazed heavenward toward the ray of sun he was convinced the Lord shot in his direction for him alone.

Archbishop Torner could best be described in terms of what he lacked, from a strong chin to a strong nose, to any color in his face or eyes. He was an agglomeration of negatives, of things missing given form. He was a vortex of a man who took when he spoke and could not give. What he did not lack was the ability to make men fear his direct path to God, and his power to bring wrath on any who didn't heed him. Famine and plague could strike at any time, but the people of Koln were convinced that it would all be worse without his holy intercession.

The archbishop held out his hands, and two altar boys in white baggy vestments ran toward him. Their costumes billowed as the wind grew into a strong gale that tilted the archbishop's miter. One of the two boys righted the holy man's headgear. The other took the staff from his master's hand, so that now the archbishop held only the books covered in the virgin parchment.

"We must now discourse on the candle girls, they of the stewhouse that some in contravention of God's will have the temerity to call a convent." His voice grew to its shrillest pitch. "It is no such thing, and such women are further from God than the seventh planet of our universe."

A man with a voice fit for town crier cupped his mouth with dirty hands and shouted, "What is the newest crime the hooded wenches have perpetrated?"

The archbishop's face contorted into what he considered a smile. "There are no new sins for those in the oldest profession. Only repeat performances and encores in the theater of the damned." He abandoned his extended metaphor in the next breath and said, "Those of you who can read, please see what Bernarda of Clairvaux says on the subject of one woman allowing another woman to feed her child the milk from her breasts."

"What does Bernarda say!" All of those who were illiterate in the crowd listened intently.

"He speaks of a noble woman, not of a woman feigning noble pretensions." His false smile became a genuine sneer now. The people on the steps of the cathedral knew of whom he spoke, and knew he would speak of her again. "Countess Ida Boulogne had given birth to a son, and forbade those of her retinue whose breasts were wet to allow her son to sup at their bosoms. One impudent maid placed a common breast in the royal mouth in contravention of the edict."

"And then what transpired?" Someone shouted.

"The righteous woman plucked the child from the harlot's breast swiftly and shook the boy until he vomited up the poisonous, common milk."

"And what has this to do with the striped hoods?" Witziger the Chandler asked from where he stood on the steps among the throng.

"I have heard from reliable sources that harlots from the stewhouse that are fat with milk are sent to wet nurse among the town's most prominent women." There was a gasp from the crowd, and Archbishop Torner fed the flames.

"Think of it!" He whispered, but his voice was so wracked by passion that his whisper carried with the force of another man's screams. "The black milk of Babylonian whores filling the mouths of royal Kinder. Our bloodlines will be poisoned and our sons will grow malformed and monstrous, no match for the next generation of Saracens preparing for another holy war. And you gentle folk know how the Saracens are with women."

"Tell us!"

"They are Scheherazade come to life, each and every one of them. They cavort through harems in shameless, sensual odalisques. They know naught but carnal splendors. The pleasures poison the soul and earn it an eternity among the coals of unquenchable fires, in the layers of Hell reserved especially for infidels who tempt good men and Christians who succumb to the blandishments of the harem. Look on this heathen tome, if you doubt me!"

"We cannot read it!" someone shouted.

"Nor can I," the archbishop allowed, in a rare show of humility, "for it is written in Sanskrit." He momentarily faltered, then resumed. "Sanskrit is a heathen tongue that predates Latin and was created solely for the written veneration of snake-headed goddesses, whose temples were destroyed in the thrust of Constantine's holy sword."

He held the volume up, brandishing its lustful images before the eyes of those who were too poor to read. The illiterate could see men and women in poses of congress that would put toads to shame. "Forget the words and the images of the book, and pay close attention to the binding."

Another of the altar boys rushed to the archbishop's side, and it was clear that this had been coordinated in advance of the sermon. "Pass it among them," he said to the boy, and then he said to them, "do not be tempted to turn the pages. Be clever as Perseus avoiding the eyes of the Gorgon, not foolish like Lot's wife casting her eyes back and becoming a pillar of salt."

"Wasn't Perseus a pagan?" Someone in the crowd asked. Since the question challenged the archbishop in no small way, his colorless eyes gathered cold force and burrowed into the eyes of the man who dared insinuate he might have an affinity for Greek heathens. The man who posed the question found his blood turn cold. He shivered from the gelid force of the stones that were the archbishop's eyes as they searched deep into his soul.

"The Greeks were pederasts and heathens, but they had many brilliant philosophers among their number." The archbishop calmed a bit, and the altar boy reached the ranks of the poor. He held his nose as his senses that were better attuned to talcum could not abide dung and rotted cabbage quite so well. "Even the Greeks knew the weakness of women and the evil that dwells in their hearts."

The archbishop pointed with the hand that usually held the jeweled scepter. "Feel the skin of the books, ignore the words." Archbishop Torner still held another volume under his arm, though he was not ready to speak on its contents.

"It feels like virgin kid!" someone in the crowd exclaimed.

"It is vellum!" one of the astonished throng proclaimed.

The archbishop took two steps down the stone stairs of the cathedral. A cloud with the color and dimensions of an anvil masked the sun, while other dark clouds began to gather and mushroom in the heavens. The clouds stained the spires and buttresses at the church until their gray became indistinguishable from that of the stone gargoyles nestled in the high pediments of the cathedral. "It is uterine vellum," the archbishop said. His tongue snuck out and licked his parched lips. He was thirsty for some sacristy wine, mixed with the blood he occasionally pricked from the fingers of one of his altar boys with the point of his knife. He found his own form of transubstantiation more thrilling than the mere conversion of wafer into flesh.

"Is it from a stillborn calf?" one of the crowd members asked. It was the fishmonger. He was blind, but the loss of one sense heightened the others and the people in his midst were inclined to agree with him if his hands told him it was calf.

"Nein!" the archbishop shouted. "When working as nursemaids these striped hoods learn the black arts under the guise of midwifery." The archbishop panted as he contemplated the unnumbered throngs of witches and hexed women who feigned Christianity and made the Devil's pact by kissing Lucifer's hindquarters in the woods on a moonless night, all unbeknownst to their poor husbands.

"What are these women taught?" someone asked. He was too short for his face to be seen while his voice was heard. The archbishop did not bother to seek out the pigmy among the ranks of the townsfolk.

"They are taught the arts of abortifacients."

A collective gasp went up from the crowd, and the archbishop continued. "The same rabbis who poison our wells with blood teach women to apply sponges soaked in vinegar and poultices laced with strong mustard seeds to the fruit of their wombs. This brings forth sons and daughters before they are fully quickened."

A rumble went through the crowd. They were ready to murder Jews, whores, or Saracens. They were even ready to murder lepers if the archbishop would only point them in the direction of the colony. "They use the skin of the quickened after the child has achieved a reasonable soul in utero. They then make their godless tomes in the skins of infants never given a chance to breathe free air."

"Stadt Luft macht frei!" someone shouted. The old quote brought some merriment to the crowd but not enough to turn them from the task of murder or at least banishing the whores from the town at the end of a pitchfork if Archbishop Torner so willed it. Whores were already obliged to buy any wares they touched at market, and they were forbidden from being at market except on certain days. They tried to get around the town's laws by sending their bastard offspring to the fairgrounds to do their bidding, but no one was fooled.

"The penitential literature is too lax!" The archbishop shouted. Some of the crowd wondered if the other volume he still kept by his side was a penitential. The archbishop wasn't lifting it and he wasn't handing it to the altar boy to pass around their number, so the people were left to guess.

Most of the throng was curious to know exactly how stringent the penitential literature was. That was the sort of thing the archbishop expected them to already know, so none dared ask. Not being able to read was no excuse either. Most of the stories of the Good Book that were worth knowing could be gleaned from pictures, stained glass, and the Stations of the Cross. The preachers were always there to spread the word, for those who were blind like the fishmonger.

"Abortion before forty days after conception involves only a year of penitence." The clouds gathered closer in the sky above the archbishop, and he looked even paler now. "Whores are accomplished in practices aimed at secretly destroying the fetus."

"Such as?"

"Such as potions, dances of Walpurgis, tightened corsets, and blows to the belly. As they allow the young nobles to suckle, they teach these wicked arts to the ladies of the houses where they work. They make harlots of once-pious wives."

One man in the crowd gripped his wife tightly as the archbishop spoke. He knew his station was too low to even afford a nursemaid, but he still feared the candle girls might whisper dark arts to his wife at market one day, or at the very least a prostitute might lean out of one of the windows of the convent and give his wife the evil eye while she was on her way to the sewing house.

"When does quickening occur?" someone in the crowd asked. The people of Koln knew Archbishop Torner was a man of chirurgery, as well as Hippocratic and Galenic stores of knowledge. He had taught the men that seed brought forth during coitus was in fact red blood from the brain churned until white in the act of making the beast. Thus a woman's sole purpose in seduction was to drain a man's mind of its vital fluids.

"We must seek out the wisdom of Saint Thomas and Saint Augustine," the archbishop said, and walked back to the top of the staircase. He came to stand in front of one of the massive oaken doors that was open, giving view onto the inside of the gothic church with its treated wood and shined marble.

"Males," the archbishop said, "are stronger than females, and this disparity asserts itself even in utero." The book had passed its way through the hands of those in the crowd. They handled the volume not only as if they believed the archbishop's words about it being made from the skin of an unborn child but as if the tome itself was a hot smoldering coal. The altar boy took the book back from the last in the crowd to peruse and thumb it, and he carried it back to his master.

The archbishop accepted the tome without a word and without looking down at the book or the boy who held it. "Because the male is stronger than the female, he quickens at the fortieth day in his mother's womb. The female is of a weaker constitution and quickens at the ninetieth." The cold stones in his head that passed for eyes now searched among the throng for the one who challenged him when he mentioned Perseus. He glared at the fellow, who dropped his eyes toward the bunched stockings on his calves and the lusterless buckles of his worn shoes in desperate need of cobbling. "Even Aristotle was of this mind and of an accord with our modern physics on this issue."

The archbishop passed off the book he'd just recently accepted to another altar boy. He spoke to the boy loud enough so that the crowd could hear him. "Light rushes, create a pyre, and burn the book."

"Yes, your holiness."

"Cover your ears," the archbishop cautioned. "The screams of the unborn are preserved in the skin stretched over the wicked tome."

"Yes, your holiness." The boy lowered his head as if just freshly anointed with oil. He walked down the steps and the crowd parted respectfully, not wanting to interrupt his holy mission to exorcise the evil from the wicked book they had each touched in their turn.

The archbishop held the other volume he'd kept until this time, and brandished it high in the air. "This Decretum commissioned by the Regent Matina Stovis is blasphemy." The archbishop opened the book and tore pages from it, casting one sheet of parchment into the crowd after another. The yellow sheaves were quickly torn to shreds by the people who caught them. The pages floated on the warm wind that had resumed its course, though the wind was now unaccompanied by sunlight as the white orb was prisoner to gray clouds.

"She has proclaimed that women whose wombs flow with blood and women whose breasts flow with milk shall be allowed in church. Not in my church!" The archbishop pointed through the door of the cathedral. The people of the crowd were mostly loyal to the anti-king, and they cheered the open sedition.

He looked in the direction of the seat of empire, as if the regent on her throne could hear him from this distance of several hundred stadia. She was said to possess the powers of an enchantress, so it was not impossible that his words might carry on the four winds and reach her ears, attuned as they were to the fine sounds of court intrigues.

"Women whose bodies leak with the fluids of sin shall not take communion in the House of the Lord!"

"Amen!"

"We do not celebrate malady. We ask that our wives, sisters, and daughters hide the impurity from the eyes of Christ. They should come to our church only when they are pure and not suffering visible effects of the original sin men carry in their hearts, those sins women carry more evidently in their flesh."

"Amen!" The women in the crowd cheered and shouted Hosannas as hard as the men if not harder. The assembled roared as if blessed with trumpets, their anger like glorious fanfare and pomp now.

The archbishop spoke in the direction of the queen's throne far to the north, beyond the high stone walls of Koln. "Lustful queen, adulterous queen, oh ye queen who offers weak and contrary counsel to foment factions in her empire, factions like those which now afflict us."

His eyes turned from the direction of the seat of the throne, and toward the clouds where he was sure his Lord hid and would hear his imprecations to smite the whorish pretender to the throne. "I issue anathema on her. You Jezebel and Athalia, so far from the model of Esther and Mary, may ye be torn limb from limb like the Brunhild who was ripped into quarters by horses in the sagas of the

Northmen who plague us for their Danegeld and raid us of our reliquaries!"

A susurrating ripple of misery passed among the famished people. Their stomachs were already sour from acorn bread pulling their contracted organs into Gordian knots. They thought of the dread square sails floating along the Rhine, passing from one Zollschloss to another until one day the barbarians might make their way here.

The people gathered there did not know that an affliction greater and darker than mere Vikings was on its way toward them. They did not know that it would sneak within their walls as easily as that giant wooden horse of ancient Trojan lore had accomplished its own work.

Chapter Seven

A Night in the Life of a Stewhouse

No one called the abbess Mother Inferior to her face, but they didn't have to do it for her to sense how they all felt about her. Martin found it hard to hide his fear and disgust in her presence. Her breath was so fetid that he had to hold his own breath when she spoke, and then he had to wait a moment for the rancid wind to pass before answering her questions.

"Did you feed the new one?" she asked him, moving closer and pulling her hood around her head.

"I did," he said. "I gave him a bit of honey water and chewed some bread and soaked it in wine for him."

The old woman's wizened features bunched together in one sour, wrinkled mass. The wart on the end of her nose danced. "He's not so new that he can't have a bit of beer."

"I'll give him a bit next time."

"See that you do." The old whoremaster walked around the basement and lifted the stone panel in the center of the floor, which led down to the catacombs beneath Koln. "We have some men here who have availed themselves of the secret entrance tonight." The abbess closed the stone portal once her point was made, and then said, "They're also wearing those dreadful Bavarian masks."

Martin shuddered and stowed his own thoughts before they became words.

That was good, since he needed a place to live and she wouldn't brook his impudence. What he wanted to say was *Worry about your own mask, wench*. He thought she looked a bit like a Baba Yaga woodcut, only she was a crone without wisdom in her years. If anything, the years of living off the blood and sweat of young women had turned her into a thoughtless turkey buzzard. He rarely saw Mother Inferior read.

She stepped closer to Martin, and he held his breath. She didn't speak, but studied his eyes with her own milky peepers that were filmed and glowing yellow like those of an alley cat. "Did ye smooth the wrinkles from the linens of the girls of the house?"

He waited for her breath to pass and said, "I did, at that."

She tried to smile and her wart danced again in the darkness. "And did you have a smell at the underclothes?"

He refused to answer the question. One of the young girls had caught him at it once, and he suspected she told the abbess. She confirmed his fears. "Lora told me she caught you with your face in a set of her underthings." The crone cackled, and then remembered there were men in the rooms and business was afoot. She covered her mouth with a wrinkled hand and said, "Lora is turning thirty in a fortnight, and we must make way for another girl."

The abbess watched his young, vulnerable face for a reaction. There was only a slight twitch to his nose, as if a bit of dander had found its way there. He cared for all of the girls. He lacked acquaintances beyond those he saw at market or at the docks, but Martin could live without Lora. It was Lyudmila he couldn't live without.

"Where will she go?"

"She will go to the cloister for penitent prostitutes. They have examined her wretched, stretched womb, and deemed her fit."

He stowed another thought before it reached his lips. The thought was *And what of your own wretched womb?* She thought not in terms fit for life. There was for the abbess neither young nor old, only fresh or worn. She had called that swaddled infant new rather than young. Lora had been with her for nigh on ten years, and could continue to work by the candle for her witch of a master. The abbess wanted her gone though, and she would go.

She leaned forward and whispered. She was so close that he had no choice but to breathe the full flush of her wretchedness. "Use the secret compartment. Keep an eye on your Lyudmila. The Mädchen has her hands full tonight and there may be more than mere revelry or sport afoot in Room Five."

"I will," Martin promised. He'd planned to spy on Lyudmila with or without the old witch's orders. Mother Inferior was more than half-blind, but it was clear she saw his affection for the young girl.

"I will be on my way, then." Mother Inferior turned, ready to escape to her own secret quarters. Martin thought of telling her of his vision, but then thought better of it. The woman was of old gypsy stock and had to wear the yellow star in addition to the striped hood when she went to market. He'd seen her reading auguries in tripe she'd bought from the butcher. Martin was sure she would have some sound advice if he were to tell her of his vision, which was the first he'd scryed in his thirteen years. Still he wasn't sure if he should relate the dream to the abbess. He didn't think she deserved to hear it.

She was gone in the next moment. Martin walked toward a secret passage in the other direction. He decided he would tell Lyudmila of what he'd spied in the heated marble globe he used to smooth the wrinkles from her underthings. He would wait in the wall all night, peering at her in her room through wattle and daub. He would sleep in the wall at the figurative foot of his queen.

Martin tapped the stone in the wall before him. The rock sheet drew aside and allowed him to enter the cold shaft. He stepped into the wet chamber, and pressed another stone that brought the wall sliding back into place as easily as a bookshelf on rollers. He padded softly past a dormouse that Merlon had yet to catch. He walked in his soft leather shoes on the bed of straw until he came to the wall before Lyudmila's chambers where she entertained her male guests for the night.

He felt with his soft hands along the thatched bits of mummified dung that caulked the cold wall, looking for the space where he could plant his eye. As he searched, he ran over the vision one more time in his mind …

He'd put the other young bastards to bed, from the oldest to the newborn who would be headed to the foundling home in a few days. He'd made the boys say the Lord's Prayer in Latin and recite the Nicaean Creed, Paternosters, and Ave Marias from memory. David was younger than Oliver, but he was a faster study. Martin was sure that when the day finally came for him to set sail, the boy with the crooked teeth would be able to read *Parzifal* cover-to-cover without help.

The polished stone had been heated in the hearth, and Martin had been running it over a bit of linen that one of the girls would wear in the morning. The stone had grown cloudy of a sudden, as if filled with dripping white milk. Martin had watched it, as transfixed by the white nectar as Merlon was by the milk in his saucer.

He had seen a vision in the stone. More women than men were burned for their visions, but he would tell no one outside of the house what he'd seen, just to be safe.

A little man, a dwarf of some kind, had walked with a staff tipped in a dunkel-glazed pinecone of some sort. The dwarf walked through the countryside, over hills, mountains, and dales. Martin had never been far beyond the city walls, though he knew enough to know the ruins the dwarf passed were Celtic. He also knew that the other rubble was left by the Romans as they built fortifications to aid them in their war to Christianize or kill the barbarians of the ancient land.

Martin understood little else about the vision he glimpsed in the shewstone, except there was the nagging suspicion now that the dwarf was headed for him. He wanted to know why.

Loud sounds from Lyudmila's room brought him from his thoughts. His fingers finally found the hole in the wattle-and-daub, attaining purchase like the nervous digit of a lad entering his girl with forefinger for the first time.

There was a new moon, and little light aside from what the candles in their tripod provided. Between the heat from the hearth and that produced by the candles, the chamber was as warm as a calefactory. Martin shook the thought as it came to him unbidden that his poor beloved Lyudmila now occupied one of the outer rings of Alighieri's Inferno.

It was a point of jealousy with the other women how well-appointed Lyudmila's room was in comparison to theirs. It was through none of her doing, though. She tried no charms on men, though her natural beauty cleared a path for her wherever she went. Her breasts were ever heavy, pendulous, and maternal. They caused men to lose their speech in her sight and avert their eyes.

It was on account of both her beauty and kindness that her floor was always appointed with rushes fresh as wintergreen mistletoe. The feathers for her mattress and the pressed leathercraft wall hangings came gratis from the tradesmen of the town who assuredly thought of her as they made the beast with their own wives and whatever women they kept in private concubinage.

"Come now," one of three men in the room barked.

Martin was so shocked by the timbre of the voice that he jumped back until his spine slapped the far, cold wall of the passageway. His heartbeat slowed, and he brought his eye back toward the warm hole in the wall.

The abbess hadn't been lying. The men wore smaller versions of the

Schwellkopp ceremonial heads the villagers sometimes bore over their faces for their fairs and carnivals. The masks were unmoving, made of druidic wood, and carved in the form of satyrs and devils. The hideous woodwork masks caught light from the burning rushes. Martin fought the urge to burst through the wall and save Lyudmila from the demonic men in her midst.

The second of the three pulled a shining dagger from his belt, and held the knife in the light of the flames from the hearth. Red light flickered off his papier mache mask. The mouth of the mask didn't move as he spoke.

"Can you accommodate three, young whore?"

Lyudmila hid her fear, or had none. Martin admired her. His terror was strong, even though there was a wall between him and the three men. Lyudmila breathed deeply once, her white breasts heaved, and Martin wondered how men could treat her so. "The abbess stipulates that married men and underage youths are to be turned away from assignations."

She glanced from one masked man to the next, and Martin pressed his face flush against the wall until his eye virtually swam through the hole. He forgot in his terror and curiosity that the wattle and daub had more than its fair share of petrified waste making up its substance.

"I can accommodate up to four men, provided they are not related by blood."

The third of the men who had not spoken until now said, "We are related by trade, though not bound by blood."

The one with the knife split her Chainsil gown without another word. Martin wanted to brain him to death with the polished glass he used to clean the clothes, the same one in which he'd seen the dwarf earlier. He was relieved to see the man put the knife away after unclothing the damsel. He hoped the blade would be put to no further use.

When Martin was only nine years old, he had spied through the walls as three villeins played half-penny prick with a knife on the body of a whore. He'd forgotten her name, but her face was seared into his mind as deeply as a woodcut carved into a book. They'd sliced her form and made a bloodied pincushion of her naked body, but none of the cuts were deep enough to bring suit against them in coram publico. The men were syndics of estate, and could have carved her like a turkey without much racket being raised within the fortified walls of the town.

All three men now shed their particolored gowns, each garment festooned with fine silks and lined with ermine. They left their masks on, which only confirmed his and the abbess's suspicion that they had much to lose by having their identities found out.

One of the men massaged Lyudmila's heaving breasts, and spoke through the demon mask with the dancing horns. "Now my love, we are married for the night." Lyudmila remained standing, flush against one of the posts of her bed as if she were a saint tied to the pillar.

Another of the men leaned down, spread her legs, and inspected every inch of her naked white flesh like a physic. Lyudmila closed her eyes, and her mind drifted off. Martin knew she hid in thought as much as he did. Her work soured her on men, and there were too many years between them, but he was certain their mutual visions gave them a bond that could not be broken. She could go across town and work as a nursemaid for some nobles, or she could take to the road and work as an itinerant midwife, collecting guineas and roasting hares over wooden spits in gypsy camps. They could even part for years, but he was sure they were bound by the dream they shared.

Martin closed his eyes and saw himself on a clinker-built cog bound for the far waters of Iceland. He would navigate by the Greek fire of countless lighthouses until he'd collected his store of Norse herring and brought it back to market to fetch a worthy price. He'd spend the profit on courting his queen Lyudmila. He knew she didn't dream of him, but she dreamed with him, as she ignored the cocks now assaulting her body much as that whore of years ago had ignored the stings of the three villein blades.

She saw herself as the long-haired damsel in a drum tower who leaned out of the window and allowed a knight with his white steed and lance to serenade her with his song.

One man filled her mouth with his rancid priapic horn, while another plugged her rear and slapped it. He repeated, "We are married for the night." The third man with the demon head prepared to spill seed onto her naked back.

He maintained more of his senses than his two brethren, perhaps because his prick remained in hand and outside of her body. He could still speak while the other two moaned and stroked. "A pity Grotius could not join us, for she did say she could accommodate four."

Martin listened to the man speak. He knew no Grotius, but he was eager for the disguised men to commit some kind of error. He wanted them to betray the specifics of their estate in a way that might make them vulnerable to blackmail, and give Lyudmila a chance for revenge. There was nothing that Martin with his single eye pinned to the wall could divine from the clothes or the shoes that told him exactly who the men were, so he kept his ear attuned as well as he could without forsaking the vantage of the hole with his eye.

"I have my doubts about old Grotius," the third man said, speaking more since his brothers could only grunt. "Either he buggers boys or he keeps a mistress elsewhere. He is one of the Jungen and when nature moves him to sport, surely he must have an outlet of some kind."

The two men with deeper purchase on Lyudmila's body gripped her and thrashed like fish flopping and starved for air. The third looked heavenward in his wooden mask, turned his head, and Martin's heart froze. The demon with the red, fixed features stared with its fierce eyes and snarling mouth filled with sharp teeth in the direction of the wall. Martin blinked once. He wondered if the fellow saw him, if he might not now reach down for the dagger among the underclothes of his other friend who pumped poison into Lyudmila. Martin's fears were confirmed, as the man with cock in hand now searched among the discarded underclothes for his knife and found it.

Martin pulled his eye from the wall, lest he be rendered a cyclops as punishment for his peeping. All in the town would see him without an eye. They wouldn't know how he lost his peeper, but the maimed were always suspected of theft or some manner of roguery unless they were given a letter from the courts that explained their affliction to Christian satisfaction.

The knife did not come prying for the wall, and now Martin had another fear that was strong enough to make him forget the sacrifice of his own eye. He pressed his peeper back against the wattle and daub. He saw the man with the demon head use the hand not stroking his cock to stab at the featherbed. Goose quills scattered into the air. The man laughed, shouting to the rafters, "Pity we have no tar to add to the feathers that grace this little whore."

His two brothers giggled through their own satyr masks. They tilted their horns heavenward as they debased the woman stuck between them like a spit-roasted rabbit. Martin could not see who spoke next because they all faced away from him and their real mouths were hidden by the ersatz ones of their masks.

"Forgive the scattering of feathers." Lyudmila's breasts shook as violently as butterfly wings. "Cock must ever be master of hen, and thus you deserve to have your feathers ruffled from time to time."

"We will pay for the damage, and the price of a new bed. Tell Mother Inferior that."

The two men in her body slammed against Lyudmila with all of their force, as if they intended to break her like a spiteful child jealous of his brother's toy.

"After this, we'll go taunt the night watch," one of them said.

He counterpointed his promise by slapping Lyudmila on the rump. Her white flesh rippled a moment and then settled. Martin saw in the flicker of the waning lights that tears were silently streaming down her cheeks. He pulled his own eye from the hole in the wall now since he needed it no longer for spying but rather for his own spell of crying.

He didn't want to alert the three demon men or Lyudmila to his presence at the wall, so he slid down into a crouch and pulled himself into a ball like a mortal sinner preparing for judgment. He cried silently. He knew the priests called what the three Jungen were engaged in venal, but he thought it a profanation greater than blasphemy against the Holy Spirit.

He thought no more of his ships as he cried. He thought no more of Lyudmila's courtly verse, her lofty drum tower, or her secret roses. He thought now only of the dwarf, who could not come soon enough to rescue him from this wretched place, this stewhouse, this town, and this life.

Chapter Eight

Petitioning the Fairies

The next morning Martin was sweeping breadcrumbs from the kitchen floor and gathering them for Merlin when Lyudmila came storming into the room. She cried and snatched the broom from his hands.

"Lyudmila!" he shouted, and looked after the girl. He followed her, sidestepping the younger boys as they ate their crunchy morning trenchers.

"Come," she said, as he stood on the threshold of her door. She hadn't lit a fire for the morning, and her chambers were cold. The only thing that saved the floor from being freezing was the even scattering of feathers torn from her bed last night by the three monster-headed revelers. She swept the goose down into a large pile. Martin noticed a big purple bruise swelling above her left eye.

"Let me help," he said, and he walked forward to take the broom.

She shoved him back and fidgeted with her torn Chainsil whose lace material she'd tied in place with a swath of taffeta from the newborn's swaddling. "You can help," she said.

He stood in place. She pointed. "Get for me one of your shepherd's overcoats, and your little gispere sack you carry about when you leave town."

Martin left the room without asking to what purpose she would put his things. He walked to his dim chambers, grabbed his things, and carried them back to Lyudmila. When he found her, she was standing above the hearth whose flint she'd struck. A flame danced in the fireplace and warmed her milky skin.

Lyudmila had dropped the broom and now held her knotted aiguillette in her hand. He feared for a moment she would throw her whore's badge in the fire, a crime he knew to be punishable by death unless she'd already been accepted into a convent.

"Don't do it!" he hissed. She shared none of his fear, took the things from his hands, and said, "Turn around. Once your back is turned, answer me true."

Martin spun, an automaton with no choice but to obey her commands. Many of the men had teased him about being unter dem pantoffel, but he suspected they were secretly jealous that he got to live among the whores.

"Now answer!" Lyudmila said, a bit strongly.

"You haven't asked me a question." Martin's nose crinkled in puzzlement. He wondered what she was doing behind his back and what she was going to ask him.

"Forgive me," she said. "I am somewhat distraught this morning, though I intend to shortly change that state of affairs, and I will enlist your help."

"What do you need my help with?"

"I know you smell my underthings, and that you pleasure yourself at a chink in the wall when I bathe and I hold neither act against a ripening young man. In fact, I take it as a compliment."

He turned red as a cooked swine, and was glad his back was to her so that he could hide his face. "You must tell me," she said, "have you known a woman?"

That made him even redder, and he spoke low. "No, never but in dreams."

"Good," she said. "This ritual requires virgin blood, and thus mine won't suffice."

"What ritual?"

"You can turn round now," she said.

Martin spun, flabbergasted to see Lyudmila wearing his shepherd's clothes and stuffing the down sliced from her featherbed inside the garment. "Help me stuff this coat, please."

His gispere sack lay on the deflated remnants of the bed. Martin stooped down and picked up handfuls of cold feathers from the floor. He stuffed them beneath her clothes as if she was a scarecrow who needed filling. She undid her aiguillette, and cinched it around her waist like the simple hemp belt of a monk.

"This little cloth of ignominy will finally be put to a better use." She adjusted the feathers beneath the shepherd's coat until she looked like a fat, jovial merchant. She pulled the hood of Martin's cloak over her head, and it was impossible to tell she was a woman. "The Jews have their rouelle and the lepers have their rattle, but I will announce my trade no more when I walk."

The flames in the fireplace roared behind them. He turned and saw her striped hood going up in smoke. Martin looked back toward the girl he loved with his mouth open wide. "Then Archbishop Torner will burn you on the pyre."

"Not until other men burn first." Her eyes were fierce, living coals. She gritted her teeth, and pulled back the blanket of her bed. Martin saw the dagger from last night there, along with three beeswax candles melted and formed into the guise of tiny white poppets. Martin knew she had skill with a loom, but he didn't fancy her a toymaker. He wondered to what end she intended to put the little men she now stuffed into the gispere sack she'd asked of him.

She headed toward the door, and Martin followed after her. "It is not too late," he said, bile rising in his stomach. He followed at her heels and spoke. "The Calendar of Saints is filled with the ranks of reformed candle girls." She ignored him as she walked for the front of the house. She stepped spryly over Merlin, who one of the other bastards had let out of the basement. "Saint Pelagia," Martin said, "Saint Afra and Saint Mary the Egyptian," he added.

Martin ran until he was in front of her. He stood in the doorway, barring her path to the outside world. She would look like a fat man to the passing scrutiny of the marketgoers. If the light winds of yesterday roared with banshee shriek today, her cowl might come off and the false fat of the feathers might scatter to the four winds.

"Let me marry you," Martin said.

Her eyes softened, and Lyudmila shifted the gispere sack from one arm to the other. She touched him on the cheek with her soft hand, and a lightning bolt passed through him. "Oh, Martin, what trade can you learn?"

He lowered his voice because he didn't want to get Witziger in stocks any more than he wanted to get Lyudmila on the pyre. "The chandler has offered to induct me into his craft under the shroud of bohnhaserei."

She looked at him with pity, as if he were a stray cat maimed in combat with the local hounds. "What will you do? Make candles to keep track of how many men storm me nightly like a castle keep?" She shook her head, forced her way past him, and he followed at her heels. "If you would help me in truth, then come with me beyond the gates of the town and give me a bit of your virgin blood."

"Hush," he said, and followed her onto the cabbage-strewn cobblestones of the street. "Must the whole of Koln know of my innocence?"

He walked until he was alongside of her again. Luckily there was not much wind today, and the streets were too crowded for them to call much attention to themselves. She tickled his ear, and the writhing maggots of young lust crawled beneath his skin. "You speak of virginity as if it were a weakness, as if it meant you were more eunuch than unicorn."

Martin was one of the few well-read people he knew, and Lyudmila was the only woman who knew who could read, aside from Mother Inferior. His anger melted at her last comment, and he discoursed as they walked along between the crowded rows of fachwerk homes. "There has been many a storied eunuch in history. I would not mock the men. They are said to possess special powers."

The mention of magic made him think of the dwarven mage he'd seen in the scrying glass the other night, and he wondered when the little magician or whatever he was would come for him. "Eschenbach speaks of King Anfortas, the guardian of the Holy Grail, as having been wounded in the scrotum after a display of courage in battle."

Lyudmila pulled the dagger from the sack she carried and placed it in the loose belt she wore around her waist. "You and that silly book," she said. "Say the word and I can unman you and make you like your precious king."

He thought of getting in a sour word in retort, but he did not want to disparage her *Roman de la Rose*. It was her one respite from this horrid world, aside from her twice monthly baths she enjoyed. Instead he cited more proof of the manhood of the supposedly unmanned. "Francois Garin speaks of the royal guard of the Sultan of Egypt, and how they were fierce warriors notwithstanding their caponage. He said that they could still poke the fire with what remained."

"Really," Lyudmila said, and shook her head. Her anger seemed to be tempered by the city air, and Martin saw the tears were dry on her white cheeks. "Can we talk of something else?"

Martin was about to mention Clinschor, the magician eunuch in the same Eschenbach text, but he kept his hole sewn shut. He tried to think of other subjects. She spoke now in a deep voice, adopting her role with the verve of one in a mystery play. "The town is alive today. From mill and from market, from smithy and nunnery are the tidings brought. I wonder what is afoot?"

Martin's beloved docks loomed to the east, the carbuncle-laced wharves made from split tree trunks floating among the black volcanic tufa that rose like freshwater coral beyond the ships.

One of the moneychangers looked up from his work, and spoke to Lyudmila as he switched a clinking stack of trientes and denarii for a roll of sceattas. "The Spanish Jew Ibrahim Jakub has just arrived at the wharves. He brings tidings from Arabia and goods to trade."

"How auspicious!" Lyudmila said in her newly-acquired man's voice. It was easy to fool the moneychanger, since he was curious about naught but coins. They passed the stalls where live hens and ducks fluttered in crates while their less-fortunate friends hung without feathers from hooks. They passed barrels of salt beef whose bloody brine scent reminded Martin of Mother Inferior's breath. He thought of the money she made off the girls of the convent and he felt like biting the wart off her nose. Whatever Lyudmila's ultimate design, he prayed she'd made a wax poppet of the old crone.

"Poppets are witch trinkets," Martin whispered, pleading as he walked along at her side. He spoke his next sentence louder, since he was well-within the Word with it. "Vengeance belongs to the Lord alone. Give Him time."

She shook her head. She spoke in her own voice, whispering, "The Lord works too slowly for me. I need vengeance in this life, not in the next. I will petition the Goddess with your virgin blood, and she will make those three masked demons pay for the sport they made of me."

"You have nothing to be ashamed of," Martin assured her. He looked up ahead at their path, and saw they were near the wall where he usually exited to gather moss for caulking the clinkers on the shoreline. "Your infamy is far from irredeemable. Do you do what you do for pleasure and carnal enjoyment? Or do you debauch yourself out of need?"

She gazed at him with eyes steely as flint, and he knew he shouldn't have asked the question. He also knew the answer, and that in the Word she could be cleansed and saved. Maybe she could not be saved in the Word as preached by Archbishop Torner, but one look at his snaky, jeweled scepter was all it took to know the man served Mammon and not Yahweh.

"Speak to them," Lyudmila said of the guards on the ramparts, "for they know you."

Martin looked up at the two garrisoned soldiers on the walkway. They stood on either side of the crank that lifted and lowered the grated portcullis. They wore oversized hauberk mail coats and conical spangenhelms that draped awkwardly over their forms. It would have been easy for any assaulting party to see they were drafted burghers who came up for rotation on watch duty, and not real warriors of any kind.

"Edgar!" Martin shouted up at the wall. One of the two men turned, his Aventail flapping as he shifted to see who had spoken his name. The metal nasal bar over his nose twitched and his helmet rose a little on his head, until it looked like a miniature papal miter.

"Martin," the man said, smiling, "going out to gather moss?"

"Aye!"

The other soldier hoisted his checkered kite shield and shifted it to his other arm to give his sore arm a break. Edgar looked from his old friend Martin to his new companion with a curious gaze. "Well, take care."

"I always do," Martin said, and tapped Lyudmila once on the rough material of her feathered shepherd's coat to give her strength. "One is always to encounter two monks, two asses, and two whores when he crosses a bridge. I myself find all three classes agreeable works of God's creation."

The other soldier on the walkway laughed at that and looked down. His breastplate was cast in the Greek manner and gave the effect of musculature, though his Cock Ale belly protruded beneath the metal plate.

"No, lad," Edgar said, his tone a bit more serious now. He turned the gears that controlled the gate even as he spoke. "We've word that a Zollschloss was razed to the very foundations not a fortnight ago. If whatever man or beast responsible should cross your path, you'll be worms for the mandrakes."

"We'll take care," Martin said. He and his companion walked through the groaning portcullis, and Martin spoke to the men at his flank without turning. "I can come back with some lard or tallow and grease those grates, if ye like."

"I wish ye would," Edgar said. "The sound sends shivers down my spine and makes me think I'm guarding a dungeon rather than a Freistadt wall."

Lyudmila walked out ahead of Martin, moving so fast that he feared her feathered disguise might scatter to bits.

"This isn't the way I usually go," he said as he followed after her. "They'll be suspicious."

She ignored him and gave not a fig for his words now. She walked toward oaks large enough to house hamadryads, their swollen and petrified wooden hollows resembling her own breasts and belly when she was large with child. Mist blanketed the dark conifers in a lattice thicker than heavy snow, making tiny white dolomite mountains from the trees. They entered the tree line, and Martin followed Lyudmila to a ravine where boughs of glowing red holly mocked her with their cheer.

A murder of alpine ravens scattered at their approach. Lyudmila sat among the rustling understory, opened the pack, and set the poppets down on the bed of dead leaves. She took the dagger from her waist, and reached underneath the shepherd's coat. She brought out an unlit length of rush.

"Can you not petition the courts for vengeance?" Martin was surprised by how weak his voice was now, and how dark her laughter.

"The magistrates fear urban insurrection," she said, "that men will have all wives in common if they aren't allowed to go sporting and whoring. What happened to me last night or what has happened to me the last thousand nights is naught but the natural order and a rite of passage to the men who make the laws of the League."

She drew in the pile of leaves on the ground. She spoke words that had hurt her heavy heart a long time ago, when she finally discovered what she was worth. "Women are either pure or public. I am public."

Clouds gathered above the treetops at their heads. The branches of the firs trembled slightly in the wind, as if even they feared the woman. She continued to draw in the ground with the knife. "Let us say that those three sons of privilege end up in shackles. It is customary upon the formal entry of a member of the royal house in the town to free all but the debtors."

She shook her head, and removed her hood. She exposed her aureate locks that shined even without the sun's presence. "They'd suffer a fortnight in shackles, less time than a drunk in stocks. Their cruel sport will not affect their honor, which remains intact. My honor must be retrieved by intercession." She looked at Martin with those glowing jade eyes. He yearned to fall under her spell, and if she be a witch, to cook in her cauldron if she so willed it.

"Give me your hand," she said.

He did, and felt the knifepoint jab like a sharp tooth biting into his skin. Blood oozed from his palm. He thought, *Hurt me. Hurt me for what men have done to you. Take my life if it will heal you. I will see the sea in Heaven.*

Lyudmila grabbed his wrist and Martin could not control his breathing, his bleeding, nor the force with which his propagator rose.

He looked down at the pile of leaves where his blood dripped, and noticed the leaves were arranged in the form of a pentagram. He also noticed that features began to arrange themselves on the little wax poppets. He now saw the faces of the men of estate who'd hidden their visages behind Bayern demon masks last night as they made a rotisserie rabbit of Lyudmila's poor, milky body.

"The Earth in its fivefold path," Lyudmila spoke to the trees. Their branches danced as she held Martin's hand and moved its bleeding form from right to left over the star written in the dead leaves. "The deosil path the blood follows doth quench ye star of Bethlehem, ye druid's foot, ye Solomon's seal, and ye witch's cross."

Martin's hand stopped dripping blood. He gazed around, dizzy and confused. It felt as if the trees around them had gathered closer, forming the ring of a covenstead. "I call on you," Lyudmila shouted to the sky, her nose tipped heavenward. "Juno Lucina, Mother of Light, take this boy's virgin blood and redeem me."

She dropped the dagger and held the candle in a two-fisted grip. It caught on fire without aid of flint or tow. In the flash of flaming light Martin caught a glimpse of a goddess with drooping, massive breasts who wore only a goatskin over her naked form. Lyudmila's back arched as if tickled by a feather. She gripped her own breasts in her left hand and stabbed the first of the three poppets arranged on the pentagram. A pool of red blood formed in the white wax, thick as sap as it dripped over the sides of the little doll.

Martin cupped his ear and leaned back in the direction of the city. He swore that he could hear the men over the sounds of the wind, the creak of masts in harbor, and the bells of the cathedral. He knew beyond all shadow of a doubt that it was the threesome from last night screaming as Lyudmila renounced her whoredom and stabbed each of the little wax statues in their turn.

Chapter Nine

A New Arrival in Koln

They had buried the bloody poppets beneath a mound of moss, and then filled the leather gispere with fungus in order to throw off the guard of the town upon their return. When Lyudmila and Martin came back to the wall, they found the portcullis opened and the wall untended.

They stopped at the nearest market stall where a merchant held three spaniels he'd purchased from one of the ships that had come in bearing the famed Ibrahim. Martin asked him what was afoot in the town.

"Murder," the man said, and stroked his dogs. "A son of a powerful Hansa suzerain was counted among the three men stabbed to death."

Martin hid his horror, and Lyudmila stowed her joy. She lavished affection on one of the three panting dogs heeled at the merchant's feet. She turned the golden spaniel's ear inside out and stroked the pink innards much to the dog's delight.

She still wore her disguise of feathers presenting her as a fat merchant, and she spoke in a man's voice with the hood still pulled over her head. "How much for this fine animal?"

"Well," the merchant grunted, and lifted his hidebound *De Canibus Britannicis* onto the barrelhead he used as a tabletop. "This gentle spaniel exists mainly for idle companionship."

"Can he hunt?" Martin asked. He imagined sporting in the fields and dales with the beast by his side. Lyudmila shot him a sidelong glance, scowling. It was clear from the dirty look she gave him that she wanted the animal for a personal companion, and not for hunting.

"He is mainly a comforter," the merchant responded. The church bells rang from the center of the city, and guards in chainmail wandered with their pikes and broadswords toward the yard of the hall.

Martin hid his bleeding hand, which had already started to scab over. The merchant spoke to Lyudmila while she stroked the dog's dappled coat. "I call this beast Henry on account of his English pedigree. He is meant as an instrument of folly, and of vain disport."

"I wonder how he'll get on with Merlin?" Lyudmila said, continuing to ignore Martin. She stroked the dappled coat of the retriever and spoke a last word to the merchant. "Perhaps another day."

"Perhaps."

She tugged Martin by the hand that wasn't bleeding, and bade him follow her back to the stewhouse. The abbess was standing on the front steps of the house as they arrived home. She lowered her voice, and the wart on her nose wobbled as she spoke through clenched teeth. She seethed with rage as she stared daggers at Lyudmila. "If it was witchery on your part that brought those men low, I'll see to it myself that you burn."

"Whatever do you mean, Mother?" Martin thought for a moment Lyudmila would call her "Inferior" to her face. That would have led to a fight in the street that would tear her disguise of feathers apart and end up with both women burning on the greenwood pyre.

"A curfew's on," the abbess said. "That means we won't get many customers tonight or any other night until the murderer is found out."

Lyudmila displayed hands stained with Martin's blood. He panicked, fearing the one woman he adored was about to confess to murder. "The flowers have been brought to me for the first time since I gave birth." The abbess stood back, as if afraid of menstrual blood. "So you see," Lyudmila said, "I couldn't service the rowdies and rakes even if there were no curfew on."

"Get in the house," Mother Inferior seethed, "and take off that ridiculous disguise."

Lyudmila obeyed, but pulled Martin after her. They walked through the house, passing the kitchen where the bread oven glowed. They moved through the main room, walking until they came to Lyudmila's chambers. She closed the door behind them, and Martin's heart beat in his chest like a drum.

"Light a fire," she ordered. He obeyed, went to the hearth, and struck flint until the unspun tow caught fire and lit the bundled wood. Flame danced, and warmed them.

"Tell me," Lyudmila said, and Martin turned to see his queen naked. Her large breasts bounced like buoyant white swans about to take flight. He watched her with an open mouth, as she took the feathers from the shepherd's overcoat and stuffed them back into her bed.

"What?" he asked.

"Do you believe animals have souls?"

"You're still thinking of that little spaniel?"

"I need some sort of companionship in my new home."

Her words hurt his heart worse than the knife had hurt his hand before. He'd forgotten for a moment that she was going to work as a wet nurse. He wondered if she would return to the stewhouse when her time there was done.

"Answer me," she said, and fell backwards on her bed. She sunk into the feathers and giggled. She held her naked feet toward the fire, then planted her toes on the floor and rustled her feet through the fresh rushes scattered there.

"I have read," Martin said, "in *Quaestiones Naturales*, what Adelard of Bath has to say on the subject."

"Oh?" Lyudmila giggled again. "What does he say?"

Martin was frozen in place. He feared her nakedness, her giddiness, but most of all he feared her because she was lying on the bed. He harbored no ill will or judgment toward her for what she'd done to the three men, since he'd seen and heard what they did to her last night.

"Animals can desire and avoid things, like Merlin," Martin said. He looked at the space beneath the doorjamb, where he sometimes saw the shadow of the cat pass. "Such judgment, even in something as simple as judging the quality of milk, comes from the soul and not the body."

"This man …" Lyudmila said, still kicking her bare feet through the rushes. "This Adelard," she pronounced the word as if it was an absurdity that warranted laughter. "Is his the final word on the subject?"

"More lettered men than he have their own opinions," Martin said. He fell to his knees, not knowing what came over him. He crawled toward Lyudmila's dirty feet and spoke. "Thomas Aquinas and Aristotle were both in agreement that animals have souls, albeit not immortal."

He gripped the calloused padding of her heels in his hands and found himself massaging them. Her giggling increased and she squirmed like a piglet. "Augustine," Martin said, kissing her toes, "believed that animal souls are not rational, so they would disappear when the animal dies."

She sat up on the featherbed and smiled, displaying teeth as white as her skin. "What of your soul? You can no more keep your mouth from my toes than some wretched cat like Merlin can keep from scurrying after mice."

"I am an animal," Martin conceded, and stripped his shirt from his back. "When you are not about, I am a young man of sound reasoning skills. When you are near, I am a mindless beast."

He yearned to feel the bottoms of her cold, naked feet on his back. She placed them there without his having to ask, and he feared she truly was a witch who could divine his thoughts with little trouble. "Would you see me burnt for the power I wield over you?" she asked.

He lowered himself, placing his nose in the rushes at her feet. He felt the need to sneeze, and could not bring himself to meet her smiling mouth or sneering eyes. "No, I would worship you. I would live at your heels like the little Hundchen you saw at market today. I would let hen be master of cock."

Martin feared that his last statement would be too much, and that she would connect it with the words the three rapists of last night had uttered. He was scared that she would know Martin's eye was at the wall while she was violated in the heat of concupiscence. His words startled no fear in her breast, though. His words only warmed her heart as the hearth warmed both of their naked bodies.

"Stand," she said.

He trembled. "I cannot." He was content to remain unter dem pantoffel, to live beneath the shelter of her feet like a brownie housed in a shoe in an old Märchen.

"You can." Her voice was softer now, more coaxing than mocking. She was amused by his shyness, but she didn't want his fear. She leaned forward, and took his hands in hers. "Let me see your little horn, satyr."

Martin closed his eyes and wept silently. She wiped the tears from his cheeks with one fine hand, and grabbed his propagator with her other hand. It was swollen with veins and he felt himself on the point of bursting, of boiling over with white blood like a cauldron left too long unattended.

"I owe you pleasure for the blood you gave the Goddess today."

"You owe me nothing," he said. His voice was weak and he didn't trust himself to be able to continue speaking aught but grunts if she kept up with her stroking. She cradled his balls, and he was without strength.

"Since the embargo, the men of this town can have a girl for the price of an egg. It is not right for you to give me your blood and to receive nothing in return."

"Let me …" he panted. She pressed her lips to his ear, licked the pink nautilus, and breathed hot air into him. He shivered and tried to speak. A bit of spit fell from his mouth and fell to the warm rushes carpeting the floor of her chamber. "Let me kiss your nether regions. I have smelled your bouquet when I cleaned your underclothes. Bitte, let me taste you."

"My, my," she said, and leaned back on the bed. He felt her bare legs ridged with gooseflesh. They snaked over either one of his naked shoulders. He lifted his arms and felt his strength return to him now that he was enslaved as he'd so long wished. He pulled her thighs against the sides of his head, and licked the hairy nest above her rose as it filled with wet dew. "My God," he said. "I …"

"You what?" she said, her voice deep but feminine, filled with a power and contempt that overjoyed him.

"I…" he said, and could say no more. She locked her legs around his head, folding them like a yogi in the forbidden sutra praying to an idol. He licked her and tasted the dirt, must, and intimate juices that gave him life. The fertile soil was a warm mystery. He wanted to drown in it, sleep in it, hide from this cold town and cold world. He breathed in her scent, and her voice came to him as if he was submerged in a river and could hardly hear her.

"What would the theologians say of this? Is man's rightful place under woman's slipper?"

"I cannot speak of man," Martin said, between licks. "I know this is my rightful place. I have found my purpose."

His head swirled in a ritualistic motion, as if his tongue were a wand with which he cast a spell inside her body. Now it was Lyudmila's powers to speak that waned as his tongue grew in force and confidence. He spoke and licked with equal skill. "Thomas Aquinas in his *Summa Theologica* denounced men who fail to remember they are men and those like the heretics who refuse to believe in the union of body and soul."

Her rose grew warmer and larger. It became engorged with blood and swelled so that it overtook him like Merlin eating a mouse. His whole mouth was inside of her body, which was warm with fine dew.

She fanned her legs, beat her naked feet against his back, and panted. "Jean de Meun in the *Roman de La Rose* told his readers to obey nature unreservedly."

Martin sucked now as if it were not a sin to do so, but a virtue. Lyudmila shuddered, bucked against him, and tore into his hair with the strength of a shopkeeper who'd caught an urchin poaching an apple from his cart. They both froze, as if in a death rictus on the gallows.

Lyudmila let out a sound, an utterance of cleansing and healing. Martin had licked the wounds of her womb clean and sucked the sin from her body. She unlocked her legs from the back of his neck, tapped him once on his backbone with her dirty foot, and then curled up in a ball on the bed. "Come to me," she said, "little spaniel unter dem pantoffel."

"Your lapdog is coming." He stood and hopped onto the bed, sending a scatter of feathers into the air. He placed his nose in the back of Lyudmila's neck and kissed the errant strands of hair that had scattered from her bun as she writhed in pleasure against his lips and tongue. He batted his eyelashes against the back of her neck to produce more gooseflesh, which he felt rise on her cold, naked skin with his own fingers.

"Do you think Mother Inferior will report you?" he asked.

"No," Lyudmila said, and leaned back into Martin so that they were as well-conjoined as monstrous twins. "For the simple fact that I know secrets of hers as well."

"Such as?"

She yawned. Martin realized he might be allowed to sleep with her in the featherbed, and his heart stuttered harder now than when his mouth was pressed against her flower. "Secrets such as you would be safer not knowing." After a pause, she said, "I will tell you one, if you want to know it. If you can keep it…"

"I can keep my tongue in my mouth."

Lyudmila laughed. "I should hope not, for a dog whose tongue does not wag will not have the pleasure of my featherbed."

He paused, laughed, and said, "Very well. I know when to wag my tongue and when to hold it."

"Do you remember the executioner, Pierpont?"

"Yes, I remember that king of debauchery." He sometimes went through four or five girls per night. Many were convinced he had the aid of some Saracen poultice or potion to give him such strength, though he maintained that swinging his axe against the enemies of Christendom kept him hale and hardy.

"Have you seen him of late?" Lyudmila turned to him.

"That I've not," he allowed.

"Aye," she said, whispering in his ear with her hot breath. "He paid Mother Inferior to cut his own head off. She says he burst forth with seed as she swung the blade and beheaded him. His lust was for the loss of his own head."

"My God," Martin whispered.

"Yes," Lyudmila said, "and he lies buried beneath one of the padstones in the cellar."

"I can't believe it." Martin shuddered and then thought of how sometimes he would go into the cellar and see Merlin padding after a certain spot on the ground.

"That is just one of many secrets I keep in my breast, any one of which could earn that warty crone her place beneath the mandrakes."

The mention of her breasts caused Martin's glance to drift southward. Lyudmila sighed, dejected to realize that the boy who'd pleasured her so a moment ago was a mere man again. She covered her naked breasts. "I'd much prefer your attention elsewhere, and I grow tired of men always staring."

He didn't want to be thrown out of her room, cast out of the Eden that was her featherbed, so Martin switched his gaze to her eyes. He found their warm jade comforting. Lyudmila said, "I am not saying that my bosom does not allow me certain liberties with men from time to time. I can reduce a king to a swaddled infant with one tremor of them." She shook her breasts from left to right, and admired their fat contours a moment after her admonition to Martin. His eyes drifted back down, his mouth open. She giggled rather than being offended.

"Will you be a wet nurse for the king's child?" he asked.

"Nein." She went beneath her eiderdown pillow and extracted a book. Martin could see that this one was not her prized *Roman*. He sat up, curious. "That scrivener was so in love with my breasts that he gave me the royal records to peruse. See what they pay."

She opened the ledger to Martin's gaze. He stared at it, not comprehending much aside from the prices. He looked at the tinted and dried ink in the light from the fire. "What is it?"

"This," she said, "is the price the King paid for each of the nurses sought and the length of time each child nursed."

Martin read the names. He squinted until the cipher became a little bit less of a code, and he could understand bits of it. "Why are the girls weaned sooner than the boys?"

Her tone was harsh. "Why are women whores, and men whoremongers? The life of a girl is worth less. So they receive less milk, and more perish while still swaddled."

He said nothing for fear of further angering her. Instead, he placed his head between her breasts. He nuzzled. The warmth of her body combined with the warmth from the fire to make him feel as if all of time could be an opiate if only he could remain frozen in this pose.

"I don't know why men are so eager to have sons and then to send them off to die."

Martin spoke into her breasts, growing drowsy in the shadow between the pallid mounds. "Perhaps they have read too many chansons de geste." He heard the book closing in her hands. He caught a pungent whiff of her odor as her armpit rose above his head and she hid the tome behind the overstuffed eiderdown pillow.

"I will not be nursemaid to the king's child," she said.

Martin had to hide his joy, thinking that she was saying that she would remain in the stewhouse with him perhaps until the dwarf came and rescued them both. She dashed his hopes in the next moment. "I will be a wet nurse to foundlings in a charity home established by the royals. Think of it," she said, "to have such a hefty purse that you can pay the poor to give their milk to those even less fortunate." She laughed bitterly. "They would not let this whore's tit too close to a royal mouth, not in the reign of Archbishop Torner."

He trembled at the mention of the wicked man who roared from the pulpit and church steps daily.

A thundering noise came from the front of the house, and both shot up so quickly in the bed that feathers scattered. "Who?" Lyudmila asked. Her shock was too total for her to finish the question, and her mouth remained an owl-like aperture.

Martin whispered. "I'll go." He looked toward the window. "Be ready to run."

He stood and walked toward the door. He padded softly and grabbed the doorknob with the hand covered in new scabbing. He breathed deeply once. If indeed there was a curfew on, then the only visitors were either members of the night watch or ruffians brash enough to visit the whorehouse when being out on the streets could place their head on one of the pikes guarding the town.

Voices echoed in the hall, and Martin walked quietly as far as he could toward the main chamber without alerting either of the parties to his presence.

Candelabra threw wicked shadows over the crossbeams nestled in the ceiling, and Martin saw the man to whom the shadow belonged in the next moment. He wore a houppelande broidered and crusted with gems. His pageboy curls were recently primped, and smelled of lavender even from this distance. Mother Superior's warty nose was curled. Her eternally harsh features softened as much as nature would allow, as the boy produced a handful of precious metal that shined true. It was of curious denomination.

Martin walked a step closer and felt something brush against his foot. He stowed the urge to jump and shout. He bit his tongue, remembering his promise to Lyudmila. He wanted to return to her, but not until he saw what was stirring here. He looked down and saw that it was merely Merlin at his feet.

"Those are coins," the abbess said, "but they've been cast into ingots, in the Viking style."

"Aye," the sneering lad said. Martin could see his features in the golden, faded glow of the beeswax. He was not ugly, but there was something so impudent and bitter about him that each element of his beauty struck Martin as somehow corrupted even as it was appraised. The nose was perfect, if a bit too effeminate. He looked like someone who had others do his fighting, and Martin wondered just as much as the abbess how he got his hands on Viking booty.

"Very well," Mother Inferior said, accepting the ingots in her withered palm. "I will fetch the girls for you and have you select one. Our house is two short, as one is preparing to go to the convent and another has been visited by the rose."

The lad stepped forward. "Give to me the one who is bleeding."

The abbess drew back like a vampire retreating from garlic. "There are laws against that. Congress with one who suffers the menses brings plague." She held out the ingots to him, entreating him to be gone from her house and her sight evermore. "There is not enough geld in the world to make your wish so."

He held up his hands and spoke as if he hadn't just made his licentious request. "Very well. Bring the other girls forth."

"I will." She turned toward the hall where Martin stood. He hid in the shadows, clinging to the wall and sliding back toward Lyudmila's room as if he stood on the sheer face of a cliff from which he might plummet if he wasn't careful.

The abbess turned back toward the young sport, giving Martin his chance to open the door to Lyudmila's room and yet spoiling his chance to hear the tail end of the conversation. "Who shall I say is calling?" The abbess asked.

"Casper," the boy said. "Casper Namlos."

Chapter Ten

Bursting Forth with Worse Seed

Working as a procuress meant that Mother Inferior was used to strange requests, on top of which Casper Namlos had paid enough to earn his druthers. Still she had trouble working out his demand that the girl procured for him have wide, childbearing hips.

The old crone's hand was weighted with ingots. She said, "Usually men request the youngest girl in the house, the freshest. It sounds to me that you are asking for the opposite." She'd cocked her head to the side like a Haustier encountering a new sound for the first time.

He'd ignored her prodding and added, "I also want to be in the cellar."

Mother Inferior had nodded in the direction of the doors of the rooms of the stewhouse, behind one of which Martin and Lyudmila stood with ears cupped to the door. "Our rooms are furnished with rushes and hearth. The cellar is cold."

"Furnish me with a rug," the rake had said, and weighed her hand down with more coin. "Bring it to the basement." He'd grinned and cryptically added, "I wish to be closer to the earth when I make the beast."

He'd descended to the basement without another word, and the abbess had inspected the coins he'd piled on top of the ingots he'd given her. He'd claimed his trade as a shipwright, and the coins looked to be ancient looted booty. They were Byzantine pieces dating back to the early days of Christendom.

The curfew was on, so she could not have the coins appraised by the one-eyed Jew today. The mineral content of the coins passed her tooth test, though.

What's more they tasted old enough to date back to the days when the Roman senate was in session. She wondered again who this lad was.

She went to Gloria's room after the boy disappeared to the basement. She hoped he didn't get into the victuals while he was down there. She was certain that even if he did raid their stores, there was no way that he could eat more than he'd paid for already.

Gloria stood primping her blond locks with a bone comb in front of a bit of warped glass in the corner of her chambers. "Many is the time," the abbess said, "that I've told you to stop gorging yourself on bread, for your form is too large for most men."

The girl stopped combing her hair, and turned. "Tonight," the abbess said, "your extra heft will come in handy."

"I don't understand."

"There is a man in the basement. Not much more than a boy," the abbess added, taking a step forward. "He has paid sumptuously, and requested a woman with childbearing hips."

Gloria smiled at the odd request. The abbess was less amused. She was losing two girls this week, one to a convent and another to a foundling home. She didn't need to risk a customer deliberately setting out to make one of her girls big with child, even if it was a less sought-after charmer like Gloria.

"After you make the beast with the boy in the cellar …"

"Why is he in the cellar?" Gloria's nose scrunched. She set down the bone comb and gathered her robe around her.

"He is in the cellar because he requested those accommodations, and he has paid well for his peccadillos."

Gloria accepted this with a tacit little nod, her mouth slightly open. Mother Inferior thought there was something downright bovine about the girl, that she was as dumb as a mud fence. At least that meant she could follow orders. "After his candle has burnt down to the wick, you are to come *directly* to me. Do you understand?"

The abbess waited for her words to sink in. If Merlin could learn to do tricks with yarn, she thought this whore could at least heed her words. "Good. Now, wait here." The abbess left with that. She hadn't bothered to explain to the girl what she would do with her after she was finished with the customer, but Gloria had her suspicions.

It was known that Mother Inferior kept a sponge soaked in vinegary abortifacients and that she had poultices soaked with asarum europaeum and celery that were said to steal the breath of life from the man's seed seeking purchase in the womb. The girls who had her poultice lain on their vulvas were bedridden for days, and were also rumored to be able to quickly fill chamber pots with blood.

It was even said that Mother Inferior had sufficient maleficium to snap her fingers once and expunge a quickened fetus from the womb of a pregnant whore. The only reason the holy men of town hadn't put her on the pyre was that too many of them visited the stewhouse themselves under the cover of masks.

The abbess returned a moment later with a handful of things to take to the boy in the basement, along with several golden shimmering ducats for Gloria. The girl accepted the money and stowed it beneath the pillow on her bed, before accepting the other artifacts from the abbess's hands. Kindness was not part of Mother Inferior's character, which made her newfound generosity troubling.

"Take these candles and this rug to the boy. He must be cold."

And he must have paid quite a song, Gloria thought, *for you to play human all of a sudden*. The abbess retreated and said, "I will bring more." She disappeared for the moment. The girl studied what she held in her hands. There were beeswax candles as gold as a honeycomb and large enough to be mistaken for corn dollies. *No tallow for this boy.* There was also a brown bearskin rug, the one whose fur Mother Inferior often boasted was warm enough to protect a gypsy caravan as it rocked its way along the frozen spine of the Carpathians. *What*, Gloria wondered, *is that old, childless heifer up to now?*

The procuress returned a moment later with a stoppered vase in one hand and a bottle of corked wine in the other. She held up the vase in her left hand, and the wine sloshed around. "This is cheaper steeped hippocras, with cinnamon and piment. It is a good companion of a cold night, and you may drink of it as much as you will."

She handed it to the girl. Then she spoke of the other bottle, which she stroked as lovingly as an alchemist cradling a new concoction. "This is Goldenengel."

"Oh!" Gloria said, cheering up. "From the Moselle!" She was so homesick for her land that she took the bottle from the abbess without asking for it. She remembered the fruited vines in winter, how they would be strewn with candles for the Weinachtsfest in her little village of Anger near Stoissberg. The men who called themselves Christian would drink themselves into a Bacchanalian riot, crown the heads of the alpine cows with flowers, and then drive the garlanded beasts from the pastures and into the stables for the winter months. Gloria hoped the boy would share some of that stuff with her.

"Go now," the abbess said. "I will make soft spundekas for you with lots of paprika, so that you may warm your insides when you are done. Just let me fire the oven."

Tears welled in Gloria's eyes at the new kindness she was being shown. The abbess opened the door to the basement, and Gloria walked down the stone steps of the cellar until she stood before the young man in his finery. He took the items from her hands one by one. He set down the bearskin rug, wine, and candles on the stone floor. When she was unburdened, she saw his only design in relieving her of the items was so that he could study her form, with which he was pleased.

"Good," Casper said. "You are fit for my seed."

She didn't know what to say to that, so she asked "Would you like some wine?"

He kicked the stoppered vase and the wine bottle swimming with golden liquid to the side. "It impairs the senses, and we need ours." He shed his houppeland, scrunched his stockings up, and shed his clothes without another word. Gloria thought she could have a go at the wine alone at some later point, and was thus pleased with the teetotaler's abstention.

The naked boy stood back, smiling. "Let me show you a small trick." He snapped his fingers. Each of the beeswax candles lit of its own accord. The head of the bear rug awoke and roared once, making her heart jump like a songbird trapped in a cage.

"My Lord, what manner of spell mongering is that?"

He snapped his fingers again, the skinned brown bear was dormant, and the lights extinguished. They were in near-total darkness. "It is a very petty form of magic. I have a humble store in my fingers." He took a step forward. "A far greater supply exists here." He pulled her toward his prick. She had accommodated many, but the sudden rudeness of his gesture jolted her and hurt her sheath as he slid inside. He leaned into her and forced her onto the rug, holding her skewered in this missionary position. He made love to her with all of the passion and delicacy of a frog with no chance of ever achieving princedom.

Indeed, he stroked not as if he enjoyed it, but as if it was his conjugal duty to burst as quickly as possible and then to turn over and sleep. He fucked like a ploughman. He may have sensed her lack of verve or dim appraisal of his skill, for he began to boast of his deeds as he panted and corkscrewed against her like a mere apprentice in the art of love. "You should know who you have the pleasure of tupping with."

He was young, but his breath was sour with age. She didn't want to open her mouth to ask him who he was, since then she would get more of his dragon's breath in her gullet. She waited for him to illuminate his lineage and deeds without her prompting. "I sank a Viking vessel with an enchanted dragon as its figurehead. Without my intercession, every Zollschloss along the Rhine would lay in ruins. Those Vikings would be on their way over the wall now."

She grew curious. The gossip was on the grapevine, and she knew there was at least a small measure of truth to his story. Everyone had heard at this point of the razing of the little castle, and she wondered what manner of man she presently had thrusting his sword into her worn scabbard. A question came to her, and she couldn't help but ask it despite the force of his rancid butter breath. "How did you get through the wall guard? They have been instructed the last few days to admit no newcomers."

He laughed at that and shuddered as he continued to stab her. "Men are greedier than Odin's Freki. They can no more be sated by coin than the god's dog can be sated by gristle in Valhalla."

When he next spoke, his voice took on a darker tone. It was no longer his voice or his throat even. "Abhadda kedhabhra."

"What?" Gloria asked of the strange imprecation.

Inverted Latin spilled from his lips, and her body froze in terror. He thrashed harder against her like a necrophiliac excited by her deadness. "What are you doing!" she shouted. "What are you saying?"

The backwards words continued to stream. She thought of the roomful of bastards presided over by young Martin, and she remembered the Lord's Prayer and Nicaean Creed young Martin had the boys recite before they fell asleep. It occurred to her now as the monster on her seized and squirted seed into her body that the words he was saying were those of the Pater Noster, only in reverse. He went through a final spasm on her form, and then stood. His prick dripped fat dollops of seed onto the bearskin rug. The candles relit again of their own accord and Gloria stood up.

"What is going on!" she shouted. The abbess heard her shouts from above. Mother Inferior attempted to open the door to the cellar, but it was locked through enchantment. Whores came from their rooms and the bastards awoke in their bedchambers.

Casper Namlos looked at the girl. He spoke not to her, but rather to something she already felt kicking inside her. "Come forth Eurynomos," he said. "Rot your way into this world like worms brought forth from the sour core of a spoiled apple."

Whatever he spoke to inside of her body obeyed him, and she felt the flesh wilt on her arms. She stared down at her hands. They were covered now in flaming boils and pustules, spilling maggots that crawled through the decaying flesh and left trails of pus and slime as they slithered. She tried to speak, but was too terrified to form words. An infantile groan escaped her lips, but no more. Her eyes were wide saucers of blank terror.

"Help me!" The small blond hairs on her arms became thick lycanthropic fungus, smelly as ergot blooming on black bread. The ailment that was leprosy compounded by Black Death tore all of the skin from her frame. She was a clean mass of naked musculature, like a skinned rabbit hung by a hook in market. She exploded in the next moment, like a pelting of rotted cabbages thrown from the crowd at a poor performer. Eurynomos came from the flesh he had corroded.

His bluish-black skin was the color of a dragonfly that had soaked in swampy, sulfurous marsh for a season. He grinned and his wings flapped. "Thank you for bringing me here."

Casper nodded. He ignored the shouts from above and the rain of fists beating at the basement door whose enchantment held. The demon said, "I grew tired of devouring flesh in Hades."

Casper was about to speak, but the demon held up a staying hand and the boy listened. "Hark," Eurynomos said, "the Bell of the Three Kings which crowns Koln Cathedral doth now become the Bell of Girardius. It is a necromantic chime to summon the dead, whether they passed on the gallows or from plague or while in sickbed."

There was a resounding gong from the direction of Koln Cathedral that carried through the whole town. The sound swept through the gables and reverberated off mansard roofs and slate chimneys.

The boy picked up his clothes, and began to dress. His work in this town was done, and he had more seed to sow in other locales. His stockings were halfway up his knees when the ground beneath him erupted. This caused both him and the demon to take a step back. A rotted corpse with its head draped in a black hood emerged from the ground. The man was a shirtless executioner.

He wore a pitch-colored Cucullus attached to his head, closed at the neck, and tied to a cape draped over his back.

He looked at the demon and boy. "How is my head back on my body after I asked that old crone to behead me?"

The blue-black demon looked at him and smiled, baring its hollow viper fangs. "You sound disappointed."

The revenant executioner had no fear of the demon, and spoke to him as if he was an insolent pup. "I was lopping heads in Hades, and doing a mighty fine job of it until you came and interrupted me." The executioner looked around his form and down toward the mound of dirt that had erupted after the demon had raised the dead. "On the subject of lopping heads, where is my precious axe?"

The demon extended a single long black fingernail that was more like a talon, and a felling axe emerged from the same crater where the executioner had been buried all this time. "Ah," the head lopper hissed with satisfaction as he gripped the short shaft of his tool.

The demon and Casper appraised the axe. The demon spoke first. "That axe seems better for felling trees than cutting heads."

The executioner nodded. "That was its original purpose, true. And I prefer an axe that does not cut cleanly. I like to have multiple chops at the head. Thus, the woodcutter's implement."

The demon and Casper grinned at this remarkable show of sadism. There was a moment of silence in the basement. It allowed the three demonic presences to hear the shouts on the street, where the dead were awakening from cemetery plots and crypts and vaults. They were walking the cobblestones and terrifying the night watch.

Fists continued to beat the door above, and the demon spoke to the executioner. "Would you like to lop off the heads of the whores?"

"Nein," the Scharfrichter said, "I would prefer to terrorize men with my blade. Their deeds are usually worse than those of mere whores, and they warrant more attention from my axe."

"Very well," the demon said. It pointed its elongated, sharp talon toward the door at the top of the dressed stone staircase. "The door is open." It looked to Casper. "Flee, and spread more seed."

"Aye," Casper said.

The executioner was on the steps before the young man, while the demon held its place. The abbess stood at the top of the steps with several whores flanking her. The girls got one look at the hooded man with the naked chest carrying the bloodied axe. They turned in terror. They ran back into their rooms or bolted for the street, curfew be damned. The abbess remained fixed to the spot, frozen as if mired in horse glue.

"You begged me for death," she said, hoping he would spare her life.

"I've no quarrel with you, old crone." He shoved her aside, and headed for the open front door. "You gave me the deliverance I sought, and I shan't forget your kindness." The executioner disappeared into the street, impervious to the shrieks of the living and the moans of the dead as they shuffled through the boulevards of Koln.

"What of Gloria?" Mother Inferior asked. She was a whoremonger, but not totally without heart. She prayed she had not delivered the girl unto the executioner's blade. She attempted to take the first step toward the basement. Casper Namlos rushed past her, fleeing after the executioner into the street.

She turned and shouted after the particolored blur of a boy running past in his finery. "You little worthless bastard! Cur! You've brought infamy to an otherwise-tolerated house!" She was sure she was ruined. She thought there was also a good chance she'd earned a place on the pyre as a witch.

She looked down the stairs. She saw a mess of wilted, exploded leprous flesh. She knew there was no amount of ingots worth this unholy nightmare. The abbess walked down, and reached the final step of the basement. She looked at the shards of skin and bone that once were her full-hipped Gloria. The bluebottle demon with flapping wings picked his way through the shattered bits of matter and offal, tasting the banquet to his hellish heart's content. His fluttering translucent wings were stained with blood. He was too busy gorging himself to take notice of the abbess standing behind him, though he did smell the vomit as it came from her mouth. He yearned to eat the puke with a spoon when he was done supping on the corpse of the whore before him.

Things were in a hellish state on the streets above as well. Unearthed corpses fought off Holstein pigs that escaped their cages and chewed on their flesh as they rooted with their snouts and grunted. Cobalt-skinned hordes of the undead climbed with necrotic, decaying fingers out of burial vaults and scaled the ivy-clad walls of the cemetery.

Archbishop Torner stood on the steps of Koln Cathedral, shouting at the dancing procession of the dead as they passed him and the two cardinals accompanying him. He pointed his jeweled scepter at the dead and quoted scripture to no effect. The bell above the church continued to ring, and he turned to one of the cardinals. "I believe the bell is enchanted. Make your way to the belfry and drape it in cloth to silence its sounds. It is drawing the dead from the crypts through some form of wizarding."

"Yes, my lord." The cardinal tipped his red miter forward and then walked back into the church, moonlight streaming through the stained glass and splashing over the fan-vaulted ceiling.

The archbishop stood on the steps with the other remaining cardinal. He reached inside of his purple and gold filigreed liturgical vestments for his crucifix and rosary beads.

Three of the dead left the procession that shambled along the cobblestones. They turned toward the archbishop, who was terrified but could not show it. If he were blamed for this, then he might be defrocked, excommunicated, banished, and pronounced anathema.

"Christ in Heaven," he said. The three dead men were recently deceased and not far along in putrescence. As they approached, the cardinal at the archbishop's side attempted to flee. The archbishop held him to the spot, laying his scepter across the man's path to prevent his departure. Archbishop Torner was convinced he needed a witness to whatever words the three undead had to impart. This was assuming they didn't just want to taste the flesh of the living.

"Do you recognize us?" one of the three men asked. They were not far along in decomposition, and it did not take the archbishop long to remember.

"Yes," the archbishop said, "my condolences." He remembered the funeral from earlier today. The cortege was impressive enough to be mistaken as a Corpus Christi procession carrying the host in monstrance on Whitsun. The three men who'd perished recently were of a high enough estate that the archbishop himself performed the Rite of Extreme Unction for them. They were dead, but they were rich dead men and he felt it best to accommodate them now.

"We have passed through this realm into the afterlife and seen what lies beyond," one of the three moldering ghouls said.

The archbishop tried to muster a smile. "How was it, being seated at the right hand of the Father?"

They ignored this, and one of them spoke through a broken jaw. "We know who killed us."

"A witch," another said.

The archbishop and the cardinal could barely contain their joy. Usually charges of witchery had to be fabricated. Now there was a real one in their midst. The archbishop looked up toward the belfry where the unholy chime continued to sound and make the dead dance. "Who is this witch?"

"A prostitute," another of the dead said.

Now Archbishop Torner was elated. If it had been a woman of estate, organizing a burning might have been out of the question and he might have had to settle for banishment.

The bell above them stopped ringing. The cardinal had virtually mummified the ringing bell in vestments and white linen virginal enough to make the gong look more like a dovecote than a chime.

The archbishop was about to ask the name of the whore. The last of the three dead men had been silent until now, but he cleared his throat to speak. "Her name is Lyudmila Stein. She made poppets of our forms and plucked them with a knife, pricking us to death."

The dead man opened his shirt and exposed a chest pocked with bloody stab wounds. "She is in the tolerated house, and she has been given a plum assignment as a wet nurse in a foundling home run by the royalty of this town."

The archbishop nodded. That made matters more complicated, but only slightly. He stared into the filmy eyes of the dead and gave them his promise. "I will see that her wretched, black milk touches not the lips of the children of this town."

Chapter Eleven

Hell Loosed in Koln

Half the candle girls had fled the stewhouse, and the other half remained sealed behind their doors. Martin couldn't wait any longer behind Lyudmila's door, despite the Abbess's shrieks that a devourer of souls was loose in the cellar.

The booming voice of Eurynomos followed Martin as he ran out into the hall. "Poor milksop trying to defend his houseful of whores and bastards!" the demon cackled. "I know the secret of your little concubine, and soon the whole town will know of the whore's sorcery. Look in the door's threshold! Behold!"

Martin stopped, dagger in hand. He stood in the kitchen and watched as the three, tiny tallow poppets danced in blood and shadow. Each of them bore the likeness of the men who suffered as Lyudmila stabbed them. They howled with laughter and danced like marionettes.

"Be gone from my house!" The abbess picked up her broom and thrashed the three little boggarts with the willow bristles in a sweeping motion. The hair on Merlin's back stood on end, and the cat hissed and clawed at the three little brownies. Mother Inferior looked over at Martin. "Hide the children! Quick!"

"I intend to!" He ran into the nursery and left the abbess to fend off the little monsters, while the voice of the emissary from Hades rang in his ear. "Enjoy my malevolent little genus loci, boy. They will make your Merlin lame and cause the milk in Lyudmila's breasts to curdle and go sour."

Martin was tempted to turn again, head into the cellar, and fight the fly-winged beast with the measly dagger in his palm. The cries of the youngest forced him into the nursery, however.

Oliver and David guarded the other children, who wept and stood in a confused huddle. David looked up at Martin with a mouthful of crooked choppers. He wiped the sleep from his young eyes. "What is happening?"

"I don't rightly know." Martin shook his head and walked to the hearth. "You must hide in the wall until this madness has passed, and peace has been restored." Martin reached for one of the two swords crossed above the mantle. He usually didn't like to divulge the secrets to the youngest denizens of the house, since he feared they would abuse the nooks and crannies for their own ends. He also knew they were too young to bear witness to what went on in the rooms through the cracks in the walls, but this was not the time for great caution.

He moved his hand up to the latten sword coated in monumental brass. He pulled at the wheel pommel, and a secret passage opened in the wall.

"Go!" Martin shouted. "Hide in there until I come for you!" The younger children scurried quickly for the hole. David and Oliver remained planted where they were. "Food!" was all Oliver could say.

"We haven't eaten in a dog's age," David said, "and if the babe has nothing he will cry and give away our location."

"Scheise," Martin said. He tousled the lad's curls, proud of his forethought. "I'll be right back," Martin said. He was so caught up in the moment that his hand still gripped the sword's pommel that opened the secret passageway as he ran. He almost pulled his arm free of the socket as if suffering the strappado, and the sword was ripped from the wall. The heirloom that was given to Mother Inferior in her widowhood clattered to the floor.

Martin dropped the dagger and picked up the sword. He studied it for a moment. He held the blade up in the light of the new moon streaming in through the window's glaze. The sword was a souvenir, but it had a sharply-enough tapered point. "Wait," Martin said, "and I will bring you food."

He walked back through the open doorway into the kitchen, where Mother Inferior had skewered all three poppets to the wall on a sharpened blackthorn stave covered in leper bells. The little monsters screamed and squirmed, and she laughed. Martin feared the warty hag for the moment more than the demon in the basement, but he worked up the courage to speak to her. "The children need food while hiding."

"Here ..." A voice came from behind him. The voice was dulcet and honeyed, but was so close and unexpected that he almost sliced Lyudmila as he turned with the sword in hand. She jumped back, startled. He smiled at the abundant bounty in her hands.

"You thought ahead," he said.

"I keep a few victuals in my room. I was hungry when I was with child, and my appetite has not totally abated." Whatever wizardry the demon in the basement intended to use to sour her milk had not yet taken effect, at least not by Martin's reckoning.

She filled Martin's free hand with wastel bread and a half loaf of cocket, along with dark plum damson and rosehip preserves. Mother Inferior looked over at Martin. "What would you intend to be doing with that sword, young man?"

He nodded toward the basement where the demon smacked his lips on the morsels of the whore's scattered form. "I intend to send him back to Hades after I feed these children." Lyudmila touched his ear once with her warm pale fingers before Martin was gone, sprinting down the hall to the secret passageway. The hands of the children reached out for the jars filled with fruits and the slices of hardened, stale bread.

"Here," Martin said. He handed them the food and then shut the children in the passageway. He turned around, gripped the sword with two hands, and marched back toward the kitchen. Dogs barked in the distance, and Euronymous bellowed, "Cu Sith comes from the ramparts. He will abduct the first nursing mother he finds and bring her to the fairy mounds to give milk to the babes of the flying nymphs." The demon shouted over the squealing of the skewered poppets, in whose direction Lyudmila now spit. "Do you know how many fairy babes a mortal breast can feed?"

"To your room," Martin said to Lyudmila, "and lock the door."

Lyudmila, for all her fear of the demon, stood her ground and squared herself to Martin. "Boy, behave not like a knight nor treat me like a helpless damsel. Forget not that your face was buried in my fine rose but a few hours ago."

He smiled, and bowed his apology. "I cannot forget. The scent and taste lingers in my nose and on my tongue, thankfully." She smiled, mollified. She returned to her room, slamming the door.

Mother Inferior looked over at him in disbelief. "You tasted the deflowered fruits of a stewhouse maid?"

"Aye," Martin said, proud where she thought he should feel shame. "That I did."

The scent of a different flower filled the air, drifting on the current of a cold draft that came from the basement. Martin thought it odd that such a heavenly scent should come from such a putrid place. Mother Inferior was well-versed in the black arts, and she knew better than to believe the charm of fairy glamour. She shouted to Lyudmila, "Bury your face in your eiderdown pillow, and do not breathe of the Milchdieb."

Martin took a deep breath, and prepared to rush down the stairs. He posed his question to the abbess without taking his eyes or the point of his sword from the basement where the wings of the bluebottle wretch were abuzz. "What is this milk thief?"

"Euphrasia officinalis," she said with alchemical authority. "Better known as eyebright, it can cause milk to spoil." The abbess gazed out the window, above the staff where the leper bells jingled as the staked brownies struggled to free themselves from their impalement. The wax poppets were beginning to melt. "Thank God the moon is in neither the sign of Scorpio nor Cancer. God willing we will all survive this night, save the poor girl down there who is now little more than a demonic repast."

Martin thought of Lyudmila and he ran down the stairs, shouting. To his surprise the demon backed up like a cornered cat. It shrieked and displayed black talons and razor fangs, but for all that it cowered near a beam supported by a padstone. The fur on the demon's thorax was moist with blood, and it rubbed its greedy hands together.

"I cannot believe it!" the demon shouted.

"What?" Martin brandished the heavy sword in trembling hands. He was certain he was going to die, and he struggled for footing in the wet red remnants of the rotted candle girl strewn beneath him.

"How does a boy preserve his virginity in a house of assignation?" The demon was more amused than enraged.

"That's none of your concern." Martin held the point of the sword toward the demon.

"It is." It hissed as its wings beat. "For my powers are greatly diminished in the presence of the chaste. You should thank your Christ that flower dew moistens only your lips and not your prick." The bluebottle wings fluttered and writhed. "Otherwise I'd boil your liver and your brains with one flutter of my wings, and I'd treat you as the main course to the little gustatory prelude I've been enjoying."

The demon pointed at the mass of flesh on the ground where maggots writhed and emerged from whitish pupae. "You're not pristine enough for a unicorn to rest its head in your lap." The demon circled away from Martin and his blade. "But you've still bought yourself enchantment enough to see the sun rise." The demon gazed up the steps, where the abbess stood as paralyzed as Lot's wife after being reduced to a salt pillar. "I wish I could say the same for your Lyudmila."

"What do you mean?" Martin shouted so that spit left his lips and flew into the demon's face.

"Are you learned?" the demon asked.

"I am lettered enough," Martin answered. He feinted once and then ran forward with the blade's end pointed toward the demon. The demon sidestepped in time, and Martin's sword crashed hard enough against the ashlar stone of the wall to draw sparks.

The demon laughed at the boy's show of bravery and said, "Tertullian was a righteous Christian father, and though I myself serve Satan, I must concede he was right to say woman is the Devil's gateway."

Martin lowered the sword for a moment. He feared the demon would lunge for him whether or not he was a virgin, but the weapon was heavy and his arms were sore and tired. "There is nothing in the Pauline Letters nor in the Gospels of Christ to say that woman is so foul," Martin responded, "nor that the act of lovemaking should be a source of shame."

"You theologize as well as you swing a sword, which is to say poorly." The demon could not come within a hair's breadth of its quarry and so settled for spitting a globule of greenish acid. Martin felt its searing heat as it came toward him, but he ducked and dodged in time. The slimy web splashed the wall behind him. It melted its way through the stone and produced hissing steam. Martin shuddered to think what his face would look like if the Beelzebub spit had hit its mark, but he refused to succumb to the shaking that now started in his knees.

The demon heard the clacking of the boy's fearful bones. The sound was so loud it would have been reasonable for a blind man to think he was in the presence of a skeleton, and not a man of flesh and bone.

The demon looked from Martin to the abbess up on the staircase. "You, you old bitch," the monster seethed. "You should thank the Lord that you are a widow, since your veil confers the sixty-fold reward of virginity. That is just enough to protect you from me as well." The monster turned toward the Rathskeller window, and he glanced at the feet walking along the mossy cobblestones of Köln. "The wives of this town should beware, however."

"Marriage confers no reward?" Martin asked, taking a step closer to the demon.

"Thirty fold," the demon spoke, and its leathery forked tongue dripped the acid it previously spit. The air filled with a smell like a jar of eggs preserved in lye that had shattered after sitting on a shelf untended for years. "That is only when the woman is faithful." Its wings buzzed like those of a moth drawn to a candle, and Martin suspected the creature was about to take flight through the ceiling. "Almost every wife has her overcoat and her secret lover."

"Kill him!" the abbess shouted. "Send it back to Hell, Martin!"

The demon looked deep into Martin's eyes, scoured his soul and his store of knowledge. "Remember what Martin of Chrysostom said."

"He is not the only theologian," the boy said. He inhaled deeply, and gripped the sword as tightly as was possible when his hands glistened so with sweat.

"Take heed of what he said, nevertheless." The bluebottle's wings beat like those of a dragonfly skimming the murky surface of a pond in summer. "Consider what is stored in those beautiful eyes of your maiden, beneath that straight nose, and her mouth and cheeks." The demon circled left and Martin moved with it. "You will affirm the well-shaped body to be nothing else than a whited sepulcher."

Martin spoke through gritted teeth. "I affirm no such thing." He closed his eyes as tightly as he clenched his jaw and ran forward fearlessly. The point of the sword sank into the tough pectoral meat of the well-muscled demon. Its days in Hades were spent at Sisyphean tasks that had molded it into this infernal Hercules. For all of its muscle and power though, Martin's virgin charms and his righteous rage on behalf of the women were strong enough to see his sword true. The blade pierced into the monster all the way up to the hilt and through the beast's backbone.

The demon shrieked and gazed upward with its fanged mouth toward the God it had rebuked. It wilted, like a votive candle lit too long in petition of a single prayer. "Die!" Martin shouted.

The demon smiled and hissed even as it disappeared. "I cannot die. I can only leave this realm and can be summoned again anywhere a man is willing to sell his soul. That is anywhere, from the mountains of Muhammed to the iced lands of the North."

Martin calmed somewhat, and released his blistered hands from the sword. "Then do not die. Disappear, for that is enough for now." Martin slunk to the floor and waded in the blood of the poor girl from whose womb the demon had emerged. The boy spoke to the bits of Gloria now, through whose wet remnants the vermin writhed. "This monster was not born of your womb, but born of that boy's seed." Martin looked at the spot where the demon melted from his sight. Then he gazed up the stairs, where the abbess stood. "Who was he?" Martin asked. "The one who filled your hands with ingots and coin?"

Mother Inferior walked down the stairs, and slapped Martin full in the face. "I will not brook such impudence!" She dipped her hands in the blood of her charge, whom she had sent to her slaughter in this cellar. "I am not Judas Iscariot selling my Christ for thirty pieces of silver." She brought herself up to her full height and smeared Gloria's blood over her face like heathen war paint. "I am an old whore who sells pleasure to weary souls." She pointed one of her bloody hands toward the pile of gristle. Merlin came mewing down the stairs two at a time. "Had I have known what this night would transpire, I would have barred the lad entry from my house."

Martin stood and bowed his forgiveness. "I am sorry."

She regarded him with a look that was as kindly as she could muster. "I am sorry for slapping you." The abbess now touched him softly on the cheek and left a bloody palm print there. Martin did not try to stop her, nor did he wipe away the red smear when she removed her hand. "Thank you for being brave enough to banish that demon, and for protecting my house."

"Who was he?" Martin asked again of the boy who'd paid for cellar accommodations and requested a woman with birthing hips.

"He told me stuff and nonsense, fibs about being a shipwright."

"You didn't believe him?"

She shook her head. "He lacked the hands of a shipwright. He was someone and something else."

"It is a trifling matter," Martin said, stood, and picked up the abbess's sword. The weapon was covered in slime from where it had impaled the demon. "The dwarf will explain it all."

"The dwarf?" Her face was a mask of confusion.

Martin took a deep breath, his eyes aflame and his face bathed in blood. "He will be here soon."

Chapter Twelve

Retribution of the Mob

The dead had fallen where they stood after Martin slayed Euronymous to the extent that the demon could be slain. The party was already set out on their path for the stewhouse when the revenants had dropped in their path. The archbishop had spoken to those who were gathered around him on foot, from his perch in the horse-drawn carriage. "You see, it was my admonition to clad the church bells in leather that put a stop to the whore's wizarding."

Most of the mob around the holy man was ragged and poor. They were outfitted in rough homespun hemp tunics and cloaks that appeared to be inside-out no matter how they were worn. Their humble clothes contrasted harshly with the vestments worn by the archbishop. He was wearing his robe woven with a royal escutcheon bearing both the Imperial Eagle and the Bohemian Lion. This garment along with the golden labrum he clutched in his white hawking glove announced him as the living link between the Holy Empire and the Hanseatic Guild.

He pulled aside the royal purple baldachin to glance down at the throng gathering around him. He looked pleased for a moment before allowing the Arabian curtain to fall back in its place. The horses clattered along the cobblestones ahead of him, and pitchforks smelling of rank manure were brandished high above the heads of the peasants on the march. The fire of hessian torches soaked in lime filled the night and cast illumination where the new moon couldn't suffice.

"Will you burn her?" one of the marching peasants asked. The archbishop thought about this and shifted on the pillows where he lay in the covered coach. His mind lingered on the soft, white breasts of the whore. She was the same whore he'd seen who influenced his last sermon before the steeple.

"No," he said, "she will be kept as a special prisoner in the bergfried tower."

There was some grumbling from the crowd. There hadn't been a proper burning for some time, but Archbishop Torner's word was as good as papal bull. The holy man pinched his nostrils with his hawking glove, and remarked to any who might listen, "So many bodies strewn on either side of the road, it reminds me of the Lubeck plague." He grinned. "The gravediggers will have their hands full returning these corpses to consecrated ground."

He parted the curtain of the carriage again, and shouted down to the people, "Inspect each of the corpses for living blood before reburial. If warm blood is found in any corpse, fill its mouth with garlic cloves, behead it, and drive a stake through its heart."

The mob grunted its approval, and the archbishop allowed the curtain to return to its rightful place. *That*, he thought, *will sate their bloodlust enough to leave the whore in my care.*

The procession passed the Forum et Taberna, and revelers poured from the inn to watch the passing assemblage. Lit fires announced the workplace of the blacksmith, as well as the stall of the jeweler who made artifacts like candelabra from antlers. It was early morn, and they were preparing their wares for market day. A butcher with a bloody apron of tanned leather tested his scales with a bit of freshly cut joint.

Those who didn't join the assemblage looked on from windows and owl holes beneath thatched roofs. The firefly glow of numberless torches was warm enough to singe the hair off the arms of their bearers. This light was joined now by the seaward estuary beacon, the *olla vulcani* of a rumbling Vulcan's pot that acted as a lighthouse where it was sandwiched between the tufa and guided ships toward the quay. Smoke trailed up from the torches and coated the clapboard storefronts with soot, begriming the windows and smearing everything in a layer of ash. It was easy to imagine the city as a giant kiln in which all of the sinners would soon bake.

A fasting group of mendicants poured out of their friary to drop their untouched dinners into a woven basket meant for the paupers. One of the tonsured lot broke regula and walked toward the procession. The man had flabby jowls and it looked as if the fast was especially hard on him. He spoke to one of the peasants. "What is going on?"

The peasant was porcine enough in his own right. He looked back at the mendicant and waved his torch in the direction of the stewhouse. A few smoldering embers rose toward the lunar scimitar of the new moon. "We're closing down the joyous abbey, and we're bringing out the whore who summoned the dead to afflict us with plague." He covered his mouth with the long sleeve of his hemp tunic as if he suspected she may have already put the hex on them all.

The monk's eyes widened. He correctly surmised that Archbishop Torner was the leader of the rowdies, and he spoke to the man hidden behind the velvet drapery in the horse-drawn carriage. "Christ loved fallen women and welcomed them into the kingdom of the Father. Think of the Magdalenes as in need of pity, not scorn."

The archbishop didn't bother to pull back the curtain and spoke unseen. "A tolerated house is tolerated until certain boundaries are transgressed. Poppets were fashioned and witchcraft performed." The archbishop's snow-white hawking glove reached out and parted the curtain. Herr Torner had a look at the friar. "Anyone who would defend such a whore as would engage in witchcraft would himself be defending heresy." The archbishop winked at the monk. "Brother Moue, isn't it?"

The friar's blood turned cold, and he shivered. "Aye."

"I know the names of all of the people of this town. I could have your own friary closed as easily as I could shutter up this house of assignation. My advice is that you return to your matins." The archbishop closed the curtain again.

The friar was speechless with terror for a moment. He regained the will to speak, if only because the archbishop had shut the curtain and he no longer had to endure the piercing scrutiny of the man's cold eyes. "If soldiers have no women, they abuse men. Think of the restless garrison who've been guarding the walls these last few months."

The archbishop spoke over the clatter of horse hooves on wet stone. "You should not quote a Greek heathen like Aristotle to a man of God, brother."

"Then think of Augustine's words, your holiness!" The friar pleaded with his hands, gesticulating wildly even though the archbishop could not see him through the thick purple fabric draped roundabout his carriage. "The public woman is in society what bilge is in a ship at sea." He pointed in the direction of the anchored ships floating among the carbuncled pylons. The friar then cast his hand back toward the keep. "The whore is what the sewer pit is in the palace. Remove this sewer and the entire palace will be contaminated."

The friar was tired from walking alongside the procession. He paused to gather breath. His face was red. The peasants close enough to hear the conversation were less sure in their step now, torn between the wisdom of the archbishop and the common sense of the friar.

"The house will not be closed then," Archbishop Torner said. "Its business will be halted until inquisitors can assess the extent to which it has been corrupted by the black arts. Once the practitioners of witchcraft are removed, and only common whores remain in business, its doors will be shuttered no more. Satisfied, oh quoter of interlinear glosses?"

The brother couldn't see the man's face, but he somehow knew the archbishop was smirking. He stood speechless, rooted to the cobblestone. He watched the torch-lit throng clatter along the street.

The carriage halted in front of the whorehouse. The horses snorted in place and they stomped their hooves recently freed from fetterlocks. "Pull the curtain aside!" the archbishop ordered. Two peasants with hands unencumbered by torches or pitchforks obliged. "Contemptus Mundi and Contempt for the Flesh are the righteous path." Archbishop Torner pointed toward the cracked Backstein front of the whorehouse. "Bring forth the Jezebel, the Lilith from this filthy, diseased rampart of Jericho."

The front door of the whorehouse opened before the peasants could batter their way inside. The abbess pulled at the shirt of a young boy covered in blood, who brandished a sword and frightened a couple of rabble-rousers into dropping their pitchforks. The tines of their forks clattered and made a din as the newly weaponless peasants scattered behind their torch-bearing compatriots.

The archbishop spoke directly to the young milksop. "Stand aside, little bastard. Do not pervert the course of justice unless you wish to languish in the motte and bailey with the harlot."

"See?" Mother Inferior whispered to Martin, her face so close to his that her wart was in his ear. "They will take her to the donjon. They will not burn Lyudmila."

Martin's stance relaxed enough for two peasants to steal his sword from him by the pommel. He tried to rush back into the house to grab the other ceremonial sword from where it sat above the hearth, but the dirty mass overwhelmed him. They swarmed over him until he felt himself underfoot. He heard everything and saw nothing, blind and panicked. "Lyudmila!" he shouted.

"We have her familiar!" someone screamed. Merlin lighted out of the house, and one of the peasants raised his pitchfork to stab the cat. Martin managed to kick the man in his shin. The man hopped on his limb that was aflame with pain, and the cat sneaked away.

The offended party looked down at Martin, and kicked him flush in the face. Martin's nose streamed with a crimson flow of blood that leaked into his mouth and made him cough.

"We have her!" one of the voices announced. Martin tried to look up, but his eyes were filled with blood.

"Lyudmila!"

An old biddy with a sour face wrapped in a veil leaned down to Martin. "She has cast a spell on you, lad. You will soon be free of her witchery."

"Your witching days are done!"

One of the wall's garrison heard the commotion and entered their midst. He and another guard in a chainmail hauberk gripped Lyudmila's arms. They pinned her arms behind her back.

"Confess!" the archbishop demanded. "Or languish in the donjon until such a time as you are willing to admit your blasphemy. Admit that you kissed the devil's hindquarters and signed his parchment."

Lyudmila lifted her head, sneered, and shot a projecting stream of spit in the archbishop's direction. One of the guards slapped her with a mailed fist, and she hung limp and unconscious. Martin attempted to stand, but too many feet covered in leather shoes and curled slippers were on his back. He wept, silent and powerless.

"She will be revived later," the archbishop promised. The two guards lifted her as she sagged deeper into sleep. "Since she slumbers now," the archbishop said, "are there any here who wish to make confessions against her that can later be recorded for the official court records? These will be sealed and sent by carriage to the Holy Seat in Rome."

"I'll go first," one of the guards holding her said. Martin couldn't see him, but he recognized the voice as belonging to Edgar.

"Speak!" the archbishop said, and stepped down from the carriage. He walked toward the two men holding the woman, to better hear their words.

"A few days before she went out of the town's wall dressed as a man without her whore's braid or striped hood."

"That is enough to earn death!" someone shouted from behind the flame of his torch. The archbishop held up a hand, entreating the crowd to stow their anger and for the guard to continue.

Edgar pointed his blade point toward Martin, who was still splayed out on the cobblestone. "She was accompanied by this young bastard, who oft enough leaves the walls to gather moss for caulking ships in port."

"He's an accomplice!" someone shouted.

Martin tried to speak and gagged on his own blood and the smell of the recently risen dead that was still on the fetid wind. He wanted to confess, as long as he could languish in the stone keep or burn with Lyudmila. He wanted their souls to forever rest side-by-side, entwined beneath the screaming mandrakes.

The archbishop waved his crosier in the direction of the crowd as if imparting blessings. "Man is ever led astray by woman. The boy was but a pawn in her designs. Eve entreated Adam to eat of the apple. The bastard is not worth our time."

If he'd had the strength, Martin would have risen to his feet and rushed for the archbishop. He wanted to pummel him until he found himself either pitchforked and burned by the mob, or reduced to bits of diced mince by the guards. A foot remained firmly planted in his spine, and he had to be content with the measly grace he'd bought Merlin. He'd spared the cat a scapegoated death as a familiar. He'd also successfully kept the other bastards in the crawlspace even as the clatter of hooves and the glow of torches grew ever nearer and the curiosity of the children stowed in the wall grew stronger. He didn't want them to see any of this, and he was glad they were hidden still.

Another man came forward and spoke in a booming voice. "I saw her in the woods, as I was felling on behalf of a noble."

"And?" the archbishop prodded.

"And she gathered moss," the man said, "but not for caulking ships."

"To what end did she gather moss?"

All was silent for a moment save for the ripple of the flames of torches. Martin suspected the man hesitated because he needed to invent a crime for the girl. Lyudmila never left town before her last imprecation to the fairies. Of this Martin was certain.

"She formed a Green Man," the fellow said, "of mushrooms, fungus, moss, and fir. His foliage face spoke blasphemies. He said that Christ was not born of a virgin."

A horrified gasp rippled through the ranks. "There were poisonous oak clusters that served as his locks, as long as those of Samson. Branches formed the heretical mouth."

"I saw it also!" another seconded. "I was with him coppicing!"

"It pains me to say this," yet another man said, stepping forward, "for I frequented the stewhouse myself."

The archbishop's crosier glowed in the light from the torches, and his face was dappled with golden reflected hues. "'Tis a venal sin," he said, "easily remedied by confession. Nothing mortal to damn your soul."

The man was emboldened by this reassurance and cast off some of his sheepish manner. He looked over at Lyudmila. He believed that she wouldn't awaken to contradict him anytime soon, so he said, "She would ask men to undress, a violation of ancient protocol."

Archbishop Torner waved his wand over the crowd and then spoke to the man making his accusation. "Many here are unacquainted with the loose ways of the stewhouse, thankfully the lion's share of my parishioners. Please clarify your position for them, dear sir."

"Certainly," the man said. A bit of his sheepishness returned. "Men usually have women undress so they can judge their potential companion for the night most judiciously. That she would choose her companion based on his own endowments proves that she whored for pleasure and not out of need."

The archbishop looked behind him in the direction of the friar who'd crossed theological swords with him a stadium back in distance. "Not even the apologists of the Magdalenes would excuse such behavior." He shook his head.

The man continued, emboldened by the archbishop's sanction and the rapt attention of the crowd. "They do not obey sumptuary laws behind closed doors. They eat fine bread while the workers threshing the fields and guarding the ramparts at night subsist on dogmeal."

A volley of accusations shot now from new lips, like arrows flying from a bow. "She showed her breasts in the streets to entice customers!"

"She prodded men to bestiality, spellbound a burgher, and used her glamour to make him tryst with a she-ass he mistook for his wife."

Martin spoke under his breath through a bloodied mouth. "I've seen the wife of the burgher in question, and a she-ass would be an improvement." The peasant standing above him heard his words and removed his boot from the boy's back. He then stomped Martin's head into a brackish, stagnant puddle.

"Just now as the dead rose, this Fata Morgana took on the form of a crow and feasted on their flesh."

"I saw her go to the smithy's once and pull a scalding horseshoe from the fire with bare hands and straighten the glowing steel fresh from the forge!"

"She has a tail, like that of a cow or fox. She conceals it beneath her lavish robes."

"Come," the archbishop said, placing his hand into the drooping crevice between her white breasts. "I have heard enough evidence, but I must have it corroborated by her." He spoke to the two garrison guards. "Bring the whore into my carriage. When she wakes, I will begin to extract a signed confession from her. I am skilled in such arts." The archbishop walked back to his carriage and pulled aside the purple Arabian curtain, allowing the two guards to hoist the girl inside.

The archbishop followed the girl aboard. Once they were in darkness, he cast a glance in all directions. Assured of their privacy, he stuck his tongue out and licked her exposed nipple. He circled the areola with his toad-like tongue from left to right. Lyudmila moaned in her sleep. The archbishop stowed his tongue back in his mouth, lest he wake her.

He spoke to one of the horsemen astride the steeds. "To the donjon!"

"Yes, my lord."

There was the crack of a whip, the neigh of a horse and then the clatter of shoes. Some of the crowd followed the carriage. Others dispersed to prepare for early morning work or to spread gossip about what had transpired this night to neighbor and friend alike. When they were all gone, Martin's half-crushed and bloodied form was revealed to the abbess who still stood in the doorway.

She looked down at him. "At least they didn't burn the stewhouse down."

"What great fortune," Martin said. He struggled to prop himself up, but his palms were too bruised and the padding of his hands too sore for him to brace himself. He remained where he was, rolled onto his back, and gazed up at the stars in the heavens. He gripped a smarting rib and hissed from a jolt of pain that coursed from his toes to his eyeteeth. He spoke through a pair of swollen and bruised lips. "The dwarf will come."

Mother Inferior snorted. Then she slammed the front door to the stewhouse closed, leaving him out in the cold, but not before getting in a parting jab. "You and your damnable dwarf."

Chapter Thirteen

The Dwarf Comes to Koln

"Blasted involution of fate brought me home," the dwarf cursed, gripped the iced dragon's egg that tipped his amber staff, and then walked on. So far he had sighted no other rock heads, but a heavy snow was falling and they tended to stay underground in mines and catacombs in the best of weather.

He had promised himself he would never visit Koln on account of all the stone he and his brothers had brought up from the mines and down from the mountains to build the damnable cathedral. The dream foretold by the giantess said he must come here though, and so here he came. Roderick promised himself that even if he went into the town to see the bastard he'd scryed in his visions, he wouldn't get within a stadium of the cathedral. If he did get close, he was certain he would start to chip away at it stone by stone until the town guards carried him away to the chambers of the dungeon.

On the path before him, there was a gothic cloister seated across from a monastery. The buildings were perched atop the next hill. Both were hewn from sandstone, which he and his brothers had never been forced to chisel. It was soft stone, the kind a rock head could even digest in his stomach. It was perfect for mortal purposes as well. It was malleable enough to carve secret chambers into the rock with some ease, and its high mineral content gave wells and cisterns a fresh taste when they were filled with clear water.

He passed some ivy-clad ruins and then came to an old mill adjacent to three tanner cottages. A ram with a hoary coat chased several sheep up a steep hill. A farmer stood by the side of his frozen millpond and watched Roderick with curious, heavy-lidded eyes. "Hallo!" Roderick shouted.

"Guten tag," the man said, and smiled. His face was like dry parchment, filled with creases and lines.

"You are quite finely-attired."

Roderick looked down at his pleated red gown and shifted the pack on his padded shoulders. His sleeves billowed as he pointed toward the town wall where two guards stood sentry. "I plan to make my grand entrance into the town."

The farmer shook his head and looked over his shoulder as a sheep bleated behind him. A ram mounted a sheep and prepared to stud. "Koln's under quarantine."

"The Death?"

The irony brought a bout of wry laughter from the farmer's chapped lips. "The dead rose, though there was none of the Death of which you speak afoot."

The dwarf was puzzled by that, so he waited. The farmer said, "A whore with a great store of witchcraft at her command summoned the dead to plague the town. They rose, but the holy Archbishop Torner laid them quickly to rest with his own chants and invocations." The farmer pointed toward the snowcapped bergfried visible even at this distance, high above the town wall.

"I see," the dwarf said. He suspected more was afoot, but it never did well to publicly cast aspersions on an archbishop or to defend a whore's honor. He looked back in the direction of the wall. He saw a mass of rubble and a crack in the town façade, through which he could see baroque houses that were tiered like cakes and colored like chocolate boxes. "There's a hole in the bucket, so to speak." A light wind picked up and tousled the billowing crimson sleeves of the dwarf's coat.

"Yes. Three poppets danced their way through the wall, little dolls of evil design. They smashed their way through."

"I'll be." Roderick looked back in the direction of the firs behind him, their pinecones coated in glazed ice. "What of hunting rights on the land?"

The farmer pointed a half-frostbitten finger at him and said, "You are wise to ask. You don't want to earn a place on the gallows."

"Nein."

The farmer pointed where the dwarf's eye had strayed before. "The farmers such as I have turned our pigs into the fields to fatten up on acorns. My advice is to steer clear of the swine unless you wish to share a cell with the whore in the drum tower, or you wish to get lanced like some hero of yore."

"What of other animals?"

"The countryside is overrun with rabbit. If you kill a few for your dinner, not only won't you incur the wrath of the shire reeves, but you'll receive a reward for each pelt you bring."

"How much is the bounty?"

The farmer shrugged and shivered as a bracing wind crossed their path. "Enough to buy a loaf of bread."

Roderick didn't say anything to that, but he wasn't interested in such petty ante. Properly dressed and oiled hare skin could fetch a good price among the priesthood who used the pelts as coverlets for their altars. He had a feeling that he'd learned all of value that the farmer had to impart, and he bowed to the waist. "Thank you for the talk. I have been in silence for the greater part of this long trek."

"It was my pleasure." The farmer bowed back, though nowhere near to such a degree as the dwarf. "Heed my advice," he said, straightening back up as much as the rickets eating his ancient bones allowed. "The town is quite skeptical of strangers right now. Even if you mean no ill, and on the off-chance that you make it inside, you may end up as a sacrificial goat."

"I may at that," Roderick said, and he turned. "But my fate is in Koln, unfortunately."

"Let me not keep you," the farmer said to the man's back. Roderick continued onward. The well-packed snow crunched underfoot until his boots found purchase on the macadam. This trail led to the portcullis next to the hole hewn by the evil little dolls, at least according to the farmer by the millpond. It was near sunset, and Phoebus threw her last rays over the dales, and caused the snow crystals to glisten with adamantine brilliance.

The guard finally took notice of Roderick. They would have probably seen him earlier if he'd been taller. "Halt, Knee-High," one of them said.

"Yes, Half-Pint. Stand and state your business, unless you wish to be cut down."

Roderick sighed, not used to such abuse. "Very well." He thought now that his chances of getting passage were probably as slim as the farmer promised. "What would you like to know?"

"Your name first," one of the guards said. His helmet was ill-fitting. The steel nose guard stopped just short of his nostrils, from which cold snot leaked.

"I am Roderick, the Dwarven Illuminator."

"Dwarven Illuminator!" The other of the two guards sneered, and spoke to his partner. "Did you ever hear of such a thing?" He looked back down at the dwarf, his condescension amplified by his vantage on the catwalk. "Aught but one in a hundred men can read. I've never met a rock head who could spell his own name except with piss in the snow."

Roderick sighed again, this time more deeply. "I am a glossator, illuminator, and scribe. I studied in Cambridge shortly after the Oxford schism prompted several masters to leave the older university."

"Our little dwarf is well-traveled," Snot Nose said to his compatriot. He turned to Roderick. "Tell us some of the places you've been."

The dwarf saw now that there was little chance that he would gain entry through dignity alone, and so he decided to rile the men a bit. "I've travelled farther on foot than you have in your dreams."

"Balderdash!"

"I have never been to Balderdash, though I have been to the lands of which Marco Polo spoke. I saw the armies of Prester John marshalled on the field of battle." He scryed in the air with the dragon's egg that tipped his amber staff. "He had constructed a phalanx of copper automatons, filled their bellies with fire, and placed men with bellows at their backs. I saw ranks of Mongols flee in a mass of flames from bronze dummies. I saw with my own eyes that what legend speaks of Cathay is true."

"Which is?" the guard without the runny nose asked.

"Which is that it is a land where men never grow old."

The gentler of the two guards lowered his voice and said, "Maybe he is who and what he claims to be." There was a general order to disallow mercantile traffic in or out of the town, but this pigmy struck the guard as perhaps special.

The guard looked on Roderick now with merciful eyes. His meaner partner asked, "What gave you your verve for travel, rock head?"

"I tired quickly of being called rock head for one." The gentler of the two guards laughed at his show of wit but quickly stowed his smile when the other mailed guard on the walkway shot him a dirty look. "So, I yearned to flee the mines." Roderick turned. He looked back beyond the trees and little buildings, past the frozen water to the mountains turning blue in the foggy distance.

"I ran until I came to a monastery where I acquired knowledge of Christ, and of his Book." Roderick stabbed the frozen earth with the end of his staff. "Once I read the testament of our Lord, I read whatever else I could get my hands on."

"Forbidden tomes?" the meaner guard asked.

"Forbidden tomes can be read, though not copied."

"You read them?"

"Aye." Roderick saw no reason to lie. "I read of the Blemmy, who had mouths in their chests and eyes at their shoulders. I read of Hyperborea, the land beyond the Boreas where the Northern Winds slept."

"Where did you read such things?" the guard asked, sternly. He had never learned to read and was vexed to think the squirt knew more than he.

Roderick wasn't aware that his words stoked the jealousy of the guard, and he continued. "In the works of Hecataeus of Miletus, who lived six centuries before the birth of our Lord. He claimed it was possible to count every crater in the moon once one crossed the threshold into Hyperborea."

"I find it hard to believe that a book from so long ago could survive into the present age."

"Survive, it did," Roderick assured him.

The guard pointed his sword's tip toward the gathering of heavy firs, which gave off musk strong as myrrh. "And survive you will, beyond the walls of this town."

"Edgar," the other guard said, softly.

Edgar fixed the other guard with his cobalt eyes. The guard lowered his own gaze and couldn't bring his eyes up from his armored boots until the dwarf's form had grown small on the horizon. Roderick disappeared in the swirl of snow into the cluster of trees.

It was the dwarf's custom to speak to himself in such times of setback and tribulation. He did so now, setting down his pack on an ancient boulder large enough to serve as a cenotaph for the squirrels who failed to find a hollow on the cold nights. "Very well, Roderick." He nodded. "A rock head with dignity is too much for these giants to abide. So let us give them their fool. But first, let us have something to eat."

The snow was still falling, but not so thickly that his expert jaeger eye couldn't discern the deep furrows of a rabbit run. He pulled his ballock dagger from his belt and gripped it tightly by the Maplewood handle. Its blade of alternating coats of damascened silver and gold was unreflecting in the dim light from the fading sun. He sliced some stubborn greenwood from a nearby branch. Then he knotted a snare, which he hid in the snow where the trace was deepest.

He kicked with his soaked leather boot at the ground, uncovering a circle of stones where a previous fire had been lit. He spoke now not to himself, but to the young boy in the whorehouse he'd seen in his vision. "You'll have to wait a bit longer, lad. The rock head needs his minerals." He cursed himself for calling himself that and for regarding himself the way men were bound to regard him if and when he made it through the wall on his next try. He would have to feign humility, not throw his knowledge in the faces of the unlearned curs next time.

There was a bit of flint and unspun tow in his pack, but the dwarf was too tired to play with it. In fact he was too tired to abide nature's pace while waiting for the rabbit. He sheathed his blade and gripped the dragon egg atop the staff. It glowed warmly for a moment, like a jar of honey heating by the hearth.

Flames rippled in the old campfire and a rabbit all but danced into the snare where its foot caught. "A quick twist, my tiny friend." Roderick ran to the squirming mass of white fur, gray against the blinding white snow. He broke the rabbit's neck and it lay still. He opened his mouth and put those rock-biting molars to work, tearing each of the rabbit feet off in their turn and spitting them out into the snow. Some men made trinkets from the paws, but he had bigger game on his mind.

He flipped the beast on its back, dropped the staff against the side of a heavy oak tree, and retrieved his ballock dagger from the sheath. He slit the rabbit's belly. The warmth of its intestines coated his hands and fended off frostbite. Steam rose and filled the air. He pulled the innards and organs free and flung them into a nearby snowbank. Roderick briefly paused to wipe his bloody hands on his coat. The mantle was red and would mask the blood, leaving no one the wiser.

He lastly eased the rabbit pelt away from the lean meat. Roderick used the same scrutiny he reserved for the scales at market and figured that he could use the ballock as a skewer while he was at it. He slid the pricking end of the blade through the rabbit's rump and shoved until the knife poked free from the hare's mouth that was frozen in the moment of death. The red, glassy eyes of the rabbit popped and sizzled when Roderick held the hare over the fire. The dwarf breathed a sigh of deep satisfaction.

He looked back at the dragon egg and spoke a compliment to the little totem he'd stolen from the slumbering beast so many moons before. "The wood you brought forth is of a most excellent quality." He stared into the blaze. His hands were harder than the pads on the foot of a wolf, so Roderick had no qualms about holding the hare just above the licking flames and turning his wrist like a poor man's spit.

"Good driftwood," he said, breathing deeply of the forest potpourri. "It smells old." He looked through the stand of trees, toward the wall where he noticed the guard was changing. Hopefully the men who spoke to him would not instruct their relief to turn him away. If they did, he would have to gain entry to Koln through some form of chicane.

He looked back at the snare he'd made from the living branch he'd sliced off a nearby tree. "Greenwood's good for burning witches, as it creates a lot of smoke and knocks heretics out before they can feel the flames." He only knew this on account of a reformed Cathar who'd converted after watching several others of his sect burn at the stake. It was something he would hopefully never have to discover firsthand, though the caution of the farmer by the millpond was still lingering in his mind.

The scent of charred meat reached his nose and made his stomach growl. It made him behave like a werewolf as he brought the roast hare from the fire. He pulled it from the heated blade, ripped the rabbit in half, and cracked the bones. He held the shattered frame of the hare over his mouth and sucked the scalding marrow as it dripped into his mouth. He drank like a vampire suckling from a virgin's femoral artery.

"Ah!" he hissed, and threw the gamey meat into the snow where he'd earlier discarded the other bits of the rabbit. The moon was high in the sky, a pale discus thrown across the heavens. He sheathed his knife, still hot from its use as a makeshift spit, and he walked over to his staff.

"Now," he said, "since the giants cannot tolerate a learned dwarf, let them meet the fool."

He closed his eyes, envisioned an outfit, and felt himself transformed as the dragon egg glowed atop the staff of Prussian amber whereon it perched. All nearby water was too frozen to let him see his reflection, but he sensed the floppy jester ears atop his head, and heard the bells jingle on the mummer's hood. He felt the satin horns with his greasy fingers, and then looked down at his feet. They were covered in galoches whose toes were too pointy to belong to any race save the elves. No rock biter would be caught dead in the things, but here he was. He had to get through that damnable wall.

He walked toward the two guards on the walkway. He stopped once enroute, before embarking on the frozen macadam path. He slid his staff into the pack on his back, reached down to his feet, and gathered a handful of walnuts nestled next to the curling toes of his shoes.

"Look!" one of the guards shouted. He took his hessian torch from where it was nestled in a brass cradle on the parapet. It dripped flame over the wall, which melted the snow it touched.

Roderick juggled the walnuts. "I am but a simple fool who wishes to ply his trade in market."

The two men roared with deep belly laughs on the catwalk, and Roderick continued to speak while the walnuts sailed from hand to hand in a rainbow arc. "I know no songs of the Minnesanger, for my memory is not good. I know the trade of a fool quite well, though. See!"

He prayed his magic would work upon the three walnuts rotating from palm to palm, and he wasn't disappointed. "That's a right nice trick," one of the two men said, pointing. Roderick looked at his hands and at the little cabochon rubies that floated in the stead of the nuts.

"I am quite the amateur lapidary."

The guards wasted no time in going to the crank that controlled access to the portcullis. "Our town has been afflicted with witchery and other forms of misery of late." The rusted door lifted by fits and starts. "By Christ, it would do us all well to enjoy your mirth and folly."

Roderick tumbled through the gate, rolled into a tight ball, and did a backflip despite the cumbersome pack on his back. He bowed to the applause of the two men on the catwalk. "I aim to please," he said, smiling. The men smiled back at him, and then returned their gaze toward the snowy horizon. All were still waiting for the monster who'd razed the Zollschloss to arrive. They had no way of knowing that he'd already been here and had also left.

It was dark inside the town walls, and the buildings were crowded close together. *Stadt Luft macht frei indeed,* the dwarf thought with a grin. There was the creak of a wheelbarrow finding scant purchase on cobblestone. Roderick stepped aside for a mason whose cart was filled with mortar and topped by a brass trowel.

"Guten Abend," the man said.

"Abend," Roderick replied.

The man nodded at his cart. "Have to brick up da wall where da poppets broke through, 'fore a real monster makes his way to Koln."

The dwarf looked beyond the laborer, past the market stalls, and the fachwerk homes. He gazed toward the lone spire of the cathedral piercing a veil of clouds set before the moon. "Too late," Roderick said, and pressed on toward the stewhouse.

Chapter Fourteen

The Bastard meets the Dwarf

The fool changed back into the illuminator in an alleyway up the street from the stewhouse. He bid adieu to the floppy-eared hat and silly shoes, though he kept the walnuts-turned-jewels to be made as an offering to the lady of the house. Roderick saw that he might need a bribe of some nature as he approached the steps where Mother Inferior swept.

He paused to allow a man with a cartload of dead bodies to wheel his way past him. The sun had risen over Koln, and the putrescence of death was on the air. "Hallo!"

"We're closed," the abbess said, still sweeping, "by order of the archbishop."

The dwarf walked up the steps, and held his palm open to her. The reflection of the gems glowed in her eyes, but she made no move to take them from his hand. Roderick had yet to meet a procuress as discerning as this one.

"The last time I took a handful of riches from a man, it cost me my house." She pointed behind her.

"Oh?" Roderick leaned forward. He could see much in visions, but it never hurt to supplant that with a bit of inquiry.

"Some cur came here claiming he was a shipwright, filled one of my girl's bellies with demon seed, and then he absconded." She swept the final step, and then made to turn back into the house. "I've lost three girls this week," she added. "One to the cloister, one to the dungeon, and another to a demon."

Roderick continued holding out the gems to her. They shone in the morning sunlight. "I want nothing for these, save for you to tell the one who calls himself Martin Stolzer that Roderick the Dwarven Illuminator is waiting for him."

The abbess snatched the gems from his hand, opened the front door, and shouted, "Martin! Your precious dwarf is here!"

The Bastard snuck his way past her and looked down at Roderick. "You came!"

"Aye, I came for you. Now come with me. We have work to do."

Martin looked back at Mother Inferior, who averted her gaze and said, "Go. Oliver will tend the other bastards for as long as these gems and ingots hold out."

Martin left without another word. He walked alongside the dwarf as he continued down the street, as if joined to the man at the hip.

"Where are we going?" Martin asked.

Roderick pointed the egg tipping his staff in the direction of a rusted onion dome rising from the fog. "My water witching nose tells me there is a bathhouse there."

"Yes," Martin said, following his new master like a faithful dog. "Why are we going there?"

"For two reasons," the dwarf said. "Firstly, I need to make ablations. Secondly, I must do more scrying in the volutes of steam. Tell me," he said. "is this bathhouse also a place of assignation and procurement?"

"Aye, mostly for sodomites," Martin said, "The bathhouse has paid for all of the stained glass in the cathedral, so the archbishop turns a blind eye"

"The less I hear about that cathedral, the better." Roderick didn't feel like delving into his rock head history at the moment. He produced a handful of coin for the man guarding the door to the bathhouse, who wore a toga and a garlanded crowd tightly fastened around his Caesar curls.

"Thank you."

They entered the main atrium, where two boys similarly attired unburdened them of their clothes and pack. "I keep my staff," Roderick said firmly, and the boys pressed no further on that account. Martin gripped his hands to his naked form, and the dwarf smiled. "No need to be bashful. The sodomites won't ambush you with me by your side."

One of the two attendants who took their clothes spoke to Roderick. He'd correctly assumed the dwarf was leader. He probably also assumed Martin was his young catamite. "Welcome to the Wasserstrasse Bathhouse."

"Thank you." Roderick nodded, glancing around the room. The atrium was covered in tiles depicting Roman athletes in various gladiatorial poses. The bathhouse was a strange hodgepodge of styles. There were ionic columns and Byzantine tiles with Islamic touches and Greek Orthodox accents.

"Allow me to give you the tour," the boy said, and they followed. He pointed to a room from which loud screams emanated. A man shouted, as he was held down by four strapping attendants in togas. A rotted cavity was pulled from his mouth. A jet of blood shot from an adjacent bed where another patient was being treated. A barber with eyeglasses that shone like semiprecious beryl looked up at the new arrivals with a pair of scissors in his hand.

"We have tooth breakers, hernia cutters, and blood letters."

"No thank you," Roderick said, unfazed while his partner did his best to stow his terror. The dwarf looked over at him. "Blood cupping is not without its charms, but I'd advise you to avoid the letters and their blades."

"You mustn't tell me twice," Martin said with a gasp.

The attendant stopped before another room where men rubbed the flaccid, doughy flesh of two Hanseatic burghers who talked business through a haze of sauna steam. "Massage?"

Roderick stopped, and thought about it. "Yes, but may we have a private chamber?"

The attendant winked. "I understand."

Martin wanted to protest that he wasn't a Uranian, but the attendant's back was to them as he led the twosome to a room built of redbrick. Steam hissed like brimstone from pipes in the walls, and a small footbath shimmered with golden light as if a treasure chest might lie sunken on its floor.

Roderick seated himself on the terraced stone that served as benches. It was slick and humid, and it was hard to find purchase as he sat. The dwarf settled down and breathed deeply of the healing vapors. Another attendant came and laid new water on the smoldering grated sheet where coals burnt.

Martin took his seat next to Roderick, who placed his hand around the lad's shoulder. "I could be wrong, but I believe this is the bathhouse where Tanchelm himself once had his ablutions."

"You are right," the attendant said, without turning from his work with the steaming rocks.

"Who?" Martin asked.

"Ah," Roderick said, "he was a monk who served in my monastery a hundred years before I fled the mines and found salvation in ancient tomes. He was murdered by a priest at sea, but not before accumulating a large following. His bathwater was held sacred, and they drank of it after he made his ablutions."

Martin shuddered. He couldn't imagine drinking anyone's bathwater, save Lyudmila's. *Lyudmila* …

Roderick sensed his thoughts. "A woman," he said.

"How did you know?" Martin sat up.

"The faraway look in your eyes. It was the look my own eyes bore as I lay with my head betwixt the legs of the giantess a fortnight ago."

Martin stared at him, confused. The dwarf waved his hand. "Never you mind that. Woe betide the fool who stands between a young man and his beloved."

Martin leaned closer to Roderick, not wanting to speak of such a sensitive subject in front of the bath attendant. Being a denizen of a house of intrigue himself, he suspected the walls here had cracks for ears and eyes. "The archbishop has her in his tower," Martin said. "He's the most powerful man in Koln if not in the whole League. His keep is sealed as tightly as a pharaoh's tomb."

Roderick patted Martin's leg. The thigh was unclothed, but Martin felt nothing amorous in the man's touch. "We will get your damsel back from that dragon in due time, sapling. We have other, more pressing matters to attend to first."

Martin couldn't see what was more important than rescuing Lyudmila from the archbishop's clutches, but he didn't want to disrespect the old dwarf. "I saw you," Martin said, "in the hemisphere of glass I use to clean the clothes of the girls in the stewhouse."

"I saw you," Roderick said, "in the Pyromantic flames in the cavern of the giantess."

Martin didn't know what that was or what it meant, but it sounded more dramatic than his own scrying vision. The dwarf looked up, and saw the attendant had left the room. "Let us waste no more time, for we have already wasted enough." Roderick dipped his hands into the footbath as reverently as if the waters were meant for baptism. He carried the handful of water over to the grille where the coals roasted. He un-cupped his hands and the air filled with a haze of rippling steam.

The dwarf's voice came to Martin's ears, though the boy could see nothing. "Never underestimate the power of water. Think of the rabid dog. Have you read Montville?"

Martin heard his own voice answer, "No." He felt himself feverishly weak, as if he had taken up the blood letters on their promise and his incised veins now leaked with his lifeblood.

"The Norman claimed you could take a rabid dog or a man bit by a rabid dog, and bathe them in saltwater and they would be liberated from their ailment. They would be at peace, docile, and easily led."

"I see," Martin said, though he saw nothing.

"Of course, one could seek out the shrine of Saint Hubert in the Ardennes forest. He is said to cure such rabidity, though that would take much longer. Do you understand?"

Martin shook his head. He realized the dwarf couldn't see that, and said, "No, I don't."

"What I mean is that scrying can save us a long journey, if indeed the solution to our mutual tribulation springs from the source I suspect. We shall soon find out." The dragon egg appeared and disappeared in a rippling mist of ghastly smoke. "Oh," the dwarf moaned, "my lost youth."

A stone chatelet appeared mounted on a hill in the midst of the fog before them. The vision of the castle was as small as a ship in a bottle. Each detail was perfect in miniature, as if fashioned by the hand of a master craftsman. The vision took them inside of the chatelet, where a young dwarf in habit stood in the vestibule fronting a room where another monk worked at copying.

The seated monk wore a long eremitic beard that contrasted sharply with his youth. His hands were stained in ink. Roderick spoke of the seated man. "Meet your culprit."

The little man in the cloud was no larger than one of Lyudmila's poppets. He looked up from his desk as if he heard them. Martin stared at the copyist, as did the tiny dwarven illuminator. The little man had eyes that were possessed, which in turn possessed anything they locked on. His naked head was pointed like a miter. He had the harried look of one tormented, who for all of his pain feared he had earned his misery.

"Who is he?" Martin asked.

"He is Lord Herzog." Roderick laughed. "I should add his title is self-conferred. He lives now at the dread Magnetic Mountain. He was once an illuminator and copyist like me, until he went from reading Cathar and Gnostic texts to copying spells and incantations."

The dwarf's scepter of Prussian amber snaked through the fog again. The staff aimed for the little tableaux, which looked like something fixed inside the glass of a snow globe. "Here you see me finding him out."

"What was he copying?"

"A Goetia for summoning demons and angels mentioned in apocryphal books." Roderick strained to remember the details that were as hazy now to him as the shroud that lingered around them. "I believe I caught him when he was copying a spell to bind Saraqel, who taught men the course of the moon in a time when such knowledge was forbidden."

The miniature dwarf turned from the vestibule and disappeared. Roderick watched his smaller self and said, "I'm no tattler, you must understand. It's just that his transgression was a bit steeper than pilfering ale from the cellar on a Sunday."

A moment later the vision showed the tiny dwarf appearing with a group of other monks at his side. They had taken the vow of silence, and so gesticulated wildly to let Brother Herzog know by signs that he was banished and that he must leave his sandals and habit in the basket on his way out of the chatelet.

The scene disappeared from the smoke. "He never forgave me," Roderick said, "and apparently he wants revenge."

A vision of a darkened castle appeared suspended in the fog now. The gathered crenellated drum towers looked like giant rooks jealously guarding a queen from an enemy checkmate. The vision drifted until it revealed the inside of the castle's highest room. A much older Lord Herzog walked among his forbidden tomes, and there were no monks here to stop him now.

He passed earthenware pots filled with urine and blood, where fetid worms drank and slithered until fatted to their hearts' content. The wizard slunk among burbling crucibles and flaming aludels where sublimation took place.

"His power is growing," Roderick said, "but a man like that will eventually be devoured by his own magic." Lord Herzog was dressed in a blue gown lined with marmot and ocelot tippets. The cloak was spangled with golden stars fit for a French king's coronation. The coat was embroidered with the signs of the zodiac. The Eye of Horus was nestled inside of each sign. The magician wore a hat pointed like a dunce's cap, though Martin suspected he was anything but dumb.

The tiny necromancer walked to a corner of the room where a mirror with a lead back showed visions of time. Clouds rippled past and storms gathered in the blink of an eye. The wizard spoke into the mirror. There was a resounding clap of thunder and a blinding fissure of lightning that crackled, after which a boy stepped through the glass.

"I saw that cur at the stewhouse the other day!" Martin shouted. He was angry enough to reach into the cloud of fog and snatch the boy up in his palm, though he knew even in his rage that his fists would be left clutching only moist ether if he tried.

The cur in the vision obeyed the wizard like a somnambulist, mute and with his hands resting at his sides. The wizard spoke. His words were an inverted incantation. It was beyond Martin's grasp to understand, since his knowledge of Latin was limited mostly to prayers even when it was spoken right.

"What is he …?"

"It's from Genesis," Roderick said, interrupting him. "The first book of the holiest of books." The dwarf shook his head at the audacity. "It's backwards, but I've read it, recited it, and copied it enough times to know it by heart forwards or backwards."

"What is it?"

The dwarf quoted, "'And you, be ye fruitful, and multiply. Bring forth abundantly in the Earth, and multiply therein.'"

Martin stood up from the slicked bench of the sauna in a panic. "We must slay the sower before he spreads his demon seed further."

Roderick shook his head and pointed at the tiny wizard knighting the somnambulant bugger with a wand made of ivory tusk. "We must do no such thing." He looked at Martin. Their eyes locked, notwithstanding the fog. "We must go to the Magnetic Mountain, and we must break that ivory wand. We must also smash Herzog's spine to shards for good measure." The walls around them perspired as if alive. Roderick said, "Kill the brain, and the body dies. All men of the black arts are powerful from a distance. Get me in a room with him and I won't need the aid of magic. I'll beat the little runt to death with my bare hands." The dwarf's form was so engorged with power now that he dropped his own beloved staff to the floor of the bathhouse, where it rattled among the tiles. He closed both of his fists. "Let him feel the wrath of a rock head."

"How will we get there?" Martin asked.

Roderick recovered his senses. He leaned down to pick up his scepter, a bit abashed now. He composed himself and said, "It is far, far from here. It would take too long to get there the old-fashioned way."

"Do you know a shortcut?"

Roderick nodded. "I do. It is not by land route." He paused. "Tell me," the dwarf walked close enough now for Martin to count every bead of perspiration that bled from his brow, "do you have any lust to take to the open seas?"

Martin smiled from ear to ear, happier now than he had ever been in his life.

Chapter Fifteen

The Dwarf makes his Peace with Koln

Utrecht's Alehouse was a giant folly of a building, meant to resemble a massive hogshead cask laid on its side with the entrance to the establishment in the form of a barrel keystone. The effect of a beer barrel was actually accomplished by using strakes from broken ships in lieu of barrel staves. Roderick admired the construction of the pub while he and Martin sipped wayfarer honey refreshers in a corner.

"Why, we haven't left shore and I feel like we've already put out to sea." The dwarf slaked his thirst from the giant mug, belched once, and waved as he tried to get the attention of the alewife. She was at the opposite end of the bar, talking to a jongleur who agitated the catgut on his vielle.

Roderick stood on his stool and hummed along with Greensleaves. He looked at Martin. "It makes me want to change back into the fool's bells I was wearing before we crossed paths."

"I don't understand," Martin said. He stared into his own untouched, foamy drink. "Why are we drinking? I thought we were going on a voyage?"

Roderick slapped him on the back. "In due time, my boy. There are a couple of matters that need attending to, things that need a bit of explaining before we go filling our sails with wind." He leaned over to Martin and slid the boy's drink across the stained oak bar. "If you're not going to quench your thirst, then I may as well have a go." He tipped the glass until his head was facing the ceiling. Martin thought he looked like a wolf baying at the moon. A moment later the dwarf set his mug down with a loud roar that finally got the attention of the alewife smitten by the minstrel. Honeyed mead spilled from the mug Roderick had set down harshly, and she walked over to him.

The alewife wore her tresses arrayed in fine chestnut plaits. She frowned at Roderick and glanced at the countertop. "If you spill enough for me to cup your runoff in my hands, there's a shilling fine."

"Forgive me," the dwarf said. He belched and produced a shilling. He gave it to her. "I'm not sure whether or not there's enough foam for you to wrap your hands around, Mädchen. If there isn't, consider that a bit extra I'm spending on account of your charms." She took the coin from the countertop without another word, and walked back down to her troubadour. Roderick now looked and spoke like a man who was stone sober. Martin had heard that rock heads had hale constitutions and could never really be drunk or cold. "I have to pay a visit to the church that buried my father."

Martin's eyes widened. "I didn't know they allowed dwarves to be buried in Christian cemeteries, since I was given to understand that most of your race hews to the old Northern ways."

"You're too bright not to understand when I'm speaking figuratively." Roderick hefted his staff and tapped the countertop with the dragon's egg. "No, us rock heads quarried the stone that built that precious cathedral. For that reason I swore I'd never set foot in Koln." He glanced around the room and waved his wand about. "I am here, and since I've broken one promise I might as well see the heavenly house that misery built."

He glanced into the two empty earthenware mugs before him. "A proper Benedictine breakfast, it was."

Martin's voice was meek when he next spoke. "I didn't mean to imply all dwarves were heathens. I understand you're not."

Roderick patted him on the shoulder. "I believe no offense was meant, and you can rest assured none was taken." The rock head winked. "Tell me a little of your pedigree. Speak of your lineage, who you are, what you want, and so forth."

Such questions always made Martin uncomfortable, as rarely as they were put to him. *Better not to lie,* he thought, *especially not to one with such proven powers as this dwarf.* "I'm the son of a candle girl who died in childbirth. My father could be anyone from a stableman to a duke."

"We are both men of little estate," the dwarf said. He pulled his ballock dagger from his belt and set it on the counter.

The alewife saw the glint of steel and shouted from across the bar. "Only guards of the city are allowed to carry weapons indoors."

Roderick turned the knife so the Maplewood handle faced the maid with the plaited locks. "I'm surrendering it." She nodded. Then she looked back at the minstrel who sang improvised verse in praise of her beauty.

Martin looked down at the knife. "You don't think you'll need it?"

"This is all I need." Roderick held up the staff of Prussian amber. "Herzog lives atop a magnetic mountain. Any chainmail or longsword will be pulled inextricably toward the rocks. Anyone unfortunate enough to be carrying a weapon or wearing armor will find themselves dashed to bits, like a sailor lured by a siren. No, my boy." Roderick shook his head. "I would divest myself of anything metal I was carrying before we pay a visit to Herr Herzog."

"How will we reach his mountain?" The sauna had been quite foggy with heat when Martin saw the magician's castle, but the Schloss appeared to be surrounded by harsh rocks and sharp reefs. It also looked to be bordered on all sides by stormy seas.

"We will go through a portal, which will take us there in the blink of an eye."

"Portal?"

"You admitted your bastardy without shame, and I admire you for it," Roderick said, ignoring Martin's question. "Now you must betray an equal measure of honesty to my next question."

"I will," Martin said. He had yet to lie to the dwarf, and was not one for lying in general. He would perjure himself to save Lyudmila if someone asked him if she'd fashioned poppets of those three men.

"Are you a virgin? Is your unicorn horn still white?"

Martin sighed, thinking back to the demon in the cellar and its own infernal inquiry into his chastity. The dwarf laughed, correctly deducing from the sound what the boy meant. He slapped Martin on the back. "That is nothing to be ashamed of, since it confers a certain amount of magical power. Keep your maidenhead my friend, at least until we settle accounts with that old evil illuminator."

Roderick wiped foam from his lips and pondered something a moment before speaking. "Why are you so far unter dem pantoffel then, if you and she have never made the beast?"

Martin's eyes dropped and his voice lowered so that he could barely be heard over the sound of the minstrel's playing. "I tasted her flower."

"Aha!" Roderick laughed hard enough to stop three or four conversations at the bar. More than a few pairs of eyes were on them, and Martin's face reddened until it looked like a ripened radish. "You're luck you never tasted of the giantess's ambrosia, boy. Otherwise you'd be lapping up her honey for the remainder of your days."

The dwarf stood from the bar and left a couple more coins next to the dagger. He walked toward the front door of the alehouse. Martin followed after him and asked, "Who is this giantess of whom you speak?"

"Never you mind." Roderick moved over the cobblestone quickly. His legs looked to Martin like fatted drumsticks pulled from a chicken, but the young boy found he had trouble keeping up with the dwarf all the same. "There she is, the harlot!" Roderick pointed his staff at the cathedral.

Martin kept his voice low and hissed in the dwarf's right ear, leaning down to speak to him. "You've got a thing or two to learn about Koln, dear sir! That cathedral is the jewel in the kingdom's crown."

"Tower of Babel," the dwarf snorted.

They walked toward the cathedral. The steps of the church were surrounded by onlookers. Martin knew that meant the archbishop was speaking to the peasants. The whole of the building looked like it was one wave of a necromancer's wand away from waking up and storming the streets like a giant monster. Martin imagined the church impaling men on its pinnacles and roof. He saw the church in his mind's eye devouring them by sucking their screaming forms into the vortex of its open vaulted nave.

"I'm used to humble forest churches," Roderick said. He felt dizzy in part from the drink, and partly from being so close to the stone palace.

"You still haven't told me how we're going to get to this portal," Martin said, hoping to draw an explanation out of the drunken little dwarf.

Roderick stopped in the street, next to a stall where a man plucked feathers from a squawking white goose. "If I haven't told you, then maybe I made a promise not to tell anyone."

"What do you mean?"

"I ..." Roderick faltered, and looked up toward the cathedral. Then he spoke to the sky. "Forgive me Schreckschraube, my beloved."

"Who?"

"She was a beguine and I was a monk. We had a chaste marriage, though a marriage of any kind was in contravention of our mutual vows." Martin listened. "It wasn't ascetic enough for her tastes. She decided she wanted to be a hermitess, and so she found an island and never divulged the location to the sisters of the convent that she fled."

"Is she still a beguine?"

"I'm not sure she ever really was. She knew more forbidden lore than old Herzog. She copied more than him, too. If she were to walk through this town, she would soon probably be sharing a cell with your lovely Lyudmila." The dwarf pointed toward the far tower where the candle girl was held prisoner in the motte and bailey.

"Is she a dwarf like you?"

"No," Roderick said, "She wears the skulls of brownies as earrings and she is tattooed with enough kabalistic symbols and futhark runes to be a one-woman coven. So even though she's not a dwarf, she'd draw more attention than me."

"So why haven't they already burned her?" It was true that Martin wasn't well-travelled, but he didn't know of a land in Christendom where an old woman could flaunt her pagan ways without ending up at the stake.

"They can't," Roderick said, and resumed walking. "She is as impervious to flame as an element."

"She sounds like someone who should come with us on our journey."

"Dammit, boy! Are you deaf? She is a hermitess. She will not leave her house, let alone her island."

The voice of the archbishop rose in volume as they approached the cathedral.

"Does she know where this portal is?" Martin asked.

Roderick licked the last bit of wayfarer's honeyed mead from his lips. He giggled. His nose glowed like a bulbous cauliflower that had been dyed red. "The portal is wherever she wants it to be. Her store of magic is admirable. I am a dunce or a novice, by comparison."

The dwarf pointed toward the tower where Lyudmila languished. "Do not be a fool like us, boy. Drown your unicorn horn in the sweet wine of that maiden's pool once our work here is finished and she is freed."

Martin's heart beat like a caged bird as he imagined rescuing Lyudmila. Still, he thought maybe they should wait until their wedding night to make love. "Is chastity not a virtue?" he asked.

"Chastity is a mockery of that most holy union."

A couple of the poor folk on the steps of the cathedral turned back to hear Roderick's blasphemy as it intruded on the archbishop's cant. "To be celibate is to mock the perfection of the marriage between Mary and Joseph." Roderick's left eye danced as if made of glass. "Are you saying you are as good as the mother and father of God?"

Martin shook his head, and the dwarf pointed his staff toward the drum tower. "Then unsheathe thy sword in her womb the moment we have her free again, and order will be restored to this otherwise wretched universe."

Roderick fought his way through the throng to get a closer look at the archbishop. Martin all but rode his coattails as he followed with the next in his endless barrage of questions. "How will we reach your hermitess?" he whispered.

"By ship," Roderick whispered back, coming to stand in a place that gave him a good look at the archbishop in his royal vestments. "I will give the coordinates of the island to the captain of the vessel we board, and to the captain alone."

Martin kept crouched down at the dwarf's side. "With what will we pay him?"

The head of the dwarf's scepter glowed, and Roderick spoke as his face was reflected in the orb's aureate light. "Rock head magic," he said. "Thor and Odin will turn valueless minerals to fine stones if a dwarf can plead his case well enough. They will not intercede for greed. The gods of old will sometimes help a dwarf, even when he's abandoned his pantheon and lapsed into Christianity, as I have. The cause must be good, though."

Martin shook his head, confused. Roderick ignored him and stared up at the bishop speaking in Latin. "It is a mighty fine gown he wears."

A woman in a Norman veil of bridal white said, "It belonged to one of the three Magi, and was a gift from Barbarossa after he looted it from a Saracen stronghold."

"My word."

Archbishop Torner lifted his hawking glove above him. A golden eagle rested with its talons nestled in the cloth. The raptor screeched once, and its plumage ruffled. It alighted from the archbishop's fist and flew toward one of the stained glass windows in the face of the gothic clerestory.

Roderick leaned down to Martin. "Quite a show."

The archbishop reached into his vestments and produced a crucifix made of cypress wood. He held it out in his hawking glove and reached it toward the ramparts around the keep where Lyudmila was held as a prisoner. "See, Christ, how we have punished those who would encroach upon your divinity and raise the dead by the black arts. Display thy gratitude now, if ye approve of our holy campaign against the dens of iniquity and those whose work furnishes an ever-greater number of souls for hell." The archbishop held the crucifix now toward the sun, as if it was the True Cross and they all stood before its wood at Golgotha.

The risen sun cast its golden rays over the cross, and blood began to flow from the rough wood. The people stepped back from the crucifix as the red flowed like wine from a bung.

"Stigmata!" someone shouted. Ripples of terror and joy went through the throng, who were certain now that they were witnesses to a miracle. The blood dripped over the archbishop's white hawking glove, staining it pink.

Roderick tugged on Martin's sleeve. "Come with me, boy." The dwarf kept hold of Martin's sleeve, dragging him through the mesmerized throng to the side of the church.

Roderick paused before the cobblestones at his feet and glanced to his left and right. He was satisfied that no one was watching them, that all idle folk were either drinking or praying. He raised his scepter above his head. "We will do some old-fashioned geomantic scrying, the rock head way."

He tapped the dragon's egg to one of the cobblestones. The two of them watched a vision of the archbishop boring a hole in a wooden crucifix, slowly whittling the innards away with a shaving knife. Archbishop Torner then selected a black cat that Martin, to his horror, realized was Merlin. The archbishop stabbed the cat in the belly and then held its bleeding form over the crucifix until the now-hollowed cross was filled with blood.

"I'll be," Roderick said.

"Merlin!" Martin bit his lower lip until it bled, and he clutched his fists tight until his nails left deep impressions in the palms of his hands. "A fatherless nothing like myself has few friends." He pointed toward the vision scryed in the stone and then pointed toward the fortifications looming in the distance. "I counted that cat and that girl as my only two companions in this world, and now that charlatan has taken both of them from me." Martin got closer to Roderick. He was so impetuous now and fed up with the man's antics and mirth that he was ready to fight him, rock head or no. "Why are we delaying?" Martin wished he'd brought the sword from the stewhouse along, the one he hadn't ruined slaying that demon in the cellar. Steel accomplished things, sorcery and magnetic mountain be damned. Patience and portals be damned, as well.

Martin turned to run back to the front of the cathedral. "I'll give him his stigmata. It'll flow from his nose 'til he resembles his bloodied Christ!" Martin spit as if rabid, and in his anger he realized for the first time that he had referred to Christ as someone's Lord besides his own. What an irony it would be if the dwarf remained Christian and he turned pagan!

Roderick grabbed him around the waist and repeated the words he'd spoken in the bathhouse. "Kill the brain, and the body dies. Galen and his humors of the bowels are balderdash. The brain is the soul of man." Roderick spun Martin while he had a firm grip around him, and he pushed the boy back toward the cobblestone. "There is still more to scry, far more. My worst suspicions are confirmed."

Martin leaned down with him, so curious that he now lay on his belly in the middle of the dirty street so that he could get a better look at the vision.

"Remember," Roderick said. The vision of the blood being drained from the cat disappeared. "Christ admonished his followers to be wary of signs and wonders."

Martin took his eyes off the newly-arranged scene taking shape on the cobblestone. "So you don't believe in miracles?""

"I've seen one I've believed." Roderick held up a finger on the hand not holding his precious staff. "In Saint Mary's in Rostock, I saw a bloodstained host form at the feet of a marble pieta."

"And you believed?"

"I believed." He pointed back toward the stone where he'd performed his geomancy. "Behold!"

A look of pity washed over the dwarf's face, and Martin wished he had the man's wisdom. He wished he could pity evil rather than hate it. He wondered what he had to see or how long he had to live before he could feel what was so plainly written in the flesh of the dwarf's scarred features. "This poor bastard of an archbishop has damned his soul as assuredly as Lord Herzog has sealed his own wicked fate."

Martin was acquainted now with one demon and knew another when he saw him. "Who is he?"

The dwarf gave his appraisal to the wicked red figure with the black horns, cloven hooves, and forked tail. "That is Old Nick, the devil himself."

Martin stepped back. The dwarf giggled. "It is a mere vision, and you needn't fear him. He performs the Lord's work as much as you or I do."

The boy trembled like a leaf. "I wouldn't want to be heard uttering such things within earshot of a church."

"Come off it, boy. He forces no one's hand. Why, look!" Roderick pointed his dragon's egg at the archbishop, who was of a lower rank and in a much smaller church in the vision.

"Bitte, build me a church," the tiny Torner in the vision pleaded. He followed the devil around the modest sacristy of his windowless chapel. Old Nick turned, and held out a hand beneath which living coals burned.

"In exchange for a soul, I will build you a fine church."

"Yes," Torner panted.

"Know this," the devil said. His tongue slithered quickly in and out of his mouth, like that of an asp. "Your church will be built on the backs of the lowest of the low. They are a flock of sheep that are loyal to the Gods of the North, but they also have the blessing of Christ. They are meek despite their outward shows of rancor and drunkenness."

"Yes," the young priest said, not swayed from his course.

"Their sins are venal, while the one you ask of me is mortal. Look." The devil waved his hand over the closet where vestments hung in the sacristy. The tunics disappeared and another lesser demon with gryphon wings appeared.

"Who is that?" Martin asked. "What is it?"

"Baal," Roderick said.

The demon crawled from the closet, wearing a crown inlaid with fine jewels. Its legs were hairy and eightfold, like those of a tarantula. The spider-bodied man with the sorrowful eyes and the royal ducal crown walked until it stood before Father Torner. The holy man was in no way repulsed by the spider before him, his greed so deep in his marrow that he would rather count the jewels in its crown than the legs beneath it.

He saw moveable jasper, glowing carats of sapphire, cut and polished chalcedony in the crown. There were emerald gemstones, and precious bands of sardonyx. There was ruby sardius and topaz facets fit for a queen's wedding band. Chrysolites diffracted the entire prism at the priest's approach, showing him every color of the rainbow in the glowing jewels.

"Take each of the eight jewels from their fittings, from the crown of Baal," Old Nick said. The furry tarantula legs tapped the ground of the sacristy without sounding. The hairy limbs moved quickly enough to spin silk, as Baal got ready to acquire another soul through no force stronger than natural greed.

The priest obeyed. He reached into the crown, plucking the gems from the man-spider's head while Old Nick looked on. Roderick shook his head. "Dumb." He looked back at Martin, while the priest sold his soul by eight degrees. "You know the devil can be tricked."

Martin took his eyes from the cobblestone. A bird screeched from behind them, returning to its perch on its master's arm on the cathedral steps. "What do you mean?"

"Even common villagers know that when Old Nick says he wants a soul in payment for building something, he can be satisfied with any soul. It needn't be the soul of the one who petitions him."

Roderick pointed toward the little priest in his sacristy with the two demons, floating in the dream cast in the cobblestone. "He should have bolstered his theological training with a trip away from the seminary to learn a thing or two from the old wives and the ploughmen." Roderick winked again at Martin with his walleye. His ale-tinged breath made Martin's stomach turn a little sour, but despite all that, the boy heeded the man's words. "Do you know the village of Aachen?"

"I have heard of it," Martin said, "from travelers to the stewhouse and from Mother Inferior herself."

"Who?" Roderick asked.

"The abbess."

"Oh," Roderick said. "If you go to the cathedral in Aachen, look at the door and you will notice a wolf carved there in stone."

"Why?"

"The villagers were clever enough to know that the first soul to enter into something built by Old Nick, whether it be a bridge or a chapel, is the soul that is surrendered to the devil. They let a wolf run into the church first in Aachen." Roderick looked back at the cobblestone. "It's easy enough to trick the devil, unless a formal pact is made. Reneging is possible when there is nothing in writing."

The Torner in the vision now dipped the bone of a flight feather into an inkwell filled with blood. He signed on the parchment with the hand that wasn't filled with jewels he'd plucked from the ducal crown.

"We will take care of your archbishop," Roderick said, and Martin saw from the look on his face that the rock head's word was his bond. "You can rest assured that those of my race who toiled and slaved for his glory will have their revenge." He pointed one of his meaty fists toward the gray parapets in the distance. "We will both see that this miracle worker gets his just desserts, as surely as you will have your Lyudmila back."

Roderick waved his staff over the cobblestone, and the vision of the priest who sold his soul disappeared. The dwarf patted Martin on the shoulder. A light snow began to fall. "We had better take to the seas," the dwarf said, "before they begin to freeze over."

Chapter Sixteen

To the Friesian Waters

A wave of the wand turned the same cobblestone in which they scryed into a goldbrick. Martin carried it beneath his shepherd's coat as he followed Roderick back to the giant alehouse.

"What next?" the boy asked.

"Next, you wait in the tavern while I secure us passage out of town."

"Must it all be so clandestine?"

Roderick stopped in his tracks then. "I wasn't just slaking my thirst in Albrecht's. I was listening to every conversation that took place around us." He pointed at his ears, which were pointed like those of an elf. "A dwarf's sense of hearing must be keen, for he must be attuned to the workings of the mines and mountains. If he cannot read the orphic signs, he will soon have his fate sealed in a rockslide or cave-in."

They came to the giant hogshead barrel stood on its side, and paused on the threshold where golden candlelight from within spilled out onto the street. "What did you hear?" Martin asked.

"All traffic in and out of the bay is barred on account the Zollschloss that was razed to its foundation the other night. No one knows what manner of beast was responsible for the carnage, though they know enough to know it wasn't the work of Vitalienbruder or Vikings."

A man staggered out of the alehouse vomiting. Martin and Roderick took a step back to avoid the rancid spray that spread like wet oatmeal from between the man's fingers as he attempted to keep the contents of his stomach from the sidewalk. "How do they know?" Martin asked, checking the leather of his shoes to make sure they weren't stained with the drunken man's bile.

"A foot patrol found a bunch of the sea's hardiest marauders torn to fine gristle inside what was left of the castle's walls, along with a royal elector and the savaged remains of his wife."

"I'll be."

Roderick whispered now as he spoke, even though the drunken revelry from inside the tavern probably provided enough cover for their doings. "Now you see why this must all be very cloak and dagger."

Martin cast a skeptical gaze in the direction of the freshwater shores of the entrepot, which were visible from here. He wondered if Roderick was just trying to get rid of him. Maybe the dwarf didn't trust him to keep the secret location of his celestial wife's island quiet. "What about that?" the boy asked. He saw a crane working by lever to lift heavy goods onto a ship pointed away from harbor, and out to sea. The crane hovered high above the forecastles and fighting towers of the wooden cogs anchored in port. "The general ban has no bearing on those with diplomatic status, among whom is numbered Ibrahim the Jew. He has been in port these last few days and now intends to leave."

Martin nodded. The story was credible. The last few days had been hectic, but he still vaguely recalled hearing word of the visit from the famed Sephardic Jew.

"Alright," the boy said, and turned toward the pub.

Roderick choked up on his staff. Then he took the brick from Martin and hid it beneath his vestments like a loaf of hot bread. "Do not quench your thirst with anything stronger than mead. You need your wits about you for the next fortnight or so." Roderick pointed in the direction of the motte and bailey. "Drink to your heart's content after the archbishop is food for the worms, Lord Herzog's magical mirror is shattered, and your head is at Lyudmila's breast."

"I have no interest in drink," Martin said, and he meant it. He was thinking about that chess set he'd seen beneath the woven tapestry near the far wall of the alehouse.

"Good." Roderick turned, and headed off toward the docks where the army of masts rose in the night beneath the glow of the moon.

Martin walked inside the keystone-shaped door of the public house. Men crowded around the alewife, vying for her favors so hard Martin was sure fisticuffs were soon to break out. The floor was made of sawed lumber and was slicked with spilled beer. So many voices competed to be heard that the sound of the minstrel's lyre and song were lost in the din. It gave Martin the impression that the poor jongleur's voice had been siphoned from his throat by the hand of some jealous, tone-deaf sorcerer who begrudged him his glorious pipes.

He wasn't surprised to notice there was no one seated at the chess set, which was propped on top of a cask that smelled as if it once held aged cognac. The musk of a working fireplace along with the perfume of fine whiskey created a pleasant odor that dominated this corner of the room.

Martin took the chessboard in his hand by the corners, and turned it around. He admired the fine craftsmanship that went into making the thing. He picked up a piece, a Roman centurion. He studied the board beneath the pawn. It felt to his finger to be made of aged elm burl. When he tapped the centurion's breastplate, he heard a hollow echo and tried to guess whether it was marble or not.

"Dragon's tool enamel," a voice said from behind him. The man wore a surcoat sooty enough for Martin to imagine his trade was that of a chimneysweep.

"Is that what it is?" Martin asked.

"'Tis," the man said, and sat across from him. "Care for a game?"

The seats were made of finely-woven wicker. "Most certainly," Martin said, and sat in the matching chair on the other side of the cognac barrel.

The man sat and ran his fingers over his own pieces, touching each of the heads in their turn. His set consisted of Spartan Hoplites. The queen was dressed in fine white linen and could be none other than Gorgo, Mistress of Sparta. The fellow made the opening move of an orthodox gambit, bringing one of his knights out of position early. "Do you know the difference between the way we in Christendom play chess, and the way the Saracens play?"

Martin didn't say anything. He preferred not to speak when playing chess. He pursed his lips, pressed a finger to his frenulum, and shook his head. His opponent said, "They call the queen the vizier. I learned as much when I was in a lodge where a wounded Templar was recovering from the slings and arrows of the Holy War."

"That is interesting," Martin said. He played more cautiously than the chimneysweep, bringing a pawn out of position. He slid the piece across the length of a single enamel square.

"The heathens keep their women under lock and key." The man brought his other knight out in a second move that mirrored his first. "Is it little wonder that they balked at making their most powerful piece a woman?"

The fellow leaned across the chessboard. If he leaned any closer, Martin thought there was a good chance that he would risk upsetting the pieces on the board and they would have to start over. "What is your opinion of Domina Matina and of her endless war of attrition against the anti-king?"

Martin was mute. He spoke as freely as his estate allowed in public, which meant he could merely shrug. He gleaned what he could by eavesdropping at market and at the stewhouse. It sounded to his own ears like Koln was evenly divided between those who supported the dead king's brother in his campaign and those who supported Lady Stovis in her task of keeping the royal throne warm for the infant future king.

"I don't know much of such matters," Martin said. The man smiled a cagey grin full of mischief. Martin found the man's face to be unpleasant. He stared over the stranger's bedraggled shoulder at the tapestry that depicted the Norman Conquest of England.

A hand touched the top of his head. He turned, saved in that moment by the dwarf. "Beg your pardon," Roderick said, bowing to the curious man.

"Have you any news?" Martin whispered.

"News?" Roderick grinned and whispered back, "I've more than news, my lad. I've a boat."

"Is she worthy?"

Roderick ignored his question and studied the chessboard. "Make your move," he said to the chimneysweep. The man obliged, pressing his pointer finger to the bristled tip of his hoplite pawn's head. The dwarf moved his queen through the space Martin had provided in his opening play.

"Mater," Roderick said.

The man stood from his wicker chair, scraping the wooden floor of a sudden and causing the enamel pieces to tremble. "It can't be."

"Believe it," Roderick said. He turned and walked out of the public house without bothering to look back and see if Martin was at his heels.

The boy followed him out into the street, where night watchmen roamed in pairs with torches. "Abend," the dwarf said to one group, who nodded and passed on.

Martin kept his voice low. "Is she seaworthy?"

"The island Schreckschraube calls home is but three days' journey from here. It is not as if we are sailing to the river of Oceanus." Roderick held his amber staff aloft, pointing the dragon's egg in the direction of the Vulcan's pot and the burning Greek fire.

The lighthouse keeper in the highest room of his custos lucernae waved a torch to a couple of cogs limping rudderless into harbor. The white canvas of their sails was shredded to ribbons, *probably by the claws of a demon*, Martin thought.

"It goes without saying that we need a small vessel," Roderick said. He pointed toward the blazing fires that glowed among the ripples of the choppy waves of the black waters. "It is now as bright as the antipodes when the midnight sun shines."

Martin was scared. He feared they would drown in some rickety bucket. He cast a last eye back toward the town in the distance behind them, with the slate and thatch roof of the stewhouse visible even from here. He then lost his sense of fear. It was better to die young on the open waters than to grow old among the filth, priests, and prostitutes of the big city.

"Stadt Luft macht frei, mein eye," he said, and Roderick slapped him on the back.

"That's the spirit, my boy." He resumed his quiet lecture. "I found a sailor eager for gold and adventure." Roderick walked along the docks toward a shadowy figure, who was untethering a length of hemp tied to a deep-prowed boat shaped like a sickle.

Water softly lapped against the side of the ship. Five seamen were at their oars, but they were silent and with their heads downturned. Each of the sailors and the captain wore similar attire. Their dark cloaks and black Lirapipes made them appear as living shadows from the netherworld, or the Grim Reaper refracted five times in a prism.

"Are you sure?" Martin asked. His blood felt as cold as he imagined the waters would be if he were to test them with his toe.

"His main ship's been in for repairs for a month." The dwarf pointed toward one of the new arrivals in harbor. Gangplanks were being laid ashore so that freight and men could make their way again onto dry ground after a long journey. "A cog dropped anchor too close to his ship, tore through the hull, and he's been waiting on restitution a full lunation."

Martin pointed at the motionless oarsmen. "Who are they?"

The men didn't speak or even turn. The captain walked up to Martin, removed the hood from his Lirapipe, and said, "It's a good thing those church bells didn't stop ringing until after those corpses decided to leave their crypt and stow away on my ship."

The ancient mariner pointed at the five oarsmen, still motionless. "Tis also good fortune that I got them ashore before the ship sank. Otherwise they'd be laying at the bottom of the bay by now."

"I don't understand," Martin said. Roderick was less confused. The boy suspected they'd talked about quite a bit in the short time they'd had the pleasure of each other's acquaintance.

The mariner clarified. "The other day when the dead were summoned, I used a bit of my enchantment to bind them for my own purposes. When the rest of the dead dropped in their tracks after the archbishop locked that wench in the tower, I managed to do enough wizarding to keep a few of the dead for myself." The mariner pointed back at the five silent soulless men.

Martin thought of punching the man for calling Lyudmila a wench. He wanted to knock him into the water, but he stowed the urge. The easiest way to get Lyudmila back and to see the archbishop laid low was to do what the dwarf said. That involved getting a ride aboard this stygian rig with this old ferryman. It was also a bit harsh to expect the man to know the full story. Martin was privy to many details and even he was a bit confused at this point.

The ferryman offered Martin his hand, and the boy took it. It was a hale and hearty shake that went all the way to the elbow in the old fashion. "Mondhund is my name, and pickled herring is my trade. At least it was before your dwarven friend placed a gold brick in my hand. Come," Mondhund said, and held his hand out to the boat bobbing in the water. "Your friend has supplied me with gold, and with coordinates for a tiny island. I have seen it before, but have never deigned to visit." He gathered up his hemp rope in a snaking coil aboard deck and helped Martin onto the ship. "Let us leave under the cover of whatever darkness the lighthouse allows, lest we all be put in stocks for such fecklessness."

Martin's stomach lurched as he felt the ship list beneath him. This was his first time in the water, and he didn't want to admit his seasickness. Fortunately, there was a more ready alibi at hand. He pinched his nostrils and pointed at one of the five dead men. They began rowing in unison, to a drumbeat throbbing in their empty skulls that made them work.

"I know corpses reek," Martin said, "but these smell as if they're bloating at high noon."

Mondhund pulled his funereal cloak tighter around his body, took up his post at the stern rudder, and helped angle the tiny craft between two giant cogs that created a canyon in the shadow of their gargantuan wooden forms. "You should have smelled them earlier."

The moon lit a necklace draped around Mondhund's throat that Martin hadn't noticed earlier. Its string was composed of a snaking length of black Palatinate pearls. An oversized cameo medallion with Pegasus in flight was engraved on the shining pendant. "I salted those bodies well enough to pickle a thousand barrels of Nordland herring." Mondhund pointed at one of his revenant rowers, as the shore slowly disappeared from sight behind them and the moon grew larger on the horizon. "If I were to push them overboard, the water would be briny enough for Tethys to spawn."

Martin looked to Roderick for some help. The dwarf looked at the mariner and clarified, "It is the boy's first time at sea. This is all new to him."

"Can he read?" the mariner asked. Martin wished they'd stop talking about him while he was present. He wasn't dead like the rowers. Something slimy and muscled slithered past the ship, and his heart jumped in his chest.

"Aye, I believe he can," Roderick answered.

Mondhund looked down at Martin and gripped the sternwheel rudder with both fists. The man's eyes were filmy and glazed in the moonlight, opaque as semiprecious stones. Martin glanced over at Roderick, locked eyes with him, and mouthed the words *He's blind*. The dwarf nodded and the bastard's heart did some more dancing.

The river grew blacker and the moon grew whiter. Mondhund said, "A seaman should start his education with Pliny and then proceed forward in time until he reaches Marco Polo." Mondhund spit into river. The smell of saltwater was getting more potent in their lungs. "You have much to learn, assuming you don't perish on this voyage."

Martin thought that between the paltry size of their vessel and the man's lack of sight that death was not only possible but certain. He looked over at Roderick, who betrayed no sign of fear. Martin dreaded that his companion was mad, and fear was unknown to the bulk of madmen.

"Who is ..." Martin prepared his salty lips to try the name he'd heard earlier, "Tethys?"

"She is a goddess of the ocean," Roderick said. "She is more than mere legend, though we would have to go halfway across the Earth for me to show you her lair."

Martin settled down onto a slightly wet plank bench and gazed toward the stars waking in the heavens, each of which was visible now that they were free of the lights of the shoreline. "I will have to go there sometime," Martin said.

Roderick guffawed. "Don't take Lyudmila there."

The blind man laughed as well. Martin thought the corpses would have laughed too if it were within their power to do so. "Is she some serving wench?" the ferryman asked. Martin thought of shoving the man overboard for the second time, and for the second time he stowed the urge.

"She is his betrothed," Roderick said, rising to his care's defense. Martin smiled at him. The dwarf grinned back at Marin and said, "Tethys emits a cloud much like an octopus. Since she is a goddess of fertility, all women who swim or even venture toward her lair and find their ships splashed with spray become pregnant, usually with twins."

Mondhund nodded and left his place at the rudder. He checked a geode device, something that looked to Martin's eyes like a complex shewstone combined with an astrolabe. The mariner said, "Barren women are willing to pay through the nose for so much as a dram of the goddess's fertile waters."

"I'll be," Martin said, gripping his cold knees to his chest. His teeth chattered a bit and he sniffled. Mondhund produced a bearskin from beneath one of the benches, and handed Martin a rough wedge of biscotti he'd gotten from heaven knew where. Martin cloaked himself in the cloth, bit into the hard ship biscuit, and regretted his former designs at mutiny. He realized it would have been especially shameful to attack his host, considering the man was blind.

Roderick spoke to the captain of the vessel. "Any more word of the terror sweeping the land?"

The blind man nodded. "Aye, another Zollschloss torn brick from brick." Mondhund retrieved a second furry pelt for Roderick and draped it around the man's shoulders as if it were a royal coronation gown. "These castles are white elephants." He spit again toward the dread waters and said, "The oceans teem with all manner of beasts more fearsome than anything spoken of in Revelation." He tapped the wooden side of the boat and it emitted a hollow thud. "At least we are mobile, though. Those gryphons and demons will terrorize anything on two feet, but they have their own reservations about swimming the waters where the Jonah swallowers dwell."

He took a chunk of biscotti for himself and bit into the hardtack. "Anyway," he said, "they found a Vitalienbruder ship and another fire ship scuttled after they drained the bay where that first Schloss was turned to rubble." He shook his head, amazed by whatever devilry now swept the land. "It has been a dog's age since I've seen a ship filled with Norsemen lose in a grapple or a siege. Perhaps the Great Khan got resurrected along with all the dead of

Koln. I'd wager the sea's far safer now than dry land."

Mondhund stopped talking and turned to Martin, who was trying to find purchase with his molars on the biscotti. "We're still in fresh water." Mondhund pointed at the waves chopping alongside the vessel. "Soak your bread until it's soft enough for your baby gums."

Martin endured the hazing with good humor. He figured it was better than sodomy, the lash, and the other legends priests and busybodies peddled to keep boys onshore. He dipped his hardtack into the water, keeping an eye peeled for the streaking scales of the eel or whatever it was he had seen skirting the side of the vessel a few moments ago.

He asked, "Are there any freshwater women of the sea?"

"Most are mirages," Mondhund said, "but I sighted a coven of Rhinemaidens one night while floating in a convoy with Eustace."

Roderick was so stunned that he dropped the bearskin and it fell from his shoulders. The dead rowed around them, and he asked, "You knew the Mad Monk?"

"I lost my sight in the Kaperkrieg," Mondhund said. He was so capable that Martin had forgotten for a moment that the man was blind. He'd heard that men who lost their sight gained acuity in their other senses, which probably served the seadog well. "We were freebooters and we crossed paths with Eustace himself."

"Why didn't you flee at the sight of an enemy sail?" Martin asked. Both the dwarf and the blind man looked down at him with a mix of scorn and pity written in the scarred meat of their unholy faces.

"What sail?" Mondhund asked. "There was no ship or sail to be seen until they were alongside us and we were being brought to the forecastle to plead for our wretched lives."

Roderick looked away from his novice toward the old seadog. "So it was true, then? That he could render his ship invisible at will?"

"Aye," Mondhund said.

"He spared your lives?" Martin asked. He knew of the Black Monk only from secondhand sources. All of the parchments made it plain that Eustache spared no one, and that he raped and plundered the way a farmer stacked hay in a loft.

"He wouldn't have spared us," Mondhund said, retaking his place at the rudder. "Row, you damnable dead lot!" he shouted to the oarsmen. Then he said softly to Martin, "He saw the Rhinemaidens, who were as eager to see him as he them."

"Indeed?" Roderick asked.

"Indeed," Mondhund affirmed. "It is not often that a legend and a myth cross paths, but that was one such day." He pointed at his glazed eyes. "Thank Odin, Jesus, and Allah that I got to see it before I lost my sight."

"To Eustace?" Martin asked.

"Aye, he poured a solution of lye in my eyes. He said I would live, but would never be able to point the way to the old Wolf's Head's vessel just in case we came across another League ship while he was busy plundering the Rhine." Mondhund had tended to the needs of the other two living crewmembers and now tended to his own needs. He picked up another fur for himself and wrapped it around his body while he chewed his hardtack.

Martin was so intrigued by the old dog's tale that he had forgotten his biscotti in the riverine water. It had gone from something as hard as a trencher to something softer than a maggot worming its way through leprous flesh.

"Scheise," he said, and threw the sopping biscuit into the black water. The muscled eel emerged from the water and took the biscuit in its sharp jaws in one quick motion before slithering back underneath the water. Martin's skin crawled.

Mondhund laughed. "I wouldn't stick my hand overboard for a spell, if I was you and you aimed to keep all ten of those pretty landlubbing fingers of yours. That eel will chew through your bones like a starved man through tallow."

Mondhund rummaged beneath one of the plank benches, and grunted as he lifted a barrel. He spoke now mainly to Roderick who was an old enough dog himself to appreciate his store of wisdom a bit better than a young boy who only knew of Eustace secondhand. "The Duchy of Mecklenburg put quite a price on Eustace's head. Pity the black monk lost his head on the edge of a trebuchet to another crew. I could have used that geld." He lugged the barrel. Martin heard him straining and stood up to help the blind man.

"If I'd captured the bounty on Eustace," Mondhund said, "I certainly wouldn't be taking chances moonlighting while a ban's on and some demons are flying around wild." Martin helped unscrew the top of the barrel, which was filled with salt. "Here," Mondhund said. He looked at Martin with his sightless eyes that still divined all, like those of Isaac the Blind. "Take this salt and scatter it over those corpses while they do their rowing."

Martin took some of the salt from the barrel in his hands. The grain was white as Bavarian snow and so pungent that his eyes watered as he handled it. He looked back once toward land or at least where land was the last time he had scanned the far horizon.

There was only water all around the vessel. He realized that the musk came not only from the acrid salt in his hands or from the mummified sailors around him, but from the foamy tide lapping at the sides of the boat. He was finally at sea.

Chapter Seventeen

And the Sower Keeps Sowing

It was an experiment of sorts to see if his seed could find purchase in other soils. It was the cellarer's poor fortune to come to the basement for a cask at just the moment when Casper woke from the pallet the brothers had been good enough to give him. He brained the monk with a heavy, leather-bound devotional book. Casper removed the man's sheepskin mantle, and undid his coarse woolen tunic. Then he slid off the leather belt that girded the man's meagre vestments to his body.

The monk wept softly as the boy raped him. Casper bunched together the man's flaccid cheeks, which were rosy enough to look like they just weathered a bout of corporal punishment. "Don't cry," Casper said, and pumped harder.

He realized when he next spoke that the words coming from his mouth were not his own. They belonged to the demon whose form was taking shape like crawling quicksilver in his loins. "Oh, how the humble lay brothers must search the forests like huntsmen, seeking pheasants, partridges, pigeons and other game with the cunning of a fowler." Casper let loose of the man's flabby rump, and reached a hand around the front of the man's body and grabbed the rolls of his paunch. "Heaven forbid God's faithful servants should die of hunger."

He shivered and went through paroxysms as if someone had put the lash to his back. He grunted and pulled his swollen prick free from the monk's rear. The veined mushroom tip of his penis emerged covered in a dollop of feces, leaving the rectum with a suctioning pop like a barber's blood cup.

"Now," Caspar said and backed away, "let us see what comes forth, or if anything comes forth for that matter."

It wasn't that he was turning bugger, or at least that wasn't what he thought. The truth was that he had made the beast with so many women over the course of the last few days that he wanted to see what happened when he stuck his prick in a different kind of hole. He wanted to see whether or not the demon needed a womb to emerge from his seed and bring new life into the world.

The monk continued weeping, his face buried in the cowl the sower had stripped from him. "Stop crying," Casper said. "You shouldn't have been down here trying to sneak a draught."

The monk glowed as if the Holy Spirit itself was filling his body. His eyes and mouth radiated a light strong as that of a pure halo. Casper feared that he and Herzog had finally managed to provoke God into a reaction, and he braced for judgment. It didn't come. The light grew hotter until the monk shrieked with a cry so piercing that even Casper's skin crawled. The door to the cellar opened, and several monks and lay brothers in habits crowded around the scene at the top of the stairs.

"A miracle!" someone shouted, pointing at the monk aglow.

Casper sneered and looked up at the dim, shadowed forms in the doorway leading up into the abbey proper. "I wouldn't wager my life on it." He grinned. "That's what all of you in essence did the moment you opened the door, though."

The screams stopped as the monk burst into a spray of volcanic ash, which rained down over the form of a newborn demon. It stood several hands high and bore the bullhead of a Moloch idol. The demon's skin was translucent and thin, looking as if it could be shed as easily as that of a snake. The living fire that burned its way through the sodomized monk now coursed like lava flows in the channels of the brute's hardy veins that rippled like earthworms beneath its muscles. The demon's biceps alone were the size of Nephilim skulls. The creature struggled not to scrape its head on the stones lodged in the ceiling of the cellar.

Casper was at eye-level with its knees, which were hairy as a troll's chest and spiked with what looked like dewclaws.

"Run!" One of the monks shouted. The monks closed and bolted the cellar door. The demon looked over at Casper Namlos. Then it looked at the sooty remains of the man through whose rump it burned to earn passage into this world.

"You could have planted me in a womb, but you decided to put me in a rectum." The demon raised a claw to him in a threatening gesture.

Casper was unfazed. "You know you must obey Lord Herzog as well as I do."

"Aye," the demon allowed. "I was sprung from the *Key of Solomon* to do his bidding. What wouldst he have me do?"

A Cheshire grin snuck across Casper's face, which was sullen except when sadism was afoot. "Bring chaos."

"Thy will be done."

The demon raised its smoldering arms in imprecation.

"What are you doing?" Casper asked.

"You will know soon enough."

The demon sniffed the wind. Its nose was flattened enough for the nostrils to touch the red flesh of its angular cheekbones. Steam billowed from the holes in its nose.

"Why do I smell women?" It asked. "Is this not a monastery?"

The room was much warmer now than it was a moment before. It was hotter even than when the demon had first burnt its way into the world. Casper wiped sweat from his face and said, "There is a nunnery a quarter of a mile from here. The monks told me about it over supper last night."

Piercing screams echoed through the sheltered arcades of the monastery. The cries carried through the chambers and passed with a hollow resounding shriek through the Chapel of the Holy Virgin. The wails were as senseless as those ripped from the throats of beasts in death throes, but they could not be mistaken as belonging to anything but men. Casper thought nothing earthly could elicit such tortured cries from men, not the branding irons of the Inquisition or the sharp pierce of a Saracen's mace. He smiled, and realized he was responsible for the hell that had been brought here with a little help from the wizard and his ivory staff.

The demon shared a smile with him and said, "My, how you repaid these monks for their kindness."

Casper shrugged. "You turn one cheek to me after I slap you, then I'll slice your other one with the knife I was hiding all along."

"An apt philosophy for a barbarous world."

"We are on the far side of Heaven," Casper answered.

The molten demon's smile grew darker. "Your spirit will find its fate even more brutal after it sheds its mortal coil."

Casper shivered as he thought of that. No matter how long it was delayed, final judgment would eventually come for him too. He changed the subject to cease the shivering. "The monks said the Duke of Northumbria dedicated his young daughter to the church of the nearby convent on her second birthday."

The wails of wracking pain continued, but the demon spoke now as if all were as peaceful as the drip of a clepsydra in a scriptorium. "So she is still but a child?"

"Aye," Casper said.

The demon pointed its finger toward the stone wall, several stadia beyond which was the nunnery. "Then you should find another to sow with, assuming I don't kill them all tonight or they don't all flee in terror."

"Why?"

"Her flower," the demon answered, "is not yet in bloom."

Casper pointed toward the pile of ashes, a small bit of dust that looked like the remnants of a vampire who had gazed upon the sun. "He had no flower, and yet he bore fruit from my seed."

The hollow horns of the Moloch glowed green like the eyes of an owl. "So you would rape a child?"

"A child and a hermaphrodite are about the only things I haven't raped."

The demon patted him approvingly on the shoulder. "You will do well in Hell."

"I plan to," Casper said, and turned from his work. He ran up the stairs and shouted "Open the door!" to the demon behind him, who snapped his fingers and produced a bit of brimstone that ate the wood like termites. The door dissolved and Casper walked into the monastery where chaos reigned as he so willed it.

He shouted at the top of his lungs in an effort to compete with the screams of the monks, who boiled like live chickens plucked of feathers and cast into pots of scalding broth. "Such luxury has now become such misery!"

The demon he'd brought forth had worked his hexed blessings on the main cistern of the monastery. The freshwater spring simmered with scalding water. The burning liquid fed into tanks that led to a well and produced steam wending through ceramic pipes and aqueducts. These were diverted to the latrines, the bathhouse, and kitchen. Flesh peeled from the scurrying novitiates and lay brothers. Muscle became liquid and the monks didn't so much die as they did drip and melt like wax.

The books burned, while all else cooked. Works of Hellenic antiquity burst as if from spontaneous combustion. Three monks busy washing their hands in the lavabo in preparation for their meal found their hands fried to crispy batter that exploded the moment they withdrew their fingers from the basin. They ran handless around the courtyard and passed out from shock, their cauterized stumps steaming in the cold mountain air.

Those in the Chapel of the Holy Virgin learned what was happening last. Their Gregorian chant continued. The sweltering brimstone gathered force around the church in the next moment and the glazed windows started to sweat, and then pop like bits of grease in a vat of lard. The stained glass cracked and fissured. First the Old Testament depictions shattered as the panes grew superheated. The explosions mounted in force and succession until finally the figure of Christ burst apart and jagged shards of glass shot toward Mary.

The monks ceased their chanting. Rosary beads glowed like charcoals, making the coarse wool of their habits catch on fire. One monk had the misfortune to look up as the gold leaf burnt in bubbling layers from the inside of the beaten dome of the chapel and spilled into his eyes. The liquefied gold seared through the soft tissue of his eye and ate a scorching path all the way to the stem of his brain. It burned and put him out of his misery.

Dollops of hot gold dripped onto the form of the statue for whom the Chapel was named. The glowing precious metal collected like fat-bellied tears cried from the eyes of God himself, until the Roman stone and Riga softwood collapsed. A sinkhole formed in the earth that pulled more than a few of the monks into its vortex, where they had their flesh scorched and were then were buried alive. Their screams were trapped with them and they were then covered by mounds of silent earth.

The demon was content to remain in the basement of the monastery. He was himself living flame and could not be burnt. He could not be brought to fear anything mortals could summon except perhaps the wisdom to slay his maker and thus make him disappear.

His maker had his own fears brewing in his mind now. Casper ran out into the snow while the monastery behind him burned, and wondered why he suddenly felt afraid. He had stumbled onto the corpse of a Hanseatic merchant many months ago while still making a meager living as a grave robber. He'd picked the man's fingers clean of rings and stripped his neck of jewels. He'd also taken a Goeteia that the dead man gripped tightly in his skeletal fingers.

The book was filled with Latin gibberish, which Casper read before a mirror in the plain room of a humble inn where he sometimes spent the night. Usually he was in the company of a local candle girl, but tonight he wanted to see if the book that the rich man took to the grave might actually be able to make him into something other than a pauper and a robber of the dead.

The spell had worked. The magician had entreated him to step into the mirror, and into the lair where he resided with his numberless books and green and red potions. Lord Herzog had promised Casper Namlos power, and he had delivered.

Casper had felt nothing approaching fear for the last few months, not even when he was cooped up in a barrel in the hold of Forkbeard's square-sailed ship, and where the Vitalienbruder had promised him death. It had all been fun and was still great sport. Yet some doubt was taking root in a corner of his mind. Not only that, but he could feel the wizard's voice carrying over the thrash of the stormy seas. The voice told him to beware, it told him that …

"No." Casper laughed. "It can't be." He'd faced pirates and crusaders. He'd seen them fold like dog-eared playing cards. The words which reached his ears had been repeated so many times now that there could be no chance he hadn't heard them correctly.

Lord Herzog shouted down from the highest turret in the ruins of his ivy-clad castle perched on his mountain that was fashioned of lodestone, cobalt, and other manners of rare earth.

"Beware of the Bastard and the Dwarf. They can bring our wicked works to ruin and reverse the course of the spoiled fruit until it is made ripe once more."

"Balderdash!" Casper shouted.

Forms walking through the flames and shadows moved toward him now. The first of the three men was too short to be the flaming idol that had brought the monastery to a boil. Two shapes flanked the main one approaching Casper

Namlos. The moon was low, but the fire danced high. The flames revealed the abbot and twin monks who were doing great reverence to the man, bowing and kissing his hands.

"Forgive us," one wept, "for not protecting your monastery." They fell to their knees in supplication and kissed the abbot's sandaled feet.

"It was my fault," one monk said, still on bended knee. He pointed in Casper's direction. "I was the one who welcomed him in. I gave him mead and bread."

The abbot gathered the two monks to him like sheep. He quoted the Bible to the two men from memory. It was a bit of Luke, one of those less esoteric verses that even Casper Namlos had heard before.

It was the Parable of the Good Samaritan. The sower turned and ran.

Chapter Eighteen

Amid the Archipelagos

The fogbank was white, heavy, and smelled of ricotta cheese. The young dwarf stuck his tongue out and exclaimed, "It *is* cheese!"

His father patted him on the shoulder. "Right you are, my boy." His father waved his hands, waxing in the direction of Widdershins. "Let us see what other wonders this land has in store for us."

Roderick looked up at his father and said, "I almost died the last time I was here, Papa."

The old man laughed and pointed at the valley ahead of them. "You may yet die if you don't know how to swim."

A river coursed toward them, breakers splashing against the sides of the Parmesan Mountains. The water smelled sweet as malmsey. The old dwarf licked his lips as he waited for the river to rush toward them, so that he could drink his fill of the muscatel wine. "I could think of worse ways to die." He turned toward his son. "You're a bit young to slake your thirst with the blood of Bacchus, but this is but a dream and no harm shall come to you."

"Papa," the young dwarf said, "if this is only a dream, then …" The sweet wine enveloped them, picked up their forms, and lifted them along the waves.

The young dwarf watched his father troweling with his mouth open like a whale taking in its fill of krill. The wave deposited them on the shores of a land made of mascarpone cheese. It was so soft and creamy that there was no way they could be dashed from the force of the rippling wave, no matter how powerful it was.

Their feet sunk in the cheese as they struggled to find purchase in it. The father was still licking wine from his lips. His son reached down and dipped his hand in the white cheese, eating a handful. He looked toward his father and smiled.

"Wipe your face," his father said, and then he cleaned his son's face for him. The old dwarf sampled some of the cheese. Then he pointed in the direction of a tree where Mortadella sausages thick as brickbats dangled from the branches. An idea struck the young dwarf and he ran, churning the cheese beneath his feet in an attempt to reach the tree where the meat dangled.

He stood under the shade of the sausage canopy, picked up a handful of the mascarpone, and spread it over a wurst he plucked from the tree. "A most industrious little rock head," his father said, and followed suit. "I believe I will try some of the spread you're using."

There was a roar from beyond the cheese hills and sausage trees. The younger dwarf gazed toward the horizon where a thunderhead cloud towered and promised rain. The cloud moved toward them, and the young dwarf asked, "Why would clouds intrude onto such a beautiful dream?"

His father spoke through a mouthful of cheese and sausage, letting loose a coarse belch. "My son, there is nothing to fear from storms here. The hailstones are sugary pecans. Should there be rain, hold out your palms and tilt your head upward. Collect as much gravy as your gullet can handle."

The young dwarf no longer feared the cloud looming on the horizon. He couldn't wait for it to reach them now. The father hoisted his son on his shoulders, and he spoke to the fruit of his loins piggybacking on his broad back. "This land of contraries offers many wonders, which I shall now show you."

The boy covered his father's eyes with his hands, which did nothing to alter the man's course. The old dwarf knew the overland route by heart. "What will you show me, Papa?"

"We will watch the fish catching men in rivers. We will observe men drawing plows for their oxen. A miller will carry the packsaddle for his donkey." The boy giggled at that. "We shall go to the Tiergarten and watch animals gaze on men trapped in gilded cages."

"What else, Papa?"

"The most beautiful and important scene of all will be a feast for your young rock head eyes."

"What will it be?"

"You must wait."

"Tell me!" the boy begged.

"Very well." The dwarf pulled his son from his shoulders and swung him by his ankles like a felling axe. "We will watch all manner of men work in the mines and quarrying in the mountains, while we dwarves dance round the maypole to our heart's content."

"How far is it from here?" The boy grew dizzy as his father swung him around, and his elation was such now that he feared he might pass out.

"It is hard to count the miles my boy, for we travel while we sleep. The deeper we sleep, the faster we go."

Young Roderick had heard his father tell of this land many times, and he said, "The less we toil the more we earn."

His father disappeared and Roderick opened his eyes as a bit of saltwater spray splashed into the boat and hit him flush in the face. His lips had an alkaline taste to them now, and the stench of the undead oarsmen was like a bog since the sun had risen.

He looked behind him and saw Mondhund gazing into the distance. Martin Stolzer scattered handfuls of salt over the revenants up ahead of him. Apparently the boy wasn't enjoying the stench of the oarsmen any more than he was. Roderick looked back at Mondhund. "What is new?"

"Much," the blind man said. He pointed forward.

"Are we still Upp der Trade?"

Mondhund nodded. "That we are."

Roderick tapped the side of the ship. "How's the vessel been holding up?" He knew they were done for if they hit one bad breaker or stormy patch. He also knew that the whole of the land was doomed if he and the boy didn't make it to the hermitess and get her to conjure up that portal.

"She has given a good account of herself thus far," Mondhund said of the ship. "She's been involved in no feats worth chronicling, and I still miss my main ship and hope that the Hansa gives me some restitution when I return." He pulled his bearskin tightly over his body now, so that the head portion of the trophy clung to his scalp. It looked like the blind man was about to be devoured by a Bavarian black bear or like he was a Berserker clad in the skin of a conquered foe.

Mondhund gazed with his blind eyes at his mummified rowers. He shouted to them in Low German. "Bleiben sie upp den richtschen trat jetzt."

"Jawohl," they spoke in unison to their liege.

"I smell land," the blind man said. Roderick looked toward the front of the ship. He thought it was good to have a blind man on board. The sightless could still hear well enough to be prey to a siren's call, but mirage enchantments were useless against them. If Mondhund smelled it and Roderick and Martin saw it, then the dwarf figured there was a good chance that it existed.

Roderick scanned the horizon, and then looked down with a jolt of fear as something bumped the side of the boat. He jumped, and Martin turned to see what had startled him. The bastard pointed at one of the barrels that floated in the water. "Do you think someone threw them overboard?"

Roderick shook his head and said, "No, I think those are channel buoys." He looked back at Mondhund.

Small islands appeared from the fog around them on their sides, jutting black stretches of jet corral that rose lifeless from the water. No vegetation grew and no seabirds perched on their craggy basaltic forms.

"We are approaching the island where the hermitess dwells," Roderick said.

"Good." Martin had already vomited twice on the journey, and he was ready for his feet to touch land soon. He wondered silently to himself if he had the makings of a real sailor.

Mondhund retook his place at the stern rudder. "We will approach from the right side."

"If memory serves correctly," Roderick said, "there is anchorage on the left side."

"Aye," the blind man said. "That's why I prefer to approach from the other side. I prefer moorings these days and I'd rather tether than anchor."

Roderick remembered Mondhund's tale of having his prized vessel shorn by an anchor in Koln harbor, and he found it hard to begrudge the ferryman his druthers. "Very well," he said, and nodded.

The salted dead altered their course and Martin stifled the rising sickness in his stomach. All of the biscotti had already been retched from his gut. There was nothing but bile left for him to pitch overboard if his belly lurched again and he vomited once more.

He was as miserable as ever he could remember and were there a pallet available, he no doubt would have been bedridden. His misery faded as seafoam that smelled of jasmine suddenly burbled impossibly from among the colorless and harsh rocks. Two creatures with the bodies of women merged with fish splashed through the surf on the backs of glistening dolphins.

"My God!" Martin shouted.

One of the dolphins whistled and clicked, and Mondhund smiled. The women had white skin. The ivory and alabaster demigoddesses made Martin forget about Lyudmila, which he thought would have been impossible up until now. They combed their honeyed hair and reposed in glorious languor, even though the dolphins and giant seahorses they rode moved fast enough for them to be a blur that Martin's senses could only half-comprehend.

"Mermaids," Martin said, breathless.

"Daughters of Aphrodite," Mondhund answered. Martin looked at the reanimated rowers and thanked Christ that he was still alive. If death meant that one could be in the presence of such beauty without being moved, then he didn't think he could ever bear to die. He knew it wasn't as if he had any choice in the matter, though.

"I believe they may be Nereids," Roderick said. The mermaids and their mounts broke through the water one more time. They were close enough to the ship for beads of water from their glorious locks to splash Martin. The water that spilled from the bodies of the half-women smelled like talcum to the bastard and he drank it in, sucking it down like honeydew.

Martin turned around in the hopes of seeing the mermaids emerge once again, but they were now deep underwater. He'd have to content himself with this rare glimpse, which he thought well worth the misery of the dead rowers and hardtack and seasickness.

"Why," Mondhund asked Roderick, "do you think they were Nereids, and not mermaids?"

Roderick squared himself to the blind man, preparing to discourse. Martin hoped the debate stayed civil. He'd seen theologians break out in fisticuffs in the market square back in Koln.

"They were too friendly," Roderick said. "You suggested that the boy read Pliny the Elder, did you not?"

"Aye," the blind man allowed. He feared he was being lured into a rhetorical trap, but for all that he would not deny that he said something if he said it.

"Pliny claimed the bodies of mermaids were rough and scaled all about." Roderick pointed toward the rippling white wake behind their tiny craft where the creatures had submerged after a quick show. "They were scaled only from the waist down." It was perhaps a bit petty, but he added, "I have eyes to see such things. Your nose may be acute, but it can only see you in such good stead."

Mondhund laughed rather than taking offense. "I suggested the boy start with Pliny, but it was not my intent to suggest he finish there."

Roderick was not prideful unless taunted as a rock head, and he smiled back at the blind man.

"He should read the *Physiologus*," Mondhund said, "which clarifies many of the misconceptions laid down by Pliny."

Martin wasn't sure whether or not it was his place to pipe up, but he found his tongue wagging of its own accord. "Archbishop Torner once spoke on the subject and claimed mermaids caused shipwrecks. He said they seduced sailors, dragged them into the water, and drowned them."

The mirth was sapped from the blind man at the mention of the archbishop. His tone was so wrathful now that foam formed in the corners of his lips and spittle flew from his mouth as he spoke. "I've heard that old pontiff's pustule pontificating from his pulpit on occasion."

Roderick looked over at the blind man as if he'd just morphed into a slithering asp, and he asked him, "Why would you enter than damnable church?" The dwarf considered himself a good Christian, though he thought that Archbishop Torner's church was more like Matthew's Den of Thieves judging from the man's jewel-studded staff and gold-filigreed gown.

Mondhund spoke defensively. "I was there because I enjoy the way the colors hit my eyes when the sun touches the stained glass. I cannot see shapes, but grace allows me to glory in other consolations."

Roderick nodded, satisfied. Mondhund couldn't see the gesture, but he was more concerned with Martin now since the lad had brought up the damnable archbishop. "That suckler of Satan's hind tit won't be happy until every beautiful woman is either locked in his keep or burned at the stake."

Martin thought of Lyudmila again. His teeth bit into the flesh of his lower lip, and his fingernails once again sought purchase in the soft padded flesh of his palms.

"There's no winning with that kind of holy man," Mondhund said. "If a man goes impotent, he blames the woman for hexing him. If his cock grows hard and rises for the morn, he claims that to be witch's enchantment as well." He clutched the wood of his stern rudder and squeezed as if wringing the archbishop's neck. "The world would be a better place without him."

Roderick looked at Martin, winked, and said, "The world *will* be a better place without him, and soon." That seemed to pacify the lad and Mondhund a bit. Roderick looked toward the shoreline.

Another sound rang out. It was a homophonic texture of voices that soothed the blood and came to the threesome now. "Now that," the blind man said, "is neither Nereid nor mermaid. It is the voice of something else altogether."

Martin looked around in a panic, searching for something with which to stuff his ears. The sound he created as he searched the small vessel was mostly drowned by the aural ambrosia ricocheting off the reefs around them. Martin's rooting around was still loud enough for Mondhund to hear it though, and the blind man laughed.

"What are you doing, boy?"

"The song," Martin said. He wanted to share no kinship with the archbishop or other men who thought women vessels of wickedness and debauchery, but as he felt his own cock swell, he wondered if he wasn't about to jump out of the ship, swim toward the heavenly voices, and find himself taken under by the tide where he would be drowned.

"Those are undines, my boy," Mondhund said. "They aren't sirens. You can rest easy, tiny Odysseus."

Roderick shared a laugh with the blind man at Martin's expense. Martin had to hide a smile as it crept across his own face and he realized how silly he was acting. The dwarf stared at Mondhund now much like Martin usually looked upon Roderick, as a pupil looks upon the master. Roderick was a wise illuminator who'd risen above his natural station by pure dint of will, but he still thought it best to acknowledge Mondhund's mastery of the sea realm. Roderick saw himself as a jack-of-all-trades and the blind man as master of at least one trade.

"Was Paracelsus right in his assessment of the undine?" Roderick asked. Mondhund contemplated that for a moment and nodded. "Aye, he was." The blind man looked over at Martin. "You have naught to fear from such gamboling maidens." He grinned. "Unless you fear marriage."

"No," Martin said, "but I am betrothed to another." He knew it was usually a woman's place to speak of to whom she was betrothed, but he was tief under dem pantoffel and saw no need to pretend to these two men that he didn't yearn to be enslaved by Lyudmila's charms. The hen could master the cock for all he cared, for the hen laid the eggs. He was still curious, and asked, "Why would they want to marry me?" His prospects were dim, he thought. He was a boy of negligible estate who knew only the life of a whorehouse.

Roderick spoke up, confident enough to offer his own counsel, since Mondhund had seconded the wisdom of Paracelsus. "Elementals envy mortals.

If they join in holy union with man, they cease to be elements and they gain a mortal soul."

Martin thought of that for a moment. He considered life to be little besides pain even though he'd only endured about thirteen years of mortality. He wasn't sure if a mortal soul was something to envy.

"Just don't betray them," Roderick said. The dwarf coughed on the odor of the decomposing oarsmen, who rowed unthinking while the conversation carried on around them.

"I don't plan on marrying one," Martin said, fighting to hold down the horn in his pants. The undines had ceased their song, which echoed now on the wind like a single note blown on a shofar horn. "When I do marry, I plan to remain faithful to my love."

"Good," the dwarf said. "One king took an undine as wife, and thought that his royal office meant he could sow as his heart desired. He discovered otherwise."

"What happened?" Martin asked. The ship listed a bit. The waves around them were growing choppier, but the boy thought nothing of it.

"She said that since she found him asleep in the arms of another woman, she would ensure that he should never sleep again."

Roderick thought of the dream from which he'd recently been awakened, where he romped through Cockaigne with his father. "A man who cannot sleep cannot dream. A man who cannot dream will lose his mind."

"Aye," Mondhund concurred. "Even I see when asleep." Mondhund kept an ear cupped toward the shore, which rose now before them. Its cliffs were sharp as jagged fangs, and upholstered in moss. Martin and Roderick gazed toward the island before them. It looked foreboding and ominous, like one of the Pillars of Hercules.

Mondhund turned to Roderick. "I heard a tale similar to the one you told, although I heard that the king was fond of hunting and harsh to poachers. When the undine found him sporting with a chambermaid, she had him changed into a stag and set his hunting dogs loose on him."

The two men shared a laugh over the king who'd gotten his comeuppance. The laughter stopped a moment later as did the lapping of the waves. All was silent, and Roderick mused, "The last time I was here there were many swans this close to shore. Something …" He paused. "Something is wrong. Mischief is afoot." He hopped up onto one of the plank benches and closed his fists. It was a futile gesture, he knew. The seas teemed with life he was no match against.

"Come to think of it," Mondhund said, "that was not an ordinary call those undines made. I'm not well acquainted with their ways, but I believe it could have been a warning of some kind, a …"

The ship rocked and a swirling whirlpool formed starboard. Mondhund lifted his stern-rudder from its hole. He moved with incredible force and speed, lugging the thing like a quarterstaff. He swung it so that Martin had to duck and would have had his brains turned to gravy if he hadn't reacted so quickly. One of the rotted rowing corpses did actually find his head taken off, and shattered bits of skull fell into the water. The headless revenant continued to row and Martin admired the dead man's dedication.

"Scheise," Roderick said, and then turned to Martin. "Give me my staff," he hissed. Martin searched among the gunnysacks filled with hardtack and handed the dwarf his amber staff tipped with the dragon's egg.

"Is it a monster?" Martin asked. He suddenly wished he was back onshore. He saw himself hearthside, playing chess against that chimneysweep beneath that Bayeux Tapestry replica. That alewife's breasts were a pale imitation of Lyudmila's, but they were nothing to sneeze at, either.

Roderick clutched his staff and Mondhund held his rudder. Both men waited against the silent sea. The dwarf spoke first, though his voice was low. "Most mappaemundi are drawn by charlatans to discourage sea traffic. The guilds of each land don't want their catches being poached by foreigners, and so they stock their oceans with monsters the way a fat king stocks his ponds with fish."

"Aye," Mondhund seconded, "but as a Christian you know what the Church Fathers said themselves of the diverse creatures with which the dark waters have teemed since the days of Genesis. I'm sure," Mondhund added, "that you've seen with your own eyes what manner of life one can encounter at sea."

"Aye," Roderick replied. He knew that Augustine himself said monsters contributed to the beauty of God's creation. As the whirlpool grew now and a mouth large enough to swallow galleons emerged, he had a hard time believing that the sea was the Lord's domain.

"My God!" he shouted.

A triple row of teeth as triangular and sharp of those of piranha gripped the roof of a hideous gaping maw that was as fleshy and putrid as the deflowered rose of a giantess whore. The head of the dead rower that had been sent into the sea was drawn into the vortex of the hungry maw. The monster smacked its lips together, which were as rubbery as clam meat.

"What is it?" Martin shouted. Their tiny vessel was quickly being drawn toward the mouth large enough for Martin to believe it belonged to the very Earth. He fought the rising suspicion that it was the razor-toothed, diseased cavity that gave entry onto Hell itself.

Roderick shouted as loud as he could. His voice was barely heard over the roar of the beast. "It has the teeth of a manticore, but they are land animals!"

Something sliced Martin on his shoulder and he turned. He'd been so engrossed with what was before him that he didn't notice the reptilian tail of the underwater creature, which had slipped around the tiny ship and skewered several of the rowers. The tail had also impaled the blind Ferryman.

Martin fell to the berth of the ship in terror, spilling the contents of the salt barrel onto his body as he tumbled. Sucking lamprey mouths filled with wretched human teeth drank the dead blood of the rowers and savored the living blood of the screaming blind man. The tentacles writhed and sought more flesh, living or dead. Martin shuddered to think what the flopping, coiled appendages would think of his own virgin blood if they found such succor in the putrid flesh of the dead rowers.

The only thing that saved him so far was the barrel of salt. The tentacles felt in his direction, tasted the mineral rubble, and retracted in disgust. The lamprey mouths were ringed with crystalline scum from where they had accidentally sucked salt while trying to taste flesh. Martin picked up a bit of hardtack and chucked it at the nearest mouth, which watched him like oculi.

The biscotti sailed through the air and out of the ship. Several of the floppy, constricting feelers reached after the ship's biscuit. Martin had a revelation. "It hunts by judging motion!"

"That's all good and well," Roderick said. Martin could not see the dwarf in the eclipse of the ravenous limbs that blotted out all sunlight. "That big mouth is going to suck this ship down and those sharp teeth are going to slice us until we're soft as gruel, whether or not these damnable ravenous arms here have us for their bread."

Roderick crossed himself on account of the blind ferryman, who'd been a hale and hearty companion on this voyage and a man to the last moment. Quills and spines danced from the limbs that slithered like the body of a boa constrictor. The tentacles danced like proboscises searching for an orifice to rape.

"Draco marinus," Roderick said, though it was a little late for taxonomy.

"What?" Martin whimpered. His eyes were filled with salt and were burning. He could see nothing, and it was just as well. He would prefer to meet his death with eyes as blind as the man who'd taken them this far, only to meet his maker so close to shore.

"It's a sea dragon!" Roderick shouted.

The Word of the Good Book came to Roderick, as he remembered what as a young monk he first copied from that bit of Psalms. "Yonder is a sea!" he shouted, so that Martin could hear him. The words he spoke weren't the last rites, but they somehow felt more apt for a death at sea. "Great and wide," he continued, "which teems with things innumerable, living things both small and great. There go the ships and Leviathan, which thou didst form to sport in it." He laughed against all reason and will, parting with sanity as the tentacles lifted the ship on high so that the chain of islands below them were as field mice to birds of prey. The mouth now loomed below their tiny craft, looking much larger than any of the coral islands around it. The two men prepared for their flesh to be sheared by the serrated teeth as easily as lumber by saws.

"Hail Mary," Martin said, "full of grace, the Lord is with thee." They were held aloft, high enough to kiss the clouds. Martin felt urine stream down his leg, melting the barrel salt stuck to his thigh and shin.

The tentacle aimed the ship for the manticore mouth. There was a piercing shriek as the marine behemoth let them loose. The ship flew through the air and crashed against the sea. The wood of the tiny boat broke into splinters too numerous to count, and Martin felt himself slammed deep beneath the waterline.

Flotsam from the shattered ship and the dead, rotted rowers floated above him. The bubbles of terror floated freely from his nose and mouth. He watched the many tiny toothed mouths surrounding the great mouth of the undersea manticore as it shrieked in terror. Martin closed his eyes in the next moment, thinking of Lyudmila as he slept and felt his lungs fill with water. His mind became a blank purple slate.

Roderick was with his father among the rivers of wine and mountains of Lubeck marzipan as usually happened when he was unconscious.

Chapter Nineteen

Among the Venerators

The cultists stood around the little man and the young boy, who lay on the ground before them. The dwarf woke first, shouting, "I am not a gnome!" He repeated his assertion, screaming until the surf lapping the rocks seemed to curdle. The boy awoke beside him.

Martin placed his hand on Roderick's arm. "It was just a dream. We are still alive." He looked around the jagged promontory at the strange assemblage of men around them, and he wondered why they weren't dead.

The boy stood first. His shepherd's coat was torn to shreds, and ribbons of flesh dangled from his back and his palms. He hissed in pain, and helped Roderick to his feet.

"We made it," Roderick said, and groaned. He looked toward the sea where the monster had attacked their tiny vessel. His tone grew sad. "It doesn't look like Mondhund made it."

Martin was only half-listening. He didn't know what to think about the men around him, and his mind was telling him that they had been saved from the leviathan only to be prepared for the cannibal's pot.

Roderick's voice was soothing now. "Easy, boy. We are in the right place, and are among friends."

"Friends?" Martin had a hard time believing that. The natives in loincloths held radiant swords ringed in sharp dragonfish teeth that glowed like jellyfish. The blades sent out signals to each other, pulsing as the men gripped them in their hands. Their armor was made of sea urchin and starfish, with breastplates made of sheets of interlaced, smoothened sand dollars.

The leader of the group stepped forward. He had spiked epaulletes made from the tines of underwater hedgehogs. He spoke to Roderick in perfectly modulated German. "It has been a dog's age since we saw you last."

The man extended his hand and Roderick accepted it. The dwarf checked the urge to pat the man on the back, lest he mutilate his palm on the Oceanian armor. "Aye," Roderick said. "The journey was not easy, but it was necessary."

The footmen remained silent around their king. "I suppose," he said, "you want to see Schreckschraube?"

"That is why we came."

"Then come."

The leader turned, and his tribe turned with him. Roderick followed the clan, and Martin limped alongside his keeper. He spoke to the dwarf with a tongue swollen with saltwater. "How do they speak such good Deutsch?"

They looked to Martin like heathens from a distant land, where such vernacular was not in use. Roderick gripped the staff he'd retained in all the commotion. "Schreckschraube taught them naturally, after she freed them."

"She freed them?"

Roderick aimed the dragon egg at the end of his staff toward the wreckage of a ship up ahead. "She was content to live as a hermitess on the island. When one of her shewstones showed a vessel laden with a cargo of slaves, she interceded on behalf of the Oceanians and dashed their ship on the rocks."

One of the party turned, lifted his loincloth, and exposed a tanned and uncircumcised propagator. "She gave us our foreskins back as well, after our overseers had us shorn of them with sharpened oyster shells."

Martin shivered and reflexively touched his loins as he felt a phantom pain there. "So they are loyal to her?"

"That we are," the leader said, turning his head. He fell back so that he could speak with young Martin without having to eavesdrop. "Roderick is a friend of hers. Once we spotted him, we figured it would not do well for that monster of the deep to swallow him whole. You're lucky you were in his company."

The young boy shivered again as he thought about the triple row of choppers, the suckerfish mouths with the teeth of men, the writhing and scaled limbs. "What was it?" Martin asked.

"We have no name for it," the islander said, "though we have killed them before, and made good use of their parts."

"I wouldn't eat one of those if I was starving," Martin said.

"You'd be surprised what you'd eat when there was no other food about. It is not prized so much for its meat as for its other parts."

"What parts are those?" Martin asked. He prepared to heave the bile remaining in his stomach if he had to hear about how the thing's gonads were cooked and eaten as an aphrodisiac.

"Its spines make good darts, and its teeth make good spearheads." One of his soldiers held up his implement of war to offer proof of his leader's words. Another warrior said, "Its stomach has a poisonous sack that helps paralyze prey."

"It is immune to its own venom," the leader said, "though of course men aren't." His eyes grew tight as flinty arrowheads, and he smiled with a mouth of equally sharp teeth. "Any man who has intentions of burning the hermitess as heretic or witch will get a bellyful of quills until he looks like a right porcupine."

Martin was glad they came here as friends. He kicked at the ashen tundra beneath his heels. Roderick was equally curious about the barren land around him. "I perhaps misremember, but I thought this island teemed with vegetation the last time I was here."

"Your memory serves you well," the islander said. He shouted something to the men around him in his native tongue, which neither Martin nor Roderick understood. The tribe quickly coalesced around them in a sharp formation, and speeded up their pace. "The witchfinder broke through our ranks and managed to disturb the hermitess while she was slumbering."

He lowered his head in shame, embarrassed that he and the other cultists failed to protect their queen who allowed them to reclaim their freedom and manhood. "He made to drive a stake through Schreckschraube's heart, but she sensed his presence and cast a spell on him." The chieftain looked at the parched earth around them. "This beast she made was part basilisk and half cockatrice. He fled her abode, and now roams the island breathing fire wherever he goes."

"We will kill him yet," another of the swiftly-moving clan said.

The chief pointed at his men before him, and then waved his glowing sword studded in shark teeth toward a runic pile of stones. "I decimated my own ranks to atone to Schreckschraube for our laxity. All of my men volunteered to be beheaded, but only one in ten had the honor to die for his mistake."

Martin's eyes were wide, and he grew fearful again. If Oceanians were willing to do that to their own, then he wondered what they might do to him if he made the slightest mistake. He moved a bit closer to Roderick and farther from the royal guard of the hermitess.

"Such loyalty unto death is not unheard of in other lands," Roderick said, though his words did nothing to assuage Martin's fear at the suicidal zeal of their escorts. "Do you know of Alamut, the Saracen's castle which can only be reached if one is willing to allow themselves to be carried in the talons of a giant eagle?"

Martin shook his head. The Oceanians were as well-traveled as the dwarven illuminator, and their leader said, "It was considered impregnable until the Mongols finally took it."

"It appeared that way when I first spied it," Roderick said. The men picked their way over a slab of fallen boulders still warm from when the witchfinder turned cockatrice had scorched the land with its breath. "I myself witnessed the Old Man of the Mountain demonstrate his fearsome power when I approached the foot of his castle," Roderick said. The dwarf grunted as he picked his way through the fallen rocks, and Martin helped him along. "I saw the man point to one of his followers and make an all but imperceptible gesture. The man jumped from the drum tower and tumbled to his death. Those soldiers were willing to dash themselves on the rocks at the slightest whim of their protector."

"Why?" Martin asked. He was still a bit winded and sore from being thrown about by the sea and the monster therein.

The chieftain was equally acquainted with the story, and he supplied the rest of the details as his men crawled over the stones. "He took his men from childhood and kept them stupefied with blandishments of soft cakes, wine, and hashish."

"Women too," Roderick said. "Never forget the role played by the harem."

"He clouded their minds with perverse bliss," the chieftain said. They had attained the summit of a hill.

"Then," Roderick continued, "he exposed them to the humdrum life of a dirt-poor Saracen, away from the pleasures of his mountain keep." They picked their way down the monadnock, among the loose scree and crumbling stones at their feet. "He told them kill for me and die for me, and you will dwell among the hashish, whores, and cakes in a realm of eternal delights."

"It worked well enough," the chieftain said, "until the Mongols came."

"There is no force on Earth that could resist the army of the Great Khan."

The chief came from a proud tribe of warriors and usually wouldn't admit that he could lose in combat, but even he nodded silently. Then he said, "The only thing that stopped the hordes of the steppes was the death of Genghis. Had he lived, the Kingdom of Lady Stovis would have much greater woes than what the demons bring to the realm."

When they reached flat land, Roderick said, "So you have heard then of the plague that stalks the land?"

"Aye," the chief answered. "That is why I surmised you had come."

"You surmised correctly." Roderick dug the end of his staff into the fissured ground beneath them.

Martin looked out at the plain ahead of them. A longhouse was shrouded in milky fog and perched on a tumulus mound in the distance. Shattered bits of scuttled cargo and nautical implements were scattered all around them now.

The mist was growing thicker, but the glowing swords provided more illumination than any whale blubber lantern could. The chief explained the wreckage through which they walked. "The fate here for the slave traders was worse than what befell any wrecked ship in the Jutland Bay of Sorrows."

Torn lattices of wainscoted board crunched under Martin's foot, so precious and yet so charred that it looked to him like the aftermath of a peasant's revolt against a fatted regime whose day of reckoning finally came. Split masts and spar remnants showed among the detritus, along with unraveled and threadbare cordage and fine Brittany silk stained with blood that once made up the sails on the vessel.

One of the former slaves saw an oriflamme, bits of red streamer, and the French fleur de Lys. He found himself compelled to stop and make water with his uncircumcised member on the pile of crests and coats of arms meant to foster espirit de corps.

The chief lifted up a bit of softwood, and ripped it in two with his hands. "These righolt boards give quite well after they've been wet for a time." The wood splintered in his hands, and he threw it back to the ground. "Here," he said, stooping again, "was the cargo that wasn't us slaves."

He hefted chunks of soapstone, enough to fashion statues, and then he slammed the blocks of steatite against blocks of Swedish iron the islanders had left on the ground. Roderick looked to Martin and said, "If all men were like these islanders, I suspect I would have never been forced to toil in the mines." He pointed at bullion stacked in pyramids. "They have no use for anything the ocean does not provide."

"T'was a pity," the chief said, "that the ship was not put to better use. It was a glorious sight to behold." His eyes tightened until they were sharp as arrowheads again. "I must say its construction was hard to admire while manacled in the berth."

Martin was so caught up in the effects littering the ground at their feet that he didn't notice they had entered a gated area, surrounded with pavises. The convex shields made from giant tortoise shells were linked together to form a great curtain wall around the fortification. The wall of shields was pulled closed from within once the chief, his retinue, and his guests were safely inside the hamlet.

"You are safe here from all monsters," the chief said. "You are also approaching the settlement where the hermitess has her abode." He pointed down into a valley where huts made from wood with thatched roofs were settled, and the smell of cooking fish rose from chimneys made of coral that glowed like the blades and armor.

"Are these houses fashioned from the wood of the ship?" Martin asked. For the first time in a while, his nerves felt sturdy, and the Gordian Knot of terror in his stomach slowly unwound now that they were within a walled area among heavily-armed men.

"Whatever didn't break upon the rocks we used to help fashion the huts," the chieftain said. The wives of the Oceanians came from the small dwellings, bearing young babes in fur-lined papooses. The cradleboards were front-loaded, and the women walked with swollen bellies. A scent as rich as opium resin filled the air and Martin truly felt relaxed now.

The chieftain ignored the adulation of the people pouring out from the huts and he continued to speak to the inquisitive youngster. "The shipwright's Tagebuch was recovered from the wreckage. From it, we discovered that it took almost three thousand oak trees, fifteen ash, twelve-hundred beech, and twelve elms to fit her for slaving." He gazed around his fiefdom, beaming with a mouthful of sharpened teeth. "You can see we got much better use from the wood, and that we ask no one to be our slaves." He pointed toward the hill that was raised so high Martin had seen it from several stadia away even through the fog. "We are happy to live in service if it is in service to something truly divine and our reverence is given of free will."

His arm was outstretched now in the direction of the longhouse on the hill extended like a fingerboard pointing toward an inn. "The path is safe. Follow it to see the hermitess."

The chieftain halted. Flowers and wild mushrooms grew in this protected realm where the monsters could do no ill. "You're not coming?" Martin asked.

The chieftain shook his head and said, "We only go to the top of the hill once a month to pray and make offerings to Schreckschraube."

Martin wanted to ask if the offerings were live sacrifices like goats or maybe men, but he held his tongue.

"Very well." Roderick bowed and said, "Thank you for saving our lives."

"Bitte," the chieftain said. He continued to hold his arm outstretched, entreating them to carry on. Martin stuttered, found no words in his throat, and passed awkwardly through the ranks of the villagers. He walked with Roderick past the crackle of a roaring blaze where sturgeon cooked and a baby cooed as it dreamed in its papoose.

He cast a single glance back at the hamlet. Then he looked ahead toward the longhouse growing larger as they walked faster up the hill.

There were so many questions, but one bubbled in his brain above the others. He asked it before he knew what he was saying. "Why did you shout that you weren't a gnome?"

Roderick acted as if he hadn't heard the question. He pointed toward the longhouse. "We're almost there, my boy."

Martin took the hint, and spoke no more. He didn't know it, but he had reopened a wound with his words. Roderick heard his father's voice on the wind, which disturbed him. The voice and the visions usually only came to him in sleep, in the dreams which caused him to cry out and had betrayed him to this young boy.

"Stay away from the children of the town," his father warned. "Stay among the rock heads."

He hadn't listened. It had happened on a rare day when there was no work in the cave because the overseer had died in a mine collapse. Roderick went to the fachwerk village alone, where all of the gabled houses had balconies draped in springtime sunlight. Window boxes garlanded with pelargoniums and petunias overflowed with glorious color like whirling fair carousels.

"It's a gnome!" a boy suddenly shouted. Roderick remembered how the child towered over him like a giant. The fear made his knees knock and he realized that the children were at least as tall as his own father. That his father was stronger and could bash their heads like summer squash was no consolation. The children were bigger than the man who he respected above all others.

"Kill it," one of the boys said.

"Blessed are the meek" a mother admonished from a box window, but the boys ignored her. They answered only after they collected a handful of rocks. Roderick was frozen to the spot. "Gnomes are elementals," one of the boys said.

"They don't have souls, so they're like fish or hare. They're something God gave us to use."

"I'm not a gnome!" Roderick shouted. "I'm a dwarf!"

"It speaks!" One of the boys was so shocked that he dropped his rocks. The others were so terrified that they threw their own stones without further delay. One rock sailed past young Roderick's ear, slicing the earlobe so that it stung as if frostbitten.

Roderick finally turned and ran, though the stones and the voices followed him. Somehow the voices were worse than the stones. "If you kill it, it turns back into whatever element it started out as."

Poorly-cobbled shoes clattered on the stone behind him. Roderick felt a rain of rocks hit his back, stinging like a nest of disturbed hornets. He wished he'd heeded his father's words. This was so bad that he would have rather been lugging rock from the quarry at the moment.

"What if he was gold?" one of the boys asked.

"Then we'll be rich if we kill him," another said.

They passed through the gates of the town out into the country where green Bavarian hay shaggy as witch hair lichen was draped in soft mounds. Roderick made for the dense cluster of oaks. The trees were stained such a dark shade of brown that they may as well have been black.

"Don't let it get to the trees! It can disappear into a stump."

Roderick wondered why they called him an "it" as he fought back tears. He thought they could see he was a boy at the very least even if they mistook him for a gnome. A stubborn part of him that sometimes got him labelled as a troublemaker made him want to turn, pull down his trousers, and prove his boyhood to them. After he brandished his rock head's propagator, he'd promise to return and leave their mothers with dwarven offspring or at the very least halflings.

The smarter side of him won out. His father's voice grew louder and urged him to safety. He knew that if the town rowdies stoned a rock head to death that the court would rule in their favor, especially if one of the fathers of the rock-throwing lot was a prominent merchant.

The young dwarf ran through the woods, zigzagging between the branches until the sound of the boys softened behind him and they gave up the chase. His mother saw him first when he returned to the lair. She doused his wounds with strong drink from her husband's store, and the young rock head finally worked up the nerve to ask, "Mama, are we gnomes or dwarves?"

She had set down the bottle of drink, and slapped him across the face. "Gnomes are loyal to their king only, not to the Gods of the North." She held out her hands, which were covered with calluses. Then she inspected the pads of her son's palms that were already coarse and blistered. "Those servants of God are tricky little cowards who've never done a day's fair work in their lives."

He'd let the subject drop at that point. He knew not to bring it up with his father, since what merited a slap with Mama usually warranted a closed fist with Papa. He'd asked his father other questions though, when the man returned from his work at the rock pile where the collapse had previously happened. The bodies of dwarves were still being recovered.

"Where do we come from, Papa?"

His father dipped his fingers in a tallow candle, waxed the ends of his moustache, and said, "We come from Nidavellir, where we were craftsmen before the men aboveground made us into slaves."

"Can we still make crafts?"

His father smiled and recovered a whittling blade. He also picked up a smoothed and sculpted wooden model of Sleipnir, which was the most glorious of all Viking mounts. His father shaved a few more flecks of wood from the horse of the gods and said, "We are of the same bloodline as Brokk and Eitri."

"Who?"

Roderick's father looked at his wife, who was tending a cauldron loaded with broth of bat guano in which velvet worms and phantom cave snails simmered. She said, "Brokk and Eitri made the hammer that always returned to the hand of mighty Thor."

The young dwarf's father nodded, attesting to his wife's words and smelling the rich aroma of her cooking. He then looked down at his son, scrutinizing him closer in the failing light. "Why are you bleeding, my son?"

Roderick came back to the moment, walking alongside Martin toward the top of the hill. He suddenly had to pause, out of breath. He walked to a mossy boulder, sat, and offered his friend his apologies. "I am getting older." He stifled the tears as best he could, and when they fell from his eyes he hoped Martin mistook them for profuse sweat.

The young bastard looked away from his idol, not understanding how or why his question had hurt Roderick. He regretted that he'd asked it in the first place. Never again would he say the word "gnome" in Roderick's presence, not if he could help it.

Roderick remained silent on the subject of his secret journey to the town of the giants, and of the way they mistreated him. He never asked any of the other rock heads to discourse on the differences between gnomes and dwarves. It was a taboo too great to breach, whose mysteries would only be unraveled for him in the codices of the monastery where he first took to words. It was in the monastery where he had one uncanny puzzle after another unlocked for him after he learned to read and gained his freedom thusly.

He learned Paracelsus thought that gnomes were malicious, while others believed they were helpful to humanity. Gnomes were said to live in massive underground castles fashioned of alabaster and marble. They could not only cut crystals and rocks like dwarves but could actually develop lodes of tungsten and veins of ore.

Roderick had never encountered a gnome outside of the pages of books, but for his part he always wondered if they were larger or smaller than dwarves. He didn't exactly know why he wanted to know. He didn't want to consider himself given to the vagaries of a bully, like the whims of those boys who threw rocks at him. Still, he somehow thought that if indeed gnomes were smaller than dwarves, then he wanted to see one, if only to know what it felt like to stand above someone who was smaller than him.

Chapter Twenty

From Cathedral to Castle

Vespers had ended, and the lingering echoes of the evensong drifted on the night air. The sun was setting. Faded orange light coruscated through the tracery of the gothic windows and splashed across the Vitruivian marble of the floor. Two guards stood on the other side of the hinged triptych, whose three panels depicted the Last Supper in frescoed polychrome with blues and reds predominate.

Neither of the two guards knew exactly what Archbishop Torner did behind the veil of the three of panels, but they knew when he spoke there that his voice was lower and more secretive than when he heard confessions. They thought it odd that he spoke since there was no one there that they could see. Had they been on the other side of the triptych, they would have seen the archbishop walking to the Shrine of the Three Kings said to hold the bones of the three Magi. The reliquary was as detailed as a Venetian music box. There were intaglio designs across the three sarcophagi compartments, and more jewels in its studded face than a Sunday processional cross.

The archbishop opened one of the three compartments on top of the box. A tiny cloud like the one bearing a genie rubbed free from a lamp billowed up into the air. A wizard in a gown covered in sigils appeared in the rich plume of unfurling smoke. The room behind Lord Herzog was visible, a shelfful of books lined up in the background. Many of the books were tomes the excommunicated illuminator had taken with him after Roderick reported his misdeeds to the abbot. The vision was detailed enough that if the archbishop squinted, he could read the titles of the books. There was everything from Dicuil's *De Mensura Orbis Terra* to papyri volumes that were priceless on account of their having survived the blaze of the Alexandrian Library.

The wizard looked at the archbishop and asked, "Did you pick the root?"

"Indeed, I did." The bishop held up the mandrake he'd ripped from the ground. He clutched it in his white hawking glove.

"Ah," the wizard said, letting loose a pleasured little sigh. "The love apple has long been held to be one of the most powerful aphrodisiacs, if not *the* most powerful. The Egyptians called it the phallus of the field."

"Will it work?" The archbishop was less interested in the grotesque root's history than its present use on the woman who made his own heart swoon, rotted though he knew it to be.

"I will ensure it works," the wizard said, "if you will indulge my whims."

Archbishop Torner nodded and listened. He'd already promised his soul to Baal and Old Nick, but he could labor in service to other lesser evils while alive if it would grant him pleasures while he yet breathed.

"The sower is returning now from a monastery and its sister convent that he has razed to their foundations." The wizard's face glowed and rippled in the smoke. "Have you rounded up a sufficient number of women?"

"I have," the archbishop said. "The stewhouse has been closed and the whores have all been brought to the mural tower, all except for the one whose love you promised me."

The wizard pointed at the mandrake that the archbishop held. "If you place that beneath her pillow, she will be yours."

"I will," the holy man promised.

"Good, and in return-"

Archbishop Torner cut him off. "When Casper Namlos comes calling at the city gates, I will tell the guards to allow him passage into the Freistadt of Koln. I will invite him to make the beast with each of the whores in their turn, twelve in all." He grinned as a thought occurred to him. "The abbess has the same number of whores as Christ has disciples."

"I have already cast the spell," the wizard proclaimed. "One of the twelve, I know not which, will birth the Great Beast. He will take the throne from Lady Matina, and you will sit at his right hand." The wizard's voice lilted as he addressed the man's vanity. "You will be one of the most powerful men in all of the Holy Land by the Holy River in return for your loyalty."

"Good," the archbishop said. "Then let us waste no time." He made as if to close the box, when he thought of something. "What of the abbess herself, the thirteenth?"

The wizard had more pressing matters that needed attending, and he was vexed by the question. "What of her?"

"She has gone through the change of life. She cannot bear fruit. Perhaps I can burn her to appease the peasants? Their blood is very hot right now, and a sacrifice might quench the fires of their rage."

The wizard howled with laughter so hard the archbishop feared his image might fracture in the smoke. "The sower has already proven that there is no soil barren enough not to bear his demon seed. Let the old crone live and let him fill her with his wicked fruit, or burn her if it be your druthers."

The archbishop would think on it for a night or two. He would speak with Lyudmila. Perhaps if she felt fondly toward Mother Inferior, he might spare the hag and thereby gain some of the girl's favors in the old-fashioned way, through simple extortion rather than witchery by root of the mandrake.

He made as if to close the top of the treasure chest again, but this time the wizard stopped him. "Before we cease this session, you should know that there are two who have designs of stopping us."

"Who?" the archbishop asked. His face tightened into a grim mask.

The wizard paused. He was perplexed by his own words, but his second sight never failed him. "A bastard," he said, dubiously. "A bastard and a dwarf."

The archbishop's face relaxed and he closed the reliquary with a slight titter. *A bastard and a dwarf indeed!*

He walked from behind the screen to his two guards, who stood there oblivious to what just transpired. The special detail of two men was marked by their riveted, scaled armor made from the squamous hides of dragons. They were faceless behind their sallet visors. Their parade armor terminated in billowing metal skirts that might seem feminine if their edges were not razor sharp.

The archbishop spoke to the two faceless knights. "Is my carriage ready?"

"Yes, Your Holiness."

"Good." He gathered the hem of his flowing robes around him. He walked with his bodyguards out to the horse-drawn carriage, which was draped in a fresh purple canopy of state. The horses were clad in armor for the special occasion. Spiked steel chanfrons covered their equine faces, spoiling their beauty and making them appear as steely automatons.

One of the two knights unfolded the footstep for the carriage. The archbishop climbed up, drawing the curtain around his form and settling into the sumptuous luxury of the cushions plump with goose feathers. "Los!" he shouted. The driver cracked the whip and turned the beasts in the direction of the castle.

Archbishop Torner stroked the mandrake in his gauntleted palms. "You will be mine," he said to the distant Lyudmila. He'd been smitten with her from the first time he saw her in market with her striped hood. Her large breasts inflamed his mind and fueled his sermon on the evils of midwifery and nursemaids. It was his hope all along that he could have her diverted from her appointment in the foundling home whose details he discovered through his network of spies and emissaries.

He parted the purple curtain with a gloved hand and saw the man in the watchtower wave his flaming torch toward the guards on the catwalk. One of the men in hauberks moved with deliberation toward the winch and turned it with a mailed fist. A groan resounded throughout the town, and the archbishop had to shout to be heard. "Driver, take me to the Great Hall!"

"Yes, Your Holiness."

The castle grew larger as the horses clopped along. There were usually children playing around the outer wall of the motte and bailey, even at this late hour. The lands around the looming granite and slate defenses were empty now, though. Even the townspeople suspected something was afoot. They probably thought the whores would serve as sacrifice enough, but perhaps more than a few denizens of Koln decided to lock up their daughters for the evening lest the night watchmen snatch up more to swell the ranks of the donjon.

First, however, the girl …

Lyudmila walked the length of her room in the Palas above the Great Hall where the sounds of merrymaking caused the floor to rumble even though it was built of strong stone masonry. Heat rose from the dirnitz on the floor below her, warming the vault of the ceiling beneath, so she could pad across the rock slabs barefoot without getting the chills. There was no one to talk to here save for the snowy little Melita. She'd been given the dog as a companion when they transferred her from the cold, high tower to this warmer intimate building. The little Canis delicates would have to do. She spoke to him as she touched her recently coifed and primped hair encased in a golden net on her head. Someone must have placed the lace crespinette over her head while she slumbered.

"I hope he burns me." She picked the little dog up in her arms and stroked his Himalayan fluffy coat. "I'd much prefer that to being forced to make the beast with the man." She shuddered. "There aren't enough guineas in the world to make me pretend to love him."

The little dog wasn't much help. He merely stuck out his reddish tongue and lapped her soft white hand. She kissed him on his nose that was cold despite the nearness of the Palas to the dirnitz, and then she set him on the floor. "Off you go." She didn't know his name, and so didn't know how to address him.

The little pup was nice enough, though she missed Merlin and wondered where he was. She'd exhausted her patience with the purebreds, since she suspected that golden retriever she'd petted at market a few days ago with Martin perhaps scented those poppets. Maybe the dog dug them up and exposed her witchery, leading to her sorry state here.

Martin, she thought. She walked to the window, wondering where he was. Several of those dreadful knights had come in earlier with all of the stewhouse girls manacled together in a daisy chain. She'd watched as the soldiers marched the ladies up the spiral staircase of the donjon where she'd languished until recently. She hadn't seen Martin among their number, and she wondered what would become of him and all the other little bastards now that they had nowhere to live. They were probably headed off to the foundling home. She should be breastfeeding there now rather than wasting her milk within these castle walls. Of what use was an archbishop anyway, when he was naught but a eunuch for Christ? At least the laity forgot not their brothers or sisters when they remembered their God.

Martin. He was just a boy, but his name came to her again unbidden. She felt the absence of his tongue on the petals of her rose. She thought his name and touched herself. She stroked beneath the curling mound of hair, tickling her pearl and patting the entrance to her womb with fingers that danced like busy spiders spinning webs. She thought his name once more, and then there was the screech of a hawk.

She looked toward the windowsill. It was that verminous bird of prey that the archbishop kept. He watched her with the wretched patience of a vulture waiting for his quarry to waste away to carrion.

The whim to pleasure herself was all but extinguished, and she pulled her hand from her womb. Her fingers were gluey with her own secretions. She intended to slap the bird full on its beak with her dewy hands if only she could get the thing in her clutches. She might even wring its neck as otherwise partial to animals as she was.

"Be gone," she shouted. The feathers of the hawk ruffled and it screeched hideously so that the little dog barked and came running to her side. The bird lighted from the window, loosing its talons from their grip on the windowsill and flying toward the white luminous saucer of the moon hanging over the Rhineland.

"Pest!" she hissed. The bird had alighted so quickly that it left a nest of discolored feathers in its wake. She picked one up, and a thought occurred to her. The Melita cocked its head to the side as he watched his new mistress stab herself in the palm with the quilled point of the feather she held. Blood poured from her hand and the frightened dog skittered away from her on his little claws.

"A bit of magic," she whispered. Lyudmila walked with her hand dripping blood and the quill equally doused in red. She came to the bed covered in Burgundy brocades and fine Egyptian silk.

She pulled back the cotton duvet covering the bed, and wrote a single magic symbol the abbess had taught her in the blood. "Martin Stolzer, I Lyudmila Heyne do thee wed." She pulled the cover back over the bloody writing she'd quickly accomplished, and then lay in the canopy bed. The little dog sensed her bloodletting session was over and padded quickly over the heated stones at his feet. He lunged for the bed, failed to make the leap, and fell on his back.

"Oh," Lyudmila said, "poor thing!" She leaned over the side of the bed. "Come to your mistress's lap, little fellow."

The dog panted, his tail wagging. He made another play for the bed, and Lyudmila caught him in mid-jump. She cradled him to her bosom and stroked him with the hand she hadn't pricked with the quill. "He's no great chivalrous knight," she said, of Martin, "and certainly a candle girl like me and a bastard like him are not commonplace in courtly literature."

She lay back on the pillows and lifted the little Hund high above her head, smiling. "The boy knows how to kiss a rose, though."

The drunken revelers continued to shout from the great hall below. The bang and clatter of foaming steins slamming against an oaken tabletop made her ears rattle, even at this distance. "I hope it works," she whispered of the bit of pillow magic she'd just cast. Mother Inferior had said the spell was best aided if a girl could either sneak a few beads of menstrual blood into her target's stock of port wine, or if she had a sprig of myrtle bound in scarlet and white ribbon.

She lacked both menses and myrtle that night, and hoped her meager imprecations alone would be magic enough to ward off whatever wizarding the archbishop had planned.

His carriage was rushing toward the castle in the night. He was thinking only of her with a bit of enchanted mandrake root in his hand.

Chapter Twenty-One

The Hermitess

Her home was built like a Norse stave church, with palisade walls of standing split logs that smelled of smoke and saltwater. The structure was one single open-aired room, and it was as cluttered as a Wunderkammern. The contents of the shelves were almost enough to send Martin fleeing in the other direction.

Glass jars lined the walls. They were filled with staring, bloodshot human eyes and tongues dried as peppers. The eyes watched Martin in unblinking horror as he tried to pretend they weren't there, or that they didn't frighten him. Schreckschraube missed nothing.

"Those oddments are the remains of the slavers whose vessel crashed on these shores." Her voice sounded to his ears like the caw of a crow. She wagged her head from side to side and moved around the room on a gnarled staff of driftwood. She had a hunchback. "I tried to stop the Oceanians, but their bloodlust was insatiable the day I liberated them." She walked toward them. "Hello, Roderick," she said to the dwarf without looking at him.

"Hello, Schreckschraube," her old celestial husband said, timidly.

Martin took a closer look at the ancient woman. She wore a hooded cape made from the shagreened skin of some kind of sea monster, maybe like the one that had attacked them. It could have been a shark or a stingray. A necklace hung around the slackened skin of her throat that was as tough and dry as jerked elbow meat. The necklace was strung with sawfish teeth similar to the ones ringing the swords of her venerators. Her earlobes dangled with heavy rings made to look like skeletons. At least that's what Martin thought until he remembered that in Roderick's description of the woman he mentioned she had baubles made from skeletons of dead little brownies.

He shivered and looked around the room as Roderick and the woman embraced and spoke quietly to each other. He didn't know what they were talking about. He thought that it seemed like it was none of his concern, else they would have spoken louder. Besides that, the room held a sufficient abundance of wonders for him to have no trouble paying them no mind.

There were ancient Greek terracotta gallipots, whose sides were covered with meanders and from whose mouths volutes of steam billowed. There were jadeite dragon statues used to prop up books on shelves, and there was a freestanding Roman centaur statue that was missing its head and arms.

Martin was a bibliophile at heart, and naturally drifted over to the unfurled scroll that was held open on a wooden desk. Its two dogwood rollers were stretched to their limits so that the entire parchment could be read. A bleached skeleton sat next to the desk, propped in a corner next to where the scroll lay. He thought the skeleton made the room look more like the study of a physic or apothecary and less like the lair of a hermitess.

Schreckschraube's voice came from behind him. "You can look, but please do not touch. I need that book open to that page."

Martin turned to her. "I won't touch anything." He studied her worn features now. He thought she looked a little like Mother Inferior if the procuress had spent her life questing after knowledge rather than marrying and burying husbands one after another in quick succession. There was something guarded in her voice when she spoke, a solipsistic casuistry that smacked of riddles and madrigals. Martin thought it would be hard or maybe impossible to get worthwhile information out of her without the dwarf at his side.

She looked somewhere above his shoulder as she spoke to him and grinned. "In love are we, young man?"

He wondered what Roderick had already told her in whispers. Still, he thought his feelings for Lyudmila were nothing that should cause him shame. "Aye," he said, "I'm in love."

His lack of reticence pleased her. "Perhaps we can remedy the situation, in a moment." He hoped so. Martin found his eyes drifting back to the tiny skeletons dangling from the woman's ears. They were by far the most unsettling acquisition in the old antiquarian's collection after the eyes and tongues. She seemed to Martin as blind as Mondhund had been, but she must have noticed his scrutiny, for she said, "I couldn't tolerate the sounds the little hobgoblins made as they ran around my house." She pulled at one of the little skeletons dangling from her ears. "I have reading to do, and I must not be interrupted." Schreckschraube turned to the front of the longhouse, and pointed down the hill, in the direction of the village where her venerators dwelled. "They understand that, and bother me only when it is absolutely necessary."

She turned back to Roderick, and the two spoke to each other in low tones again. Martin looked back at the unfurled scroll on the desk. His Latin wasn't stellar, though he knew enough to be able to read what was on the parchment before him. The red and brown paintings of the fat worms supplied enough information on their own, even if he hadn't been able to read Latin. "The Best Segmented Worms to use for Leeching Practices," was the title of the page in question. Martin studied the slimy, colorful little worms. He didn't touch the tome, remembering Schreckschraube's admonition.

A bloodcurdling roar came from somewhere beyond the walls of the house and the coral barricade erected around the tiny settlement. The bellowing groan made the hairs stand up on Martin's arms and on the back of his neck. He looked back to Schreckschraube who was only amused.

"Some witchfinder had it in his mind that he would capture the old hag on the island where she lived and bring her back to the realm of Christendom and burn her at the stake. It was not to be."

Martin pointed in the direction from whence the sound came. It continued, something like the baying of a werewolf on the moors when the moon was at its fullest. "That's a man?"

"Was," she said, walking toward Martin and stabbing the floor with her driftwood staff. "I turned him into something that doesn't even have a name." She snorted as she laughed. "Even someone as well-versed as I can sometimes mix a spell up."

"You have to be careful," Roderick said.

"You do," his wife said. "One letter falsely transcribed in an incantation, one word mispronounced can get the caster devoured by their own magic." She lifted her staff from the ground and pointed in the direction the howling came from. "I wasn't sure whether I wanted to turn him into a cockatrice or a basilisk, and so now the old witchfinder bears the worst traits of both."

"He has destroyed much of the living foliage on your island," Martin said.

Roderick shot him a dirty look, but the hermitess held up a staying hand to her husband. "It is all right, Roderick. I admire the boy's honesty." She looked in Martin's direction with an expression lighting her eyes that was as soft as the pain of her years would allow. "Yes, I intended to enchant and enslave the beast for my own purposes, but he fled before I could recite the words. So now we have a small problem on our hands."

"Perhaps," Roderick said, "we can do something about that monstrosity after we attend to our own business."

"No," Schreckschraube said, emphatically. "The Oceanians must take care of that." She grinned at Martin. "You are in love, and I am told right now that your love is kept in the castle keep of a wicked man who professes to be holy."

"Aye," Martin said.

"We will see what can be done for you. We will see what can be done to the men who've brought this curse upon the land of which Roderick told me."

"If the curse is lifted," Martin asked, "will you return to the Holy Land by the Holy River?"

"No," Schreckschraube said, "I am more than happy here, among the Oceanians and my antiques."

"Why did you leave in the first place?"

Roderick gave his apprentice another piercing stare. Martin only amused the old hag, as with his previous question. She turned to Roderick. "Don't punish the boy for his curiosity."

"Still," the dwarf said, "he should learn not to ask people questions about their past and allow them to speak in their own time." Roderick was thinking especially about the fresh wound of being mistaken for a gnome and pelted with rocks in childhood. Martin should have kept his words to himself and not asked the dwarf the meaning of imprecations shouted out in sleep.

"I left your Holy Land because I had no desire to burn at the stake. Let us say that we kill this man who keeps your love at his leisure. Let us also say you were to slay Lord Herzog himself. I am an old, unmarried woman with only a passing interest in Christianity. I would still stand a good chance of being burnt at the stake. I don't wish to die among the greenwood and to be buried among the mandrakes, so I am more than content to stay here."

"Why did they want to burn you in the first place?" Martin asked.

"Boy!" Roderick shouted. "Hold your tongue or I'll see to it that it ends up on the shelf over there with the tongues of the slavers." The dwarf pointed in the direction of the jars, just in case Martin doubted his threat.

Schreckschraube was unmoved. She placed a wizened hand in the small of her husband's back. "Asking questions is hardly as bad as man enslaving his fellow man, however impertinent those questions may be." The hermitess pointed to one of the pots from which smoke curled. "I was known for my pessaries that helped cure sickness and cramps once upon a time. Your precious Archbishop Torner was but a parish priest then. He made false accusations against me."

"So you know the archbishop, then?"

Schreckschraube ignored his question. "He and his busybody crowd of churchgoers claimed I was making abortifacients to snare quickened fetuses from the womb, and that I slayed them after ensoulment had commenced." She shook her head at the ludicrousness of the charges. "Those men understand nothing of science or religion, save how to abuse and misquote both." She sighed as she exhaled. Martin thought she sounded more disappointed than enraged with humanity. He couldn't say that he blamed her for keeping to this hermitage, or that he could blame anyone from fleeing the world. He loved the woods himself, where he sometimes collected moss to help caulk the planks of the Hanseatic ships harbored in the waters of the Rhine. Many was the time he thought of fleeing to a cavern or a mountain himself. The only problem was that he wasn't sure he knew how to survive in the wild alone, and he didn't have a royal guard of Oceanians with sea urchin armor and swords of shark teeth to help him.

"Men believe much that is false," Schreckschraube said.

"Such as?" Martin no longer feared asking her questions. It was clear that Roderick's celestial wife would take Martin's side over the dwarf's objections when it came to satisfying the boy's inquisitive nature.

"They claim male and female fetuses quicken at different rates. Any midwife worth her salt who's been unfortunate enough to witness miscarriages of both sexes will tell you that's a lie."

Schreckschraube walked over toward Martin, and passed him without comment. She set her staff against the desk where the open leeching tome rested, and continued to speak. "Men of science and religion also believe that the female's nature is hotter than that of man." She gripped a leaf of the book she'd told him not to touch, and turned the page.

The pages were no longer covered in Latin, but in Greek. "The word *femina* itself comes from the Greek word for fire I'm told, though I am not sure of the etymology and would need more corroboration." She continued to turn pages. Thunder rumbled across the expanse of the sea surrounding the island, the foreboding sound quaking in the distance. "Why do men burn women at the stake?"

Martin shrugged. "Fear?" he tried.

Her smile let him know she approved of his guess ventured. "Why would men fear women?"

"Because women make men."

She looked at Roderick. "Have you been having words with him?"

"The boy has lived all of his life in a stewhouse. He was born there. He can probably teach me as much about women as I can him, despite my learning and the many years of living that I can claim."

Schreckschraube looked back at Martin. "Do you intend to marry this fair maiden?"

"I do."

"Was she a whore?"

He was tempted to get angry at the question. Then he remembered the hag hadn't begrudged him his own inquiry, and so he remained respectful. "She was, but she will be a whore no more after I marry her."

"Well," Schreckschraube said. She interlocked her fingers and cracked her knuckles. The crepitus sound clacked as hard as teeth in the mouth of a skeleton wakened from the dead. "Let us see if we cannot give this Hausmärchen a happy ending, shall we?"

She reached toward her ears with her bony fingers, and extracted the pendulous brownie baubles that had dragged and stretched her earlobes since she'd taken to wearing them. Martin saw that the aged flesh of her ears was studded with little holes, as was her nose.

She handed one of the earrings to Roderick, and the other to Martin. He accepted the little skeleton trinket with a queasy feeling mounting in his stomach. "Do either of you men know who Mertiel is?"

"No," Martin answered.

"He is the demon of transportation," Roderick said. "He can send any man to any locale in the world in the blink of an eye."

"Not just men," Schreckschraube chastised him. "He can send women anywhere he wills as well."

"Forgive me wife." Roderick bowed, as was his custom. She returned the bow, accepting his apology. Then she pointed back at the baubles. "I have imbued those little brownies with powers derived from incantations to Mertial."

"Where did you hear about him?" Roderick asked. Martin was glad his caretaker had asked the question, since it was forming on his own lips. He thought he'd already done enough asking.

"I once encountered this demon's name while reading the forbidden tomes in the monastery, although his name was given as Inertiel." Schreckschraube giggled. "It is a good thing that I neither copied nor spoke the name Inertiel."

Martin piped up. "Because if you mispronounce the name or transcribe it wrong, it can result in death."

"Your boy is smart as a whip, Roderick."

"He has more than cheese between his ears."

"Yes," she said, in answer to Martin's question. "Mispronouncing or misspelling the name of a demon is a good way to die, and the death usually comes painfully at the hands of the demon insulted by the conjurer's ineptitude. Fortunately," she said, "I have imbued the skeletons with the spirit of the demon, and you must say or write nothing."

"What must we do?" Martin asked. He suspected, but he hoped his suspicions were wrong.

She proved them right in the answering. "You must pierce your ears with the brownie earrings and close your eyes. Then think of the location to which you wish to transport, and you will find yourself thusly transported there."

Martin thought of all the holes and punctures he'd seen in the woman's ears and in the cartilage of her nose. "We must pierce ourselves every time we wish to go to a new location?"

She nodded. Roderick patted him on the back. "Come boy, you've already shed quite a bit of blood." The dwarf stuck his hand through the tattered material of Martin's shirt, which had been shredded by the underwater manticore. He held his young surrogate son's palm. The hand still bore the marks of Lyudmila's blade, although the flesh was scabbed over. Martin had no way of knowing that Lyudmila now shed her own blood on his account to undo the spell of the archbishop and to make the boy with the magic tongue her betrothed.

"Very well," Martin said. He lifted the earring to his dirt-encrusted and waxy ear. It had been quite a while since he'd last bathed. That was one of the things about being in the whorehouse that he missed. He wondered how Oliver and the other bastards were doing, and how the candle girls were coming along. He wondered if Gloria had made it to the convent for reformed prostitutes, or if the baby had been given to the orphanage yet.

"Come," Roderick said, and pierced his own ear without further delay. Blood trickled down his earlobe. "It will hurt either way, but it won't be as bad if you go fast." The dwarf stepped toward the boy. "Do you want me to do it for you?"

"The magic won't be effective that way," Schreckschraube said. "He has to do it for himself."

Martin took a step back, embarrassed and a bit salty over how Roderick was willing to impugn his courage after he'd already seen the boy's mettle in action. Martin closed his eyes and felt the sharp end of the earring with his finger. He took a deep breath, placed the pointed metal against his earlobe, and pushed in. His shriek rivaled that of the monster stalking the tiny island and burning everything in its wake.

"Agh!"

Both the hermitess and the dwarf laughed. The worst part was that the earring had only half-punctured his ear, and the dull metal point gripped the soft flesh and throbbed painfully. It felt to Martin as if he had been swimming for an hour and had water trapped in his head. He wriggled the bit of metal with his now-bloody fingers as he struggled to get the earing to go all the way through the flesh. The little legs of the brownie skeleton danced a jig and the bones clicked and clattered.

Martin spoke to the ancient woman as he pushed the earring in and winced. "When was the last time you used these?" He didn't doubt her store of magic, but he knew the effects of charms could wear off if they were used too many times or if their mana was allowed to rust.

Schreckschraube gripped her ears, and felt the holes. "Oh, I've been to more places than Hannibal and Caesar combined. That Christian who came here intending to bring me back to Germania said he was going to break my broom in half so that I couldn't do anymore flying. I don't need any damn broom, not to fly at least." She looked around the room. "I'll admit this place could use a sweeping. I'll get one of the Oceanians up here to help their goddess with her chores once you two have taken your leave."

"Which we intend to do now," Roderick said. His words were hard and his gaze a bit harder as he locked eyes with Martin. He finally asked the boy, "Do you want to see Lyudmila or not?"

The name worked like a charm, and Martin pushed so hard that the hole he made in his ear gushed with blood. The sharpened needle went all the way through the flesh, finding purchase like an angler's hook in the mouth of a fish.

"Good," the dwarf said. "Now close your eyes and think of the Magnetic Mountain."

Martin shut his eyes, as instructed. He thought of the lair of Lord Herzog. He saw the vision of the castle perched on igneous and metallic rocks above a tempestuous sea. The waters crashed and hissed as if they intended to break the boulders of the island, reduce them to rubble, and cast them to the bottom of the ocean.

All was black, though the voice of Schreckschraube the Hermitess followed the two men through the dark void. Martin somehow sensed Roderick's presence at his side, even though he neither saw nor smelled the man.

"I was given the grimoire in which I found this spell by a member of a confraternity of knights," Schreckschraube said. "They got the book from a group of peaceful idolaters, followers of the one they call Buddha."

Martin wasn't familiar with the name of the strange god. He knew of Greek gods like Zeus. He knew Allah, the god of the Saracens. He didn't know Buddha. He would have to ask Roderick about him when there was time.

Schreckschraube's voice continued to follow them through the blackness. "After you two settle accounts and the sapling has the love of his life in his arms, you might want to return to the island to try some of my zweibelkucken."

"I love onions," Roderick's voice without a body said, "almost as much as I love garlic." He smacked his lips together and the noise of his watering mouth echoed through the darkness. "I quite miss your cooking, wife of mine."

"I quite miss certain things about you," she replied, "things it would be indecorous to enumerate before your companion. Whether he grew up in a stewhouse or no, there are certain subjects not meant for young ears to hear."

"Aye," Roderick agreed.

The twosome floated farther and farther on an astral trajectory away from her tiny island.

"I'll go to Carnival in the Pfalzerwald," the hermitess said, "sometime before the Lenten season. I'll pick up some more recipes there."

"Aye," Roderick said. He and Martin blinked again. They found themselves side-by-side, perched on a jagged rock made of rich ore. Above them was the castle where Lord Herzog lived.

"Don't worry," Roderick said, removing the earring from his ear. The brownie skeleton was covered in a new coat of blood brought on by the piercing. "Herzog is a coward. His confidence grows with distance, and we are near." The dwarf tapped the legs of the skeleton dangling from Martin's ear, and the boy hissed as a shock of searing pain went through his temple and his ear throbbed.

"Take off the earring and stow it where someone won't find it," Roderick said. "You'll need that enchanted earring to get out of here and back to Koln, where your princess awaits you."

Martin pulled the hook from his ear as quickly as he could, hoping the swiftness of his motion would dilute the pain. It didn't. He stowed the skeleton, lodging it safely beneath the golden buckle of one of his shoes. "I'm not sure if we should be availing ourselves of witchcraft," he said. He'd seen what happened to Lyudmila when she made the poppets and stabbed them. Her magic had worked and her three debauchers were dead now, but her vengeance had come at a high price.

Roderick's staff found purchase on the rocks. He stabbed his way upward with Martin following quickly behind. "Come now, boy. Even Solomon used demons as slave labor to build his temple. A demon in service to good is a good himself, for as long as he remains in service."

"Certainly," Martin said, "but slaves rebel. Think of the greatest rebellion of all in Heaven." The whims of the sky were as fickle here as they had been on the island where the hermitess dwelled. Craggy barbs of lightning stabbed the clouds as if they intended to bleed them of the water they held.

"Satan's rebellion was successful inasmuch as he was given more power and his own realm. What the devil doesn't know," the dwarf said, "is that he also serves the Lord's purpose."

The two continued to struggle up the rocky cliff made of magnetic ore. Thankfully there wasn't enough metal in the hooks of the brownie earrings for them to get pulled toward the rocks. "How can the devil serve the purpose of the Lord?" Martin asked.

Roderick shook his head. He growled, "Now is not the time for theology. It is the hour for action."

Martin stowed anymore questions he might have asked. He followed his friend up the cliff toward the Schloss where the dwarf's old foe now dwelt.

Chapter Twenty-Two

Old Enemies Meet

The mountain was death piled on more death. The tide was high, and the ocean spray tasted especially acrid to Martin. The wounds he'd accumulated so far on this quest stung every time a wave crested against the side of the jagged rocks, and the salt seeped deep into the bloody cuts covering his body. Centuries of weathering by wind and water had sharpened the escarpment. The effect was like a whetstone on a blade. Martin risked cutting himself again every time he found a new foothold on his ascent toward the castle where Lord Herzog dwelt.

Roderick had fewer problems since his years down in the mines and high among the mountains had made his skin tough as leather. He turned back toward his care. "Come on, my boy! We're almost there!"

"I'm coming," Martin said, weakly.

"You can mend your wounds by the fireside when you and Lyudmila are together again."

The dwarf's words spurred him higher. Martin ignored the sting of the sharp rocks and the trickle of blood forming in new wounds. They were almost there. Roderick had more history with Lord Herzog than he did, but Martin intended to be the one to snuff the candle of the excommunicated monk.

The boy winced as he pulled his way from boulder to boulder. The stinging sensation was so bad now that he was convinced that it couldn't be the salt spray alone causing his wounds to ache. There had to be something in the base metalloids of which the mountains were composed that caused him to suffer so. He looked down at the rocks and the black stains on his hands.

He spoke to Roderick's backside, since the dwarf was two or three footholds ahead of him and almost to the castle's walls. "I think some of this rock is arsenic." He panted in his quest for breath. "I think I've got blood poisoning."

"Come lad!" Roderick shouted, refusing to slacken his pace or give quarter.

"Blast!" Martin shouted. "Balderdash!" He had no compunctions about shouting until his lungs were hoarse. The sea was tempestuous and the crack of waves against the rocks would drown out any sound before it reached the wizard's ears.

"This mountain needs a giant blacksmith to beat it metal hide into shape," Martin said. "I'd like to see it turned into a horseshoe for Thor's giant steed."

Roderick held a callused hand down toward the boy, and lifted him toward the wall of the castle. "Let's have no more mention of the pagan pantheon from you." After lifting Martin to the summit, Roderick pulled his amber staff tipped with the dragon egg from where it was sheathed on his back. "I was raised among dwarves. That's my alibi for clinging to the Northern ways. You," he said, pointing his staff, "were raised among Christians."

"Very well," Martin said. He wasn't sure that Christians were better than heathens, but now was not the time to theologize. Roderick had said as much earlier. The man and the boy looked up at this portion of the fortress. It was an eclectic mix of Moorish and Iberian influences. It was rounded like a mushroom and gave the appearance of a simple redoubt rather than the spired and peaked structure that came to mind when Martin usually thought of the word "castle."

This side of the wall was pocked with loopholes and arrow slits through which a strange amethyst glow radiated and cast its purplish hue over the rocks. Martin wondered what manner of sorcery was afoot inside, and he hazarded they would soon find out. Roderick walked in the purplish light spilling from the slits in the wall, until he came to a spot where a domed bartizan jutted forth from the rock wall of the fortress. He looked at Martin. "Here's where we'll make our entrance."

He touched his staff to the wall, which immediately decomposed into a gooey fromage blanc. The rock was now soft as the cheese spread on flammkuchen. Martin looked on, stunned by the wall that had gone from stone to cheese with one touch of Roderick's wand.

"How'd you do that?" Martin asked.

"I told you," Roderick said, sliding his hands between the soft mass of white cheese and parting it like a curtain. "Dwarves can sometimes have our way with minerals, provided it is for a purpose that serves something higher than Mammon and we possess the correct magic." He held the billowing cheese curtain open for Martin, who stepped through. "Apparently the Nordlanders decided your love for Lyudmila was a worthy cause. Else this wall wouldn't presently be cheese, would it?"

"No," Martin said, stepping through. "I guess it wouldn't."

Roderick walked into the wall behind Martin. The cheese became stone again, and the two treaded carefully into the main atrium of the keep. They were inside, Martin realized with a mounting admixture of dread and excitement. He thought of Lyudmila and stifled his fear.

There was the low murmur of a voice. Martin gripped the cracked limestone wall he and Roderick walked along, and he peered around the corner. There he saw Lord Herzog, facing the lead-backed mirror from which he'd previously culled the sower. Inside of the mirror Martin saw the archbishop, clutching his jeweled processional cross and wearing his gold filigreed vestments. He seemed pathetic to Martin for all of his rich accoutrements. The man in the mirror shouted at the wizard, "I used your precious mandrake, and it did nothing to win me the whore's affection!"

Lord Herzog looked into the diaphanous ripple of fog surrounding the archbishop, and he waved his wand made from the ivory of an elephant's tusk. "Then she must be using some manner of counter-magic."

"Counter-magic!" The archbishop snorted like a wild boar about to charge. "How do I counter her counter-magic? Tell me," the man threatened, "or you can forget about me letting your precious sower cast his seed on my new harem. If I cannot bring Lyudmila Heyne to my bedchambers, then one of the other twelve will have to do." It was clear from the man's tone that none of the other women would supplant his designs quite as well as the candle girl he had in mind.

Martin made to walk forward, and Roderick put a staying hand on his young companion's shoulder. "Remain here," he whispered. "He's mine." The dwarf handed Martin his staff, which stunned and confused the young man. Roderick clarified by closing his large fists and saying, "I want to beat him to death with my rock head hands."

The boy remained silent and in place, as ordered. He peeked around the corner. Roderick walked toward the wizard with his back toward the mirror. Shrill shouting, like that of a court eunuch, came from the mirror as Archbishop Torner spotted the dwarf of whom he'd been warned and of whom he'd also dreamed of late. The little rock head walked behind Lord Herzog, who the archbishop was beginning to loathe, though not enough to forego warning him.

"Look behind you!"

The whirl of smoke disappeared from the mirror, along with the magical vision of the archbishop. The wizard looked on his old companion from the monastery who ferreted out his heretical illuminations and cost him his post.

"You little rock-headed worm!" Lord Herzog held out his ivory wand, which was curved like a cutlass. "Why don't you go chew some stones and leave magic to men?"

"Traded in our tonsure for a dunce cap, did we?" Roderick squared his stance, and prepared to throw blows. The wizard circled left. The dwarf moved in time with him, like a dancing partner. Lord Herzog walked backwards until he accidentally overturned a gilded silver paten in which desecrated host swam in a marinated sauce of blood and urine. The bread and wine spilled out across the stone cracks in the floor.

Roderick unclenched one of his fists and pointed at the leaking blood puddle and made a promise. "You'll be written out of the Lamb's Book of Life for that."

The wizard was unfazed by his threats and his fists. He moved backwards now toward another heretical totem. This one was an upside-down crucifix with Christ sculpted by a goldsmith with his crown of thorns facing downward and his feet raised high in the air.

Roderick lunged once for the wizard. Lord Herzog scampered across the room, shouting as he fled, "I see the dwarf, but I don't see the bastard. Show yourself, young cur!"

"In due time," Roderick promised, and stalked the lanky wizard. Martin continued peering around the corner. Lord Herzog finally ran until he was behind his mirror, which he clutched like a kite shield that might protect him from a barrage of arrows. Roderick prepared to lunge forward when the wizard dropped his ivory wand to the floor with a clatter. The wizard waved his hand over the mirror's glassy orb. "Look," Lord Herzog said.

Roderick came to a dead stop, and Martin wondered what was wrong. In the form of the mirror there appeared a glorious vision of the land Roderick had first learned of when reading the works of Lucian the Rhetorician. It was a place he had dreamed of nightly. The tree branches blossomed with golden loaves of bread. The trees produced sap that could be lanced from their bark, from which cinnamon, cassia, and laudanum for life's pain would leak and beg to be drunk along with the roiling seas of milk and honey.

"It is yours," Lord Herzog said, and waved his hands over the mirror. "Step into the mirror, and go home." The wizard licked his lips. Martin knew it was a trap, but he had trouble taking his eyes away from the vision in the glass where the streets of cobbled gold radiated with the force of a saint's halo. Two dwarves appeared in the glass, one older and the other much younger.

"Return," Lord Herzog said. "Join your father in the uroborus, the circle from life to death and back into life. You must die first, but then eternal life will be yours." Martin could not only see the vision, but could smell it from where he stood. The sweet scent of honey and frankincense filled his lungs, and made his wounds sting less.

Roderick remained pinned to the spot and watched as the two dwarves entered a colony of other little people who joined hands and danced around the maypole. "If you were to have a son here," Lord Herzog said, "he would never be called a gnome. No one would ever dream of casting a stone in his direction. Come."

The streams of milk and honey evaporated, and there was a rushing spring of crystal clear water coursing over smooth obsidian stones covered in verdant lichen. "This spring is but one part of the paradise that awaits you. To taste of it is to be healed of all wounds. You will slake your thirst and be blessed of all rheum and aches and pains so common to the dwarf. Bid farewell to these vestiges of suffering in the mines and in the mountains. Return home, my child."

The dwarves in the mirror played in the water, wading up to their hips and hiking up their trousers. Dwarven nymphs unheard of in any real earthly realm dipped water vessels in the artesian springs and poured the cold creek water into the mouths of the little men. The meadow where the spring ran was overhung with the boughs of trees where pear grew impossibly upon pomegranate, and fig shared branches with olives that could become grapes if one so willed it. This was a land where no season save the most temperate, Mediteranean spring was ever known.

"Come," the wizard said. Roderick walked toward the trap, and Martin appeared from his hiding. A strange odor filled the boy's throat as he walked forward. He looked around at the candles burning in the atrium, their wax dripping in beads shaped like teardrops. The smell reminded him of putrescent flesh. He gasped with horror and realized that the candles were not spermaceti or tallow, but were made from human fat.

Martin ran for the upside-down golden crucifix on which an inverted Christ languished, and he picked it up in his hand. His feet slipped, and regained purchase on the wine-colored mixture of blood and urine in which consecrated host had been seeped like tea leaves. He hurled the crucifix toward the mirror, asking the Savior's indulgence as he flung the relic toward the glass where the dreamland shattered into a thousand shards.

"No!" the wizard shouted and stumbled backward. His lead-backed mirror flipped and toppled onto him where he lay on the floor. His hand groped around searching out the wand's ivory so that he could punish the bastard he'd seen in visions. He would turn the little cur into a Cornish game hen and roast him on a spit.

He didn't get the chance. Martin recalled the Latin he had seen on the page of the book in Schreckschraube's longhouse. He'd initially thought of the words as medical gibberish, but closer inspection revealed them to be a spell. The old hermitess had warned him about the perils of mispronunciation, but even if he failed in casting, he thought the consequences couldn't be any worse than whatever Lord Herzog had in store for him and Roderick. The dwarf was now waking from the spell that the mirror had cast on him.

"Coniuro exercitus herudines!" Martin shouted.

"No!" the wizard shrieked. His voice was as high-pitched of that of the archbishop with whom he had commiserated in the cloud that took shape in the mirror.

Roderick cackled like a banshee. His Latin was as good as Lord Herzog's and he knew his young ward had just done him proud. Martin watched as a numberless cluster of dark brown leeches slithered and left a dripping trail of mucus. They made their way toward the prone form of the wizard. He found himself carpeted in the little monsters just as his hand barely touched the blunted point of the ivory tusk on the wand he would never use again.

Martin looked over at Roderick, breathing heavily. "I guess all of those nights of reading Paternosters to the other little bastards finally came in handy." He wondered what had become of Oliver, David, and the rest of the little denizens of the stewhouse. The shrieks of terror gave way to howls of pain. Martin stopped wondering and looked with Roderick, open-mouthed. The thousands of bloodletting leeches blanketed Lord Herzog with their dorsal sides, which were furry like the hides of caterpillars. The leeches sank their tripartite teeth into the nooks, crannies, and pores of the wizard's crawling flesh.

Their tiny teeth sawed and incised. They splintered, sucked, and debrided like hungry nursing babes at a teat. "My God!" the wizard shouted.

Martin looked around the room where the crucifix lay among the shattered glass and the candles made from the fat of men. "You have no God."

"Aye," Roderick said, patting Martin on the back and walking until he stood alongside the boy.

The leeches imbued with magic worked faster than those of the apothecaries and physics whose powers were of this world. They sucked and ate. As they did so, they also lay eggs in hermaphroditic ecstasy. The egg sacs exploded and new life was born. Pupas supped from the moment they spawned, crawling through intestinal lining and sneaking through fissures so that they tickled the wizard as they tortured him. When they finally scattered from his form, there were only bones picked clean and slicked with wetness from the salivary glands of the hungry monsters Martin had willed into being with his spell. It was the first he'd ever cast, he realized.

The leeches were porcine with the blood of their prey. They disappeared in a mist. Roderick walked through the room, blowing out the candles made from human flesh as he stepped gingerly over the spilled, desecrated host. All was dark, save for the little bit of moonlight filtering through the murder holes and arrow slits of the fortress. Martin watched the dwarf's shadow as it slinked back toward him.

Roderick stood face to face with the boy. "Our work is not yet done."

"I know." Martin pulled the brownie skeleton from his pocket and felt for the pointed hook of the enchanted earring. He pressed the sharp metal hook to his nose, and pushed. He only emitted a slight grunt as the earring pierced his cartilage.

Roderick elected to use his other ear, remarking, "You know, it hurts a lot less going into an ear than it does going into a nose."

"Aye," Martin said. Both men closed their eyes and left the fortress of the vanquished wizard and his shattered mirror.

Chapter Twenty-Three

The Sower Meets his Fate

The wizard had been right. Casper had heard his voice in his ear telling him that he would be allowed into Koln, even though the city was under strict moratorium. Herr Namlos had not only been allowed inside the town walls in contradiction of the local ordinance, but he had been escorted to the castle in a royal carriage pulled by two armored steeds, and carried on a bed of cushions. It was so sumptuous that at first he suspected a trap of some sort. His suspicions grew even greater when the carriage stopped and he was taken to a cold donjon tower. He feared they were going to make him their prisoner for the previous havoc he'd wreaked in this town that resulted in the dead rising from their graves and walking the streets. He was doubly surprised when the archbishop told Casper he would soon be loosed in a room with twelve women. He was told that he could take his tupping to his heart's content, a ram among a roomful of naked ewes.

So much was right, and yet something was wrong. For one thing, the wizard's incessant chattering in his ear was no longer there. He wouldn't shut up earlier about the bastard and the dwarf. Now he was curiously silent on the subject and on all other subjects. Casper knew that meant one of two things: either the twosome had taken care of Lord Herzog or he had settled accounts with them.

Casper stood naked now in a room outside of the one where he was told the women were held. He looked down. His member wasn't hard when he wanted it to be for the first time since he spied the wizard in the mirror. He'd been a virile bull, a horned satyr over the course of the last few months. He'd been born with a tiny member. It was not much larger than an olive when flaccid, and it was a paltry twig when swollen and engorged with blood. The wizard had caused him to swell in size, along with the other great powers that Lord Herzog had bequeathed him. Now he was back to the old Casper, for whatever reason. He was the same one who would be laughed at and denied entry to whorehouses on account of his small member and the belief that he had to be too young to go a sporting with a prick that tiny.

He stroked it and jerked it to no avail. It was as flaccid as a deflated bladder skin. The pelts of a hundred soft red squirrels weaved into one heavy robe fell over his naked shoulders and sent shivers down his spine. The archbishop draped the mantel over him and said, "You mustn't waste your seed." Casper averted his head as he settled into the robe. "Isidore of Seville said self-pleasure dishonored a man the vigor of his sex." The archbishop settled the robe on the sower's shoulders and said, "Forfend young buck, save thy seed and leave Onan's sin to languish in desuetude."

Casper couldn't tell the archbishop that he wasn't playing with himself, or that he was merely trying to revive his dead member that was tiny again. "There will be no coitus interruptus," Casper assured him. What he didn't add is that there might not be any coitus at all that night. The archbishop was excited by the prospect of Casper sowing his seed with a baker's dozen of whores for whatever reason. Perhaps he was a pervert who wished to spy through a bit of wattle and daub, as Casper knew many holy men to be hypocrites. There was also a good chance that the archbishop knew what Casper did. Maybe the holy man had more than a passing acquaintance with the wizard himself, and wished for Casper to sow to his heart's content for that reason. If indeed there was a bond between the wizard and the archbishop, then neither man had made him privy to their pact.

"Are you ready?" Archbishop Torner asked.

"Aye, that I am."

The bishop sensed Casper's newfound meekness. He tried to gird the Sower's loins. It was important that the lad perform tonight to bring about the coming of the Great Beast so that the anti-king could depose Domina Matina and the archbishop could increase his own power.

"Woman," the archbishop said, his breath smelling like sour milk, "should always be forced to submit to man, else he might turn to his own sex for satisfaction. This is truly against the will of God."

Casper wondered if this was a veiled proposition from a catamite, but he said nothing. That suited the archbishop just fine, since he was not done speaking. He looked at the door, behind which the twelve candle girls waited to receive their rightful tupping. The archbishop's lips curled in disgust. "Remember the words of Jerome." Casper could not remember what he had never heard in the first place. "Woman's love is insatiable," Archbishop Torner said. "Even if you should quench the fires of the dozen harlots therein, their passions will burst into flame anew. The only purpose of woman is to enervate man's mind and his will."

"I will bear that in mind," Casper said. He felt uneasy in the man's presence. The archbishop was even eerier than the wizard.

"The Archbishop of Saville said that women are under the power of men because they are spiritually fickle. Thus should they be governed by man, who is head of woman. Do not heed their designs. Make them heed yours."

"I will."

"Taking pleasure is virile, giving is servile."

The sower tried to ignore the flaccidity of his member and worked himself into a rabid, enraged lather. "I will sow my seed! I will rape to my heart's content!"

"Good," the archbishop said, his tongue slithering free from his mouth. The boy was ready. Archbishop Torner turned and left, having dispensed with all of the counsel that was his store.

He wanted to visit Lyudmila in the Palas, but first he would go the reliquary of the three Magi and consult with the wizard. He had a request to make. It was a request he didn't think Lord Herzog could deny him, since he had done all that the wizard had asked of him.

"Your Holiness!" Two guards stood at attention with their halberds by their sides as the archbishop passed. He didn't acknowledge them as he walked by. His mind was too troubled by other things. Something was amiss, though he didn't know what.

He practiced the speech he would make to the wizard. He would tell the man that it wasn't enough to keep Lyudmila on the footing of a mistress. He wanted her as a wife. The wizard might laugh and tell him that the clergy couldn't get married, though they could keep as many concubines as they could count. Then the archbishop would speak up, and quote from the past. He would demand the abrogation of the rule of celibacy and use the argument of the physics who said it was good to expel superfluities to irrigate the body. It worked well enough for the sower, did it not?

The wizard was learned, but the archbishop was convinced he knew even more. He would quote the seneschal Guillaume Saignet of Beaucaire, recite verbatim from the *Lamentation Humanae* on the nature of celibacy. If the wizard wasn't swayed by these arguments, then he would take his appeal to the people. He would speak of how the Saracens multiplied at will and choked the Holy Land with their numbers. He would invoke the powers of Old Nick and Mammon, who had served him since he signed his pact. He would make Lyudmila Heyne his bride by hook or crook, and he would also tell the wizard to take his mandrake spell and feed it to the birds.

He'd visited Lyudmila's chambers after working that bit of magic. If anything she had been more repelled by his person than usual, not less. As to the wizard's assertion that maybe she had performed some form of counter-magic, the candle girl struck Archbishop Torner as dumb aside from a splendid pair of large breasts, which were clever enough. He doubted she had cast any spell. The only reason she'd gotten lucky with her poppets in the woods was because she had petitioned a green man much smarter and more powerful than she. The girl could not avail herself of such resources when she was kept prisoner at his leisure now.

Lord Herzog's powers were waning, and the archbishop's were growing. Perhaps Archbishop Torner would slay the wizard when the opportunity presented itself. Once installed as king, he could marry whomever he liked and defy the Pope's decrees. He'd do it so loudly that the investiture years would look like sport compared to the heresies and anathemas the archbishop would cast and commit once he was seated upon the throne himself. He went to the basement of the cathedral, to the reliquary filled with bones …

The girls had barely heard the murmurs from the other side of the door. Lora was bound for the cloister for penitent prostitutes run by the Poor Claires before all of this madness and plague had swept Koln. She now spoke her fears as she walked the meager circumference of the room with her eleven sisters. "I wonder whether or not they've burned Lyudmila?" The other girls had been silent for some time, and they looked up at her.

"Tis possible," one named Maria allowed. She had serene features. Her flaming red locks were plaited intricately. The hair spilled down her back onto the sheer gown she had been given to wear when yanked from the house and taken to this donjon, along with the other girls.

"I wonder how the other little bastards will get on," another girl said, "now that no one is there to tend them."

"They will fend for themselves," Lora assured them. "Martin taught them well."

"Where is Martin?" The girl giggled. "He never misses a chance to smell my underthings, and I haven't seen him in a fortnight."

"He left," Lora said, simply, "with a dwarf."

"A dwarf?" It didn't make any sense. None of this did.

Sarah was a girl with an oval-shaped face and a neck as long as a swan's. She felt the dimity of the sheer gown she'd been given, stroking the material like a housecat. "This feels like it was made on a loom I couldn't afford after a thousand hours and a thousand candles and a thousand men."

"Yes," Maria said, "but they could have spared equal expense on the bedding." She kicked at the sackcloth scattered on the floor. It was a coarse mixture of horsehair and goatshair, and smelled of fairground dunnage after a heavy rain. "Hens at market are treated with more dignity than this."

The door suddenly burst open. A young, miserable cur of a lad stood there. Maria tittered a little and covered her mouth. She'd been with enough men to know that not even the most strapping woodcutter or knight errant could have his way with twelve women, not unless he was willing to eat six roses after tupping six girls. What exactly did this little runt intend to do to her or to any of the girls for that matter?

Casper decided that the only way to reinvigorate himself and regain his bull's cock and his swagger was to work himself into a foaming rage at the twelve women with whom he must now sow. He must do it without the aid of the magic that guided him these last few months. He felt lost and terrified and tried to conceal that with rage.

"Why are you whores not wearing your striped hoods and aiguillettes?"

No one answered him. The girls merely lined up as if Mother Inferior herself had rung the bell and bade them to the parlor where they would undress and allow the men to have their pick of girls for the night. Lora wondered where Mother Inferior was right now.

The girls disrobed. Their stark, naked beauty terrified Casper. He hid his fear in another show of rage. "Look at these despoiled whore bodies." He dropped his robe of Baltic red squirrel to the floor and pointed at his limp penis. "No wonder I cannot grow hard. It is your fault!"

He pointed at them, stabbing the air before him with an accusatory finger. The girls lowered their heads and stifled their smiles at his pathetic rage and his tiny propagator. He looked like one of those ancient statues on which the god in question was given undersized genitals to show he was above earthly pursuits. That was all good and well for the gods. This cur's aim was earthly conquest though, so he was in awkward if not downright humiliating straights.

He sensed the laughter of the girls, though they did their best to stow it. Their faces grew red, they bit their tongues, and smiles crept up unbidden no matter how hard they fought against them. One finally snorted at his tiny appendage, and he turned to her. It was Maria, her cheeks as rosy now as her beautiful hair.

"You!" he said. "You worked the maleficence upon me." She said nothing, though she didn't hide her smile from him. At most they could burn her for her impudence, and she suspected they would do that whether or not she consented to the worm's designs tonight. Casper Namlos walked closer to her and said, "You worked some prestidigitator magic upon my organ and gave it the appearance of smallness and weakness it now bears. It is an illusion, a glamour." He shouted now to the wizard who had abandoned him. "You have granted me power, and now these harlots wish to conceal my glory from mine own eyes. Cock," he said, "was master over many hens these last few months, and so he shall be again."

Maria's disposition changed. The smile left her lips, and her face was no longer red. Serenity washed over her. She held her arms open, entreating Casper to come unto her naked body. "You are right," she said. "It was but a glamour, and a bit of deceit as spoken of in the Malleus Maleficarum. Forgive this poor witch, and allow me to make it right."

The apology worked like opiated ether on the boy, and his own look softened. He fell into Maria's embrace. She kissed his ears, licking the lobes with hot breath so that he shuddered and fell into her as weak as a ragdoll.

She clutched his tiny soft member in her hand and said, "My, it is large and hard as stone." Maria winked at the girls behind her. A smile of wretched vanity crossed the young boy's face. She fondled his testicles with expert tickling fingers that had him open-mouthed and dumb with pleasure after a moment. Her fingers drifted to his hindquarters, and stroked his rear so that he bucked like a bitch in heat and his panting became heavy.

He was finally hard. It was not the satyr's veined shaft that he'd wielded like a mace these last few months. It was his old small penis, a mere splinter of flesh. Maria cupped one of his balls with her soft white hand, and placed her other hand around his hardened member. Two girls came from behind him, kissed his ears and massaged his shoulders until his limbs went slack.

Maria's voice came to him as if from a distance, so deep under the spell of pleasure was he. And yet he heard the words. "You want to know where my whore's knot is? Here."

He felt something slip over his cock, the braided length of aiguillette that the candle girls were forced to wear when they went out in public. The sensation of the thing winding over his penis wasn't unpleasant, and he remained in a fog of ecstasy with merely the will to groan while the woman spoke lucidly. "Let us turn the screws a bit, girls." The eleven prostitutes pulled him to the ground, which was one massive straw paillasse. He kicked and they held his legs firm. He tried to swing his fists and they sat on his arms with their ample endowments.

His limbs prickled with nettles as his blood flow was halted by the pressure that the girls applied to his splayed form. "No!" he said. Maria turned the knot around his cock several times, so that the soft sensitive flesh of his member burned and cramped. The rope was a tight mass around the erect base of his penis, where a clot of blood now formed and a vein quaked in his flesh as if it might explode.

"Undo it, please!"

"What?" Maria asked. "Tighten it?"

The laughter of the women came to his ears where more blood rushed. It felt, after the next pulling tight of the knot, that his penis had been ripped in half. He only wished it had.

"Look," she said. Two of the women who held him down propped his head up so that he could gaze upon the ligature the whore's braid had made around his cock, which was now as contorted as a Bavarian pretzel.

"Please!"

"Please?" Maria sneered. She looked over at her sisters. "I recognize this one. He came to the stewhouse. He arrived at our joyous abbey, loaded with Viking ingots, and he plied the abbess with his pieces of silver."

"I recognize him too," Lora said. Her rage was such that she reached over and slapped the purpling penis captivus, which swelled now as if it had been left baking in a kiln for too long. "He is the reason that Gloria died. He filled her belly with demon seed."

"Thank God little Martin slayed the demon," Maria said.

"Yes," Lora said, "but think of how much more misery he has no doubt sown. Think of what he would have done to us, if given the chance." She twisted the bulbus glandis. There followed a hollow crack, as when a celery stick is broken in half.

The women covered his mouth so that his howls of pain were stifled. They kept his head tilted upward so that they could watch his eyes swim with terror, a terror similar to the one he'd no doubt inflicted on as many women as he could.

"Open his mouth," Lora said.

The girls removed their hands from Casper's mouth. As he attempted to shriek, Lora stuffed the half of his penis that had been ripped free from his body in his mouth. The girls who'd previously covered his mouth with their hands now clamped his jaws shut so that he chewed his own little member like it was an undersized wurst fresh from the griddle.

"Good boy," one said. Blood seeped from the corners of his lips. He looked down at the stump where geysers of blood pumped each time his heart beat, and then he died. The women stood. One spit on him, but that wasn't enough for Lora. She stood over the prone body. The other girls suspected what game was afoot and they moved away, lest they be splashed with their sister's golden water.

Lora parted the lips of her rose, and spoke to her sisters as she peed on the dead man's form. "He entered through that door over there." She nodded as she pissed a stream that came from her rose like water from the mouth of a stone cherub in a fountain. "See if we cannot leave through that door." The girls accepted her as their natural leader, and walked toward the door through which Casper came. "We must free Lyudmila." She finished pissing on the dead wretch, a couple of last trickles squirting from her body and onto his.

Her sisters watched her in awe and terror mixed with a bit of admiration. "Come to think of it," Lora said. "Why stop at Lyudmila? Let's free the whole damn town." The girls rushed toward her, chaired her, and chanted her name as they fled the diseased donjon where they'd been imprisoned until now.

***

The monsters had no way of knowing it, but Lord Herzog's evil powers fell into abeyance at the moment of the wizard's death beneath an army of slithering leeches. His demons that so plagued the land went into dormancy and returned to the Hades from whence they'd been called.

The bluebottle-winged monster Casper had summoned in the Zollschloss had dined on raw sheep and ruined many a shepherd in the process. He'd razed entire villages on his own, and laughed at the burghers as they tried to pitchfork him. The demon found himself in a spice shop as the life left Lord Herzog, and he slowly dematerialized. He fought against his death. He thrashed against his return to the underworld where life meant eternal torment for him rather than torment inflicted on mortals, which was quite much more fun.

He had been shattering phials of black pepper and mace, ginger and nutmeg, while the shopkeeper could do naught but hide behind his counter and weep as his wares and his livelihood were destroyed. He was sure he would probably be ripped to shreds by those black talons the demon called fingernails after it had wrecked the shop.

There were roars of laughter from the demon, punctuated by the sound of glass shattering. Then there was a groan of horror as a vortex rippled beneath the demon's feet appearing from the sawed lumber planks of wood on the floor of the shop. The whirlpool grew in strength until it pulled the demon's form inside, and then shut behind him. All was silent in the shop. The shopkeeper was confused and disheartened over the destruction but finally grateful that the monster was no more.

The demon of living lava flows that Casper sired from the cellarer's rump was having his own problems. This same demon was the one who melted the armor of knights and caused the chivalrous brotherhood to boil as they left their keep and clopped toward him on their mounted steeds. He was the same demon who laughed as cauldrons of boiling pitch were poured onto him from castle walls, and he drank the brimstone concoction like a thirsty pilgrim who'd discovered a well on his trek. His hide was pierced by a thousand flaming arrows and they were as but the stings of bees.

The people defending their Zollschloss from him were convinced the castle would topple and be raided. They were sure it would be destroyed and plundered, with every man slaughtered and every woman raped as they had heard happened elsewhere. The beast had spent hours enduring their barrages and finding their defenses naught but comical. Then of a sudden the creature of living coals collapsed in a pile. Its remnants smoldered as harmlessly as the aftereffects of a campfire doused with ashes kicked over crackling logs. Two archers hidden at murder holes had looked out at the demon that went from walking holocaust to curling little wisps of vaporized smoke.

These demons and the others that Casper Namlos sired disappeared with the wizard, and they died with the sower who joined them in Hades. There they commiserated with an Euronymous whose pride had been wounded. He was the first demon to be sent back to the Underworld. He'd been forced to admit to Old Nick that he'd been rendered incorporeal again on account of a trembling thirteen-year-old bastard with a sword that was barely fit to hang above a mantle as a decoration in a whorehouse.

All of the demons were gone now except one, and his hour was at hand.

Chapter Twenty-Four

Skeletons Put to Cross-Purposes

They had not only chosen different places on their body to pierce, but had selected different destinations. Roderick was now alone in a city he vowed to never step foot inside, in a church he despised with all of his being. He wondered where Martin had willed himself when he'd closed his eyes and used the enchantment of the brownie to travel.

It was just as well that the boy wasn't here. Roderick had no intentions of leaving this place alive and he didn't want the boy to die with him. The dwarf had a storied past but the boy had quite a future ahead of him, Roderick was convinced.

Shouting came from the streets, beyond the heavy oaken doors of the cathedral. It sounded like womenfolk. Now was not the time for curiosity however, or to step outside. Now was the hour for revenge. He walked past the empty wooden pews, and sat in one of the varnished benches which groaned beneath him as he took his leisure. He breathed in and out. He settled into the pew as if it was the mercy seat itself.

He realized that he must go on despite his aches. Roderick stood and walked onward toward the sound of a voice hissing imprecations in the vault beneath the nave. A hawk shrieked bloody murder and flitted past one of the stained glass windows. Roderick looked up toward the ribbed triforia where shadows and cobwebs lingered. The hawk flew on, and the dwarf walked to the baptismal font.

It was heresy to use the font for any use besides that for which it was intended, but his face stung from long exposure to the saltwater and harsh winds. He dipped his hands into the holy water, which was lit with a halcyon glow from the sun radiating through the gold and red of the stained glass windows.

He shook his head like a dog who'd taken his ablutions at a bucket of rainwater, and then he kept on walking toward the cursing voice. It was that blasted archbishop. Roderick treaded softly down the stairs, holding his breath so that he could better hear the holy man hurl insults at his unseen target.

"Where are you, you spell-slinging waste of life? You told me your sower was practically Pan. I saw his cock and it was a measly worm. He is to bring the Beast into this world, that little shriveled eunuch of whom you spoke as if he was the Minotaur?"

The archbishop was so aggravated that he hadn't bothered to set up the panel painting to conceal the triple sarcophagus of the Magi, as was his custom. He was usually careful to conceal his communion with the evil wizard even when alone. Some stray parishioner might wander down here looking to request confession or prayer on behalf of the sick or aged.

The situation was too dire tonight, however. He sensed riot and revolt in the air as he toured his castle earlier in the evening. It wasn't just the whores under lock and key either, or the way Lyudmila sneered at him when Lord Herzog had convinced him the mandrake would bring her under his power.

Greater clouds were forming. Confirmation came in the lengthened shadow of the dwarf that was reflected in the flame of votive candles lighting the chamber where the reliquary was kept.

The archbishop turned. "What do you want, little gnome?"

Roderick let that pass without comment. He didn't feel like waxing on the finer points that distinguished dwarves from gnomes. The archbishop would discover that soon enough. The dwarf threw the broken tusk of ivory that was the wizard's wand to the floor, where it clattered against the Vitruvian marble and echoed in the hollow chamber.

Archbishop Torner had seen the wizard wave that wand before, and he knew what the dwarf meant by his gesture. The archbishop's rage overcame his fear as he realized that Lord Herzog might not have been speaking pure balderdash when he said a counter-spell was cast against his magic. "You," the archbishop said, and stood. The cameo and gold box lay open behind him. It was filled with bones and dust and little else. The form of the wizard he attempted to summon certainly wasn't there. "You're the reason Lyudmila cannot love me." He gripped his jeweled processional cross in his hands, as if preparing to bring it down like a sledgehammer on the dwarf's skull.

"Those who cannot love rarely receive love in their turn."

"Magic works," the archbishop said, his tongue sneaking from between his teeth. "It is only stymied by counter-spells."

Roderick gripped his own amber staff and said, "I cast no counter-spells."

"You killed the wizard." The archbishop pointed at the broken shards of ivory.

"Aye," Roderick said, smiling as he savored the memory of the man's suffering. "That I did, with the help of a little bastard."

"Who?"

"Concern yourself no more with earthly matters," Roderick said. He stroked the eternally frozen dragon's egg tipping his staff. "Prepare to go to Hell."

The archbishop was more amused than frightened as of now. Roderick thought he had time to rectify that. "The Saracens," Archbishop Torner said, "are right about women, for all of their bestial heresy."

"How so?" Roderick asked. He didn't mind a bit of theology before giving the man his just desserts. He thought the archbishop evil, but there was no doubt the man was intelligent, brilliant even. The dwarf would no more begrudge him some final disquisition than an executioner would deny his victim their last words.

"The Prophet in one of his hadiths claims that there are far more women in Hell than men."

"Perhaps," Roderick said, "you can finally find love there."

"I was to rule here," the archbishop said, "with the anti-king and Lord Herzog, and the Great Beast." His tone was so pathetic now that Roderick felt his rage giving way to pity, though not enough to divert him from his course.

"Perhaps you can gain a powerful position in the infernal afterlife and rule as a palatine on the crystal battlements of Hell."

"Perhaps," Archbishop Torner said, and smiled. Roderick had meant his words in jest, but the holy man was so thirsty for power that he now looked genuinely pleased by the prospects of ruling some kind of prefect in Hades.

Roderick decided to test the archbishop's knowledge before he put the man out of his misery and met his fate himself. The fate meant for him was the one he'd dreamed of and seen betwixt the legs of the giantess. "Do you know of Saint Brendan?"

The archbishop was impressed by the dwarf. "How does a little rock head know of him?"

Roderick ignored the insult, the second one bandied his way after being called a gnome. "Have you read of his deeds?"

The archbishop nodded. "*Naugiation Sancti Brendani Abbatis* is a fascinating work."

"Oh," Roderick said, shifting his staff from right to left hand. "Then you've read it?"

"I have, but you haven't answered my question. How does a lowly miner like you know of such works?"

"I fled the mines," Roderick said, not wanting to go on a tangent of pedigree and lineage, "and I found a monastery."

"Admirable," the archbishop said.

Roderick ignored the deceptive bit of flattery and said, "Since you've read of him, and read the work in question, then you know what the great Irish navigator monk saw on his excursions."

"Yes." The archbishop's voice grew distant and whimsical. Roderick's sadness for the man increased until it felt like he'd swallowed a stone. There may have been a time when Torner was a humble parish priest and he had really believed in and delighted in the Word.

"You know then that Saint Brendan claimed he saw an island where Judas could spend Sundays and church holy days, and that he could escape from Hell for a short time?"

"Yes," the archbishop said, remembering the days when he read of the escapades of the mariner monk in his tiny ship. That was before he had soaked that quill in blood and signed his pact with Old Nick. "I remember."

"Perhaps," Roderick said, lifting his staff above his head, "you will be allowed to take your leave of the scorching flames from time to time. I doubt it, though."

"Wait!" The archbishop held up the jeweled processional cross, and its rubicund gems glowed like transubstantiated blood. "Please!"

The dwarf quoted the Bible, shouting so that his voice echoed through the stone vault and made the bones of the Magi quake in the reliquary box. "Then shall he say also unto them on the left hand, depart from me, ye cursed, into everlasting fire, prepared for the Devil and his angels."

The archbishop recognized the words from Mathew, but his knowledge of the Good Book couldn't save him. He combusted and flames melted his flesh from his form like soft wax. The fires were holy and he lived as he burned. He suffered a worse fate than those he burned as heretics and witches at the stake. He screamed, and Roderick shouted, "Fall before me, you den of thieves. Quake and crumble now!"

Roderick's rage evaporated in the next moment, and the desire to forgive all spread through his body. He saw ghostly chimeras and shades of the dead diggers from his past. He saw dwarves who'd bled to death from the whip of the cat-o-nine tails as they quarried. They slinked around him. Their ghostly shells passed through him and like wraiths through the scorching and screaming archbishop, who still melted and dripped. His form collapsed into tallowed rivulets, weeping steam and unholy water from the poisoned font of his soul.

"Arthur," Roderick said to one of the dwarves, a brother of his who got a rock lodged in his hand and died of blood poisoning. "Where is Father?"

Roderick's dead brother grinned and adjusted his stamped purse of leather boiled in oil that he always wore around his shoulder. "You will see him soon enough on the other side." His brother and the other shrouded forms scampered away. One of Roderick's uncles was among the throng. He'd been adopted by a nobleman who toured the mines one day and decided his court could use a new dwarf.

"Where are you going?" Roderick asked the retreating spirits.

"To fulfill your wishes," his uncle shouted. "I no longer do somersaults to entertain the giants or allow men to call me Half Pint."

The dwarves chiseled at the church. They attacked it with concentration as if metalsmithing even though their only aim was destruction. They were phantoms and specters, but the apparitions tore through rocks that were very real. An army of dwarves large enough to level a mountain in hours set upon the church like maggots feasting on a rotted limb.

The pews splintered as the bewhiskered and stumpy men swung anvils and battle axes. They kept time with work songs and ditties, madrigals and chants. Some of the Lieder could only be sung in the original Northern tongue, since they were insults to the giants. If the overseers knew they were the subject of sport and song, they would have taken offense and cracked the whips harder, and selected random men for the rack at higher numbers.

One dwarf was a bit cleverer than the others, and he snuck outside the church. He found out the cornerstone that had been laid before everything else. He began to attack it with his chisel.

Townsfolk who'd already started storming the castle now poured into the cobblestone streets, and watched with unbelieving eyes as the ghosts of the rock heads tore the church to pieces. Some of the whores who'd absconded from the donjon after tearing Casper Namlos to shreds came into the street as well. Others looted the royal treasury, their hands still slicked with the viscous blood from when they plucked the sower's eyes from their sockets.

The dwarf finally split the cornerstone asunder. There was a loud cracking sound, a rumble that reminded him of the workings in the mine that would presage a collapse as all the rats would scurry from the catacombs in search of safety.

He looked back at the townspeople, and beamed from tiny pointed ear to tiny pointed ear. "Achilles' Heel has been found." He took a bow and disappeared as the crowd burst into thunderous applause.

Their cheering was short-lived however, as the demon Baal himself now fled from the church. He emerged from a cathedral crawlspace where he'd nestled all of this time. He tiptoed on his arachnid legs covered in black hairs, and the people shrieked as the hirsute monster with the body of a spider and the head of an immiserated king slunk away in ignominy.

The peasants picked up loose cobblestones and flung them at the monster. Most of the townsfolk overshot, their aim spoiled by sheer terror. Several of the stones found purchase and landed with a wet thunk or plop, as they sunk into the monster's slick black carapace before he disappeared.

The Bell of the Three Kings echoed, rang without anyone to pull its hemp chain, and it shattered as easily as milk chocolate. Its shards flew down from the steeple and the people moved even farther from the steps of the church. Four tons of heavy brass landed and shattered the stones of the street, giving rise to a mist of chalky powder emitted from the rocks that broke on the boulevard.

Stained glass exploded in a cloudburst. It blew like a sneeze from the nose of a giant brought on by a man tickling the monster's nostrils with an oversized feather. The rocks of the church collapsed, and Roderick held his arms aloft. He welcomed death.

A boulder fell onto his head and his world was blackness for as long as it takes one grain to fall from an hourglass. He blinked, and found himself on a hill of rollicking green grass, where nuns in wimples and gowns and white veils stood. They cavorted and took mincing steps like ballerinas, not like women wedded to Christ. They giggled and shed their veils and their gowns.

"What?" he asked. "Where am I?"

One of the women held open the *Penitential of Bede* and shed pages from the volume. She tore leaves as she turned the thin pages of the book, while she tickled the rose of her unclothed neighbor beside her with her other hand. She spoke without removing her hand from her fellow nun's womb and without taking her eyes from the book she read. "If nun should lay with a nun using an instrument, seven years penance." She closed the book and looked back at the sister beside her. "I suppose we'd better find an instrument, then."

She removed her hand from the slicked vagina of her companion. Nectar thick as mucus dripped from her fingers as she ran to a nearby tree from which engorged phalluses dangled. They grew like fruit from the branches of the trees. They were the size of gourds or cucumbers.

Roderick looked around with mouth agape, unable to speak or close his jaw. He could not even swallow the spit gathering in his mouth. Moans of passion and ravishment came from behind him. His own euphoria overcame him as he watched two nuns who were naked now except for snowy wimples. They locked leg and joined pudenda. They bumped against each other, and one struggled to explain to him what she and her sister were doing while in the throes of hysteric passion. "We join shield to shield here, and have no need of lance. You, little pygmy, are just the right size to be of other use to us."

It would have come to fisticuffs at a bare minimum if a man had called him a pygmy. The last man to have a go at his size had burst into flames and now lay buried under the rubble of his once mighty church. He was willing to make allowances though, being as these were females and seeing as women usually shunned dwarves.

They were apparently willing to indulge his own caprices in kind in this seventh heaven from which he hoped he would never escape. There was a row of nuns, lined up as if ready to receive corporal punishment. The way they brandished their privates in shameless joy and wagged them like a mistress dangling yarn before a calico kitten made him think they'd drunk their dram of earthly suffering, and thought it wise now to slake other thirsts.

He walked toward the women, and noticed that the nun who was part of the pleasured dyad in the high grass was right. He was just the right size to stand and deliver, where another man of average height would be forced to kneel.

Roderick wiped his face, where the last vestiges of holy water from the baptismal font were still drying. He opened his mouth, stuck out his tongue, and licked the first of an endless number of roses he intended to taste for the remainder of eternity.

Chapter Twenty-Five

The Bastard Comes Home

The one remaining sword sat above the mantle. The stained impression from where the other had been removed was still on the wall, traces of rust dripping down from where the monumental brass had lain. Martin wasted no time in reaching up for the sword and taking the latten weapon in hand. He turned to run outside, intending to find the archbishop and slay him. Martin didn't care where Roderick had used Schreckschraube's enchanted earring to travel. He had only two things on his mind, killing Archbishop Torner and rescuing Lyudmila from the holy man's donjon.

"Boy, why do you have a brownie skeleton dangling from your nose?" Martin stood face to face with Mother Inferior. He touched a finger to his nose and felt blood dripping. He didn't feel like explaining the hermitess's charm to the procuress, but he was thankful that she had mentioned the hook snagged in his nose. He was so consumed by the desire to kill that he had forgotten that the tiny skeleton was dangling in his nostril, on top of which his other wounds and bruises were so severe that he barely felt the brownie. Still it wouldn't do to go walking around with the thing lodged in his face.

He pulled it free, and pushed the abbess aside. "Out of my way."

She followed him as he walked toward the front of the house. "Just where are you going?"

"I killed one demon with the other sword, now it's time to slay another. This one should be easier," Martin said. "He's a coward."

"Damn you, boy!" She grabbed the hood of his shepherd's coat and yanked him back toward her. He stayed the urge to elbow the woman in the nose and heard her out. "You already ruined one of the swords bequeathed me by one of my many husbands. Must you destroy the other one as well?"

"Aye, if I need to destroy your sword to save Lyudmila, then so be it."

"What makes you think she needs saving?" Her words gave him pause. Martin opened his mouth to speak, but no sound came out.

"I thought that she was the archbishop's prisoner?"

"I have heard people shouting in the street that the archbishop and his church are no more." The abbess gently touched Martin's hand, and he loosened his hold on the sword.

"Martin!" David and Oliver ran toward him, and he leaned down to embrace the two boys.

"Tell us of your journey," Oliver entreated.

"Yes," David said, "did you travel the seas?"

"I did," Martin said proudly, realizing that his dream of sailing had come true. He had even helped slay a wizard. His deeds were worthy of a chronicle or a tapestry.

"Did you find the Grail?" Oliver asked.

Martin suppressed a laugh. "No," he said, and tousled the boy's shiny pageboy coif. "I can see you've been reading your Eschenbach in my absence."

"Aye," David said. He spoke for Oliver, who stood in silent awe of the oldest bastard in the house. "He has read to us nightly."

"Have you recited your paternosters?" Martin asked a bit sternly.

"Yes," Oliver assured him, regaining his voice. The baby cried from behind them. Martin looked over the heads of the orphans before him to see the infant wrapped in swaddling cloth. The baby was held by another one of the young ragamuffins of the stewhouse. The tiny boy swayed and rocked the waif in his arms.

"Will the babe be taken to the home for foundlings?"

"Nein," Oliver said, "we'll raise it to be a right bastard like the rest of us."

"Don't call yourself that," Martin said. He thought there were enough people who would insult the fatherless children without them aiding the backbiters and gossips of the town.

The wry voice of Mother Inferior came from behind him. "So you didn't find the Grail, eh?" Her cackle was dry as Riesling.

"No," he said. He sensed the disappointment in the moony eyes of his two cares, and hastened to add, "I may have found the Grail Maiden."

That lifted the spirits of the two boys who brightened considerably now that they knew there was at least some accord between what they read in books and what the world held in store.

"Who?" Oliver asked, jumping up and down and barely containing his excitement.

"Lyudmila," Martin said, breathless just at the mere recital of her name as it trailed out of his mouth.

Mother Inferior clucked her tongue. "That whore is nothing but a set of large milk jugs set beneath an empty pumpkin of a head. She ..."

Martin turned and slapped the abbess so hard that her head spun. "Stand down," he said. She lowered her eyes. He'd had his fill of violence and somehow knew his quest was at an end, and that his maiden needed no saving. He dropped the sword to the ground, where it rattled against the wooden floor.

Oliver preceded him to the kitchen. David picked the sword up and followed them. Martin felt his stomach rumble, and it occurred to him that he hadn't eaten in some time.

"Are you hungry?" Oliver asked. He stood over a Harzer cheese wheel that rested on the surface of a rough wooden table.

"Aye," Martin said, and sighed. "I could use a bath, as well."

"You're bleeding all over," Oliver said, looking his hero up and down. "Your nose, your face. Your shirt is cut to ribbons."

Martin took up the butcher knife that was lodged in the wheel of cheese as deeply as the sword of Arthurian lore laid in stone. He struggled to pull the knife free of the wheel and spoke as he grunted from the exertion. "I climbed a mountain made of precious metals. I grappled with a sea monster. I slayed a wizard by summoning an army of leeches. I am hungry, and a bit bruised from the exertion."

The knife finally came free from the Harzer round, but unfortunately a cheese fly also flew free. Martin was too tired to even swat at the skipper with his knife, and he collapsed to the floor.

David made as if to lift the ceremonial sword to slash the fly and Oliver chastised him, while Martin struggled to regain his footing after the dizzy spell. "You blasted fool! You can't kill a fly with a sword!"

"He's right," Martin said, and he stood. He forced some of the rock hard cheese into his mouth and chewed. "Swords are for bigger game."

He swallowed the cheese, which settled in his stomach like a barb from a mace. He groaned and burped. The abbess was now docile, and she swept the floor with a willow broom. "You should not lay hands to women," Martin said.

He staggered from the room, out to the Backstein façade of the building facing the Strasse.

Oliver's voice followed him. "You just hit the abbess!"

"It was wrong of me to let my temper get away from me."

There was the clatter of hoofs over cobblestone. A carriage humpbacked as a nautilus drifted to a stop in front of the stewhouse. Several of the candle girls were aboard, including Maria and Lora. They clung to the carriage's body while two or three more girls were hidden in the berth masked by purple Arabic curtains.

A fair hand parted the canopy of state, and Lyudmila hopped down from the carriage. Martin noticed that she was the only one dressed in more than a sheer gown, and that she was the only one not covered in blood. He had no way of knowing that the fingers of the other girls were stained with blood on account of the throats they had torn in their feverish madness that was unleashed from their breasts after they slew the sower.

The other girls hopped down from the carriage. Lora looked Martin up and down and said, "You are covered in blood."

"So are you," he said, queasy now from the curdled cheese swimming in his stomach.

The roar of a thousand denizens of the city filled the air, and Lora had to shout to be heard. "The friars and the Carmelites broke from their charisms and contemplations to help us drive the archbishop's lackeys from the town."

"Is he dead?" Martin asked.

Lora nodded. Gloria came to her sister's side and wiped blood from her palms onto the sheer material of the gown she'd been provided with when she was taken prisoner by the royal guard. "The archbishop is dead. His witchfinders and other maleficence-sniffers have been driven into hiding."

"Justice," Lora said, "has finally come to Koln, and not a moment too soon."

A monk in habit walked through the streets, holding a link of heavy chain in his palm. Martin saw the metal was attached to the throat of a well-known Hanseatic slaver. Two of his previous chattel walked behind him. They were a Slav and a Saracen captured in the course of the Holy Wars. They flailed his back raw with bullwhips while peasants rubbed handfuls of salt from the royal coffers into the wounds of the screaming man.

The monk quoted from the Pauline letters as he led the slave master through the street like a dog on a chain. "There is neither Jew nor Greek. There is neither slave nor free. There is neither male nor female; for you are all one in Jesus Christ." He tugged at the slaver's leash. "You shall truck in human cargo no more."

David and Oliver looked on. Martin turned to them and snapped, "Get back in the house. It is justice, but your eyes are too young to endure it."

He raised his hand as if to strike them, and the boys were too terrified by his threat to admonish him for his hypocrisy coming so soon after he spoke out against violence. They ran back into the house, passing Mother Inferior where she swept.

Lyudmila walked toward Martin. He barely heard her words. His heart beat as if it were about to cease its rhythms in his chest. "It is not just the witchfinders and fatted priests and slavers who are getting what is coming to them."

He gazed into her eyes, looked at her breasts, and decided he could no longer endure being on equal footing with her. He fell to his knees. The bruises he'd endured as he climbed jagged slopes now went from crimson to purple as his knees touched cobblestone. He had no concern for the pain he felt.

He clutched her around the waist and pulled her body to his. He buried his face in the woolen mound above her rose, whose smell he could barely discern through the fabric of the garment she wore.

"Poor boy," Lora said, "unter dem pantoffel."

"Aye," Martin said, proud of his weakness. He nuzzled Lyudmila's cherished jewel whose scent and taste he had so missed these last few tumultuous days. She petted him on the head, in indulgent strokes that were as deliberate as a farmer broadcasting seed. "Those unscrupulous merchants who previously had the protection of the guild have now been driven from market." He kissed her rose and heard nothing. He forgot he was in public, and she continued speaking. "Those scales found to tip in their favor were shattered on the spot. Bread laced with chalk or bone was force-fed to underhanded bakers."

She lifted Martin's face toward hers and said, "If someone calls you a bastard or me a whore, he will have his tongue removed for him."

Gloria opened the doors of the carriage wide, exposing a berth filled with clothes and jewels. She took a handful of aiguillettes and striped hoods in hand, and walked toward the house. She passed Martin and Lyudmila. "Hopefully no one's using the oven, because we have some whores' hoods, some Jews' hats, and some braided aiguillettes to burn in the fires."

David's voice came from the house. "There's no bread in the oven. We've been living on cheese since Martin left and the guards took you away."

"Yes," Oliver said, "Martin doesn't like us to use the oven when he is not around."

"Good," Gloria said.

Lora walked to the steeds pulling the carriage. "Poor beasts," she pouted, and began to remove the steel chanfrons masking their gentle features "There is no reason for you to be accoutered in such brutish fashion. We are now at peace."

"Peace," Martin said. He didn't believe it even though he knew it He felt it in his bones as surely as Lyudmila soothed him with her strokes of his head or Lora salved the galls and sores in the currycombed hides of the horses. The beasts' eyes watered in gratitude at the first kind touch they'd felt in some time.

The clouds lifted from the skies as the dolor lifted from their hearts, and the sun appeared with the force of a mandorla carrying the Virgin to her mighty ascension.

"I love you," Martin said.

"Silly boy," Lyudmila replied, though her eyes were serious and she suspected he meant it.

"Silly man," he amended, and she nodded. He took her hand from his head and put it to his lips. He kissed each of the white knuckles in their turn, and then he placed his face in the warmth of her palm.

"I love you as well," she said.

Gloria returned from the house, where flint had been struck to tow and the kiln was now heating. "Look at what we raided from that damnable castle!"

"Yes!" Lora said, equally excited. She left the side of the horses she'd been mending with her touch. The two women went into the carriage, and emerged with handfuls of treasure. They groaned as they carried sacks weighted with golden bezants struck in the Levant. They risked herniation as the boys came from the house along with the abbess who knew when loot was in the neighborhood. They carried coins minted in Tripoli and Venice, and Lora paraded for a time wearing a crown inlaid with diamond lozenges and golden fleurs-de-lys. She pranced and touched the crocketed golden arches, as the boys jumped upward in an attempt to touch the points of the crown surmounted in heraldic trefoils.

David finally got the crown in hand when Lora made the mistake of curtsying, and he pulled it free from the candle girl's head. He and Oliver disappeared back inside the house with the stolen crown, and Lora shouted after them playfully. "How dare you take Queen Matina Stovis's crown from her head while she sits in regency for her son, the future king!"

Her bon mot reminded Lyudmila of something, and she lifted Martin from his crouch to tell him. "The mandrakes will drink their fill of traitorous blood in a day or two."

"What do you mean?" Martin laid his head upon her ample bosom, and listened to her heartbeat.

"A plot was revealed against Domina Matina in which the archbishop was to act as the anti-king's functionary."

"Is the archbishop dead for certain?" Martin asked.

"Aye," Lyudmila said. "His mighty church collapsed about him."

Martin, so serene since the moment he reunited with his love, now went bolt upright. "The dwarf!"

Lyudmila was so confused that she pulled his head from her breast. "The dwarf?"

"The dwarf," Martin whispered, and wondered.

The young fatherless boys of the house, the candle girls, and the abbess continued to carry treasure from the carriage. The sight of it could not assuage Martin, not until he knew what became of his friend. Yet he still watched, as helpless to pull his eyes away from the parade of riches as anyone else born to no estate would be. The women and boys were heavily weighted with white gold and silver bars as they brought the treasure into the house. It looked to Martin's eyes like they stumbled not only onto the treasury of the castle, but had found the Philosopher's Stone itself, or that they now knew secret alchemical concoctions for turning any plain mineral into gold. If that were not the case, then maybe they had somehow acquired the touch of King Midas.

Pearls followed jeweled brooches meant for the mantles and furred chaperons of nobles. Aquamarine finger rings wagged from digits, the stones glowing like faceted ornaments fixed in tiaras. Necks were draped in lustrous necklaces. Plaques and pendants dangled. One of the jewels had belonged to a countess who the archbishop burned as a witch, before acquiring all of her possession and requisitioning them for his church.

None of it meant much to Martin though, certainly not as much as the presence of Lyudmila's breasts straining in their corset, or the absence of the little man who had taken him a from humble origins to a life of glory.

"Roderick," he said, and his heart sank.

Chapter Twenty-Six

Chandler, Lovers, und Kinder

Snow fell on the heather thatching of the wooden-framed cottage. The cold night was made colder by the winds picking up force as they cascaded over the Rhine and drifted above the tiny hamlet. Things were warmer inside of the house. Food was cooking on a fire and pelts and furs were nailed to the walls made from lime plaster wash and woven twigs. The loft was overflowing with hay. The little dog Mondhund spread extra warmth whenever he deigned to come down from his hayloft and frolic among the two little girls and their parents.

The man of the house sat at a trestle table that was long enough to accommodate a meal for his family and some of the tools of his craft, which was that of a chandler.

The two daughters, Gloria and Mary, kicked their stockinged feet under the table. They tangled their legs together as they sat across from one another and played with the pottage in their pewter bowls.

"Eat," their mother said, looking up from the Bible she held. "Don't play. Many are starving."

"Listen to your mother," the man said. The girls stopped kicking their feet, sinking their cow horn spoons into bowls filled with steaming fish.

"Tis bland," Gloria said. She was the younger of the two. She looked more like her mother. She had the same milky skin and always looked impassive, as if just roused from pleasant dreams to which she planned to soon return.

Her father stood and walked to the spice pouch above the hearth where the fire glowed. He reached into the dried sheepskin bladder and dug out a handful of salt. The man walked it over to his daughters and scattered the white grains over their steaming bowls.

"Where did you get that, Father?" Mary asked. She was named for the Holy Virgin, and bore more than a passing resemblance to the Mother of God. The girls knew he'd purchased the salt from the market, but they asked in the hopes that he would furnish some embellishment. They weren't disappointed. "Why, I once used my little brownie skeleton to travel to meet the Tuaregs of North Africa and I halted their caravan of fifty-thousand camels and I said, 'Wait, I need salt for the soup my daughters intend to eat.'"

The girls laughed, growing so giddy that they started kicking their feet again. Martin thought they laughed because they believed he was fibbing. They didn't know the brownie skeleton he'd gotten from the hermitess so long ago was real and did possess magic. He didn't need magic anymore, though. He had a family, and found that was magic enough.

Martin Stolzer wiped the remaining salt grains onto his chandler's apron and sat down to his own stew. He was about to take a bite when Mondhund sat up in the loft and hopped down on his stubby legs. The dog barked. His fawn colored coat bristled and his tail curled like a scimitar.

"Someone is here," Martin said. He stood and looked at his wife. Lyudmila Stolzer quickly hid the Bible. It wasn't stolen, but it was a relic from a revolt that happened long ago. The Stolzer family lived a comfortable enough existence, but the royal plunder was too out of place in their humble cottage. It was the Wenceslas Bible, the same one commissioned by the King of Bohemia. Martin had been able to resist most of the jewels the candle girls had plundered that day so far in the distant past. He had ignored the crowns and coins. He had even refused a ring, though the one he used to wed his wife took him three years of labor as a journeyman to purchase. But being as he was a bibliophile of the most passionate sort, he snatched the royal Bible for his very own when he saw it. He'd refused to sell it even when things were roughest for the newlyweds.

Martin opened the wooden door of his home. A night watchman in chainmail and frog helmet walked toward the hut. He headed through the fence cobbled together from stone Martin had carted away from the cathedral on the day it was razed and the archbishop was buried inside.

"Guten Abend," Martin said.

"Abend," the guard said. He removed his helmet with his mailed gloves. He looked down as if ready to beg pardon. Martin was far from a lord, but he had grown into a reputable merchant in the days after the laws were changed. He'd been allowed to apprentice under Witziger, even though he was not of the manor born and didn't even know his father's identity. The same Witziger who had promised to teach him his trade while moonlighting ended up instructing the boy in the full light of day. He guided him through his apprenticeship and helped him achieve good standing with the guild after he passed his exams.

"Won't you come in?" Martin asked. He held the door open for the guard who looked eager to escape from the cold. "Please, warm yourself by the hearth."

Mondhund continued to yap until Mary picked him up in her arms. She cradled him, at which point he became impassive as a lamb rocked to sleep in the arms of a shepherd. The guard removed his mailed gauntlets and held his frostbitten fingers over the fire.

Gloria clearly wasn't going to finish her soup, and she held up her bowl of pottage to the guard. He took it and gobbled it wordlessly.

There was silence for a time. Martin finally broke it, walking to stand beside the guard. He spoke in low tones so that his daughters wouldn't grow sick with worry about those things beyond their control. "The plague which has swept Italy, has it made it here?"

"Nein," the guard said, slurping up fish from the pewter bowl with the spoon made from cow horn. "That is not why I am here."

Lyudmila struggled to stand, her swollen stomach a fertile mound. A chaplet of dried flower petals was laid on her head. The girls had arranged the rose petals on their mother's plaited hair while she slept, and the baby kicked in her stomach.

"Surely," she said, "you cannot be here for the yearly dues?"

"No," the guard said, and turned. "Naturally you all are exempt from such tithing while the woman of the home is great with child." He pointed at her swollen belly. The woman sat back down in her chair, realizing only too late that she had exposed the Bible hidden beneath her bottom when she stood. The guard didn't seem to notice.

He looked at Martin, and grinned. "Do you think it will be a third daughter?"

Martin grinned back at him. "I love my daughters with all of my heart." The father scooped his offspring in his by-now burly arms, lifting the girls who stroked the dog they kept between them. "But I think it is time for a son, lest this whole den become a Gynaeceum."

The guard finished slurping his pottage and handed the drained vessel back to the girl in her father's arms. Then he looked at the pregnant wife. He spoke in a somewhat apologetic tone, as if he felt guilty for making her stand in such a state. "Well, my lady, if it be another daughter, then may she sew, spin, weave, and be brought up to a life of good deeds."

"If she so chooses," the wife of the house said, faintly.

"And may she marry well."

"If she so chooses," the wife repeated. The guard was a dense sort, but he relented with his backhanded well wishes.

Martin didn't like anyone to stir his wife, or to upset the evening ritual, which consisted of a pleasant fireside meal, followed by some reading of the Good Book and then a bit of idle chat. He mustered as much politeness as he felt the fellow was owed. "To what do we owe the honor of your visit?"

"Oh!" The guard snapped his cold-benumbed fingers, remembering why he'd been sent on this errand. "There are housebreakers about. We've caught a couple, but we believe there are more in the town."

"Well," Martin said, "we have but one window, and Mondhund will bay if there's any stranger who sets foot where he's not wanted."

The guard reached out a hand to stroke the dog and patted its belly. "Yes, he proved as much when I came here to pay my visit." The man turned, donned his gauntlets and helmet again, and stepped out into the night. He belched once more as if he'd just left an alehouse rather than a cottage home.

Martin closed and locked the door behind the man, and his wife pulled the Bible from beneath the soft contours of her rump. "He just wanted to get warm and have something to eat."

"I know it," Martin said, "and I don't blame him." He looked at his two daughters, who held Mondhund by his four limbs. "Let the beast be, and sit down at the table."

"Aye, father," Mary said. She and her sister lowered the corgi to the ground. "We should teach this turnspit to do more than dance, you know." She looked back at her mother, who had flipped the pages of the Good Book to Psalms. "Mother could use the extra hands around the house. I saw a dog at the fairgrounds that could wash underclothes in a bucket."

"Liar!" Gloria said, a bit too loudly for such a late hour. Martin picked up both of the girls again before they could further disturb the peace already disrupted by the guard.

"Forget the dog," Martin said, "and listen to your mother read."

The girls were still too young to do much reading on their own. They preferred to marvel at the historiated initials gilded in vermeil leafing, where a knight errant sat in the book. Or they might trace the page with their fingers and feel the gold leaf depiction of a dragon whose tail formed the border curling around the Psalm in question.

They studied the blue magpies and the angels strumming harps, the inexplicable images of nondescripts that their father claimed looked much like a monster he wrestled with on the open seas so many years ago. It was a tale they didn't believe but loved to hear anyway, because he told it so well.

"Save me, O God," Lyudmila said, "for the waters have come in even unto my soul."

"Which book is that from?" their father asked. Their mother held her white hand over the page to keep the girls from cheating. Mary and Gloria in tandem tried to pull their mother's milky fingers away from the Bohemian Bible. When they were unsuccessful, they had to concede defeat to their father. They smiled and shrugged.

He feigned disappointment. "David and Oliver could read Eschenbach by the time they were your ages."

"Who?" Mary asked.

Martin ignored the question. He didn't want to dig back into the stewhouse days. He was a chandler now and hadn't seen himself as a bastard for some time. He walked back over to the trestle table and sat down. He fished a bit of meat from the bowl of pottage that the guard hadn't devoured. He snuck a morsel to Mondhund, where the dog begged silently at his feet.

"Candles come in two basic types," their father said. He looked back at the girls. Their mother restrained a smile. She liked the idea of her daughters becoming chandlers more than she liked the idea of them becoming wives.

"Wax from honeycombs," Gloria said.

"And tallow from sheep fat," Mary said.

"Good." Martin knew that both girls knew the answer, but they were willing to share credit, and allow each in their turn to speak. He and Lyudmila were doing a good job raising their children, especially considering how he and his wife had been left to fend for themselves in the joyous abbey in their own right.

"What about rushlights?" Mary asked.

"Those have their uses," their father allowed, "but those are mostly for the poor." He knew in which direction Mary intended to steer him, and he obliged by asking, "Do you know the fable of the rushlight?"

Neither girl spoke. They were afraid that if they admitted they knew it, then their father might not recite it again. "A rushlight was on fire, bragging that its light was stronger than the sun, the moon, and stars. Then a little, teeny tiny breeze came, and snuffed that rushlight out. That doused light begged the chandler to relight it."

"Did he relight it?" Gloria asked. Mondhund snoozed at her stockinged feet.

"He did," her father said, "but not before he warned the rushlight to be a little humbler the next time it was lit. Do you understand?"

The girls nodded. Martin glanced at his wife. He saw that her eyes were alive with flaming passion, despite the swollen belly. "Upstairs, girls," he said, hoisting the children toward the hay-strewn loft. It was natural and inevitable for them to learn about making the beast when homes were so small and animals were rutting in heat during the mating season. He still wanted to delay the day that his daughters learned for as long as possible.

Gloria and Mary settled into the hay up above, and Mondhund rose from his sleep and climbed up to be with the girls.

Martin resituated himself on the trestle table so that he was facing his wife. She set the Bible down and made as if to stand. He rushed to her side, aiding her as she pulled herself from the chair with a groan. She walked until she came to stand before the table, where a wax candelabrum glowed. She removed some of the dead petals from the crimson chaplet on her head and held the dried bits of flower over the flame of the candle.

She spoke now with the power of an enchantress. There was no man present to see her husband's weakness that was theirs alone to enjoy and share. The petals burned in the flame of the candle. "You know I worked a bit of flower magic on you to make you mine forever, don't you?"

"Yes," Martin whispered, and fell to his knees. He kissed his wife's engorged belly and the blood quickened to his virile member as she recited. "Strew five red roses along the pathway between your home and your lover's home." He didn't feel that he was low enough on his knees. He fell to the stone floor, crawling on his belly like the asp denied its limbs after its betrayal in the Garden.

"Then call your lover's name," his wife said, rubbing her foot across his back. His breath came in heavy gasps. He struggled to remain silent, lest he pique the curiosity of his daughters in the hay loft. "Then from the sixth rose burn five petals in the flame of a beeswax candle while chanting."

She paused before reciting the last bit of verse. She spoke in a harsh tone that melted him. "Burn a pathway to my door. I burn the rose. Love no hesitation knows. The spell is done. Come lover," Lyudmila said. "Come."

He placed his head between her legs that he spread until the limbs were squared and he could feel the warmth of her rose hotter than that burning in the fire.

Martin Stolzer pressed his lips to his wife's womb and kissed the lips, licking them. "I love you."

She rubbed his head with her hands in strong swirling motions, pulling at his hair hard enough to make strands shoot errant like cowlicks. Power moved back and forth between them, a surge that neither really controlled or understood. "I love you, as well, husband." But something disturbed Lyudmila. Her husband with his face buried between her legs wagged his head from side to side like a ravenous dog, yet she found her eyes drifting back toward the front door.

Martin looked up from his joyous labor on her behalf. "What is it, my love?"

"What if the demons come again?"

"They won't," he answered.

"But if they do?"

Martin kissed her belly, massaged his unborn third child. "If they come again, we will hang a magical trap, a cleft blackthorn stave with a lighted candle inside."

"I hope it will work," his wife said. She guided him back toward the petals of her flower that grew like a night-blooming cereus. Martin had gone from apprentice to journeyman to master in more than chandlery. His licking brought moans of blasphemy from his wife, who whispered, "Christ in the manger."

He felt her pulling away from him again. There was another distraction she kept in the corner of her mind. He ceased his labor and said, "What now, wife?"

"A name," she said.

"A name?"

"Yes. If it is another daughter, what shall we call her?"

He wiped her honeyed juices from his lips with his sleeve. "I leave that up to you."

"If it is our first son?"

His face grew rigid, as if he'd just gotten lockjaw. She knew now that she asked him for his opinion that he would give no quarter on this subject. "Roderick," he said. He massaged his wife's belly, preparing to taste her fruit once more. "If it is a son, we will name him Roderick."